Jadesola James loves summer thunderstorms, Barbara Cartland novels, long train rides, hot buttered toast, and copious amounts of cake and tea. She writes glamorous escapist tales designed to sweep you away. When she isn't writing, she's a university reference librarian. Her hobbies include collecting vintage romance paperbacks and fantasy shopping online for summer cottages in the north of England. Jadesola currently lives in Long Island, New York. Check out what she's up to at jadesolajames.com!

Emmy son wrote her first book at the age of seven, pooky ghost. Her passion for romance novels few years later, with the discovery of a worn c Kathleen E. Woodiwiss's *A Rose in Winter* buried nother's bookshelf. She lives in the US Mi untryside with her husband—who's also her ex d!—their baby boy, and enough animals to star own zoo.

This is **Jadesola James**'s debut book
for Mills & Boon Modern

We hope that you enjoy it!

And check out Jadesola's debut for Carina Press,
The Sweetest Charade!

Also by Emmy Grayson

The Infamous Cabrera Brothers miniseries

His Billion-Dollar Takeover Temptation

Discover more at millsandboon.co.uk.

REDEEMED BY HIS NEW YORK CINDERELLA

JADESOLA JAMES

MILLS & BOON

To Aunty B, who gifted me my first stack
of Harlequin Presents so long ago.

I hope you love this one!

CHAPTER ONE

LAURENCE JAMES STONE hadn't eaten alone in a hotel dining room in years.

He had no idea why he'd chosen to do so tonight. The Park Hotel's quiet elegance, shrouded in greenery on the north end of a mid-Manhattan street, possessed the sort of shabby opulence that was no longer favored by the rich and young. However, the food was sublime, the service impeccable—and in a manner of hours he would be hosting the biggest social event of the season in the Grand Ballroom.

His advertising firm, recently gone public, would be the talk of the evening. He and his business partner were so close to hitting the billion-dollar mark that he could taste it. That number had eluded him for years, and though his personal fortune was vast, this was different. He wanted to be able to *pay* himself that amount, created by his own hand.

This, in a way, was their debut.

Laurence had arrived and been ushered to the penthouse suite in plenty of time to rest and dress for the evening's festivities, after an eight-hour flight from Berlin, but his stomach had started growling thirty minutes after his arrival, even though he'd been offered a bewildering assortment of food on the flight.

He'd showered and thrown on a sweater and wool trousers, then taken the penthouse elevator down. He'd looked forward to this quiet meal. Perhaps it was because he'd be forced to make small talk with hundreds of people in only a matter of hours, not to mention playing nice with a particular client he was hoping to sign...

He was dreading it like most people did the dentist.

"Oh, don't be such a snob," his partner Desmond Haddad had said dismissively, when Laurence had complained earlier.

Desmond was everything Laurence was not—youthful, flashy, and bafflingly optimistic. He was tall, slim, and debonair, in contrast to Laurence's solid, grave steadiness, and always up for a party, when all Laurence really cared to do was work. Upon their arrival at JFK, Desmond had seized his friend's laptop, tablet, and work phone, despite Laurence's protests, then waved him off.

"It's for four hours," Desmond had said, mockingly. "You won't go drinking with me, I know that, so you might as well get some rest, look fresh for tonight. Surely you can make do without looking at a single ad campaign for four hours? Come on, Laurence. I find it hard to believe you grew up rich. You work as if you're millions of dollars in debt."

Yes, fine. He'd grown up fairly well off. After all, he'd met Desmond at Exeter. Hardly a high school for the impoverished, although his senator father's fortune paled in comparison to Desmond's dynastic oil money. Still, he could not explain to Desmond, who spent the money from his family coffers with gleeful abandon, the need to make a fortune that was completely his. And even when he *did* try to explain—

"Yeah, yeah, yeah...poor little rich boy, innit?" Desmond always said scornfully, his English accent cutting like glass. "Your problem, Laurence, is that you're too damned serious."

Well. Perhaps he was.

Laurence was relieved to see that the dining room was empty, except for a young woman seated alone at a table in front of a large stone fireplace.

"Do you mind, sir?" A harried-looking waiter ushered him to a table close to the young woman's. "We're short on staff right now, as there's an event taking place in a couple of hours. They've closed off most of the dining room."

"Very well."

It mattered little to him, and as the waiter fussed about with clean linen and water glasses, and a long, rambling recitation of the wine list, he found his eyes lingering idly on his dining room companion. She was tucking into an enormous meal with so much enjoyment he stifled a smile. She hadn't skimped on quality, either. On her table he identified the remains of a caviar starter, oysters, and a steak smothered in fresh mustard greens.

"Sir?"

He blinked, looked up. "A glass of whisky and water, please. And those oysters—" He gestured at the young lady's table. "Are they grilled?"

"Rockefeller style, sir."

"I'll have those, and the new potatoes in cream."

"Very good, sir."

The waiter swanned off, and Laurence was left to feel annoyed at the fact that he'd have to log into his email manually, since his rarely used personal phone had none of the many apps he used to keep his work organized. He hadn't used it in a couple of weeks, and he felt a rush of physical relief as he switched it on and began to scroll.

He was halfway through a report on viewing statistics for a motorbike ad when the waiter came back with a bread basket, dropped it off with little ceremony, and headed over to the young woman's table.

"Are we all set, then, ma'am?" he heard the waiter say solicitously.

Laurence listened with half an ear; he was curious to hear what such a voracious eater's voice sounded like.

"I am, thank you."

She spoke quietly, almost inaudibly. Her voice possessed a low husk that, despite himself, made him look up. It was familiar, in that elusive kind of way that nagged until finally the brain identified it. He registered wide eyes in the clearest shade of brown he'd ever seen, a full, bow-shaped mouth painted berry-red, and a dimpled chin before he looked back down at his phone.

Pretty, he thought idly. He'd look up again when she stood, see if the body matched the face. And there it was again—that sense of déjà-vu. Who could she possibly be? He'd gone to university abroad, so that was out. She looked far too young—and too broke—to be a client. Perhaps one of the many interns who filtered in and out of Laurence & Haddad each summer? No, it couldn't be that; he avoided them like the plague.

"Shall I charge it to your room, ma'am?"

"Oh, yes, please." Again, in that soft, cultured voice. "I'm in Suite 700."

"Ah, the penthouse. Very good, ma'am."

At *that*, Laurence did look up. He knew for sure that the woman wasn't staying in Suite 700, because that was *his* room.

Brazenly, she signed the bill with a flourish, and took a long, last sip of champagne with every indication of pleasure before looking up. She had the gall to shoot him a shy smile and lowered her lashes, touching the napkin to those soft, full lips.

Laurence was torn between being amused, annoyed, and appalled. If the menu was any indication, she'd just charged at least a few hundred to his room, and the little grifter hadn't even blinked.

He half considered going after her, but his phone buzzed just at that moment. His last impression was of subtle but definite curves shrouded in soft faded denim as she headed toward the door, hips swaying gently.

Laurence cleared his throat and looked away. He glanced down at the message, and what he saw was enough to drive all thoughts of beautiful, dinner-scamming women from his head.

* * *

"What the *hell* do you mean, you're in Dubai?" Laurence demanded. The dining room was thankfully still empty, so he didn't bother to leave. "Aurelia?"

On the other end of the line Aurelia Hunter—*his girl-friend*—yawned, and loudly. Laurence did a mental calculation: Dubai was nine hours ahead of New York. Most importantly, it was much too far away for her to show up that evening in formal dress as expected.

"Aurelia!"

"Hold on."

Aurelia sounded irritated now. He heard rustling—bed-clothes, probably—and her soft dulcet tones speaking to someone else. Then she came back, sounding only slightly more awake.

"What?"

"You're. Supposed. To. Be. Here," Laurence said, emphasizing each word. "What do you mean, *what*?"

There was an incredulous pause, then Aurelia began to laugh. Loudly. "Are you serious?"

He was serious. He was also convinced that he was missing something very, very important.

"This is hardly a laughing matter," he snapped. "We're seated with the Muellers during coffee, Aurelia, and you know how important that account is—"

Her laughter finished on a gasp. "You really have no idea, do you?"

"Not unless you choose, very *kindly*, to fill me in. Why are you in Dubai?"

Aurelia's voice changed from incredulous amusement to something he was more familiar with: a studied cool-ness. "I see you didn't get any of my messages. I *know* you didn't return my calls."

"Obviously not," Laurence snapped.

He fumbled with the phone and opened his text notifications. Immediately messages began flashing up on the screen—messages that he hadn't checked. He squinted down at the screen, mouthing the words as he read them, then swore eloquently.

"Charming. I see you've seen it."

Laurence hated being taken by surprise, but this was outrageous in the extreme. "You're—*ending* this?"

She sighed. "I'm sorry, Laurence."

"Via *text message*?"

She snorted. "How else was I supposed to do it? You've been fielding my calls all week. Not much of a boyfriend, are you?" she added sarcastically. "And, as good as your assistant is at making you look genuinely busy, she isn't *that* good. I'm not going to fall for the 'in a meeting' line more than three times."

"But why?"

"I met someone."

Laurence stared at the screen, struck dumb. His arrangement with old school friend Aurelia Hunter had lasted a year and was quite a satisfactory one. As the head of a massive tech company she'd inherited from her father, she had no time to date but plenty of occasions for which a date was needed. A chance meetup at a networking party had led to their deal. He'd beau her around to her events, and she'd come to his, smile for photographs, be an escort he didn't have to worry about or call.

That last detail had apparently been his downfall.

Aurelia spoke into the silence. "I'm sorry. I— It's kind of been happening for a month, and it came to a head a week ago. I— It's different. I don't want to do this anymore. I sent you an email so you could make arrangements for the rest of the season."

Laurence scrolled through the email, biting back another litany of curses. Were he calmer, he might marvel at Aurelia's tone. She sounded softer than he'd ever heard her, both in the email and now, on the phone.

She's really in love.

He'd be happy for her, he supposed, if she hadn't screwed him over so colossally.

"That's all well and good," he said sarcastically, "and I hope you're enjoying your desert getaway, but this is *appalling*, Aurelia. I'm courting a huge client tonight, I've got events coming up, and—"

"Go solo."

She was definitely awake now—and possibly enjoying this? He heard the flick of a lighter, and Aurelia drew a long breath. He pictured her as she exhaled, probably swathed in something outrageously expensive, playing with the tendrils of hair on her shoulders.

"And if you do find someone else to do this with answer her calls, emails and texts, okay?"

"You really don't understand how badly you've messed things up for me, do you?"

Or maybe she had, until love had snatched all reason from her. Clients liked doing business with folks who were settled, committed. Couples were comforting. It made them feel as if their accounts were safe in the hands of someone who understood relationships, understood what it meant to make someone happy, to care for someone.

Laurence did not understand relationships or want to— he'd given that up long ago. But he knew what they looked like, and he knew what he needed to do to play that role. The idea of pursuing a woman for romantic reasons was out. He had no time or inclination for that. Aurelia had been an ideal compromise: no strings, no sex, none of the messy aftermath. Still, now the faithless woman had—

"Look, Laurence—"

Laurence hung up, then scrolled to her name and blocked her. It was childish, he knew, but he had a problem to solve and Aurelia was no longer relevant. He could explain away her absence tonight, but the rest of the season still lay before him, with all the galas, the dinner parties, the weekends away—

He swore under his breath again. She'd *met* someone. Women! They really were the most *ridiculous* creatures.

If Kitty Asare knew one thing, it was that lies were much more convincing when she half believed them herself. So she recited them over and over again as she stood shivering in the ladies' lounge at the Park Hotel. It was cold—colder than she'd anticipated—but then again, all she was wearing was a black lace thong at the moment.

She unzipped the small rolling backpack she'd brought with her and extracted the silk dress inside, then held it up critically to the light. Last season's, of course, obtained from one of those designer dress rental sites. It didn't look too terribly off-season, she told herself. It suited her lanky frame and deep coloring, and had enough oomph for tonight's soiree without looking out of place. It was also in her favorite color: a deep Lincoln green with a hint of brightness that made the rich tints of her skin glow.

Blending in was essential, since she hadn't actually been invited. All that mattered was that she'd manage, for the fourth time that month, to run into Sonia Van Horn at a New York social event.

She was counting on Sonia being in a good mood. The kindly middle-aged woman was definitely a low-watt bulb, but she was current chair of the board of the Hunt Society—a social club that Kitty had been trying to get into for a year and a half.

The small, unobtrusive group of the *ton* on the outskirts of Long Island was made up of a number of appallingly horsy middle-aged people, but it was one of the oldest, finest clubs in the state, and Kitty was determined to begin moving intimately with that group—or at the very least get an audience with them. There were simply too many potential contacts there to ignore—contacts with fat wallets who liked the convenience of contributing to a cause without getting their jeweled hands dirty.

Quality over quantity, she told herself as she shimmied the dress over her slender hips. As founder of a foundation that helped foster children transition to real life, Kitty had learned over the years that cold-calling and mass-mailing brochures was not enough. The charities she'd studied that achieved the most were either established by wealthy patrons or fronted by them, with endowments in the billions. A one-time donation was not nearly as beneficial as a lifetime supporter—and Kitty wanted those lifetime supporters.

She yanked the zipper up, trying to get her shivering under control. The dress fit okay, but narrow straps held up a draped bodice that was just a hair too big. Kitty would have to remember to stay upright.

Rich people, she thought with some disgust, and as she did so she saw the strong line of her jaw jut out from beneath the skin in soft relief. She'd have to take deep breaths, settle her face before she went in.

She knew from experience that the grasping, greedy bunch inside would have spent months—and millions—planning their jewelry, their impeccably tailored wardrobes. Makeup and hair would have been done by professionals hours before, and they would have been ferried to the Park Hotel from their Manhattan penthouses and their Long Island and Connecticut mansions to a party where champagne would flow like bath water.

Kitty, of course, had no such resources. She'd done her hair herself, cringing at the heat while she hot-combed her hair as close to her scalp as she could, and her dress would need to be dropped into a mailbox before noon on

Monday if she wanted to avoid a fee from the rental company. There was no such thing as a fairy godmother—not for Kitty Asare. She had to make her own transformation.

Not that I care, she reminded herself.

She didn't want to be one of them. Years ago she'd reached for the moon and fallen hard, and Kitty, if nothing else, was someone who learned from her mistakes. Hope was futile; so was depending on people. She didn't need any of them. She just needed their money, and she needed plenty of it.

Kitty had an encyclopedic memory for names, faces and stories, and she used them shamelessly. Acquaintances became donors much faster than strangers did, and though the glitter of these people was nothing but a pretty facade on an aching emptiness, their money was extremely useful.

Other than that, the thought of all the opulence, the waste, left a bad taste in Kitty's mouth. There were people only a few zip codes away who had nothing tonight—not even a bed to sleep in. There had been a time when she'd been one of those people, and she'd been angry at the injustice of it, but now she chose to use what she'd learned over the years to take some of that money and funnel it to where it was really needed: to support the underserved.

People like the girl she'd been.

Kitty took a deep and steadying breath. She could not think of that—not right now. Thinking of what she'd lost and how she'd lost it made her stomach clench and her eyes water, even ten years later. She would not be able to maintain her composure if she dwelled on it too much.

Focus, she told herself.

She looked the part, she'd dressed the part, and she'd fortified herself with a meal fit for a king. She smiled, thinking of the meal she'd charged to the penthouse suite. It was immature, but it felt like sticking it to the Man, just a little, in a gloriously Robin Hoodish manner.

There had been another diner in the room, ordering a meal as lavish as hers had been. *He probably didn't even finish it*, Kitty thought, with a mixture of wistfulness and disdain. He'd been shrouded in shadows from the soft lighting in the room, but she'd been able to make out broad shoulders, smooth skin, fine tailored clothes. Someone accustomed to that sort of life. Probably handsome, too—they always were.

A glance at the time reminded her that she needed to head over to the Grand Ballroom—and now. Experience had taught her it was much easier to sneak into an event of this magnitude a bit late, when people were liquored up, security guards were relaxed, and groups were moving in and out.

She looked in the mirror. She should take pleasure in her appearance. The dress skimmed over her slim figure and her makeup was done to perfection. However, her eyes looked wide and anxious—too anxious. There was an odd prickling beneath her skin, as if something were about to happen.

For heaven's sake, they're just people.

Kitty picked up her beaded clutch. She'd stow her overnight bag with the concierge until the event was over and she was stumbling out to the subway to head back to Queens. She straightened her thin shoulders, set her face, and clattered out the door, moving seamlessly into a group of well-dressed, heavily perfumed people heading for the ballroom.

The soiree, Kitty knew, was "a little dinner and dance" for clients of an advertising firm that Sonia's husband worked for. Enormous floor-to-ceiling prints and digital screens showcased what she supposed were the focuses of the firm: whiskies, wines, a couple of luxury cars, perfumes, watches. Most of the women in the room wore gowns and cocktail dresses in deep greens and maroons and golds, echoing the runways of that year—she'd at least got that right.

Her mouth went dry as she identified several people she knew—well, not personally, but she knew of them. Page Six, the society columns, TMZ even. She needed to find Sonia, and she needed to do it now.

She pulled out her phone and shot the older woman a quick text message.

Hi, heard from a little birdie that you're at the Laurence & Haddad event tonight! Are you anywhere about? Would love to say hello. :)

She hit "send," knowing it was probably futile. She was fairly positive the fifty-two-year-old matron wouldn't have it out at an event like this one.

Suddenly she felt tired, and prickles of what felt suspiciously like embarrassment heated her neck, bit under her arms. It was the dreadful, suffocating self-consciousness of a person who didn't belong, and it would choke her if she let it. Audacity was probably the defining characteristic of people who were successful at this, and normally she had plenty. Tonight she didn't know what was wrong with her. Perhaps it was the heavy meal she'd had earlier.

She tossed her head and held it high, determined to overcome it.

And then she saw *him*.

The man from the dining room.

She'd only seen him for a few minutes before clearing out of the room to dress, but she certainly had noticed him—it had been hard not to. Now that he was standing, and she could see him from head to toe, she felt that same, almost involuntary prickle of excitement, beginning at her scalp and blossoming down.

He was big and solidly muscled, and the simple black tuxedo he wore created sleek lines from broad shoulders to a narrow waist. He was drinking champagne and surveying the room with a critical eye. He looked as if he did not quite approve of something.

She would not call him handsome—his features were too irregular for that. However, he was undeniably attractive...something that was unsettling for Kitty. She remembered the dark, heady gaze he'd directed at her from his table and she swallowed, then gathered her wits and began to walk toward him.

When she was close enough, she stopped and used the full battery of her eyes on him. "Hello," she said, simply.

When the man turned and looked at her Kitty experienced such a surge of unexpected warmth that she felt quite weak. The warmth was chased by panic when she looked at his face. She was now able to make out features far sharper than the hazy impression a candlelit dining room had left. Close up...

She knew him.

His was a face that was connected to her past, to the things that still kept her up at night even after ten years.

Kitty felt her whole body go hot, all the way to her fingertips. She tried in one frantic effort to make her face stony, but she knew he had seen that moment of panic. She opened her mouth, his name on her lips, but he beat her to it.

This could not possibly get any worse.

"I'm Laurence Stone," he said, "and I think it's time for you to leave."

CHAPTER TWO

"Laurence *Stone?*" Kitty whispered.

His lips curved up. "So you've heard of me."

Heard of him? She *knew* him. She'd met him only once before, at a party not unlike this one, in the massive mansion in Long Island where she'd been living with his parents. Laurence Stone. Only son of one of the sitting senators in the state of New York, or he had been in those days.

Kitty had been there as a foster child, connected to the Stones through his wife's involvement with the state's social services department. She'd been living with them for the year when Laurence had arrived on Christmas break from his place at boarding school, and they'd met at the annual New Year's party there.

Before she'd been thrown out of the house. For reasons she could not dwell on now, or she would not get out of this room without looking insane.

Laurence Stone.

As her mind raced, she was able to process how much he'd changed. She remembered him as a teenager—a big angled handsome one, handsome enough to make her seventeen-year-old heart flutter, but still a teenager. The man in front of her had grown both up and out, and what had been a rather devilish jauntiness had matured into something else entirely. He was tall—tall and broad enough to make her feel rather slight. Not an easy feat for a girl who nearly stood six feet tall in her stockinged feet.

He didn't say anything. He just looked down at her with a distinct lack of expression.

Prickles of embarrassment began to flood her neck and cheeks with warmth.

"Well?" he said finally, and the baritone rumbling from his chest seemed to penetrate every sensory nerve she had.

She took a full step back, and at that his mouth jerked upward...just a slight twitch.

He'd noticed.

She swallowed. His eyes slid down the length of her, from the crown of her head to the twenty-dollar stilettos on her feet. She felt all at once that he'd stripped her naked—not to violate her, but to assess the net worth of her outfit, if not her life, in ten seconds flat.

He doesn't recognize me.

Kitty had never been more grateful to have been little and scrawny in high school, with close-cropped dark hair that in no way resembled the jet-black waves that spilled past her shoulders now.

"I saw you in the dining room earlier, and..." She faltered.

Get out of here!

He smiled. It wasn't a nice smile. "And?"

"And I thought I'd come over and say hello." Kitty forced her shoulders back and lifted her chin. Who did he think he was, looking at her as if she'd crawled out from under a not too impressive rock? "Clearly," she said, a little haughtily, "you're busy. So I can make my way—"

"I saw you, too," he said, and with gleeful precision he moved in for the kill.

His voice dropped an octave, and despite her irritation Kitty's stomach did too, pooling somewhere low in her abdomen. She shifted uncomfortably, pressed her thighs together.

"Did you enjoy your dinner?" he asked.

"My...?"

"You know," he said, "when I confronted the front desk about my suddenly astronomical dining bill I was almost pleasantly surprised. You've got exquisite taste for a thief. Osetra caviar, champagne and peppered Kobe steak?"

Kitty swore. It was involuntary, but the word slipped out before she could stop it, and Laurence's left brow climbed to join its twin. She closed her eyes—this could *not* be happening.

"Charming," he drawled. "I think it was rather rude not to ask me to join you, considering you knew my room number." His face raked over her face and form again, but it was questioning this time rather than mocking. "And you look so damned familiar. I just can't place—"

"Laurence?"

An older man's voice interrupted them and they both turned. The mixture of amusement and irritation completely left her companion's face and it changed as suddenly as a thundercloud might give way to the sun during a tropical storm.

"Giles!" Laurence said heartily. He reached out and clapped the man on the back, then began to walk away with him.

She was forgotten. At least for the moment.

In one quick motion she whirled and, despite the heels, ran back the way she had come. Forget Sonia. She needed to get her bag and get on the subway as fast as her feet could carry her.

Laurence quickly forgot the young woman and her frightened face. As usual, business drove thoughts of anything else from his mind.

"I'm gonna be straight with you," Giles Mueller said, with that annoyingly gruff cheer he wielded like an instrument of torture.

"Go right ahead!" Now even *he* sounded idiotic. He sighed inwardly. Desmond was nowhere to be found.

"First of all, how's the Senator? Wonderful things he's doing out there!"

"He's peachy," Laurence said, no longer able to hold back his sarcasm.

"Wonderful, wonderful... Laurence?" Giles said, and his face changed. "Perhaps a moment or two?"

Laurence nodded in assent. "At least let me get you a drink, Giles."

One snap of the fingers and a server appeared with two servings of Japanese whisky, courtesy of their latest client.

Giles made an appreciative noise deep in his throat as he sipped. "Exceptional."

Laurence watched him, a pleasant half-smile still in place. Over his years in the business Laurence had identified several different types of clients. Giles was the type who adored being wooed. Desmond was better at the wooing, and Laurence usually left it to him, but an account of the Muellers' standing was one that could not be left to chance.

The man owned a private racetrack that was a new but significant player in the horse-racing industry on the Eastern seaboard, and his goal was to blow the walls off the old clubs, making the sport as mainstream as baseball. Giles had the track, the connections, the money—what he needed was an advertising firm that would create an enormous buzz, fill the stands at his racetrack with the people he wanted.

Laurence's father, the Senator, loved horses as well. The old jackass was good for mostly nothing, but at least thanks to him Laurence knew enough about the sport to have caught Giles's attention weeks ago, when he and Desmond made their pitch. Now Giles was dancing them on a string, enjoying being courted before making the decision Laurence knew he'd made already. Tonight, the thought of Aurelia's defection had soured the chase considerably.

"Very much looking forward to seeing you at the track next weekend, Laurence." Giles sipped his drink with every indication of enjoyment on his florid face, pursing his lips in a silent whistle of appreciation.

"Not as much as me, Giles." Laurence cleared his throat. "I'm looking forward to seeing your track again. My father infinitely prefers it to Belmont."

The words were bitter in his mouth, but the thought of Giles's millions made them drift out as smoothly as watered silk. However he voted, an endorsement from a prominent politician would flatter—exactly as Laurence intended it would.

Giles's chest puffed out with pride. "He's too kind. Please, do give him our regards—and let him know there's a private box for him whenever he graces us with his presence again."

"Absolutely, Giles."

When pigs fly. Or horses.

There was no way, of course, for Giles to know he hadn't spoken to his father in years, but that was a conversation he wasn't interested in having.

"Very well then, Laurence, we'll see you soon. I'm looking forward to giving you a tour of the place…hearing your ideas. Doris has some amusement planned for the women-folk, too, so tell your lady-friend."

"I will," Laurence said, more sourly than he would have liked, remembering Aurelia.

He could not tell Giles that said "lady-friend" was no more. Doris Mueller was nervous and exact—precisely the sort of hostess who'd go into a snit if her dinner table was suddenly uneven. Besides, that would open up a whole slew of questions he wasn't ready to answer. Thankfully the Muellers had never actually met Aurelia, so at least there was that.

He patted the man's shoulder, gesturing to a server to

top up his glass. "We'll be there," he said, and he shot Giles Mueller the smile that had closed a thousand deals. He needed some fresh air. "We can't wait."

Laurence took his fresh air as soon as he could.

From the outside, the Park Hotel looked very different from its posh interior. It was undergoing restoration on the magnificent Gilded Age French doors on the balconies of the rooms facing the street, and rusting gray scaffolding hugged either side of the main entrance, but it was such a common sight in New York City that no one blinked.

The wind had picked up, and Laurence ducked under the plastic sheeting that was draped on the sides of the scaffolding that served as a divider for a temporary walkway. He stared out at the street, irritated at the fact that he felt irritated. He did not want, *need* to feel anything but indifference.

When a woman emerged from the doorway of the Park Hotel and joined him in his temporary shelter he started in surprise.

Again?

"You," he said.

He felt his annoyance at Aurelia melt away; this was a welcome distraction. And what an attractive distraction she was, he noted, taking his time to look her up and down again, indolently. In the dining room she'd been wearing a hideous sweatshirt and nondescript jeans; this dress, he'd noticed inside, definitely showed off more of her. Long legs topped by slender thighs were outlined by the clinging skirt. Her braless breasts were high, full, and very visible beneath thin fabric.

To his delight she started to squirm, and suddenly looked too warm. Her hands were trembling. He wasn't sure if it was from the cold or from the lie, but he didn't care. If she was bold enough to charge Kobe beef and a bottle of

Perrier-Jouet to a total stranger's room, she should be bold enough to face the consequences.

He took a step closer to her. She did not step back, but her chest rose and fell a bit more rapidly. Laurence was close enough now to smell rosewater and something else, something richer, reminiscent of perfumed oil warmed by soft skin. It hung around her like a scented mantle, and if he did not step back right away it might be because he was trying to identify the complex scent.

He did like a good perfume, if it suited the wearer, and this one did. Gentle, insistent, without being cloying on skin that looked so soft he suddenly itched to touch it. He wondered…just a thought…what she might do if he pressed the backs of his fingers to the slender column of her throat, felt the pulse he saw beating wildly there. There was an odd feeling of intimacy that hung between them… He definitely had seen her before. But where?

The next few things happened so quickly he did not have time to process them. The young woman's face was suddenly contorted in shock. There was a faint rattling directly above his head, and then a full-bodied shove from her, so hard he stumbled backwards.

She'd knocked him off his feet completely!

The two of them tumbled into the busy street.

Behind them he heard a creak, a groan, and a crash, but right now all he was concentrating on was not getting run over by the worst of post-dinner Manhattan traffic. He blindly reached out, dragged her into his arms, rolled over. He heard a soft cry of pain, but that couldn't be helped at the moment. All he thought of was shielding her.

Feet away from them he heard screams and shouts and raised his head. The scaffolding they'd been standing under collapsed to the ground in a spectacular avalanche of dust and steel.

CHAPTER THREE

LAURENCE STONE.

"I don't know why you won't let me take you to the hospital," he growled.

The name throbbed through her head to the rhythm of the headache that was forming. They had almost died and she'd *saved him*.

"I told you, my insurance doesn't cover ER visits."

Kitty swallowed hard and closed her eyes. The first thing she'd croaked when he'd dragged her to the curb, ignoring the myriad drivers cursing them out, was, "No ambulance," and Laurence Stone had been *furious*.

"That is no excuse," he snapped. "I'd pay, anyway. It's the least I could do, considering you kept me from being crushed."

"I won't let you pay—"

"You won't let me pay for a doctor, but you'll let me pay for your damned food? Now, don't move."

She felt large hands, surprisingly gentle, run over her back, her arms, her temples. She felt violently ill. It was as if she'd suddenly realized how close they'd come to death.

"Your teeth are chattering," he said, a bit less crisply.

In a moment he'd shrugged off his jacket and she was draped in the softest, finest quality material she'd ever felt in her life. It even smelled expensive, and that made her feel even dizzier. His face was still forbidding, but he drew the sides together with enough gentleness to make her eyes well up despite herself.

She closed them, not wanting the tears to come. Crying was not a luxury she afforded herself much. Kitty wanted nothing more than to lean on him, ease the pounding in her head, but he'd probably recoil and toss her right back in the road.

She was startled when she felt the warmth of his fingers. They skimmed over her left cheekbone as if to assess any damage done.

"Open your eyes," he ordered.

His voice was decisive, but at least that nasty lilt had left it, and he sounded almost kind.

When her eyes fluttered open, she swallowed. "Are you hurt?" she managed from between numb lips.

Gosh, it seemed like the temperature had plunged ten degrees in the time it had taken for this to happen. It was early summer, early enough for the nights to still have some bite to them, but this was on another level.

"No, I'm not."

He hadn't a single scratch she could see. His tuxedo had escaped with only a little dirt streaking the knees.

"Anyway. Get up," he ordered, drawing back and shattering the moment.

She stared up at him.

"Come on."

He stood and extended a large hand. Even with all his bluster, she could see him shooting tense glances at the pile of rubble that would have buried him. People were beginning to emerge from the doorway, to stare at it, gasp, exclaim, pull out their cell phones.

"Let's get you upstairs and cleaned up."

"I'm sorry?" Kitty asked rather stupidly; it was hard to form words.

"Suite 700. I'm fairly certain you know it—you did bill a dinner to the room, after all."

Would he *stop* alluding to that? Kitty's indignation was just the shot of adrenaline she needed, and from the flicker of amusement on his face she suspected he knew it. She lifted her chin and attempted to stand, but her legs folded beneath her as if she was a newborn lamb.

She decided to stay put for the moment. "I am not coming upstairs with you, or anywhere else!"

"Don't be ridiculous." He frowned. "You just saved my life. I'm not going to repay you by taking advantage of you. And if you won't go to hospital, the least you can do is let me watch you. What if you've got a concussion?"

"I don't."

She hadn't hit her head, although blood was trickling down her arm. Her hip was sore, too, and most of the skin had come off her palms from where she'd used them to break her fall.

She probably had him to thank for her lack of really serious injuries. The moment they'd fallen he'd wrapped his arms around her and rolled. He'd *protected* her. She swallowed hard against a scratchy throat, wondering if she'd inhaled some of the gravel when she fell.

"Then come with me before the cameras get here." His eyes scanned the street and he groaned. "Hell. They're already here."

When she attempted to rise again, Laurence hissed through his teeth.

"Will you let me help you up, at least?"

She hesitated for a moment, then she nodded.

Laurence bent to anchor one large arm round her waist, pulling her to her feet. Even from this undignified position, she tried to muster all the haughtiness she could. "I don't need—"

"Like hell you don't," he said rudely, and began to walk, matching his long legs to Kitty's stride. Now that she'd emerged from the fog of shock, she took note of more elemental things: the feel of her cheek pressed to the softest dress shirt she'd ever felt, and the iron-hard muscle it covered.

"Are you all right?" he said after a moment.

She could hear his baritone rumbling low in his chest, and the sound of it stirred deep in her lower belly.

"It isn't far to the elevator."

"I'm fine."

"See that you don't trip, so I don't have to haul you up again. You women wear the most ridiculous shoes."

A thank-you would be nice, Kitty thought, dumbly letting him cart her through the double doors like a sack of flour.

She wondered if her tumble into the street had knocked all remaining sense out of her head and concluded that it probably had. That was the only explanation for why she huddled beneath his solid warmth and followed him so meekly. Perhaps she also did it because— Well. She did know him, after a fashion. He wasn't a complete stranger to her, even though there was no indication on his chiseled face that he'd ever met her in his life.

"Nothing to see here," he snapped at the throng that had collected. They scattered.

He bypassed the main elevators and rounded a corner, and then they were left alone in front of a private wood-paneled elevator. Laurence released her, saw that she was steady, and extracted a key fob from an inner pocket, which he pressed to the sensor.

In the few moments before the doors whooshed open Kitty had the opportunity to study him carefully, in a way she hadn't been able to in the poor light outside. His frame seemed to take up all the space. He had a narrow face topped by a head of tightly cropped ink-black hair. His lashes and brows were equally dark, and Kitty was suddenly struck by a memory: his eyes, soft and honey-brown, boring into hers as they spoke in soft candlelight in the ballroom of his parents' Long Island estate.

He'd been kind to her that night, taken her under his wing when she'd been overlooked, ignored by the glitterati flitting about and skimming the marble floor with feet as light as angels' wings. Kitty, young and innocent, had been thoroughly seduced by the elegance, and in despair of ever living up to it.

Laurence had crossed the ballroom and stopped in front of her, two glasses of pilfered wine in his hands—an unlikely Prince Charming in a fashionable designer suit.

"This is boring as hell," he'd said, a little indelicately, but tears had sprung to Kitty's eyes at the relief of being noticed.

They'd sipped the sticky wine and made awkward conversation, and at midnight, when bells had chimed soft and sweet, and every person in the room had turned to embrace their companions, he'd bent and kissed her on the cheek.

"Happy New Year," he'd told her a little gruffly, and she'd blushed. "I'm out of here."

And he had been gone in an instant, presumably to one of the many Manhattan parties that she hadn't been invited to.

She'd gone to bed as soon as she could get away, snuggled beneath her down bedspread, replaying the memory. It had been a small kindness, but one that she'd held on to in those long lonely days, and it was the last happy memory she had of the Stone household.

Even now it still hurt...the way she'd been dismissed. The Senator—her foster father up until that point—hadn't said a word to her about it. She'd gone to her prep school as usual, about two weeks after the party, and Laurence had gone back to Exeter. One day when she'd opened the door of the car that normally picked her up, with its enormous leather seats and government plates, her case worker, Anna, had been in the back. Kitty's stomach had immediately dropped to her feet. As a long-timer in the system, she had known that an unexpected visit from a case worker meant nothing but upheaval.

"There's been…some complications, Katherine," Anna had said, wringing her soft hands. "I'm afraid you have to come with me."

There had been a trip back to the Stone mansion to collect her things, already waiting outside on the porch. There had been a trip to a lawyer's office where she had been asked to sign an NDA. She'd listened, dumbly, as the man droned on about not talking to the press and where she should direct questions and told her that, yes, the Senator was still planning on paying for four years at the college of her choice.

At that, Kitty's head had snapped up. "I don't want it."

"Katherine—" her case worker had entreated.

"No. I don't want it."

Even at seventeen years old, Kitty had known that something terrible was afoot, and she'd wanted no part of what she realized was bribery.

"I will honor the non-disclosure agreement. If Senator Stone thinks I've done something so terrible that he can't even give me the respect of telling me personally—"

"Katherine!"

By that time Kitty had been sobbing so hard she could barely breathe, but she'd insisted, adamantly, that she would *not*, under any circumstances, accept the money. She'd only stopped shouting when the lawyer had hurriedly drafted a document waiving her rights to the money. She'd wiped the snot off her face, signed it, and walked out of her Cinderella story.

She'd graduated from public school, gotten a scholarship to City College, and now she ran her own foundation—one that raised money to help youngsters in her situation. She'd been angry, yes, for a long time, but she'd managed to channel those emotions into getting money for kids like her—kids who needed the help. She'd been around wealth for only a short time, but enough to see how much it did for people—and how much it emboldened them to be monsters. Kitty now lived the simplest possible life, funneling money to those who needed it by way of donations, grants…anything she could get her hands on.

Tonight, this chance encounter with Laurence Stone— now a man—had brought it all back to her mind with devastating clarity.

When the elevator doors slid open, he gestured. "This is us," he said.

Kitty took in a breath.

The entryway led into a massive front parlor, with a sunken floor and a lofty ceiling lined with skylights—a meeting of old and new design. In the daytime the place would be flooded with sunlight, but now she could see stars glittering as brightly and as vastly as they would have if she'd been outside. The interior had stone-colored walls and soft plush rugs in dull rusts, chocolates and siennas, all spread over a polished wood floor. The furniture she couldn't recognize, but she knew the style—very English, probably vintage, and undoubtedly worth a fortune.

Laurence turned his head when he didn't hear her footsteps behind him. "Well?" he asked, as he walked over to a rotary phone on a sofa table not too far away and grabbed the receiver. "I'll need a first-aid kit up here now, please," she heard him say. The sardonic voice was gone, replaced with a quiet authority that just screamed boardrooms and boarding schools. "And a bucket of ice…"

As he spoke, Kitty took a step, thought better of it, and then slid her feet out of her heels before creeping forward. She stood hesitantly in front of the sofa he'd indicated and began to sit—then popped up again. Her dress was filthy, never mind the blood still trickling from her shoulder. Maybe she should find a bathroom instead, and mop it up…

She jumped a little when the receiver clattered in its

cradle and Laurence looked up, frowning when he took in her half-executed squat over the sofa cushions.

"What are you doing? Sit down."

"I don't want to mess up your sofa—" she began lamely.

"It isn't my sofa, it's the hotel's. Sit," he said, in a voice that bore no argument, and then headed off into one of the side rooms.

When he came back he carried an ornate bottle, took it straight to the wet bar that occupied the north corner of the room. When she looked confused, a hint of a smile crossed his face.

"It's whisky." He took down two glasses and spun them before they hit the bar. "Japanese. Our newest client, so I've a case in my room waiting to go back to the office with me. I thought we'd toast life, since I nearly lost mine tonight. Plus, I've had an appalling evening," he added, almost to himself.

Kitty opened her mouth; nothing came out. He was twisting the bottle open, beginning to pour. "I…" she managed, then swallowed and tried again. "I don't…"

"You don't drink? That's a lie—not with the bottle of champagne you charged to this room earlier."

There he went with a reference to her dinner again. Kitty scowled. "This is hardly just a *room*," she snapped. "And if you're in it, you can definitely afford a bottle of champagne."

Her show of spirit made him turn around and lift both eyebrows. Kitty raised her chin. She should be terrified. Hell, first of all he was Senator Stone's son, and she had no idea what the ramifications of their meeting would be. She also didn't know if she could get arrested for her idiotic move earlier that evening, but there was something in those inscrutable familiar eyes that dissolved her fear.

It was… Yes, that was it again. It was faint, but unmistakable. He was *amused*. That made her feel better, if nothing else.

Laurence poured a couple fingers of whisky in each glass, then pressed one into her hand. He raised his, gave her another of those not-quite-smiles. "To good health," he said, and raised the glass to his mouth. He only wet his lips before placing it down. "I've had enough tonight," he muttered under his breath.

Kitty took a tiny sip and immediately began to choke. The whisky, while smooth, was much stronger than the cocktails she preferred.

Laurence opened his mouth to comment, but a ring at the elevator entrance had him getting up instead. Thank goodness. She watched from her seat, taking prim sips from her glass—it did taste better as she got used to it. A white-jacketed attendant entered and opened a large first-aid kit on a side table, then shook crushed ice into a silver urn-shaped bucket.

He gave Kitty a cursory glance. "Sir, do you need assistance with—?"

"Nope," Laurence replied, rifling through the kit.

He was already tugging on a pair of blue latex gloves that seemed far too small for his hands. He selected gauze and alcohol swabs and a tube of cream with great efficiency.

"Would you like any food sent up, sir?"

"She's eaten plenty," he said, with just enough of a lilt in his voice for Kitty to choke on her whisky again, then glare in his direction.

He carried the case over to Kitty and peered at her injured shoulder with real interest.

"Lower that strap," he said, and his fingers danced across her collarbone.

Kitty jerked forward, startled both at the touch and at the way her body tightened in response.

"What?" She squeezed her glass in a death grip.

"Just lower it. Don't have the vapors…you don't need to remove it." His voice was quiet, unhurried, as if he did this all the time. "Perhaps you can light the fire for us before you go?" he said to the attendant, who was still hovering. "The lady is shivering."

The man nodded, clearly glad for something to do. A flick of a switch on the wall had flames roaring and crackling in the big fireplace, and then he left.

Kitty was shivering, but it wasn't climate related. Having Laurence Stone so close was suffocating in an arousing way, and she was certain he knew it.

Laurence made a low sound in his throat as he examined her wounds. He slid a long warm finger beneath the edge of her dress, tugging it down further. Kitty felt her lungs constrict in her chest, just for a moment, at the warm jolt of his fingers on her bare flesh. She could feel her back arch of its own volition and her nipples tighten. She was positive that he'd notice. The thin silk and her lack of a bra was doing nothing to hide them.

She shifted uncomfortably.

"Don't move," he said.

His eyes flickered down and Kitty blushed. He'd noticed, all right, if the mocking curve of his mouth was any indication.

Kitty closed her eyes and inhaled deeply—which was a mistake. Losing her sight only heightened her other senses, and now she smelled something whisky-sharp, combined with the spiciness of soap and cologne on warm skin. The urge to lean into him, to simply give in to that warmth, was utterly overwhelming.

"You've got several nasty scrapes and some gravel inside one," he said, so quietly she could barely hear him. "This is going to hurt."

"It's fine," she gasped, and gulped down the rest of her drink.

It did hurt, but she wasn't going to give him the satisfaction of seeing her wince. She would welcome the pain—anything to counter the dull ache that was beginning, inexplicably, between her thighs. Instinctively she pressed them together. It was as if the adrenaline rush from their near-death experience had gone straight to her nether regions; she'd be squirming in a moment if this didn't stop.

"Do it," she said, and the breathiness in her voice made her swallow.

Laurence Stone, despite his trademark iron-fast control, was very uncomfortable at that moment.

The entire night, he thought, as he gently swabbed blood and debris from the gold-tinged silken plane of her increasingly bare skin, was a disaster. Aurelia's stunt had thrown him off, Laurence had almost *died*, and now...

He resolved to ignore how she held her body tense, or the way the soft mounds of her breasts were thrust upwards as if in offering. Every nerve-ending in his body was humming—had been since this girl had shoved him out of harm's way.

You almost died.

Even with his eyes open he could still see the pile of rubble, sending clouds of dust, shards of glass and steel into the air. He could have been crushed. Or perhaps a stake or broken glass might have driven straight into his heart. Or perhaps he might have been left paralyzed, a shell of himself—

Stop thinking.

This confrontation with his own mortality had shaken him like nothing else had ever been able to lately. Laurence was a planner. His life was a series of carefully calculated assessments of risk, benefit, and payoff. This had been a freak accident, and nothing rattled Laurence more than things he could not anticipate or control.

To keep from dwelling on this he had to concentrate on something else—and for now, unfortunately for her that was the supple curves of the dark-haired beauty pressing her knees together on the sofa next to him.

The young woman was clearly distressed—so much so that Laurence felt quite sorry for her. However, once she'd settled into the plush upholstery and lowered the straps of the green dress she wore, all the tension of the evening had gone straight to his groin.

Her soft, rapid breathing did not help. Neither did the proximity of his fingers to the soft swell of bare skin. She was slim, yes—much slimmer than he usually preferred— but everything about her promised *lushness*. One tug, he thought, and the soft bounty of her breasts would be completely exposed to him, to touch, to taste—

"Stop." He found himself saying it out loud, more to himself than to her, really, but her eyes fluttered open again anyway, and he was confronted by that lovely shade of brown.

He could see it in her eyes, reflected as clearly as his own face.

Mutual desire.

And she wasn't schooled enough to hide it—another key difference from the woman who'd just dumped him.

Laurence cleared his throat and pulled back, making quick work of fastening a clean white gauze bandage round her upper arm. She began to speak very carefully, as if she were trying not to slur her words. Another reason for him to get her out of here as quickly as possible.

"Y'know, it's rude to make a lady drink alone…"

Laurence laughed out loud, hoping the sound would drive out some of the tension and it did—somewhat. He picked up his glass and downed the liquid as coolly as he might a glass of water.

She goggled. "How is your throat not on fire?"

"I've likely had more practice than you." Laurence slid a finger underneath her shoulder strap and tugged it back into place, careful not to put pressure on the wounded area. She quivered, ever so slightly, and he tempered his gruffness. For now.

"The bandage doesn't really go with the dress, but you can consider yourself patched up." He decanted another measure of whisky into a glass. He offered it to his companion first, but she shook her head.

"I think I'd better have water this round," she said a little primly, and he laughed.

He took a long sip, closing his eyes, feeling the smooth slide down his throat. The whisky was so smooth it would not burn...not until it had settled deep in his stomach. He leaned his head against the back of the sofa. He really should get up, but something in him wanted to savor this moment, this quiet.

They sat in silence; then she spoke, softly. "We almost died."

"We did," he attested, "but we didn't. And you mustn't think that way. If you do, you'll never want to walk under scaffolding again."

She frowned. "You cannot be okay with this."

"I'm alive; what more do I want?"

She turned her head.

"Hey," he said gently.

The young woman was biting her lower lip hard. He leaned forward and pressed his thumb to the dimple in her chin, dislodging the soft wet skin from her teeth. It had plumped from her abuse and was redder than her lipstick could make it.

"You're alive," he said firmly, and there was some compassion in his voice. They did have that bond of survival, after all. "We're alive. Celebrate it and move on."

She opened her mouth and closed it—and then there was nothing else. Because suddenly the softness of her body was pressed full against his and she was kissing him.

CHAPTER FOUR

DECADENT.

That was the first word that came to mind when Kitty pressed her lips to Laurence's. He was surprised. She felt him stiffen and grow rigid. The inside of Kitty's head was awash with panic, even as her lips softened, parted.

What the hell are you doing?

She was, she realized, trying to grasp something, anything, that would assuage this tension that was winding her body taut. She'd drunk just enough whisky and it'd gone to her head just fast enough to ensure that she would do something this stupid. And now that she was kissing him—

He was kissing her back.

It was controlled, and very, very short, but it was enough for her to taste alcohol and spice and send a jolt of lust through the haze that threatened to lift her straight off the sofa.

"Please…" she whispered against his lips.

The sound of her voice broke whatever spell they both were under. A moment later he began pulling back, leaving Kitty trying to steady her breath. His eyes were carefully blank, but there was enough storminess in his expression to keep Kitty's pulse racing.

He wants you.

That in itself was something she'd never thought a possibility: the thought that Laurence Stone might ever want *her*.

"Are you all right?" he said after a moment, in a carefully neutral tone. "You've had a lot to drink."

Heat rushed to Kitty's face instantly. She knew exactly what that meant. Pulling herself together, she somehow managed to stand. She was relieved that the room did not spin, neither did she wobble. She licked her lips; she could still taste him on them.

"I'm sorry," she said after a moment.

"For what?" Laurence's face was as calm as if she were apologizing for bumping into him in a supermarket. "We went through a traumatic event tonight. Let's not speak of it anymore."

Kitty should be grateful he seemed so determined to forget, but instead she felt a rush of anger that shocked her in its intensity. She was being dismissed. She was always being dismissed.

Now you're being irrational. He doesn't even know who you are.

Kitty swallowed hard once, twice, three times, and dignity reached out its strong arm to steady her.

You need to get out of here.

The past had come back for her in the form of the son of the man who'd cast her out so unceremoniously. And she, overcome by the present and the fact that she'd nearly lost her life, had lost all self-control and kissed him.

When she thought back on it, tears threatened to well up in her eyes—tears of humiliation at her own behavior. Ordering the meal… How could she have given in to such a stupid, *childish* impulse? Despite her show of strength, Kitty was not made of stone, and in quiet moments over the past ten years she'd often daydreamed of running into the Stones as a polished, successful woman…an *equal*.

Tonight had been the opposite of that.

Silence hung heavy over them for a few moments; then Laurence spoke quietly. "Let's go. I'll put you in a car."

Kitty blinked hard, nodded, shoved her feet into her shoes. The two of them made their way to the elevator, entered at the touch of a button and faced each other, silent.

Laurence broke the silence first. "You'll have to let me do something to pay you back," he said.

She shook her head. Someone with Laurence's millions—billions, probably—would be an ideal sponsor, but she wanted nothing more than to exit his life and forget she'd met him. Again.

Gooseflesh rose up on her arms; instinctively she rubbed at them. Laurence saw this, and in a moment she was once again draped in the heavy softness of his jacket.

"No—" she tried to protest.

"Just wear it. You can give it back to me downstairs." He crossed his arms.

When the doors whooshed open, light assaulted her retinas and she blinked. Her time upstairs with Laurence seemed like an encounter from a different land…a candlelit land with whisky and soft kisses and the strong clean scent of him that now clung to her skin, blending perfectly with her own.

A couple stood in front of the public elevators—an older couple, dressed in dour but very correct evening dress. She recognized the man after a moment. He was the same one who had been talking to Laurence in the Grand Ballroom. When he saw them the man's eyes lit up, and Kitty thought she heard Laurence swear…very quietly.

"Laurence! Is this your lady-friend?" the man said effusively.

Kitty gasped, for Laurence's arm had snaked out to draw her close to his side. He spoke quickly, with increasing pressure on her hand that set out a clear message: *Be silent*.

"It certainly is," Laurence said smoothly, and his dark eyes glittered with a sudden intensity that shut Kitty up much faster than his silent imploring had.

His next words froze her in place, sent a shock through her.

"Giles, this is Katherine Asare. She appeared rather unexpectedly tonight, and she's been *dying* to meet you."

CHAPTER FIVE

"YOUR *LADY-FRIEND*?" Katherine demanded, prodding his arm. Hard.

The trembling waif who'd kissed him only minutes ago had been replaced with an indignant woman, demanding answers. Laurence ignored her.

The two of them were outside now, waiting for his car to pull round. The rubble that had nearly buried them was now roped off with sheets of plastic and orange strips that warned *Caution*.

He shook his head. He had plenty to be cautious about, and Katherine Asare had made it to the top of the list in a single leap. The fact that he'd impulsively dragged her into the Giles matter was another layer of complication he didn't need. He rarely acted so rashly. He did not like this at all. And the girl, with her incessant questioning, was not letting him think.

She wouldn't be the first woman from his past to reappear as if by chance, and the fact that she'd kissed him— Suspicion was fast overwhelming his initial curiosity.

"Why would you tell him that?" she said, punctuating her words with a stamp of her foot. "Can you hear me?"

Of course he could hear her—she was shrieking in his ear, after all. He turned slightly.

"And don't lift your eyebrows!"

They, of course, climbed.

"Why didn't you tell me who you were?" he countered. "You knew it was me as far back as the ballroom."

The shot was an accurate one; her eyes dropped in confusion. "I—"

Little Katherine Asare.

He'd known there was something familiar about her the minute he'd seen her in the ballroom that evening—but he hadn't remembered who she was until she'd kissed him, pulled back, and looked up at him with those massive dark eyes. Then recognition had slammed him in the gut; he'd barely been able to hide it.

The more she spoke, the clearer a picture of the timid teenager he remembered stood out in his head. He vaguely remembered skinny arms and legs, a deplorably flat chest, a jaw far too strong for her face, black hair cropped close to her head, and again those vivid eyes—her most distinctive feature, but so shadowed by anxiety that she'd always looked haunted.

He raked his memory for information. She'd been his parents' little foster foundling from Ghana. She'd been brought on board as the first recipient of his father's foray into philanthropy, all to appeal to a certain group of voters and to give his ex-supermodel wife something more meaningful to do than be photographed spending thousands at the French boutiques she favored. Some tragic backstory, if he remembered rightly—dead parents and a granny who'd been deported when she was small.

They'd brought her into the household months before his father's election campaign had launched, doubtless to ensure that his father was painted in the most sympathetic, most benevolent, most philanthropic light, and his mother had gone along with his hypocrisy like she always did.

Could the man have been any more transparent?

His lip curled in disgust at the memory. A common schoolgirl, an orphan, no family in the United States. A girl with ties to his own mother's native Ghana—a tacit reminder that his father had married just as open-mindedly as he'd chosen a foster child. A perfect complement to his mixed-race son, whom he trotted out for events like a dumb, obedient show puppy, but ignored otherwise!

Laurence had come home for Christmas break that year, angry and resentful, and his discovery of the real reason Katherine had been brought into their home had left him reeling, even at that young age.

Charity fraud.

His father had been soliciting donations to line his pockets, while making the public think him the best kind of benefactor, with Katherine essentially the face of the whole operation.

Laurence been horrified at first. He'd had no respect for his father, but he'd thought actual crime far beyond his capacity. Once that feeling had passed, however, he'd been *pleased*.

Finally, a way to pay his father back for years of negligence and show the world exactly what kind of man he was!

It had been easy to focus on his parents and not on Katherine, until the mingled look of awe, fear and misery on her thin face had drawn him to her side at his parents' New Year's party. She'd aroused a strange protectiveness in him that night, one he hadn't liked. Caring was dangerous, and a young man seeking to get *out*—and scorch the earth behind him as he left—must not care for anyone he might destroy in the process.

That night he'd held Katherine's trembling little hand in his and seen how innocent she was. It had kept him up all night. He'd asked himself how he could do this without subjecting her to the scrutiny and embarrassment he knew his father was in for, keep her name from being connected to scandal for the rest of her life? How could he get her out swiftly?

Warning her would do no good, he'd reasoned. She'd never believe him over the people who had given her everything for months. Katherine was shy and softly spoken, tiptoeing round the house, always with a book in her hand, and she absolutely idolized his mother. There was also the chance she'd tell her parents about his plans to expose them. No, he had to be merciless about it.

What was the absolute worst thing that Katherine could do that would make his image-conscious, hypocritical parents do away with her *immediately*?

The day after the party Laurence had purchased a pair of lacy underwear, planted it at the foot of his bed for the nosy maid to find, then sat back and waited. When his parents had confronted him, he'd managed a guilty look, then smiled.

"It happened after the party," he'd lied. "We got drunk."

He cringed to think of it now. What a little snot he'd been—and so proud of his noble intentions. He'd been exposed to so many machinations as a child that they'd come as second nature to him once he was old enough to formulate manipulations of his own.

His father had held up a hand against his mother's angry hysterics, silencing her. He'd fixed ice-blue eyes on Laurence then, for a long moment, as if assessing his story.

"Is there a chance she is pregnant?" he'd asked.

Laurence's courage had left him at that point; he had shaken his head dumbly. It had been his intention to say there was, to up the threat of scandal, but there was something ugly, something dangerous in his father's eyes, that stopped him cold. He'd always thought himself a good judge of what his father was capable of, but at that moment he'd wondered.

His father's lip had twitched, as if Laurence had verified something he'd thought all along. "I'll take care of it."

He had—and swiftly. Katherine had been gone in less than a week, and to where Laurence had not cared. He'd soon been back at school in New England where, despite the cold, his hatred for his father had been able to blossom, grow, thrive. He'd leaked the information from his tiny dorm room, sat back and watched the internet implode.

Katherine had been safely out of the way. He remembered that her name hadn't come up in the fallout. Not *once*. But now what he'd done as a teenager was coming back to bite him—and hard.

Katherine had saved his life, true, but what had she been doing at the party in the first place? She'd recognized him and hadn't identified herself. She had no idea what he'd done for her. In her head, she likely thought he'd smeared her name maliciously.

It was well within Katherine's rights to return and exact revenge for what he'd done to her so long ago. Trouble was, he had no idea what she knew. Was her contact with him made out of anger, a determination to right a wrong? Or had she, perhaps, decided she would entice the Stone heir into giving her something? She'd already scammed a meal, crashed a party, and *kissed* him.

Was it an attempt to get something out of him? A way to taunt him? A warning? A seduction? How much did she *know*?

He felt his throat tighten at the memory of their encounter—along with another part of his body. Closing his eyes briefly did not help. All he saw was Katherine's body in sharp relief, her breasts undulating under that flimsy dress with every breath she took, her eyes cloudy from their kiss. She'd kissed him, yes, but he'd felt want as sharply as if he'd been the one to initiate it.

Danger.

"Laurence?"

He blinked and she came back into focus. She looked wary now. *Good.* He preferred it that way.

"Giles is a potential client," Laurence said shortly. "He was to meet my date this evening, and she was…indisposed."

He could tell from her face that she didn't believe a word of his lie. "Is her name Katherine as well?"

He did not answer the pointed question; the nuances were too much to explain. He breathed an inward sigh of relief when he saw one of the black Mercedes in his company's fleet approaching.

"I was coming down from my suite with a very young and very disheveled woman next to me—"

She huffed. "*Young?* We're practically the same age."

He ignored her. "It doesn't look right. And looking *right* is everything in my line of work. Maintaining the charade costs you nothing, and I guarantee he won't remember you."

Hurt flashed across her face, but he ignored it. Katherine's feelings were not his concern—not when he had other things to worry about.

"Telling an outright lie and dragging a stranger into it didn't bother you at all?" Katherine pressed.

The irritation that had needled him at first grew into a full-on assault of his senses. He inhaled once to calm himself, then turned on her. Normally he would have left it alone, given himself time to plan what he would say and why he'd say it. However, there was something in her audacity that made him speak.

"I may have lied, but you sneaked *uninvited* into a private event—not to mention the charging your meal bit—to do who knows what. May I ask your motives, Katherine? Why me, and why *now*, after so many years?"

Her face blanched as his implication sank in.

Kitty's whole body was tightening, growing taut, as if in reaction to the proximity of his. It was a tightness that wound like a coiled spring…a tightness that needed release. At that moment she felt utterly miserable. She'd spent ten years freeing herself of the influence of people like the Stones, and with one look Laurence Stone had made her feel as if nothing had changed.

Instinctively she crossed her arms over her chest and his

full mouth curved up into a smile. It was a half-smile—not one of sympathy, but of resentment. Suspicion.

"Answer me," he said, and his voice was cold. "You wouldn't be the first past acquaintance who thought they could grift off me."

Kitty felt penned in, crushed by the weight of his wordless accusations. Laurence's eyes were still on her, dark with that same odd anger and with something else—something that made her stiffen.

He looked…triumphant, almost. Vindicated. As if he'd been proved right. And that made something flare up in Kitty that had little to do with lust, or intimidation, or any of the myriad emotions that had been crushing her ribcage up till this point.

She lifted her chin, uttered a short, foul phrase that made him draw back with an expression of surprise. She felt pleased for the first time that evening.

"That," she spat out, "is none of your business, and my appearing in a *public* hotel had nothing to do with you. I can see that you're still a Stone, through and through. If you want to give me a ride, give me a ride. But I will not be interrogated like I'm one of your father's staffers!"

Laurence stared at her, unblinking, then looked away.

Kitty let out the breath she'd been holding. "The name of your firm is Laurence & Haddad," she pointed out. "I had no way of connecting it to you. I don't know anything about advertising."

"It isn't hard to Google."

But some of the animosity had left his face—he knew she was right, though she suspected he'd rather be crushed by that scaffolding than admit it. They stood in tense silence for a moment, then he spoke.

"Thank you for saving my life," he said.

It was a stiff concession, but he'd made it. Kitty felt some of the tension leak from her shoulders and risked a glance at him. He was staring straight ahead, a muscle working in his jaw.

"I will see that you are suitably rewarded."

"No need," Kitty said.

Anything that would prolong her contact with this insufferable man was something she had no interest in. Despite her body's reaction to him—which was wholly physical and born out of adrenaline, she told herself sternly—he would be the worst possible person to extend conversation of any kind with.

"Just do me one favor?"

He looked at her.

"Don't tell your parents you saw me."

His face grew even more cold and still, if that were possible. It was extraordinary, the way it varied from showing those quick flashes of emotion to complete immobility, as if he'd drawn down a blind.

"I haven't spoken to either one of them in ten years. You needn't worry on that account."

Interesting.

Kitty opened her mouth, but a Mercedes pulled up to the curb at that second and a driver scrambled out of the front seat, apologizing profusely.

"I'm sorry, sir. The whole place is blocked off and—"

"Not to worry. This is Miss Asare, Mason. Please take her to—"

"Astoria," Kitty said.

"Queens," Laurence said, his lip curling faintly, as if he smelled something off.

Kitty felt a new stab of anger, at him, for being so rude, and at herself, for the flash of embarrassment she'd felt. She was past being intimidated by people like this pompous *ass*.

"Katherine…" He hesitated. "I can't say that it's been lovely to see you again."

Kitty had never in her life rolled her eyes, but she did it

now, stepping into the back of the luxury sedan. She saw a flash of amusement on Laurence's face as he bent to peer at her through the glass, lifted a hand to wave.

Thank you, he mouthed.

It was not until Kitty was home and stripping off her ruined finery that she realized she still had his tuxedo jacket, tucked around her shoulders as if it belonged there.

CHAPTER SIX

Kitty FORCED HERSELF out of bed on Monday morning, feeling sluggish and dull. She switched off her alarm, stepped into the hottest shower she could stand, and was walking out the door in the next half-hour, her dress from Friday night wadded in a parcel under her arm. She'd have to mail it back today or they'd charge her already strained credit card for the full amount. She just hoped the dress wasn't so damaged they couldn't take it back.

Walking in her black high-tops over the grimy sidewalks of Astoria and navigating around vendors hawking everything from umbrellas to hand-painted silkscreens of the Empire State Building made the weekend's encounter seem all the more surreal.

Kitty quickened her steps, as if physical movement could help her outrun her thoughts. She lived in what her landlord trendily called a "community loft." In reality it was dormitory-style shared housing reminiscent of an old-fashioned boarding house.

Kitty had a small room, with basin, bed, chair, nightstand, and wardrobe, to herself. She shared an enormous bathroom with several other residents, as well as a massive kitchen and lounge. The best part of living there—and the reason she'd gone for it, other than price—was the fact that the two top floors had been converted into shared office space that was free to use for the residents. There Kitty worked in solitude, six days a week. She occasionally had a coffee or a night out with a few of the other residents, but no close friends, no permanent ties. She was hyperfocused on her work.

Kitty could have lived somewhere else if she'd wanted

to—somewhere more appropriate for a twenty-seven-year-old business owner. However, this suited Kitty and her minimalist approach to life quite well. She didn't need anything other than reliable wi-fi and desk space. She didn't host, wasn't dating, and that meant she could funnel so much more of what she made into her foundation, One Step Ahead.

Laurence Stone and his opulent lifestyle, no matter how seductive both were, had no place in her everyday life. She needed to force him out of her headspace. Desperation had driven her to the event on Friday night. She had bills to pay, and chasing a check was the only way to get money quickly.

Although she kept her costs to a minimum, there were kids expecting their monthly allowances in only a few days. She'd just replaced her ancient laptop after it had given up the ghost two weeks before, and on-boarded two new clients at the same time. Thankfully her endowment would cover that, but she had other costs—her rent, what she ate, and her own salary, which had been more of a theory than a practicality since the beginning of the year.

Laurence Stone and his offer to pay her back for saving his life came back to her as she went over her accounts in her head, once, twice, three times, as if thinking about them again would change the balance. However, all thoughts stopped there: getting involved with Laurence never had been and never would be an option.

Kitty was so engrossed with her thoughts that she didn't see the sleek black E-Class until it caught up to her at an intersection. The back door opened and Laurence Stone peered out at her, looking incredulously at his surroundings.

"So this is Queens."

Kitty's jaw sagged downwards.

"Get in," he said.

Kitty took a very large step back.

Laurence had the gall to look irritated. "I need to talk to you. Come on. I'll take you wherever it is you're going."

The hell you will!

Kitty stared at him in disbelief, then turned and began walking in the other direction, back toward her building. Rapidly. If nothing else, there was a security guard called Rafe just inside the double doors, who'd had a thing for her since she moved in.

Laurence Stone, the psycho, she saw, had climbed out of the car, cupped his hands round his mouth, and was calling after her.

"You can do this now, or I can show up at your office! Your choice."

Kitty whirled around. "This is harassment," she spat out. "I can call the police, you know."

The look on his face was smug; he had never, she thought exasperatedly, looked more like his father.

"Call them. You can explain why you charged three hundred dollars' worth of food to my room Friday night."

Oh! What felt like most of the blood in her body rushed directly to her face. "You—" she began.

"You can call me names later, Katherine. Just get in." His voice had resumed its usual dryness. "You were in my room for over an hour with no issues, so you can't be afraid I'll take advantage of you."

The light had changed and Laurence's car still sat in the middle of the intersection. His face was immovable as cars began to honk and creep round him, and drivers leaned out their windows, swearing colorfully.

The din frazzled Kitty completely. She let out a huff, then moved forward. "I am *not* getting in the car with you."

"You don't have to. Drive on, Mase," he added, and the car lurched into motion, making a U-turn that made Kitty gasp and easing smoothly into traffic.

"You never got back to me, you know," Laurence said mildly. "I was serious about giving you something."

"I don't want anything from you."

"At the moment. Is that it?" he said quietly.

Kitty found herself locked in his gaze. Although his skin was much lighter than hers, a fine bronze in contrast to her soft sienna undertones, his eyes were darker, and they gleamed. They were the type of eyes a girl could get lost in, were she not careful, and she'd already kissed him, she thought helplessly.

He was moving nearer her now, closing the distance between them as if the presence of the people on the street mattered little.

"We may have a problem that I need to discuss with you," he said.

"We?"

"I assure you that I'm as appalled as you are." His voice was clipped. "Thirty minutes of your time will suffice."

Kitty pursed her lips, then shrugged and pointed at her building. There were no coffee shops or restaurants on this strip of sidewalk. She had a moment's hesitation, thinking of Laurence coming into her humble space, but she forced it back, angrily. If it was good enough for her, it was certainly good enough for Laurence Stone, with his Mercedes-driven arrogance!

She began marching down the street without looking to see if he followed, then punched in her door code and entered, pausing to nod at Rafe. The grizzled guard looked curiously at Laurence, and even more curiously at his identification, but waved them through without any questions.

Laurence, as expected, was not well-bred enough to keep his comments to himself, and began talking as soon as they walked into the lounge. "You *live* here?"

"Were you expecting the Ritz-Carlton?"

Kitty stalked over to a couple of distressed leather chairs

in her favorite corner of the communal lounge area. Luckily most of the residents of her building had gone to work, either upstairs or to their offices outside, and the place was virtually empty.

"You are unbearably spoiled," Kitty snapped, and lowered herself into the chair, dropping her parcel on the floor. "Say your piece. I've got to get to the post office."

Laurence looked at her measuringly and to her surprise broke out into a smile—a real one—that softened his face so dramatically she was taken completely off guard. The fluttering in her chest was equally discomfiting.

He dusted the leather with a handkerchief in a show that she suspected was for her benefit, then sat and extended his long legs.

"We've gone viral," he said.

When Kitty's brow furrowed with confusion he sighed. "That means—"

"I know what it means!"

"Very well." He extracted a slim, top-of-the-line tablet from its carrying-case and laid it on the scratched Formica table between them. "Google away. I'm going to…" his lip curled slightly as he looked around "…visit the water dispenser. If one can call it that."

Snob. Kitty rolled her eyes and tapped away.

"Can I get you anything?"

"I don't need anything from you."

It was as if he hadn't heard her, or rather chosen not to listen.

"You have a vending machine in the corner," he said, "that seems to be selling *coffee*. I'm intrigued. Would they take American Express?"

"Why don't you go over there and see?"

He said something else before he ambled off, but Kitty tuned him out. Once she looked up Laurence's name and

"The Park Hotel" hundreds of hits came up; the video, it seemed, was everywhere.

Some enterprising cellphone holder had recorded them, uploaded it to his personal account with a long thread ranting about safety. Views were gaining traction, mostly shared by indignant city-dwellers insisting that something be done about the never-ending construction in midtown, but something else had caught the attention of the public—Laurence's "rescue."

"*I* saved *your* life!" Kitty exclaimed in disbelief, scrolling past the comments.

Unfortunately no one had captured those first few moments, but had yanked out their phones when she was already on the ground and Laurence had tugged them to safety from the road. One image made her breath catch in her throat: she and Laurence, on the ground, him cradling her and looking down at her with an expression of tenderness that made her skin flush hot.

"Combined with the fact that I told Giles Mueller you were my girlfriend, it's made things slightly awkward," Laurence said, his dry voice breaking her concentration. He set down a paper cup of coffee in front of her. "This," he said, "tastes precisely as if someone has burned beans, soaked the pot in water, taken that water, added milk and sugar—"

Kitty didn't want to drink it—vending machine coffee was disgusting—but caffeine was exactly the boost she needed to clear her brain right now. She gulped, welcoming the scald at the roof of her mouth.

"I don't see how this is my problem," she said, flatly. "You have more to worry about than I do if anyone makes the connection. I didn't do anything wrong."

"Didn't you?"

"No!"

How she hated that loftiness. It was as if he'd placed

himself on some sort of invisible pedestal, from where he could look down and smirk and wield that sardonic voice of his like a lash. He thought he was better than her. They all thought they were better than her. Kitty felt her anger flare.

"Just get to it, Laurence—you bullied me into letting you come here," she added. "What do you want?"

She's beautiful. And her anger only heightened it, brightened her eyes, illuminated her skin. The thought surprised him.

They sat in silence for a moment, looking, he thought fleetingly, like any other couple. They could have been co-workers, lovers—or, hell, just friends. Laurence could not remember the last time he'd sat with a friend like this; those meetings were restricted to days long past, in high school and university—days when he'd still cared about what people thought of him, when he'd still been looking for the family he didn't have at home.

Those friends had proved as disappointing as his home life had been. No matter how long, how wild those nights were, his companions would inevitably go home, and he would be left alone.

Home. There never had been such a place for him. He'd have one eventually, when he was old and tired and needed somewhere to rest his head. For now, though, he worked and did his best to ensure he'd never need a penny of his father's inheritance. He would surpass it.

And partnering with Katherine Asare would add a significant chunk to his holdings.

Giles had already declared himself absolutely charmed by her—why, Laurence had no idea—but if he could get her to agree to this he'd not only have a stand-in for Aurelia, he'd be able to find out what had happened to Katherine—and, potentially, why she'd shown up. He still did not trust that their meeting had happened by coincidence, and Laurence knew that keeping a possible enemy close was the safest way to proceed.

Also, if Laurence was being honest with himself, there was a third reason that was far more elemental. Katherine was attractive, and he was not completely unmoved by occasional pleasures such as good whisky, good food, a soft, scented woman in his bed. It had been a long time since he'd had the third, and after the way she'd kissed him—

She was trying too hard to look unconcerned; he could feel the tension coming off her in waves. Not as much as when they were in his suite on Friday night, but very much there.

"You look so very different than you did when you lived with them," Laurence said after a moment.

"I must," Katherine said, and her voice grew just a fraction softer. "You didn't remember me."

For heaven's sake.

Laurence eyed her face. So here it was, the part where they would acknowledge their shared past. He recognized it as necessary if he was to strike this deal with her, but that didn't mean he had to like it.

"It's been a decade, at least," he said, crisply.

"Nine years and eight months," Katherine said quietly.

Over the years the thin schoolgirl's body had yielded to a softness that nudged the confines of her garments just enough to catch attention. Her enormous eyes, lined with makeup, tipped upward, heavily lashed; her lips were soft and full. She wasn't beautiful, not by any means, but she was very attractive—and just uptight enough to make him want to see her unravel.

"Lovely," he admitted. "You're quite lovely."

"What do you *want*, Laurence?" she cried out. "I signed all the NDAs… I've never said a word about any of you. I *left*. What do you want from me?"

Despite all his suspicions, Laurence could not deny one

thing: this was a woman in distress, and he was the cause of it. It took effort to focus back on the fact that she could not be trusted, and when he did he steeled his face, tilted his head.

"I'd like you," he said, "to extend the ruse that we started—"

"*We* started?"

"You didn't protest," Laurence pointed out. "It would be rather inconvenient to change the story now that we've become so conspicuous—"

"Is that my fault?"

"Would you stop interrupting?" Laurence frowned. He couldn't remember her being this argumentative in those days—hell, he didn't remember her speaking much at all then. "It will only be for a few weeks this summer, until my arrogance drives you to the point of dumping me as publicly as possible. In return, I will pay you handsomely—"

"I'm not interested in your money," she snapped.

"Don't be ridiculous." He kept his voice even. It was easy for Laurence to make his voice low, seductive, nonthreatening; advertising was based on that, in a sense. "You wouldn't be living here if you didn't need money."

Katherine's back stiffened with pride. "I live here by *choice*, Laurence. Big fancy homes mean nothing to me. Any income I get goes to my foundation. I only keep what I need to live on—the rest goes to helping people."

"You're a *businesswoman*," he said, emphasizing the word. "A new businesswoman, at that."

"So what?"

He'd done his research before coming out that morning, and what he'd found had both surprised and impressed him. Two years ago Katherine had applied for and won two prestigious grants, in order to start a charity that provided financial support and housing for young people exiting the foster care system. One Step Ahead, it was called.

She had a good model, although her reach so far seemed small. A cursory glance at her DIY website featured the success stories of some of her clients, as well as a list of names of patrons. He'd recognized a couple by reputation.

"I looked. It's an amazing idea," he admitted.

She'd been forced to make a way for herself after being cast out into the world and she had focused on helping others. It was admirable, though he'd never have done it himself. Laurence gave generously to various charities, but he'd never been one to do the dirty work himself.

Katherine looked wary, although the expression in her brown eyes had softened a fraction at the praise. "Okay. So?"

Laurence almost laughed aloud. There was something he liked about her prickliness. In the world of advertising everything was based on a company's ability to make everything seem smooth, pleasant, seamless. Katherine's irritation felt fresh.

"I won't insult you by offering you actual money—you'd probably throw it in my face."

"That's accurate." She *did* smile then, probably at the prospect.

"We're in a ridiculous situation," he admitted, leaning back into the cheap imitation wood chair, "but I was trying to think on my feet. I didn't anticipate it would escalate into something like this."

"Well…"

She was faltering; there was an uncertainty in her eyes that hadn't been there before. Katherine couldn't hide the expression in her eyes any more than a child could, and he found himself holding his breath before he remembered that he was there on a mission.

"Let me help you," he said, and his voice was a low husk, heavy with the sort of reassurance that was intended to persuade.

"I don't need your help."

But he saw her swallow visibly.

"I've never needed your help or anyone else's."

"Let me be your partner, then." He didn't hesitate. "Everyone needs somebody."

He realized even as he uttered the words how wholly hypocritical they were. First of all he didn't need anyone, and never had, and secondly it was something his father might have said, to reel in an unsuspecting voter. The thought made him feel sick, although he couldn't show Katherine that.

"What happened to your date?" she asked a little unsteadily. "Isn't she over her *indisposition*?"

Oh. He'd nearly forgotten the excuse he'd used, and he decided in a split second to speak honestly. Katherine Asare was someone who cut through directly to the heart of things; he'd have an easier time with her if he didn't dissemble.

"She dumped me," he said blandly.

Katherine looked pleased for the first time since they'd spoken. "I can't imagine why."

He decided it was time to round up the conversation. If they wandered into the weeds he'd be in danger of losing control, and Katherine Asare and those enormous eyes were digging in places they had no right to dig. Someone like her, with insight into his past, had the potential to do a great deal of damage.

"I'll speak plainly." The way he should have in the beginning, before she had him ruminating.

"All right."

"I'm close to signing the man you met. Giles Mueller. He's the owner of the Mueller Racetrack."

She nodded.

"You know it?"

"It's out on Long Island. I attended an event close to it once."

He grunted. "The woman you filled in for on Friday is— *was*—my set date for several events over the next month. Since Giles already thinks you're her, I'd like you to step in. In exchange, I'll make a handsome donation to your charity—"

"Foundation."

"Whatever you like."

There was silence between them for a moment, and Katherine looked at him again. It made him uncomfortable at once. He knew she couldn't see into his mind, but there was something very perceptive about that look. She said nothing, and he continued talking to cover the silence.

"You see, Katherine, I owe you a debt." Laurence's voice was dry. "You saved my life, and in turn I'll save your business."

She snorted. "What makes you think my business needs saving?"

Laurence laughed incredulously. "You're a one-person operation. You don't even have an *office*. Your website is one of those ghastly pay-by-month templates, you live in a boarding house—"

"I don't need an office," Katherine said proudly. "I meet clients in restaurants and coffee shops. An office is an old-fashioned and completely unneeded expense. I'm not looking to make money off this, Laurence. I want to help people. Not everyone is like you."

Laurence chose not to pursue the insult; what mattered was getting Katherine to sign. "As you like," he said dismissively, then reached for his phone. "My driver has the paperwork waiting in the car. I'll have him bring it round now—"

"No."

It took a moment for the word to register. "Excuse me?"

Katherine did not repeat herself, but she did shake her head. "It's a kind offer, Laurence," she said firmly, "but the thought of playing your girlfriend is at least as absurd as your lie was."

Laurence realized after several seconds had passed that he was gaping, and he closed his mouth rapidly. He'd anticipated many different counteroffers—all that had been provided for in the partnership proposal that was ready for her to sign—but a refusal was something he was wholly unprepared for.

"You're saying no?" he said, to clarify.

She nodded.

"Why the hell would you say no?" The question came out far more harshly than he would have liked, but he was genuinely shocked. "You have everything to gain."

She tucked a lock of dark hair behind her ear, and he was momentarily distracted by the smooth slide of it over her skin. The change in her was truly remarkable. In her element, she was an entirely different person than the frightened teenager he remembered, and she carried herself with a quiet dignity that was very attractive.

"Besides our shared past, which I'm keen to keep there," she said, "I don't want a donation based on a bribe. It's unethical."

"So is soliciting money by crashing other people's events."

She had the grace to look embarrassed at that jibe, though she sat proud and tall. "I stand by what I said."

Silence reigned for a moment and Laurence stared over Katherine's head, trying to think. How could he make the absurd girl cooperate? Inwardly, he felt some admiration for her integrity, but not enough to let her go without getting what he wanted.

He was silent for so long that she began to squirm.

"Are we done here, Laurence?"

He ignored the question. "Indulge me," he said, "by telling me again what you were doing at my party."

Her lips compressed. "One of your guests promised me a donation, and I was hoping…" She faltered for the first time.

"That running into her at a social event would be a good reminder?"

She looked embarrassed, but that defiance was still on her face. "Social events are where the people I need are, Laurence. I go to as many as possible, to network and meet people."

"Huh…" An idea was forming in Laurence's head. "And you won't take money from me?"

"No, I won't."

Her lower lip was thrust out. The petulant gesture only brought attention to how full and soft it was, although he supposed she'd be horrified to know his thoughts were wandering in that direction.

"Let's say you agree to do this—no, no, I'm just speaking rhetorically," he added, waving a hand for her to be quiet. "The first event we'd go to is the opening day of races for the summer season at the Mueller Racetrack. I don't recall the entire guest list, but the Regevs, the Davises and the Van Cortlandts will be there, in Mueller's box. It'd be a wonderful opportunity, Katherine…there on the arm of your *devastatingly* handsome escort—"

"Don't make me sick."

She was thinking, though. He could see it in her eyes. She frowned, a myriad of emotions flitting across her lovely face.

"Introductions. From me to every single one. And no need to crash. Your name will be on all the table settings. Maybe even a gift bag to take home," Laurence added. "I'd make sure you met everyone, of course, and talk up your charity—"

"Foundation."

"Foundation, and don't interrupt me. We'll get a new website up by the time we attend—yours is an amateur disgrace—and you'll have more donations than you know what to do with. In upcoming weeks I'll be hosting a dinner for the Muellers and several other clients of mine, to welcome them to the family—"

"Isn't that a little presumptuous, given you haven't signed them yet?"

"Oh, I'll sign them. There'll be golfing, and dinners, and late drinks, and Broadway shows—all the usual song and dance we do to make clients more amiable. You'll make a *killing*."

Katherine was chewing her lip, releasing its plump softness and drawing it back again in the most distracting way. He wanted to run his thumb over it, see if the touch would make her inhale the way she had the first time they'd kissed.

"You'll keep your hands to yourself," she said after a pause.

Laurence almost laughed aloud; it was as if she'd read his mind. Was that what she was most worried about?

"Are you asking me or telling me? I'll do as much as is needed to make it believable," he conceded.

"Connections?" she said, as if she were trying to convince herself.

"Connections. That's it. No money. I won't even make a donation."

"And I'll have to play your girlfriend for…?"

"A month. Six weeks, tops. I'll even let you plan your exit. Throw wine in my face in a public place, if you'd like."

She was trying not to smile now, at the thought of that. A glitter was coming into her brown eyes and Laurence found it sparked a warmth inside him that had little to do with lust.

"Well…?" he drawled.

She swallowed, then quickly put her hand across the table. He took it. He wanted to whoop in triumph, but he quelled the impulse—as well as the thought that perhaps he was more excited at the prospect of spending time with Katherine Asare than he should be. After all, would it be so hard just to say to Giles that he'd been dumped?

He pushed the thought aside, focused on her instead. "It's a deal, Katherine."

"No. Not yet." She shook her head so vigorously that her hair brushed her cheeks. "One condition—besides all the others I haven't thought of yet. Your parents can't know about this."

Laurence inhaled sharply. *His parents.* The reason they'd met in the first place, and a sore subject for both of them. "I don't talk to either of them—"

"Promise me!"

"You have my word that I won't tell them. The media… that's a little more out of my control. But I will take every precaution." That, at least, he knew he'd be able to do.

Katherine nodded stiffly, then stood. "I have to go to the post office," she said. "And, no, I don't want a ride, so don't offer."

"Shouldn't the guy you're dating—?"

"Don't push it, Laurence."

He nodded, trying to keep the satisfaction from his face. Katherine didn't respond well to smugness. "Shall we meet at my office when you're free this week? Discuss particulars?"

"Fine."

"I'll send you the address—"

"No. I'm sure I can find it," she said dryly. "Goodbye, Laurence Stone."

CHAPTER SEVEN

THE FIRM OF Laurence & Haddad was housed in a predict-
ably tall, angular glass building. Not on Madison Avenue,
as Kitty had expected—obviously too many viewings of
Mad Men—but a bit further away, tucked discreetly at the
end of a street not too far from Grand Central Station.

Safe in the privacy of her room, Kitty had agonized over
what to wear to her lunch meeting with that cool, worldly
creature and had finally settled on a black Chanel dress
with a short, pleated skirt. It was one of the last things Mrs.
Stone had given her before she'd left them, and the only
designer dress in her closet that wasn't thrifted. Kitty no
longer bought new clothes on principle.

"Every girl needs a little black dress, and you're eigh-
teen soon," the woman had said breezily as she'd towed a
seventeen-year-old Kitty through Barney's.

The former supermodel hadn't had the foresight to think
about how impractical a wardrobe such as she'd given her
would be, Kitty guessed, and most of it had gone to con-
signment shops, piece by piece, over the years. She'd kept
the Chanel dress, though, almost as a charm—for good
luck or bad, she could not say.

Ten years later Mrs. Stone's fashion advice had held
up—the dress looked as in style as it had the day she'd
bought it. Thank God it still zipped, skimming and clinging
to Kitty's subtle curves and showcasing her long slim legs.
It made everything come full circle, in a sort of bizarre way.

A rush of cool, scented air hit her when she walked
through the revolving door, and a petite blonde woman
with hair trimmed into a pixie cut appeared in front of her.

"Miss Asare?" She pronounced Kitty's name perfectly. "I'm Cordelia. Please follow me."

Kitty was glad she wore flats; Cordelia's gait was unforgiving. She hustled Kitty into one of the elevators that seemed to swoop down and open, magically, at her behest, but did not initiate any more conversation, just typed busily away at her phone with a sleek black stylus.

When they reached their destination they entered a foyer that was bustling with activity. Glass-walled offices lined the corridors, and Kitty could see people inside with computers, whiteboards, monitors, artwork on easels. Advertisements in sleek black frames lined the walls, many of which she recognized. It was mostly fine alcohol, jewelry, one very tiny foreign car. Decadent in a way she definitely couldn't afford—and yet it was refined. Sophisticated. Carefully curated.

All the things that Laurence Stone was.

Cordelia steered Kitty efficiently down the center hallway. She waved her keycard in front of one door, punched buttons on another, pushed open a third, and then—

It was as if they'd entered another world. The suite was quiet and cool, full of sunlight pouring in from ceiling-to-floor-length windows and skylights. Water ran over white and pale blush-colored pebbles in a reflection pool sunk into the floor, elegant furniture rendered in whites and creams decorated the space.

"This is Mr. Stone's private wing. We're going to be in conference room one," Cordelia said, and opened yet another door.

Kitty blinked, clutching her handbag tight to her side. The conference room was decorated much like the receiving room, except for the long white marble-covered table that ran down the center. It was covered by an assortment of dishes covered in filigreed bone-white covers, from which all sorts of savory smells emitted. At the head of the table stood Laurence Stone, looking a whole different type of formal in a sleek charcoal-gray suit and a black shirt that set off the smooth tints of his skin so vividly he seemed to glow.

His face was still. He looked nothing like the dry, exasperatingly amused man she'd shared an hour with in the office at her building earlier that week. He looked as if he could put a kill order out on someone and lie effortlessly about it—or at the very least smash a girl's heart to bits. She was glad to see him this way. It would be an apt reminder of who he was.

"Katherine," he said.

And there it was—that odd little twist of the consonants in her name. Her stomach responded with a flip.

"Laurence," she replied, after swallowing hard.

Laurence jerked his head in Cordelia's direction. "You may leave us."

She turned on her heel and left.

Laurence smiled, but the motion didn't reach his eyes. Kitty was struck by how much he resembled the Senator in this environment, with that look on his face.

"I thought lunch in the office would be nice," he said simply. "Please sit down."

Kitty did so and he followed. A man dressed all in black materialized from the background to fill water glasses and lift the lids off the dishes. There was a beautifully roasted chicken, mashed potatoes, fresh vegetables, a bright beet salad, and lemon pie with piles of whipped cream to finish it off.

"You probably would have preferred a restaurant, but the food is quite good here," Laurence said easily, carving the bird with unexpected skill. "White, dark...?"

She swallowed, determined not to appear intimidated. "A leg."

Laurence draped a linen napkin over her lap and filled

her plate before attending to his own and sitting down. The china was plain, but thin and gleaming; the silverware was heavy and polished to a high shine. All very good quality.

She took her first bite of chicken and sighed appreciatively. Fork-tender and seasoned to perfection.

"Good?"

"Wonderful," she admitted guardedly, and then paused to load her fork with the potatoes, creamy and golden with butter.

"Well, I know you only eat the best, so…"

Kitty's fork clattered down to her plate. "Are you *ever* going to stop alluding to that?"

"Not until the day I die."

"You probably would never have noticed," Kitty huffed. "And I knew anyone in the penthouse suite wasn't going to be financially ruined by a couple of glasses of wine."

"It was stupid." Laurence leaned back, clearly enjoying Kitty's discomfort.

"Well, I'm not sorry," Kitty said irritably. "And if you mention it again I'm not going to speak to you."

"Our first quarrel!"

Kitty leaned forward indignantly, but he spoke again.

"Don't be so sensitive. It only gets in the way of success. Look," he said, leaning in so those piercing eyes were squarely fixed on her face, "I meant what I said. I want to help you."

"You mean, you want to help yourself." Kitty attempted to calm the churning of her stomach by taking a long sip of mineral water. "Your father was the same way."

Laurence's hand came down hard on the tabletop and Kitty nearly leapt out of her skin. He did not shout, but his voice gave her chills.

"Listen. We won't be together for long, but while we are you will not speak of the Senator to me. Not now, not *ever*."

"Why? I'm sure he wouldn't approve of this little agreement…" She could practically feel the rage emitting from his pores, but she couldn't have stopped even if she wanted to. "After all, he threw me out."

Laurence stared at her as if he was trying to choose between shaking her or tossing her out as his father had. He settled for leaning back in his chair, and then spoke through a jaw as rigid as the marble top of the conference table.

"My father was expert at using people, Kitty. I'm sorry he did it to you."

I'm sorry he did it to you.

She did not trust Laurence; she would *never* trust him. Their shared past was enough to ensure that. He'd been kind to her once, but he was one of *them*. It would be foolish to forget that.

Kitty cleared her throat, and when she spoke there was much less animosity in her voice, though it was still guarded. "How did you get into advertising?"

"I got into the business with a schoolmate of mine, years ago—he runs the international side of things and I handle North America."

"Desmond Haddad?" Kitty said, remembering the second name on the door.

"The very one." Laurence seemed uninterested in talking about his business partner. "How'd you get into philanthropy?"

She took a breath and picked up her fork again, allowing herself to be seduced into complacency by the food, which really was excellent.

"I worked as a grant writer for a non-profit for a few years, and went solo a couple of years ago. I've been able to help about ten kids," she said, and she could not stop the pride from coloring her voice.

A man like Laurence Stone would have no idea what it meant to be able to offer stability and security to a young person who had nobody, but having the rug pulled out from under her at such a young age herself had left her with a near obsession with helping people in the same situation.

Laurence smiled, and Kitty fought the little flip in her stomach with all her strength. He was *ridiculously* attractive. More so than any man had the right to be.

Kitty was no stranger to attraction, but her life left little room for romance. Men, in her limited experience, were selfish creatures; everything they gave was tied to ego. The Senator had taken her in because it had made him look good. Men in college had approached her because she'd blossomed, gained new confidence, made *them* look good. It was dangerous to engage with men unless you were in a position where you needed absolutely nothing from them.

After all, her reliance on the Stones had caused her devastation, and even as a young girl she'd sworn she'd never allow herself to be in that position again. She could not allow Laurence Stone to run roughshod over her inner vows, no matter how warm his lips were, or how she wondered exactly what the hint of shadow she could see on his jaw might feel like on her bare skin…

"Very commendable," was all he said.

She stood, pushed back her chair, and took a full step back. He smiled—much to her discomfort. There must be something truly wrong with her, Kitty thought with some despair, that she reacted so primally whenever he was near.

She closed her eyes in order to shut him out, heard rather than saw him stand up, come closer to her.

"Are you all right?"

She nodded. "Just wanted to…" She could come up with no viable excuse, and instead chose to ignore the question. "Thank you for lunch."

"You didn't eat much."

No, and what she'd eaten was now knotted in her stomach. She placed a hand on her abdomen. "If this is going to work, I guess you should call me Kitty."

"What?"

"My friends started calling me that at university."

It had matched the new persona she'd taken on there—confident, strong, and outrageously independent, with a hint of sauciness that manifested in her attitude, her bold makeup, her graceful swaying-hipped walk. She felt none of those things, now; she felt a little like a fraud. Laurence had seen her when she was less than nothing, and she wondered now if these superficial gains meant anything to him.

"Kitty. It suits you." He paused, as if to savor the name on his tongue, then continued. "I plan on taking very good care of you during our time together."

His deep voice curved round the words, taking them from something innocent to something else entirely…something that tightened her stomach, eased down to her loins.

"Kitty, look at me," he commanded, although it didn't sound at all like a command. It was gentle, soft, with a hint of tenderness that drew her like a moth to flame. She'd always been a fool for a kind word.

She opened her eyes.

Thankfully, Laurence wasn't looking at her; he was looking at her hand, at the balled fist she'd made. He reached out, and before Kitty could stop him he took her wrist in between his fingers.

"You're bruised," he observed, and a lump rose in Kitty's throat.

One of the injuries she'd sustained that night was a bruise just above her pulse-point; it had darkened to a very nice shade of purple just yesterday. It faded for the most part into her dark skin, but was still visible to a sharp eye.

"Can I take a look?" he asked, gently.

Kitty felt heat take over her body as palpably as it had that night. It was as if every cell of arousal she had was primed to react to Laurence Stone's touch, though her brain knew it was the worst idea she could possibly hope to have.

He was touching her wrist, and barely that, and her body was reacting as strongly as if she were naked beneath his gaze. She felt a familiar tingle…one that would crest and reduce to an ache. She knew without looking down that her nipples would have swelled, puckering as if for his mouth.

"Fate brought us together for a reason," he said simply.

Laurence was still stroking her skin almost absentmindedly, much as he'd done that New Year's night. Kitty should snatch her hand away, but—

You don't want to.

That thought was enough for Kitty to yank her hand back—that and the fact that she was breathing as heavily as if she'd run up a flight of stairs to get here. She licked her lips, fighting for composure. The room felt smaller, smelled far too male. And Laurence—

Laurence Stone was smiling. He knew. He *knew*. And he was using that weakness against her—wielding it above her head like a weapon.

It was precisely, she thought, what his father might do.

Kitty shifted on trembling legs, pressed her thighs together beneath her brief skirt. The ache there now was delicious. The type of ache produced by lust and assuaged only by the type of roughness a man of his size and strength would be able to offer.

"Kitty…" His voice was strangely gentle.

"No. I'm not interested in—"

Was it normal, the fact that her chest was rising and falling so rapidly? She willed herself to calm, for her blood pressure to lower, for the heat that she knew flushed her skin to reduce. And the worst part—the absolute worst part of this—was…

It isn't affecting him at all.

There was no flush beneath that stunning copper skin, no uneasiness in his expression. All she saw was that immovable face, those stony eyes, and suddenly she felt a wave of helplessness wash over her.

Men like this, she thought, would always do what they willed. Get what they willed. The world was set up for them, and there wasn't a damned thing she could do about it.

She closed her eyes again. She could feel him getting closer, feel heat and warmth and smell spice and soap and other overwhelmingly good things. She didn't open her eyes…not even when she felt the warmth of his hand on the skin of her cheek.

"Kitty," he said, and his voice was almost kind. "Believe it or not, my goal this afternoon is not to distress you. Please, look at me."

Kitty forced her eyes open, trying her best to ignore the headache forming behind her lids. Laurence was closer than he'd been that night in his hotel room, his full mouth pulled down a little at the corners this time, hovering tantalizingly above hers.

Close enough to kiss, Kitty thought, and a sigh escaped her lips.

It was as if her mind had magic powers, or some sort of magnetic force, because Laurence wasn't looking as enigmatic as he had been just seconds ago, and his slow, hot lips were nearly brushing hers, ever so softly, and she felt decidedly, certainly, as if she were going to die if he didn't.

Kiss me.

Laurence hadn't intended this—not at all. But, by God, now that he was kissing her he was glad he'd given in to impulse.

Kitty's mouth was plush and rich and sweet, like some fruit he'd never yet had the pleasure of tasting. He only brushed her lips with his at first, giving her the room to push him away if she wanted to, but she stiffened, then melted back against the cool hard surface behind her, letting out an exquisitely soft sound that made his blood surge in response, pooling downwards.

He kissed her with a gentleness he hadn't known he possessed until this moment. This was no plundering; it was an exploration. Kitty's body had softened beneath his as it had done that hazy night in his hotel room, a tantalizing hint at what she might be like were she ever to be naked and pliant in his arms.

When it ended, she looked up at him with kiss-swollen lips. "This isn't right," she whispered.

"No," he agreed.

But he did not let that observation prevent him from running a thumb over the silken length of her lower lip… part of her that he was virtually obsessed with at this point. He had not forgotten how deliciously plump it had become at his ministrations both then and now.

She closed her eyes for a moment, as if to shut him out, and he found suddenly that he didn't want that. He wanted to see what was written in those eyes, what he knew she would be too proud, too angry, to say.

A flash of panic crossed her thin face when he pulled back to look at it, and Laurence suddenly felt regret. Panic was decidedly not the emotion he wanted to elicit from this woman—especially not when he had her in such a vulnerable position.

Though his body cried out with frustration, he dropped his hands, somehow restrained himself from gripping her hips in his palms, and took a full step back.

She crossed her arms over her breasts. "I think we need to set out some ground rules."

He lifted a brow.

"If *this*…" she gestured at both of them "…is going to be a problem—"

The only problem he had was that he wanted to lock the

door and finish what he'd started, but he doubted that revelation would be useful at this juncture.

"It won't," he said quickly.

"Are you sure?"

"Let's just say I've fulfilled my curiosity."

Her eyes clouded with shock and hurt, but he kept going. Harsh, he knew, but better. Were Kitty Asare a different kind of woman he might initiate an encounter—dirty, hot, fast. He'd done it before. However, Kitty's awkwardness indicated one thing: an innocence he had no interest in removing. He did not know if she'd had lovers before, or how many, but he would not make it his business, no matter how much his body cried out for it.

He cleared his throat. "Perhaps we should have a glass of water, and then I'll call Cordelia in while I bring you up to speed, yes?"

"Fine," she said between her teeth.

She'd turned her head to hide her face and Laurence suddenly felt an odd protectiveness—and something much more profound, much more uncomfortable.

Guilt.

The return of Kitty Asare into his life had presented Laurence with something he'd never had to deal with before: the consequences of his actions as an angry teenager, noble as his intentions might have been. He had a debt to pay—and, despite his millions, he wasn't sure he could afford the expense that wanting her would bring.

CHAPTER EIGHT

LAURENCE WAS RIGHT about one thing: her association with him did produce results. Even though she hadn't yet gone on a single public date with the man, word had gotten out. Her website had crashed from the volume of visits, and funds had come pouring in with alarming speed.

Kitty was astonished at how thoroughly a few hundred thousand dollars could completely change the trajectory of someone's life in only a matter of hours.

Life as the girlfriend of Laurence Stone was changing Kitty's look, as well. The day after their office lunch Kitty was approached in her neighborhood again, this time by Cordelia, who ferried her to a four-hour appointment with a stylist in Soho. Her hair was conditioned, cut, blown out; extensions were put in, then cut; her eyebrows were threaded.

When she protested the cost, because she was determined not to owe Laurence a penny for any of this, Cordelia had an answer ready.

"The girls who worked on you today are in training," she said briskly, "and the firm did an ad campaign for the salon's Paris location last year. Mr. Stone won't be paying a penny for this."

Kitty was suspicious, but she gave in—with very bad grace. She did recognize that looking the part was necessary, and that styling her thick locks herself always took more time than she liked...

Clothes were next. No arguments, Cordelia said. She would have a new wardrobe, and it would be supplied by Tania Lee—a wardrobe mistress who worked out of LA for a film company that Laurence & Haddad had done yet *another* campaign for.

"Laurence wishes you to appear successful," was Cordelia's explanation, after the delivery of a number of devastatingly chic designer outfits and boxes of jewelry marked for different occasions to Kitty's building.

It could, she supposed, be interpreted in several unflattering ways, but she closed her mouth against her response. Her fight wasn't with Cordelia.

"Again, no expense, Miss Asare," Cordelia continued. "These are completely recycled from Tania Lee's film closet. Same with the jewelry—and it's all insured. Mr. Stone will have no arguments."

No arguments? That arrogant son of a bitch.

Kitty was fuming. She planned to tell Laurence exactly what she thought of him, as soon as she could get him alone. And she'd have that opportunity on her debut as Laurence's girlfriend: a day at the races, to take a look at Giles Mueller's racetrack.

On the day of the races Kitty was presented to Laurence by Cordelia at the door of his office, coiffed, dressed, made up, and ready to depart.

He looked up, surprised. "It's time already?"

"Yes, Mr. Stone. Chopper's ready."

Laurence sighed, gave his desktop one last longing look, and stood. He was wearing slim-cut trousers and a matching jacket of thin Italian wool, in the gray that Cordelia had mentioned was part of the "Ascot theme," with braces and a snowy white shirt. When she set eyes on him all the complaints she'd prepared flew out of her head, and she was suddenly glad she'd agreed to dress up.

Cordelia had her tablet poised. "Do you need anything else, sir?"

"Not a thing. Thank you, Cordelia."

When his assistant scurried away, Laurence looked Kitty over from head to toe, taking in the soft floral dress with the neckline that dipped demurely between her breasts, her small belted waist, her wax-smooth bare legs, the pointy-toed slingbacks that were so high she threatened to tip forward.

His eyes then climbed up, and his mouth twitched.

"Cordelia said I *had* to wear a hat," Kitty said defensively.

"It's very fetching."

Kitty had no time to process whether she'd been insulted or not, for he was steering her down the hall at a good clip.

Laurence's opinion of her designer pillbox aside, Kitty could not help but preen a bit. The high-shine chrome and mirror decor in his offices gave her prime opportunities to look at herself, and—well, Kitty really did love to dress up, with a girlishness that hadn't evaporated with all the realities of life.

It was like a montage in a fun but slightly problematic romantic comedy—being ushered into boutiques with names far too French for everyday wear and being dressed by a rich man's assistant. She knew she looked well. The creamy floral dress accentuated her slim waist and long legs, and her skin glowed with health against the pale fabric. She'd never seen anything so delicate before. It was from a period film set in the thirties, Cordelia had told her, and it was like wearing a watercolor...all soft swirls of gray and white.

The elevator took them all the way to the roof of Laurence & Haddad, where an enormous white and silver helicopter waited, blades circling madly. Kitty had a little trouble with her skirt, but somehow managed to cross the concrete without flashing anyone.

Laurence ascended without looking back, then turned to squint when he realized she hadn't yet quite made it in. "What in heaven's name are you doing?"

"I'm wearing heels!" She got in at last and arranged herself, a little breathless, into the nearest seat.

"Towel, ma'am?"

A woman in black trousers and a matching button-down approached Kitty with a smile. Laurence waved her away, but Kitty took the proffered towel, inhaled lavender and vanilla, and looked round the interior of the—was it called a *cabin* in a helicopter?

There were oversize reclining seats rendered in a buttery tan, meters of walnut paneling, in-flight entertainment, and the attendant, whose sole occupation seemed to be to make sure the half-hour or so it would take to get to Long Island would be spent in unwavering comfort.

"Is this the Senator's?" Kitty asked, wiping her hands and dropping the towel into the waiting basket.

Laurence did not react to her mention of his father the way he had the other day. In contrast, he seemed almost bored. "No, it's Desmond's."

"How nice of him to let you borrow it."

Laurence's brows drew together. "I can't maintain a helicopter as well as a yacht and a private plane, Kitty," he said, patiently. "It's excessive. You live in shared housing. I share a helicopter."

Kitty surprised herself by laughing out loud.

Laurence smiled. "I fold. I do have one, but it's out for repairs," he admitted. "I'm trying to think of what we would have had while you lived with us," he said thoughtfully. "Did they ever take you up in the chopper?"

Kitty shook her head, then stopped mid-motion as her hat was already hanging on rather precariously. "No. It was an election year. Your mother said that you kept a low profile during those times."

Laurence's face darkened a bit. "Indeed."

"Please buckle in, ma'am," the attendant said from her seat next to the pilot, and then drew a privacy curtain.

By the time she'd attended to her belt Laurence had switched on a paper-thin tablet—one like she'd never seen in any store. Likely custom made for him, as everything else was.

Kitty crossed her legs and peered out of the window, watching as the chopper hauled itself skyward and the city began to fade behind them. She shot little glances at Laurence, but he didn't look up. She sighed, then allowed the pillowy softness of the seat to absorb her back, her hips.

So far, this was the quietest date she'd ever been on.

Despite his best efforts, he couldn't stop stealing glances at her.

Kitty looked remarkably like one of the vintage advertisements that Laurence had often gone back to for inspiration over the years, featuring a woman lounging at an airport in Havana. Like Kitty, the woman was willowy and dark-haired, with the same chestnut skin and brilliant eyes, and she wore the same look of longing...of unfulfilled desire.

What did Kitty desire—and why did he care so much? She was his father's former foster child. He'd shared two kisses with her that crept into his memory at the most inappropriate times. She'd made him, for the first time in years, relive the most tumultuous period in his life. And now she was clearly discomfited by the way he was staring at her.

He didn't stop.

"Is there something on my face?" she blurted out.

"No."

She ran a self-conscious finger under both eyes anyway, then cleared her throat. "Are we just going to sit here and not talk until we get there?"

He lifted his shoulders. "Up to you—although you're remarkably bad at making conversation for someone who runs a charity."

Her eyes narrowed as she registered the insult. He did not have time to enjoy it, however, for she rallied back. "Fine. We'll talk."

"Do your best, sweetheart."

"What happened to you?" she asked. "After I left, I mean?"

Laurence blanched. He hadn't been expecting that line of conversation, that was for sure. "I'm sure an internet search would fill in those details."

She ignored that. "It was all over the news. You attempted to throw your father's election—"

He was ready for it this time. "That's a little extreme, Kitty. It was just a couple of social media posts."

"You accused him of fraud!"

Laurence put his tablet aside. To answer Kitty, he needed to focus. He had no intention of letting Kitty know exactly why she'd left the Stones' house, or his role in it; he still needed the Muellers to sign, and didn't know how she would react to that kind of information. A break with her now would only disrupt his plans.

"I was a horror," he said, careful to keep his expression neutral. "But I was a *boy.* I wanted attention; I didn't get it. Oldest story in the book."

He had to tread carefully here. He'd tell her just enough of the story to throw her off the scent…leave her role in it out completely.

"My father was a bit lax when it came to reporting his taxes accurately." He paused. "Some gumshoe at the *Times* thought he was living a little…*lavishly* for a public servant, and called for him to release his tax information, which he'd locked down tighter than the Vatican."

Kitty's eyes, which had been round with curiosity, blinked. "What does the Vatican have to do with—?"

"Nothing, it was a metaph— Stop interrupting, will you?" Laurence gathered his train of thought. "Anyway. I thought a good way to get dear Daddy's attention would be to leak the pages the fellow wanted, so I did. You can imagine the unpleasantness that followed."

There. That should be enough to satisfy her.

He could see Kitty wavering between curiosity and tact; unhappily, curiosity won.

"So you were sent away?" she asked.

"Something like that." Laurence picked up his tablet, signaling the end of the conversation. *Sent away* was definitely an understatement of the hell his father had put him through in retaliation for his disloyalty, but that wasn't Kitty's business—or something he was interested in reliving at the moment.

"I'm sorry that happened to you," she said, after a beat.

He shrugged his big shoulders. "I'm not. If anything, it got me off my ass and made me work for everything I've got now. You did the same."

She was silent for a moment.

"We aren't the same," she said finally, and he had to look up, lean in to hear her over the blades of the chopper, the humming engine.

At that veiled accusation Laurence felt the first stirrings of defensiveness; he fought them down.

"Yes. You're far nobler," he said, dryly, wishing to God the girl wouldn't sit there, looking at him as if she pitied him.

No one pitied Laurence Stone; it simply wasn't a possibility. If anyone should be pitied, it should be Kitty. Yes, she'd been lucky to get out from beneath his father's machinations, but he was in her debt for the way he'd done it. He would pay it, he vowed inwardly. He would handle her business as if it were his own, introduce her to networks of people who would transform her financially. He'd ensure it succeeded if he had to front the whole damn thing himself.

Then Kitty Asare would finally be out of his life forever, and he could truly, completely, put their shared past behind him.

* * *

Laurence hated horse-racing, though he pretended not to. Nothing could interest him less than watching the sweating beasts gallop round the track, frothing at the mouth while veritable fortunes were made and lost in the stands.

The Mueller Racetrack was tucked into a heavily wooded part of the East End of Long Island. Unlike other tracks—Saratoga and Belmont—only certain types of horse-racing aficionados knew anything about it. The track was frightfully exclusive, and until last year had been completely private. Now that more people frequented the ground every year, for the invitation-only events Giles hosted, he'd gotten vetted by the New York Racing Association, and he needed Laurence's agency to present the track to the world in the most attractive light.

Today they'd greet the Muellers and do the type of schmoozing that he hated but was so necessary in his line of business. They would tour the track, pretend to like it, have a few drinks, take a few pictures. Then he'd be airlifted back to civilization faster than you could say Triple Crown.

They alighted from the helicopter and headed toward the main racetrack at an easy pace. Laurence kept a hand resting lightly at the small of Kitty's back, ostensibly to prevent her from swaying in her heels. He and Kitty rather stood out rather vividly; most of the crowd was as middle-aged and WASPY as his father, and all were eager to greet what Giles called "such an exotic couple."

"You look so familiar dear," Doris said upon introduction, squinting up at Kitty's face through her oversize sunglasses.

Kitty opened her mouth to reply, but Laurence cut in, placing a warning hand on her arm. "Kitty and I have been dating for a few weeks."

"Why, Laurence!"

"I know. It's very new, and I'm very fortunate."

Kitty looked as if she wanted to pass out, and he continued before she could speak. She'd have to work on not looking so horrified at the prospect of dating him if this was going to work.

"She runs a charitable foundation and has been kind enough to let me work with her on expanding her business," Laurence said, then on impulse squeezed her waist. She jumped a little, but she managed not to flinch—*just*. "Kitty provides incredible opportunities for young people in the system."

"Well, well... How lovely." The woman beamed. "It's so very important to give back to the community."

"Absolutely." Laurence tilted his head, taking on the diffident, modest tone he took when speaking to a potential client.

He launched into an abbreviated version of Kitty's story—her personal experience in the care system, her success story, her desire to give back. By the time he was finished Doris was shaking her head in amazement, a hand pressed to her bosom, and Giles was nodding gravely. He actually *clapped*.

"You are an extraordinary young lady, Kitty. Well done."

Kitty had a sour look on her face; perhaps her feet hurt. "I'm very pleased to meet you," she said finally.

"We're pleased to meet you as well! Will you join us in the box? First race is about to start," Doris said, sounding brisker.

She must be thinking about whatever thoroughbred she had her money on, thought Laurence.

"We'd love to." Laurence allowed his hand to slip to Kitty's hip. "Just lead the way."

Of all the overbearing, conceited, self-important—!

Kitty's anger had begun to mount when Laurence had

cut her off so arrogantly. Kitty had no shame over her up-bringing—it was no fault of hers, after all. However, the last thing she wanted was to be presented the way Laurence had just done. As a victim. As someone to be pitied—someone who only belonged in these circles because it would do her some good. It was the height of arrogance, of entitlement, and Laurence had proved to be no better than his sire!

His handsomeness, she reminded herself, was just a mask on the rottenness within. He'd always find some way to touch what she cherished, cover it with his dirty finger-prints, make it all about himself...

She pried his hand off her hip with as much force as she could—she didn't give a damn that they were in pub-lic. "Hold on," she said between her teeth, forcing him to come to a stop.

Oh, if he lifted his eyebrows at her in that maddening way she just might—

"What is it?" He had the nerve to look surprised, and that made Kitty even angrier.

"Why did you take over the conversation like that?" she demanded. "And tell that sob story about me—"

Laurence frowned. "I was introducing you and your charity—"

"*Foundation,*" she stressed. "And I thought the point of this was that I'd talk for *myself.*"

"What's the difference? We're here as a couple."

Kitty wondered if flames were shooting out of her head—her face certainly felt hot enough. She counted back-wards from ten in her head before speaking. "*I* talk about my business. Not you. And you definitely don't get to talk about my past, or how I grew up. Not now, not ever!"

"Kitty—"

"You know how the Senator is off-limits as a topic of conversation? My past is off-limits to you," she said firmly.

She was trying to sound calm, but she knew her frustration was leaching into her voice.

"Kitty, I didn't tell them anything," Laurence argued back.

Although he seemed fascinated by her anger as her chest heaved, her body hummed with awareness. In one irrational moment she wondered if he would reach out, grasp her by the wrists, pull her flush against his body, test her to the breaking point—

She took a full step back. "Just watch yourself," she hissed, and stalked away from him.

The defiant gesture was just a little too much for the delicate sandals Cordelia had forced on her, and she felt her ankle turn. She stumbled, but Laurence was there in a flash, his hands at her waist.

"These things will be the death of you," he said gently, very close to her ear.

"Let me *go*," she said, giving him a push for good measure. She was steady on her feet—and, thank God, there was no throbbing. She tried to take a step and almost lost her footing again. The buckle had either loosened or broken. She swore.

"Very ladylike," Laurence said, and before she could stop him he was on one knee in front of her, those big hands cradling her ankle. "Let me see, honey."

His voice was neutral, but his hands were anything but. His thumbs pressed down, and she inhaled sharply.

"Hurts?"

"No." A lightning-hot frisson went through her at the caress on her skin. His grip was firm without being constricting; his fingers were warm. Strong. She gulped. "I'm *fine*."

Laurence began to rotate her foot, saying nothing, and Kitty felt warmer by the second. It was a warmth that had little to do with the late-afternoon sun beating down on their heads.

Several feet ahead of them, Giles and Doris turned.

"Proposing already, Laurence?" Doris called.

Laurence laughed out loud and mimed removing a ring from his pocket, then turned his attention back to Kitty's ankle. "Nosy old bag," he muttered.

"I really am all right…" How could her voice go from furious to breathy in only a few seconds?

"It's not broken. The strap just slipped out from the buckle," Laurence said, and began doing up the thin strap with more dexterity than she would have thought in a man of that size.

He was also maddeningly slow, and occasionally his fingertips skimmed her skin in a way that left her insides quivering. She'd never thought of the foot as a particularly erogenous zone, but now she could sense the dampness forming between her thighs.

She bit back a groan, as much from frustration as from arousal. *I'm not going to be able to do this.* She concentrated on breathing instead, on slowing the rapid beating of her heart and not giving any sign that she felt what she did.

When he'd finished Laurence stood. As it had been the night at the Park Hotel his finery was virtually undisturbed except for his pocket square, which was doing its best to escape. The Muellers were no longer in sight, and when his eyes skimmed her face they did so as Laurence Stone, not as the manipulative businessman telling whatever story he had to in order to close a deal.

"I'm sorry," he said simply, and offered her his arm.

Kitty felt rather light-headed, both from their argument and from what had happened afterwards. She licked her lips. "It's fine."

Perhaps to confirm that this was indeed a truce, she reached up to adjust the errant square of pale fabric.

When he took a startled step back she even managed a smile. "I'm not going to hit you."

"A man can't be too careful."

Kitty went about her work and put it back as quickly as she could. It felt oddly intimate, doing this for him.

"Hey…"

She looked up.

"I'm on your side, Kitty."

And I don't want to fight with you…not really.

Laurence Stone was by far the most confusing man she'd ever interacted with. Most of the time she wanted to kill him, other times his unrelenting dryness made her laugh against her will, and at yet other times she wanted him to press her hard against the nearest surface, pin her down, kiss her until she couldn't breathe.

The possibility of feeling real affection for this man at some point was there, and it was terrifying. Unexpected.

She pressed her lips together and stepped back, then took Laurence's offered arm in silence.

By the time the races began Kitty had three new sponsors and found her confidence growing with each conversation. Laurence was much more amiable—introducing her to guests one by one and then letting her steer the conversation.

They sat side by side for the duration of the race, silent in the face of the chattering crowd and thundering hooves, and when they were shielded by the chatter and the cheers of their companions, he turned to her and smiled.

"Having fun?"

Kitty took a breath. She was glad they'd made up, in some odd way. Laurence wasn't *terrible* company when he was being…tolerable. Not nice, she told herself. She'd never call him *nice*—not with that perpetual smirk.

"I was more nervous than I thought I'd be," she admitted. "I've pitched before, but…" She trailed off. "It's different, being here as someone's girlfriend. Not crashing."

He nodded. "You did all right."

All right? Kitty's eyes narrowed. "High praise, coming from a—"

"You did *fine*," Laurence said laconically. "Two-minute list of bullet points…almost verbatim from that heinous website."

Kitty stared at him, half considering turning her glass of champagne into his lap. Had she really thought only moments ago that they might find some common ground? "This isn't my first time doing this, you know, and the fact that they committed to a donation—"

"Meant that they would do anything to get you to stop talking." Laurence smiled, an unexpected flash of white in his face. When Kitty sputtered, he shook his head. "I do this for a living. I'm not trying to undermine you every time I make a criticism."

Yes, you are.

Otherwise he wouldn't take so much pleasure in it.

However, curiosity won out. "How would you do it differently? I was concise and friendly. Elevator pitch. There shouldn't be anything more or I'd be dominating the conversation."

"And why shouldn't you?" Laurence half turned to smile at her again.

He'd donned a straw boater, tipped forward over his eyes; on him the ridiculous hat looked good, and she suspected he knew it.

"We're stuck in this tacky booth, dressed like refugees from *The Great Gatsby*, and we're both after fat wads of cash. It's all about acting, Kitty. Storytelling is a vital part of selling. I don't talk about myself, either, but I make up plenty. Just take enough of the truth to fit the situation and have fun with it."

Kitty frowned.

"Think of it this way…" he said, and shifted so he was a bit closer to her.

She could see Doris Mueller just outside the line of vision, looking at them and mouthing *How sweet*, nudging her husband. She could not protest when he drew her close.

"You've already fascinated them," he said simply. "You're beautiful, and intelligent, and compassionate, and kindness radiates from every word you say."

Each word lit a little spark in Kitty, so when he'd finished she felt as if a fire had been kindled low in her chest. It was a warmth that had little to do with desire and everything to do with— Well… She'd spent years working hard with barely anyone's notice. She'd told herself long ago that she didn't even care to have it, but—

"Are you sure that's not a line?" she said gruffly.

Laurence smiled thinly, then spoke again, this time into her ear. "Think on this…" he said, and there was the barest warmth of his lips against her ear canal.

Kitty could not think at all—not with him so close. He smelled like rum and spice, a living embodiment of everything rich and refined…and his hand was fitted into the curve of her waist as if it belonged there. She could feel her body relaxing into his as if the heat radiating from his frame was melting the ice she'd been encased in all this while. It was absolutely surreal.

Below them she could see the horses on the track, their gleaming sides heaving with exertion. Laurence was still talking, low and gentle. She tilted her head so that his nose and mouth fit perfectly into the crook of her neck and shivered as he drew her closer. Closed her eyes.

"The story of us, for example," he began.

"There is no 'us,'" she murmured.

"Quiet, you'll ruin it." He laughed softly.

Kitty wanted to pull away as badly as she wanted to stay, and Laurence's grip tightened on her as if he knew it.

"There's a moment of danger," Laurence was saying now, against her skin. "A flash...completely unexpected. There's a man, and a woman, and she's young and vivid, with perfect skin—" here, Laurence nipped at the edge of her jaw, making her jump a little before he soothed it with the softest of kisses "—and eyes that could hypnotize a man."

Oh. Kitty's cheeks warmed. But Laurence held her fast, still talking softly. All that mattered was the feel of him, how close he was, how *right* it felt.

Laurence was incorrigible, but—yes... There were those flashes of kindness sometimes, and amusement, and other things that had her studying his face when she knew he wasn't looking.

He was still talking. About *them*.

"They're still covered in dirt, see, and gravel...and they're trembling because they just escaped death. But there's a spark, and he's holding her like she's the most fragile thing he's ever touched, because at that moment she is. And the world, for that moment, is reduced only to them...lying on that bit of dirty concrete while the city races past."

His lips were hovering over hers now, and he lifted his brows. And Kitty felt a sigh emit from her lips *just* as they met. This was not mocking, or drunk, or possessive. It was gentle, almost loving, and that part of her she'd trained never to need affection roared to life.

When they parted Kitty blinked hard, speechless and trembling like a leaf...or a virgin...or at the very least someone who wasn't practically seated in the lap of the most inappropriate man in all of Manhattan.

"I think you're full of crap," she managed, licking her lips and drawing herself up.

His laughter rang in the small space, and to her discomfort it was just as warming as his kiss had been.

"I told you what I do, Kitty. It's precisely that—I sell stories. The beauty isn't in what *is*—it's in what *could be*, if we lived in an ideal world and things like that happened. It's not lying. It's giving a consumer a story they want to hear. Making them feel good about themselves. Creating a personal connection. And if they've all watched fate bring us together, watched us fall in *love*—" his mouth bent a little at the word "—they'll follow the story as long as it lasts."

As long as it lasts.

Kitty shifted, feeling curiously bereft. With every moment that passed she felt all the more foolish for her reaction. Whatever Laurence made her feel, it wasn't real, and she would do best to remember that.

"You're a fraud," she said crossly, pushing back against him, though with much less conviction than she wanted.

He laughed again, and when he slid his arms round her she didn't protest. In fact, she let her body relax against his.

She could not deny that whatever she thought of Laurence, this felt—nice.

"I'm a very rich fraud. And you'll be one too, if you play along."

CHAPTER NINE

AFTER THEIR DAY at the races, Laurence and Kitty fell into an easy rhythm—one that was punctuated by what Laurence called "small, smart affairs." There was a trip to see a jazz pianist, a night at a Broadway show, one lunch, two dinners, all with current and potential clients, or with members of New York's corporate society.

Kitty was growing dangerously used to being ferried about in a Mercedes in clothes that could have paid her rent for months, and she repeated her goal—*the success of her foundation*—as a mantra to herself every time she went out with Laurence for any reason. She'd received more donations in that couple of weeks than she had the entire previous year, and her little roster of clients was growing.

One morning Cordelia called her, bright and early.

"There's an opportunity for you to speak about One Step Ahead for the morning news," she said briskly. "Laurence asked me if you'd be interested."

Interested? She'd have to be mad not to be. "Yes, I'm interested."

"Very well. I'll send you the details."

A spot on a nationally broadcast TV program! Kitty went into a mix of elation and sheer terror.

A day later an agent from the network contacted her. She was to have a seven-minute spot with Laurence, to talk about philanthropy and her work in the city.

When she hung up Kitty dug into her files, read notes from other presentations she'd done in the past. Nothing seemed right for television, or for the easy-breezy format of the show. It usually featured summer cocktails, juggling, and dog-grooming as regular topics.

Laurence was right. Her usual speech was *boring*. It was as boring as drying concrete. It read like a brochure that you might find in the back pocket of a taxicab and read because you were running late and your mobile was flat.

Defeated, she rang Laurence.

He picked up almost immediately. "Is that the love of my—?"

"I'll never forgive you if you aren't serious about this."

"What's the matter, Kitty?" She could hear mild curiosity in his voice.

"Cordelia called me and told me about speaking on—"

"Oh, the news segment." He sounded as if he were prepared to be very pleased with himself.

"My presentation isn't right," she admitted. "And I have no idea why."

"Are you nervous?"

"The fact that I'm calling you voluntarily should tell you plenty."

"Ah."

He was silent so long she spoke again. "Laurence?"

He made a noise deep in his throat, and she fought the flush creeping up her neck. Laurence had been very good at keeping his hands to himself since their day at the races, and Kitty had been appalled at each meeting to find herself almost disappointed. Her brain recoiled at the idea of his hands on her, but her body missed it. Now even just the sound of his voice—

She forced herself to attention.

"When I make a presentation," he said calmly, "I think first about what the audience needs to know—not about nervousness."

"You get nervous?"

"Never—because that method works." For once there was no hint of mockery in his tone. "The success of my business lies on my ability to make people care about what

I'm saying. Think about your audience, Kitty. Think about what they don't know, what they need to know—and the fact that you're the expert on it, not them."

Kitty found herself nodding on the other end of the line. She knew all this, of course, but it was soothing, hearing it from Laurence's mouth. "Okay."

"And…" He paused. Then, "Don't be afraid to talk a little about yourself. Not gratuitously, but just so that people know you believe in them and that's why you're helping them. Empathy."

There was another long silence. Laurence apparently had nothing more to say, but Kitty found herself wanting to prolong the conversation, for some reason. "Are you busy?"

"I'm in a meeting with Desmond and a stakeholder."

"There are *people* there?" Kitty squeaked.

"You know I put you first, sweetheart."

Laurence chuckled softly, sending ripples of want through her body. She was beginning to associate this involuntary quiver with the sound of Laurence's voice when it dropped to that intimate timbre, and she despaired over it. He could be infuriating, but he also could be—

"I have to go," she said, her face flaming, and she ended the call.

On the day of the interview Laurence took Kitty to the studio at four, when many people were beginning to head home. They were to pre-record their segment and it would air the next day. She'd looked more relieved than he'd ever seen her when he'd told her about the pre-recording.

"I was nervous about going live," she admitted now, and he shrugged.

"I don't want to be broadcast live either," he said.

"Why? Because you're with me?" Kitty snapped, offended.

God, the woman could get her back up at a moment's

notice! He felt as if he were constantly trying to defend his motives.

"You're very self-centered, Kitty. This is my first in-person interview in over a year. I hate them, but Desmond pushed for it. Not everything I do is about you."

Kitty looked surprised at his honesty, and perhaps a little chastised, but she had no time to reply. They were immediately shown to a trailer, where Kitty was made up with pots and sticks of makeup of varying hues, then attacked with a powder puff the size of her head.

When the makeup artist who'd been assaulting her cheeks stopped, Kitty sneezed.

"You're perfect," the woman gushed, then took her basket and scurried out of the trailer they'd been assigned, eager to move on to the next guest.

Kitty wrinkled her nose, clearly trying not to sneeze again. She was wearing far more makeup than he'd ever seen on her—even at the party where they'd reconnected. He didn't like it. It made her skin look waxy and grayish, and exaggerated her eyes and lips almost to caricature.

She touched her face as if she'd read his mind. "It's not my color. I know I look like a cadaver."

He exhaled with a short laugh.

"I'm worried about talking about—about us on live television…" Her brows knitted together; she looked troubled. "I don't like lying. You joke about the food thing, but this is different. And if your parents ever found out—"

Laurence barely kept the white-hot anger that sparked in him at the mention of the two of them from crossing his face. "Even if I married you atop the Empire State Building they'd never say a word," he said sharply. "They are no longer in my life and I've taken legal action to make sure it stays that way!"

Kitty's brown eyes were as round as basketballs. "What happened?"

Laurence swore inwardly. Not many people knew about his break with his parents, and hearing Kitty ask about it had caught him quite off guard.

"Were you *listening* when I spoke about the tax fraud before, Kitty? My father is a manipulative bastard, and my mother is a spineless trophy wife," he said, allowing all the bitterness he felt to drip from every word. Instead of ducking his head, he forced himself to look directly at her. "You should know that better than anyone, Kitty. Did you *really* think you were anything but a ploy for his campaign?"

She swallowed hard.

"Think about it," he snapped. "You know how readily they discarded you. That's what they did, Kitty, when you were no longer useful."

He was saying too much…getting too emotional. If Kitty chose to prolong the conversation, to dig—

Shut up, Laurence!

He turned away from her to fiddle with his cuff. When he'd composed himself and looked back at her, Kitty had already arranged her features into neutrality.

"I'm very sorry," she said softly, as if she'd just realized something.

"It's fine." He was already regretting his outburst, but he would not allude to it now. "And you'll be fine out there. The general viewing public are idiots, mostly."

"It's more likely that people will be scared of me." She pointed to her face.

Laurence's mouth twitched. "My mother always took her own makeup to shoots," he said.

And with those words it was as if he were transported back to his childhood, watching his mother mutter about how makeup artists *"never got it right"* while handing over foundation custom-blended for the deep tints of her smooth skin. Memory was like that: it eased through the anger he felt when he thought about her from time to time, as subtle as smoke through cracks in a wall.

"Enhance, don't smother," she'd command. *"A light hand. My skin doesn't need help to glow."*

Kitty's didn't need help either. Even in the harsh fluorescent light of the trailer, even beneath that horrible makeup job, she was radiant.

Abruptly Laurence eased out of the high-backed makeup chair and crossed over to Kitty, who leaned back.

"What?"

"Have you got your own makeup with you?" he asked.

"Some—"

"You're right. It's dreadful," he said, letting amusement leak into his voice. "Hold still and lift your chin—I'll help you get it off. You might stain your dress."

As he talked he ripped open the pack of wet wipes on the vanity in front of them.

"She worked so hard at it," Kitty said, wavering.

"Up to you, but you look like you're on the set of *Dynasty*." He paused. "Or a clown."

That was enough for Kitty. She huffed as she leaned back, but allowed Laurence to clean her face with gentle swipes at her cheeks, lips, lids. The makeup came off easily, and her body, so close to his, was as tense as it was warm.

"Should I wonder why you're so well accustomed with women's makeup and *Dynasty*?" Kitty said after a moment, barely moving her lips.

He laughed without smiling. "Supermodel mother with a soap opera addiction." The woman also enjoyed shopping, and social activities, and always looked vaguely exhausted…as if the weight of wealth was far too much for her.

"Oh. That's right…"

"I traveled with her until my father decided he wanted to run for public office. Then she didn't have time for me anymore." He felt an odd pang as he said it. He'd signed his mother off as well as his father—complicity was the same as guilt in his head—but he did miss her at times.

Kitty opened her eyes, and Laurence felt an odd charge.

"Thank you, Laurence," she said, after a moment.

"For what?"

His name on her lips had sounded oddly intimate in this space, with him cleaning her skin. He reached for a small hand towel and turned on the tap in the sink to the right of the vanity. The water that came out was clear and hot. He soaked the towel, wrung it out.

"Last spa treatment," he said, and reached out to press the warm washcloth to her cheeks.

A little exhalation of pleasure burst from that full mouth and he felt his body respond. He had not allowed himself to think about how readily his blood surged in response to her closeness. It would not be right.

"That feels like heaven," she murmured, and closed her eyes again, surrendering completely to the warm compress soothing her skin.

Laurence cleared his throat and spoke to cover the silence. "You'll do great."

Her skin had taken on a rosy tinge beneath the smooth chestnut, both from the heat and their close proximity. When he set the towel down, she sighed.

"Thank you," she said again.

"Right."

She was close enough to kiss, and her lashes, long and lush, cast half-moon shadows on her cheeks. She wouldn't look at him, but he wanted her to. Desperately.

"Kitty..." he murmured, and touched her chin.

When she opened her eyes his stomach plummeted to his knees. For the first time since they'd reconnected she resembled the girl he remembered.

Her eyes were bright, and she swallowed hard before she

spoke. "I'm scared," she admitted. It was barely a whisper, but it still felt loud. "Lying? On live television?"

Laurence forced himself to laugh. He did not feel very much like laughing—not at all—but if Kitty continued down this path the interview would be a disaster, and he could not afford that.

It worked as he'd intended. Kitty's eyes narrowed, and she sat up. *Good.* Better she be angry than a moralizing train wreck.

"Why on earth are you laughing?" she asked.

He lifted his fingers to touch the base of her chin with careful fingers. "Because you're being absurd. Remember, Kitty. You're doing this to skim money from the wallets of people who don't give until they feel absolutely splendid about themselves. For most of them it's a drop in the bucket and a huge tax write-off. Kitty…?"

The turmoil in those lovely eyes and the softness of her lips and skin were altogether too tempting. He moved closer, allowed his lips to brush the sensual curve that was the corner of her mouth.

Just one kiss.

Kitty felt a wave of despair. This wasn't going right at all. She felt dizzy now—dizzy from his closeness, and the scent of him, and the fact that, yes, they were probably going to kiss again, and she wouldn't be able to blame him for it this time.

Her body was throbbing as hard as her heart was beating, and Laurence— Well… He made her so angry—the angriest she'd ever been since his father had dealt with her, years ago—but he also had a way of looking at her that made her want to cover her face and weep.

It was as if he saw straight through the facade to the girl inside, who still shrank when she thought of how she'd been abandoned by the Stones. He'd been ruthless, almost cruel, but he'd always been there so far, and that was something.

Kitty's head tilted back, as if in response to an unspoken question, and when the length of his body finally pressed against hers her body coiled with tension, but also with relief. Whatever the ramifications were, she'd never wanted anyone so badly in her life.

"You're going to do wonderfully. You are beautiful, and brilliant, and I'm honored to have you work with me," Laurence said quietly, his lips very close to hers. "Fake or not, that is real."

His hands lifted to grip her hips, tugging her flush against him. His lids were hanging so low she could not see his eyes, and that for some reason bothered her more than anything else. She gave in to an impulse, reached out and cupped the sides of his face with her hands. Her next breath came out as a sigh.

"Laurence…" she whispered.

This was a terrible idea, a ghastly idea, and in more ways than one. But here, so close to him, it all seemed so elemental. She was a woman, with wetness now pooling between her thighs. He was a man, a very attractive one, and if the hardness pressing against her abdomen was any indication he was much in the same situation. And if they didn't somehow clear the air…somehow get rid of the attraction that had dogged them both since she'd seen him at that party almost a lifetime ago—

She dropped her fingers down to the wall of his chest, sliding them over his abdomen. What she found hinted deliciously at muscle as finely carved as rock, but when her fingers dropped lower his hand flashed out, stilling her exploration.

"No," he said.

She felt a wave of mortification that only lasted a second, because he was pressing her against the back of her chair and kissing her as if he'd no other intent that afternoon. Unlike the kiss in his office, which had been slow and a little tentative, this was rougher, harder—as if he were trying to make a point or scare her off.

Well, she had her own point to make, and her frustrations vented themselves in this heated clash of lips and skin.

When they finally surfaced for air, she let out a ragged gasp and lifted her chin. For the first time ever since this whole miserable situation had begun she felt as if she had the upper hand—and it was all because of his dilated pupils, the heated look on his face. No one had ever looked at her like that, and her body thrummed with awareness.

"I think you like this," she managed, emulating the mocking tone he always used with her.

His mouth turned down at one corner and his reply was to apply his lips to her ear, let them travel to the side of her neck.

Kitty bit the inside of her cheek—hard. *Bastard.* He knew it was a sensitive spot for her. She realized that even at this early stage he was so in tune to her body that any lovemaking between them would be explosive.

"So sweet…" he whispered against her skin.

The warning bells pealing in her head faded. In this moment, she was completely and utterly lost.

CHAPTER TEN

IF KITTY DIDN'T stop squirming like that, Laurence thought, struggling to keep his breaths even and deep, this would be over before it began.

Not that he should have begun anything. He was aware of that—more aware than he'd ever been of anything. This…thing, whatever it was, had been hanging between them since the weekend they'd met, and it had to come to a head one way or another.

He allowed himself the pleasure of touching her breasts for a moment, cupping their full weight in his hands, marveling at how the softness overflowed. Her nipples hardened at his touch, even through layers of silk and lace—but they were not his target for now.

Thank God she was wearing a skirt…

His fingers dropped to her hips, gathering a handful of soft, diaphanous fabric and pushing it up her legs, revealing inch after inch of glowing rich skin.

But even in Laurence's most out-of-control moments his pragmatism reared its head, and today was no exception. If he was going to do this here, with Kitty Asare of all people, it had to be about fleeting pleasure and nothing else. He could not risk a connection. In his mind, if not in reality, this had to be as banal as he could make it. Kitty Asare was not an option for anything more.

It wasn't just that he might break her heart—he realized he'd already done that, ten years ago. It was that he couldn't risk his own. Not with someone so absolutely unsuitable.

Kitty's eyes were hazy and soft…beckoning, almost. He kissed her lightly, slid his hands up the inside of her thighs. The skin there was the softest he'd touched in a very long time, warm, quivering beneath his palms. He stroked her inner thighs gently, almost absent-mindedly, his eyes still glued to her face.

It was as variable as the sky, and as lovely. In the few moments he'd been looking he'd registered wonder, self-consciousness, irritation and—yes—arousal. Plenty of it. His own body was surging to answer hers, but for a moment—just a moment—he wanted to look at her. He wanted to give her pleasure.

She shifted. "Well?" she gritted out, breaking into his thoughts. And he laughed.

"Greedy," he said gently, and rested his forehead against hers. "This is disastrous," he added under his breath, surprising himself as the words came out.

Kitty laughed raggedly. "No kidding."

What *was* this, then? An attempt at self-indulgence for both of them?

He did not ask. Instead he cupped her through the thin layer of lace-covered silk that was his last barrier to the heat that was warming his palm. Her head tipped back. He began to trace over the feathery pattern on the lace slowly, thumbing it aside when he saw her bite her lip, then tugging it down to one ankle, impatiently. There was a downy softness first, and then, where he parted her, a silken wetness that made his own heart beat faster, the blood throb between his legs to the point of pain.

"Spread your thighs a little more..." he husked out. "There... That's good..."

Now there was a sweet, heady musk that made him ache to taste her, though there wasn't time. Damn it, there wasn't time, even though his mouth watered for her. The little bud of arousal between her folds was swollen, protruding through the soft pinkness that hid it, and so slick he actually groaned, then bent his head anyway.

Just one taste.

Kitty did cry out then, in pleasured shock, and jerked forward against his mouth. His laugh was muffled between her legs as he lapped at her sweetness, sucked gently. She'd been ready, and for much longer than they'd been in this room. Her whole body was tensed, coiled, ready to snap. He wanted her to break at that moment, to come undone in his arms.

He only allowed himself a moment, then resurfaced reluctantly. They had to finish this much faster than he wanted. Her small hands dropped down to where he strained against his trousers and he reached out and stopped her.

"No," he gritted out. Her touching him would mean she was taking control of the situation, and that would not do. He palmed her thighs, eased them open again.

She looked both agitated and frustrated, but her face contorted in shock and pleasure as he slipped a finger inside her. He felt her inner walls clamp down instantly. She cried out and he let her pitch forward, pressing her face into his neck. He would have preferred her head to stay back, so he could see her face, but she shook her head.

"That's it…ride it out," he said gently.

And then Kitty was moving her hips in determined circles, her lips warm and damp on his neck, mouthing words he'd never get to hear. It didn't take long, and yet he'd lost all sense of time when she cried out, spending herself on his fingertips.

They were both reduced to gasps for air and accelerated heartbeats and warm damp skin for several seconds, and then they began to emerge, separating back into their own bodies.

Kitty had gone limp in his arms. He withdrew his hand from beneath her skirt, clearing his throat. She was still hiding her face. He did not speak, but he nosed her cheek, her neck.

"For a fake girlfriend, I think you can be pretty convincing," he rasped after a moment.

He knew it was awful, but he had to do something about the throbbing between his legs, and breaking the mood would help.

"Oh—you!"

Kitty's voice still did not sound quite normal, but she did swat at him, scrambling for the flimsy scrap of lace still hanging off one ankle.

She opened her mouth to speak again, but exactly at that moment there was a knock at the trailer door.

"We'll need you out in fifteen," a man's voice called.

Kitty began to frantically rearrange her dress. When Laurence tried to help her she batted his hands away furiously.

"You've done enough!" she whispered.

"He said fifteen minutes, Kitty, not fifteen seconds."

She closed her eyes again. "You're not normal," she murmured.

"Yes," he agreed. "That being said, you need to re-do your makeup, and I—"

He gestured down to where he still strained against his trousers. They'd never felt so tight before, and he was using every trick he'd learned since puberty to take his mind off how much he wanted to take care of it, to bury himself deep inside her.

"This will take some time to go."

"Oh." She looked faintly embarrassed, then hunched her shoulders and reached for her handbag. She fumbled out a lipstick, a compact, and numerous little jars that he couldn't identify. "I won't take long."

He could have just stood there, with the massive erection that showed no inclination to wane, but he took pity on her instead, and turned. "I've got a couple of emails to answer," he said.

* * *

"Woman of the hour," Laurence greeted her sarcastically when the interview was over and Kitty had emerged from the trailer dressed in her street clothes.

He took in her torn jeans and black tank top with the usual hitch of his brow, but Kitty couldn't care less. She could have left on the fine designer dress, but after that afternoon she wanted nothing more than to shed the illusion, get back to being Kitty Asare.

"How did you find it, sweetheart?"

"Don't call me that." She'd intended to be curt, but her voice came out as something else entirely: soft as silk. Affectionate. Almost yielding…as if this was part of their own special banter. "There's no one around to hear, is there?"

"There's always someone around, Kitty." He reached out, closing a big hand round the handle of her garment bag, and she was startled enough to let him take it. "I meant it when I said that you did well. I was thoroughly impressed."

Kitty felt her cheeks warm despite herself. She'd taken his advice while in front of the camera, spoken slowly and carefully, concentrated on nothing but the memory of every young person she'd been able to help, and Laurence—in rare form—had deferred to her on almost every question. Their interviewer, a journalist of high repute, had seemed genuinely interested, and had followed up with an email a bare half-hour later, asking for Kitty's details. Listeners, she said, were already clamoring to donate.

"You did, too," she said after a beat.

Laurence lifted his shoulders, as if it was of little importance, then raised his phone to look at it. "I've gotten messages from people who haven't spoken to me since college, asking about you."

Kitty pressed her hands to her cheeks. "Surely you dating someone can't be that unusual?"

He shrugged. He looked as if he had something else to say, but his next words were a question. "Dinner?"

Kitty started. "Excuse me?"

"Dinner. With me." His voice was staccato, clipped. "Pretty natural thing for a couple to do after a day out, no?"

"I—I guess so."

Her heart gave an odd little jump. Was this part of the agreement? After-hours dates? He was looking at her so intensely. Especially after what had happened in the trailer. Heat engulfed her as she remembered the feel of his lips on her neck, her thighs…

"Great. We'll take the car." Laurence paused, looked at his ever-present smartphone. "I'm sure that Cordelia will want to arrange for us to be photographed, so you might want to change back into your dress."

Oh. So this *was* a work thing, then. Kitty pushed aside a feeling of disappointment.

"No," she said rebelliously, and Laurence looked up. "I'm satisfied with my outfit."

"Suit yourself."

"*Ghanaian* food?" Kitty exclaimed as soon as they walked into the restaurant.

Laurence's face creased into a smile—one that did reach his eyes. He looked pleased at her surprise, genuinely pleased.

"Do you like it? It was a gamble," he replied, laughing as Kitty stared wide-eyed at a menu.

"I didn't know there was anything like this in Hell's Kitchen!"

"The owner's an old friend of my mother's." His lips tipped up. "I know you've been in the States since you were small, so I didn't know if you'd like the food, but…" He lifted his shoulders. "Americans eat here, too. It's good either way."

The African fusion restaurant had no visible sign, no prices on the menu, and was so dark inside that candlelight danced off the planes of Laurence's face with all the drama of a black and white film. It smelled of frying meat, curry, smoke, and tallow, and still managed to be ridiculously romantic.

"It feels like a private club," Kitty said excitedly as they took their seats.

She'd had African food in New York before, of course, but nowhere this chic or trendy. The menu offered Moroccan, Nigerian and Ghanaian dishes, and the owner—a tall, thin man in a funky interpretation of traditional dress—came to pour ruby wine from an impressively dusty bottle.

"*Mema wo adwo*, sir," he said, and flashed Kitty a smile after the greeting. "You brought a beautiful lady, I see. Finally."

"I usually eat with Desmond, and they're all sick of him," Laurence explained dryly, and the man chuckled.

"Pleased to meet you, ma'am. Please relax. I will bring you some of everything."

The other diners were dressed in varying levels of casual and formal, and entirely wrapped up in their own conversations. If anyone was going to take photographs, Kitty had no idea how they'd do it discreetly.

Their food arrived: savory, peppery *jollof* rice, delicately flavored with chicken and thyme, smoky broiled fish on a bed of sweet onions and peppers, *kontomire* stew, rich with tomatoes and oil, with fork-tender coco-yam to absorb the delicious liquid.

Kitty fell on the meal with enthusiasm. It was impossible to recreate masterpieces like this in the shared kitchen of her apartment.

Laurence was a little more restrained, but he was amused. "You look as if you want to climb on the platter and roll around," he said, dryly, piling her plate again.

Kitty laughed and soaked up the last of her stew with a bit of yam. "I just might."

Laurence was looking at her as if she were a puzzle he was keen to solve, and if he had any sarcasm, he kept it to himself.

"I enjoyed today," he said after a moment.

Kitty met his eyes, and then she blushed. There was heat there, reminiscent of when he'd had her pinned in the trailer, a hand up her skirt. Now his gaze seemed to penetrate her very soul.

Perhaps it was the wine, or perhaps it was the haze that her earlier encounter with Laurence had left, lulling her brain into a post-coital fuzz of sorts. The afternoon had been a complete Cinderella moment—except the Prince was using her, and he'd teased her to orgasm with his fingers in a public place.

None of it is real.

Kitty bit her lip and shifted, feeling that now-familiar pull between her legs. Laurence Stone was proving himself rather quickly to be an enigma, and one she had no business trying to figure out.

"Kitty."

"Mmm…?"

"Tell me," Laurence said, almost too quiet to be heard even in that intimate space. "What it was like for you after you left."

The serenity of the moment was shattered. Kitty blinked. "Why?"

"Just tell me."

"It was a long time ago, Laurence—"

He shook his head and leaned forward. In the weak light of the restaurant his eyes were two burning coals deep in his face. "I'd like to know. Please," he added, and waited.

Kitty spoke. She didn't know what compelled her to

speak, but she did. "I went back into care," she said, and the words came out curiously flat.

There was no way—not even if she had the most eloquent vocabulary and all the time in the world—she could convey in a few short moments the pain of rejection that had plagued her that year.

"I lost my place at prep school." It still hurt, after all these years. "Went to public school. I was eyeing NYU, but that was out of the question. I got into City College."

"Where did you live?"

Her lips tightened. *Group houses. Shelters.* Places she'd never admit to this lofty, arrogant businessman who wanted to know far too much. She claimed that her living arrangements now were to save money, but if Kitty looked deep down inside herself she knew it was because she was terrified to look for anything more permanent. It was foolish, but she almost felt as if settling down, finding happiness, would tempt fate into snatching it from her.

"There are places," she said, "for people who need help."

"Shelters?"

"We call them group homes. They're nice," she added, staring him down, daring him to rebuff the lie. He didn't. "After that I bunked with my caseworker for a month, and then I moved on campus. Got my degree and—" She shrugged. "That was it."

A muscle worked in his cheek. "Was it very difficult?"

How the hell was she supposed to answer that question? She'd never starved, though she'd lived on the worst possible food, and she'd never slept outside, though she'd come close some nights, when there had been a shortage of beds in her group house, or other residents had made her feel unsafe.

Still, those things paled in comparison to her emotional state. She'd fallen into a depression so deep that some days getting out of bed and brushing her teeth was too hard.

She'd been lonely, and confused, and she had ached, continually, with the feeling of losing something she wasn't even sure had been hers to lose.

"Kitty?"

She swallowed. "I—I felt *rejected*, Laurence. Anyone would."

He was silent for such a long time that Kitty finally dared to peek at his face. Her insides were churning, as if being twisted by a hand. Laurence's face looked dark and forbidding. He also looked faintly sick and, despite herself, something in her cried out for him in a way that had little to do with sex. It was something more to do with shared experiences, shared trauma—and perhaps she was recognizing the pain that flitted across his face because she too had worn the same expression once or twice.

"We should go," was all he said, and he placed his fork down. Neither had eaten much after Kitty's monologue; the air was too thick with things unsaid.

She nodded, stared at her plate until he'd paid, and then walked out with him. She did not resist when he took her hand in his or stood close to her as they waited for his car to muscle its way to the curb.

"Mason will take you home," he said, looking down at her.

That unnerving softness was still in his eyes. It was as if he were looking at her, really looking at her, for the first time, and it was terrifying.

"Thank you for dinner." She forced a smile. "Not bad for a fake boyfriend."

"Right…" He cleared his throat.

"It's too bad we won't be able to—"

Kitty was unable to finish the casual sentence she was attempting for Laurence had stepped forward, closed the distance between them. His big hands closed over her arms. Firmly. Gently.

"Is it all right?" he asked after a beat.

Dumbly, Kitty nodded.

Laurence kissed her softly. She'd thought she'd experienced the full range of his kisses, but this one was entirely different; it sparked warmth without igniting a fire and it was disconcertingly gentle. He explored her mouth leisurely, retreating and coming back, as if he were trying to tell her something he had no words for.

When he pulled back, she was surprised. She wasn't breathless this time. In fact, she breathed the deepest she had in ages and the air seemed clearer. Sweeter.

"Why?" she whispered.

There was an oddly cool stickiness between her thighs, where his fingers and his mouth had teased her sex hours earlier. She wanted to shower, let the water beat down on her and wash the feeling of him away. Not because it had been bad—it had been the opposite. But she could not afford to think of it as anything more than—

"I don't know," he said, and she saw his throat constrict.

CHAPTER ELEVEN

WHEN KITTY OPENED the door of her apartment the next day to collect the newspaper she smelled the flowers before she saw them. They were excessively bright, tropical and in bloom, sitting on her front step in a delicate Tiffany-style vase of stained glass, brightening the dirty hallway with vivid bursts of crimson and yellow and blue. The colors were like none she'd ever seen in nature, and she reached out and touched a petal tentatively before picking up the heavy cream card peeking out from beneath the vase's brim.

The card was written in a thick, heavy hand. She guessed it was from Laurence before she even saw what it said.

Forgive me for my deplorable behavior.
You were remarkable.

Kitty held the card close to her chest for a moment, then dropped it as if it were red-hot. She could not afford such sentiment—not with Laurence Stone, despite whatever odd moments they'd shared.

She chewed her lip, then focused on getting dressed. Tonight was the *pièce de resistance*—an intimate dinner, hosted out on Long Island for several of his clients, introducing the Muellers to the "family."

"It's the Long Island house," Laurence had told her a week before their interview. "You would have stayed there while you were with…them."

"I did," Kitty said through dry lips.

The Stone estate. Her heart thudded in her chest.

"My grandfather left it to me. He died a few years back. I'll never live there, but I do use it for entertaining. My place isn't suitable for dining. If it isn't all right with you, though—"

"Why wouldn't it be all right with me?" Kitty spoke rapidly, cutting in to disabuse him of that notion. "Are the Muellers signing?"

"They're close."

"And what's wrong with a hotel?"

"The Muellers enjoy personal attention. Home-cooked meals. *Eccentricity*," Laurence said, as if he could not quite believe that anyone would want to socialize that way. "We did our research. One of the reasons they left their last client was that he didn't treat them like *family*."

Kitty felt a wild desire to laugh. Family? Her and Laurence? With their background? There couldn't be two people who knew less about it.

Laurence's eyes flickered over her face quickly, and he smiled.

"What?" she asked.

"I know what you're thinking," he said dryly. "We're creating a story, remember?"

"I'd almost forgotten."

He ignored that. "I thought we could talk about your work a bit. You may have yourself some ready-made investors there. If it's too uncomfortable for you, though—"

"No…" Why did she sound so weak? "No," she said, and lifted her chin. "I am fine. I'm happy to play hostess."

"Good."

A muscle worked in his cheek. She heard him take a breath. And suddenly Kitty realized.

He's as uncomfortable with this as I am.

Instead of running from what made him uncomfortable, though, Laurence barreled toward it at full speed. Perhaps he was determined to prove that certain things did not affect him anymore.

Perhaps she should do the same.

She could not stay in the protective shell she'd buried herself in—not forever. It had been fine for healing, but she had to emerge eventually. She supposed, in a sense, that there was no better time than tonight...

In Kitty's memory, the Stones' Long Island mansion loomed as an example of the life she'd lost—a representation of the fact that things, beautiful things, could be snatched away in an instant and growing too attached to anything was a mistake.

The house was ensconced in the wilds of Long Island's North Shore, among the remnants of New York's old money: geriatric millionaires. It had been built in a cool hamlet off a turnpike lined so heavily by low-hanging trees that the private road was completely shrouded from view of oncoming drivers.

Laurence had sent his car for her, and she'd spent most of the hour-plus ride checking her makeup and trying to fight back a nervousness that manifested itself in a vaguely sickish feeling—the kind of feeling that came from keeping terror at bay.

The Stones had used the Georgian-style red-brick mansion as a summer home. It looked like it had been lifted from an illustration of a Fitzgerald novel, with the sun setting behind it, washing the grounds in peach-tinted light.

Inside, it was still decorated with the grave sort of opulence that seemed more appropriate for a museum—lots of leather, and dark wood paneling finished to a high polish. As she walked in the feeling of *déjà vu* grew even stronger; she recognized pictures, figurines, even the smell of the dust.

By the time she reached the study, and Laurence, Kitty had composed herself enough to offer a tentative smile. "I feel as if I'm trespassing."

"You're not the only one." Laurence crossed over to the wet bar. "Whisky?"

"Please." Funny how she'd developed a taste for it since going out with Laurence.

"Strange, isn't it?"

He was talking to her but not looking at her, palming two large whisky glasses and then setting them down, decanting amber liquid into the bottom of each. He looked almost grim.

"What is?"

"Being here."

He handed her a glass, then downed his own in one quick gesture. He looked at it, as if surprised by how quickly he'd drained it, then shook his head and placed it back on the bar.

"I never thought…"

Kitty's hands tightened round her glass involuntarily. "Never thought what?"

"Don't' worry about it." He cleared his throat. "I'm going to get dressed. Will you be all right?"

"Haven't got a choice now, do I?"

He smiled wryly and left.

Things happened very quickly after that. Laurence came back, devastatingly handsome in black cashmere and wool, and the Muellers arrived, apple soufflé in hand, full of cheer and bluster.

Laurence took Giles on a tour of the house, while Kitty obeyed Doris's very detailed instructions on how to unpack the delicate dessert and greeted the other guests as they arrived, ensuring that the wait staff kept the glasses filled and that the table for ten was set to perfection.

It felt oddly domestic, and the feeling only intensified as Laurence dismissed the servers, sharpened knives and took to the enormous juicy roast himself, piling their plates high. Kitty caught his eye once, as she was refilling water glasses from the crystal pitcher on the table. She had to turn a laugh into a cough when he wiggled his brows.

Laurence had prepared for this so much. Had arranged the homey setting, right down to the steaming roast and the potatoes, and him with his sleeves pushed up; Kitty in her gifted finery; the beautiful mansion on Long Island; the roaring fire; the conversation; the laughter.

None of it was real. It was intended to manipulate a man into signing a deal. And if Laurence could do this for mere business, what was he capable of in other areas?

A chill wafted round the table and she shivered. She'd forgotten how cold this house could be. Laurence saw her and stood up, tugging off his blazer and draping it round her shoulders. She nosed at the soft fabric, which was a mistake; her senses were immediately overcome by soap, spice, the barest hint of custom-mixed cologne.

"I forgot to tell you it'd be cold," he said, his voice low and intimate, and he smoothed the wool down her arms before straightening up.

Everyone was smiling indulgently, and Kitty was suddenly *too* warm.

"I'm fine," she managed.

"Adorable…" Doris simpered.

Kitty could not have responded even if she'd wanted to; her senses were completely overwhelmed by the nearness of Laurence and those enormous hands resting heavy on her shoulders, by the memory of the kisses they'd shared after dinner only days ago. Her heart was heavy, too, with the realization that this—all of this—was part of the charade.

On an impulse, Kitty reached up and caught his hands in hers. The angle was awkward, so she only held them for a moment, but— Well… She wanted him to look at her. *Notice* her the way he hadn't since that night. Do something unscripted, even if it was just for that minute.

"Thank you, Laurence," she said. She tipped her head back, smiled—and let go of his hands.

A muscle worked in his jaw, but he said nothing. Doris and Giles chatted inanely. Her head hurt, and not just from tiredness. The memories were coming now, hard and fast. She wanted the dinner to be over—desperately.

She was almost there, she told herself. Giles was stacking plates in a jolly manner and handing them off to the silent server who stood in the wings. Plates of apple soufflé with piles of fresh whipping cream and apple cinnamon sauce were being passed round to guests who were exclaiming that they were *much* too full but eating it anyway.

Kitty stared at the pools of cinnamon and cream melting into each other, feeling rather dazed, and she jumped when Laurence jabbed her with his foot.

Talk, he mouthed, shooting daggers across the table.

Kitty felt a rush of anger that compressed her lungs so that speaking was impossible.

I should have never come here.

It had been a severe miscalculation, thinking she could handle this foray back into her past. Nothing superseded Laurence's need to win—and he'd never regard her feelings any more than his parents had.

"Are you quite all right, dear?" Doris was saying kindly.

Kitty managed somehow to make her lips move. "I'm well," she said, and he heard Laurence exhale. "I was in state care for some time, as you know, and I spent some time in a house in this very neighborhood."

She saw Laurence's face blanch. *Good.* He'd wanted her to *talk*, hadn't he?

"Did you really?"

Kitty nodded. "It was the inspiration for my foundation," she explained, and took a sip of wine to wet her tongue.

Laurence looked absolutely furious, but he needn't

worry; she didn't have it in her to air the details of her past just to spite him.

"So many people of means have resources they can use to help—and would if they knew how to. Sponsorship is an easy way to do good and still ensure the young people remain independent. Even the most successful people in the world—" and here she dared a glance at Laurence "—got help to start up in life, whether it was money, connections, or education. I want to help my young people with the first."

The Muellers were both nodding, as were the other guests. Laurence's face was unreadable.

"She's done a tremendous amount of good work so far," he said flatly.

The couple asked a few more questions, and conversation, dessert and coffee continued for another hour. After much effusive thanks, and a promise to see Laurence in the morning to iron out the paperwork, they left with much fanfare.

The two of them saw the rest of the group off, waving woodenly until the last car disappeared down the road, taillights dancing.

Without looking at her, Laurence turned and went back inside. Kitty's jaw dropped. She hurried behind him, closing the heavy door. Aside from the catering service, clearing up in the kitchen, the place was very quiet.

"Laurence!"

"Your ride will be here in twenty minutes," Laurence said tonelessly. "Should have been here twenty minutes ago, actually. I should fire that man."

"Are you not going to talk about—?" Kitty began.

But Laurence turned in a moment of fury that had Kitty shrinking back against the wall of the foyer. She felt his wool dinner jacket sliding off her shoulders, but she could not pull herself away from his expression to bend and pick it up. His eyes were *blazing*.

"Just what the *hell* did you mean with that line about my getting help to start up in life?"

Kitty was flummoxed. "What line—?"

"Don't deny it was a hit at me. You, Katherine Asare, know nothing about me." He spat out every word, a dark fury on his face. "I worked hard for everything I have, and I wouldn't take a penny from them. I've built everything I've done from the ground up."

Kitty laughed. She couldn't help it. The idea of what he was claiming was too absurd. "What, with your prep school education, your billionaire business partner and your trust funds?"

"I paid back every penny I took out of my—"

"Yes, but it was and is still there, isn't it? Any bank would give you any amount of money based on the fact that they exist. You didn't have to spend years building your credit and still get rejected. You didn't have to pour personal funds into your business and risk starvation otherwise. Even your motive for signing the Muellers—" Kitty's lip curled upwards. "The pretense makes me sick. It'll benefit both of you. You live *nothing* like the rest of us!"

Laurence had closed the distance between them and Kitty felt fear, but it wasn't fear that he'd hurt her. She knew Laurence was not capable of real violence. It was fear of his closeness, fear of what the stormy look on his face heralded, fear of whatever he was about to say. He looked for the first time since he'd come back into her life like the stormy-faced teen she remembered, angry and resentful.

She dared not touch him. The heat emanating from his body at these close quarters hinted at things she could not want, now or ever, despite what had happened between them only days ago.

Her mind conjured up an unfortunately vivid recollection of the two of them only days before, in that trailer. Her dress and his big hands had been sliding torturously slowly up her thighs and then his fingers had been inside her, buried in her to the knuckle—

She cleared her throat, willing the images that were coming to disappear. "Laurence—"

He shook his head. "You've made your point," he said, and turned to head back down the hallway, leaving Kitty shivering.

She bent to pick up the soft black wool from where she'd dropped it on the ground and went after him. "Laurence!"

He paused, though he didn't turn around.

"I'm sorry." It nearly choked her to say it, but she could not ignore the fact that... Well, this evening must have been as hard for him as it was for her. "I shouldn't— You can't help what you were or what you had. It was unfair."

"You did nothing, Kitty." He wasn't looking at her face.

"We were children," she said, and at that Laurence actually flinched.

"Yes," was all he said, but his face was a study.

Kitty's heart was hammering with much more than adrenaline; it was suspicion. Suspicion that made her suddenly feel sick. Suspicion that she was on the precipice of a truth that quite possibly would shatter everything she'd thought was true up until this point.

He turned around and his face was still.

"Do you—?" She swallowed hard. "Do you know why they sent me away?"

She had never seen such a change in a man before. There was a look of absolute despair on his face. It flitted across it so quickly she might have missed it if she'd blinked, but she hadn't, and it made the stoniness that replaced it completely irrelevant.

She'd seen the real Laurence Stone, if only for a fraction, and it aroused something powerful within her, pushing fear into the background.

"Laurence?" she whispered, and stepped forward, resting her hands on his arms.

The muscles there were iron-tense, as was the rest of his body.

He had to get out of here.

Kitty hadn't said another word, and he'd turned, forced himself to walk normally into the study, putting one foot in front of the other.

Now he went to the decanter, poured a couple of fingers of amber liquid into a clean glass, held it out without looking. He knew Kitty would have followed him.

"I don't want a drink." Her voice was tremulous but decided. "You shouldn't have one either. It's silly, running for the bar whenever you hear something you don't like."

"This was a mistake," he said finally. "All of it was."

He'd managed to convince himself that the past didn't matter, that he could be ruthless enough to place emotion aside and concentrate solely on what both of them could get. He'd also managed to convince himself that making sure Kitty Asare succeeded in life was enough to make up for what had happened to her.

He tipped the contents of the glass into his mouth, barely registered as they went down his throat with smoky dark heat.

"Are you really not going to look at me?" she demanded.

He turned, facing the reason for the guilt that had been eating at him all evening head-on. Her lovely face was tight with anxiety and she was twisting her hands in her skirt, in that nervous habit he remembered from the races.

"Are we going to talk about this?"

"No. No, we are not."

He was itching to leave the room, to pace in privacy until he'd managed to push down the feelings Kitty had aroused, back into the deep dark places from where they'd come.

"You brought me back to this house, Laurence," she said, and her voice cracked painfully.

Laurence felt something deep inside himself rend in two as well.

"You brought me *back* here."

"Kitty…" He could see tears slipping down the soft skin of her face, making damp rivulets. He took a step toward her, but she shook her head violently.

"Do you know what happened the day I left?" She took a shuddering breath. "My case worker picked me up from school and told me I was no longer welcome, Laurence. I couldn't even pack my own things. She told me I was being 'reassigned,' as if I was working for a temp agency."

Bitterness colored her voice for the first time since he'd met her. "I was seventeen, and I had no idea what the hell I'd done that would possibly make your father—" She stopped. "I don't know," she repeated. "I don't know…"

"It wasn't you." Laurence's tongue felt heavy, swollen, stupid, and the roast in his stomach was congealing into something rather unpleasant. "It wasn't you. They—aren't good people."

He swallowed hard and then he reached out, touched her cheek. If he'd had any doubts about her motives now, they were quickly dissipating. Not because of the tears—mere tears would never move him. It was the fact that this woman…this beautiful, poised young woman…had come through the same home he had and had been wounded by the same people.

However, unlike him, she'd become better for it.

"You shouldn't cry," he said, and his voice was rough. "It isn't worth it. None of this is worth it."

"I know." She swiped furtively at her cheeks and peered up at him, ran a small pink tongue over lips that were already wet, swollen and, he knew from experience, plush and warm.

The sudden rush of awareness in his body had little to do with lust and everything to do with tenderness, and that startled him. It sparked an ache in his chest that was as uncomfortable as it was unexpected. He wanted her close, and if the way she was breathing was any indication she wanted that as well.

"This makes absolutely no sense," he said, and he meant every word. However, his body relaxed, closing the final few inches between them.

"I know," she answered.

Kitty's slim fingers crept toward the cashmere covering his chest. He did not move, even though he knew that, by God, he should! She slowly, tentatively, pressed one knee up between his legs. He bit back a groan.

"Please take me to bed," she whispered, and it was those words, a little broken and a little defeated-sounding, that did it.

Laurence slid his hands round to her backside, drew her close so that the inches between them evaporated like smoke.

Kitty lifted her chin and looked into his face. "The past doesn't have to matter," she said. "Not tonight. And maybe if we finally…"

Her voice trailed off, but he knew exactly what she meant. Maybe if they had sex, if they finally allowed to happen what had been building for weeks, they'd finally be able to not want it anymore, in anticipation of when they went their separate ways.

A muscle jerked tight in Laurence's cheek, making his jaw go rigid. His mouth moved soundlessly for a moment, and he inhaled deeply before he spoke.

"It does," he said roughly. "It *does* have to matter. Because, Kitty, it was my fault they sent you away."

CHAPTER TWELVE

WHEN KITTY BURST OUT from beyond the immediate circle of the Stones' mansion she found herself shrouded in darkness. It was a thick, choking darkness that was nothing like night in the city—a velvety blackness that completely engulfed everything around it.

She cried out, involuntarily, and clapped her hand to her mouth. She couldn't hear a thing over the blood drumming in her ears.

This was a nightmare—a nightmare akin to finding oneself naked and exposed to the elements—and memories assaulted her as well, hard and swift.

The first few nights after she'd been sent away were sharpest in her mind. She'd been scared half out of her mind, unsure of where she'd sleep, being bounced from house to house as Anna had looked for a room for her.

For nearly a year she'd cried herself to sleep every night, and all because—

She screamed again, in terror this time, when she felt someone reach out in the darkness and grab her from behind. She knew before the scream left her throat that it was Laurence, and she whirled around blindly, struck out at him with her fists.

"Don't you dare touch me!"

"Shh…" he said, and his voice rumbled low in his throat. There was no mocking there, and more than a little concern. "Kitty, you ran out—"

"Because I wanted to get away from you!"

"Out *here?* We're on six acres, Kitty. Where were you planning to go?"

"I'll call an Uber!"

He laughed incredulously, and Kitty felt a hatred for him so violent she wondered if she'd be sick. She attempted to shove him away. He wouldn't let her.

"Kitty, don't be an idiot. At least let me take you home."

"I don't want anything from you!" she shouted, and to her own self-disgust tears began to run down her face, hot and quick.

She had no idea why she was being so emotional after Laurence's admission. All she knew was that she had to get away from him, from this hideous portal to a past she'd tried so hard to forget.

"You're shaking," he said, and the note of wonder, of compassion, in his voice was almost too much.

Kitty fumbled for her phone, finally locating it in the innermost recesses of the handbag she thankfully hadn't forgotten, and activated the flashlight. It was surprisingly strong, illuminating them both in a watery but completely adequate beam of light.

"You're still *crying*." He said it almost accusingly.

"I tend to do that when I'm upset, yes," she said shortly, taking a full step back.

Laurence was holding out his hands as if to ward off something evil—or to tell her that he wasn't going to hurt her. Too late for both. She wiped furtively at her cheeks with her fists.

"Kitty—"

"You ruined my life, Laurence," she said, and her voice was shaking, too. "You *ruined* it for years. And you have the audacity to tell me—"

"I was *minutes* away from shucking up your skirt and taking you against that wall," Laurence said huskily, "and you would have let me. I wasn't going to do that without telling you."

Kitty half turned away from him, fisted her hands as tightly as she could and closed her eyes tight as well, as if she could banish him from her side merely by doing so. He did not disappear with the night; she could still hear him breathing.

"Kitty."

"Go away!"

He swore low, under his breath. "I'm not going to leave you here."

"You brought me here."

Kitty hated how small she sounded. She hated it more than anything.

The silence that followed was punctuated by her steady breaths and Laurence's deep ones, and then he spoke, his voice heavy with something unsaid.

"You don't know the whole story. I did you a favor, Kitty. *Trust* me. My parents—"

She saw the vague roundness that was his head shake, and heard his voice, low and urgent.

"Whatever happened to you—it was a blessing in disguise. Trust me. You're much better off without having—"

Kitty turned on him in a fury.

"Don't give me your 'poor little rich boy' schtick, I'm tired of it!" she cried. "You have *no idea* what it's like to— It wasn't about the money, you idiot. Anyone can make money. It was having *parents*, if only for a short time— parents who could do anything for me. I hadn't had anyone take care of me properly for years, and then your parents did—"

"Kitty—"

"You were a selfish little bastard. You *lied* and you made me lose that—"

Her voice did break then, despite her best efforts, and she pressed a hand to her mouth. Laurence was only a vague shape in front of her, and she was glad for it. It meant that she, too, would barely be more than a mass. He would not be able to see the tears that still slid down her face, see how devastated she really was. Reduced back to poor little orphan Katherine Asare, standing in a big house where she didn't belong, begging for someone—*anyone*—to love her.

She hated Laurence for bringing that back.

Kitty barely registered it when Laurence moved closer to her, lifted his arms, wrapped them round her shoulders.

"Don't touch me," she said feebly.

"I know," he said, more gently than she'd ever heard him say anything before.

But he did not break the embrace. He held her, not tightly, not loosely, but just enough for her to feel warm, secure, without feeling restrained. He held her as if he'd done it a million times before…as if he knew exactly how she liked to be held…and that made her want to cry harder.

To be comforted by this—*this*—

"Hate me if you want," he said, and his voice was rougher than it normally was, his breath soft and warm by her ear. "I likely deserve it."

"I don't think enough of you to hate you," Kitty said. Her nose and throat were clogged and her voice sounded odd, strangled, as she told the lie.

"Kitty…"

There was enough hesitation in his voice to give her pause. Coming out of the shadows, it sounded as unlike Laurence as it could—subdued, a little uncertain, with none of the sardonic dryness, none of the superiority.

His hands slid down to capture hers, as if helping her brace for a blow. "Listen. You were brought into my father's house deliberately."

"I know. Because of the campaign."

"No—no, sweetheart, it was more than that." He compressed his lips, then released them. "My father operated three sham charities, Kitty. *Three.* One that solicited cancer donations, one for education, and one—"

Kitty felt her heart drop like a stone. "One foster care program," she said dully, and he nodded.

"It was all in the records I leaked, but— I don't know... To this day, I'm not sure how he hushed the bulk of it up."

Kitty's head ached; she was finding it hard to follow. "So—what? You got me kicked out to *protect* me?"

He was quiet for so long that she drew back, looked up at his face. Even encased in shadow it was dark and troubled.

"I should have let you leave on your own terms. But I knew I was going to leak the documents, and I didn't trust you to leave. Your name would have been all over them. He was going to name the charity after *you*, Kitty."

Did he remember, then, the night he'd been so kind to her as they'd stood together under the lights of the chandelier in the grand ballroom of his parents' home? Did he realize how much his small attentions to her that night had meant? Had that, perhaps, led to this act of mercy, misguided as it was?

She'd never forgotten that moment of gentleness, and the memory had always had her telling herself that there had been at least one person in the Stone household who'd thought she was worth regard, even for a moment.

Now, faced with his lie, the memory of her gratitude was laced with humiliation. The Stones had cared nothing for her, and if Laurence had been kind to her that evening he'd had his own motives.

When her body had ceased its trembling Laurence pulled away from her, as if he wanted to steer them back to the house. She did not move. It was safer here in the dark and, if she was honest with herself, she did not want to leave the circle of his arms, despite her anger. The rage that had propelled her from the door had faded, leaving an ache in its place that was only heightened by the fact that not only *was* he close, he *felt* close.

"Kitty?" His voice rumbled out of the dark.

Kitty pressed her hands to her face, and it was a long moment before she spoke. "Why did you help me?" she said.

He exhaled. "The New Year's party."

Kitty's throat was so tight that she found it hard to speak. "You remember that night?"

"Every minute." He shifted from leg to leg. "Listen… I was kind of an ass of a kid, but after that night— You looked so uncomfortable. I wanted to get you away from what was going to happen. It's not great, having your name tied to people like them."

Laurence's words washed over her, but only two really stuck, reverberating in her head. *Every minute.*

He remembered.

The admission blossomed warm in her chest and she licked her lips. Wild emotion was quickly fading into something else entirely, and she shifted. She smelled that mixture of spice and whisky and soap and something else—some clean, masculine scent that was absolutely Laurence. Her skin began to prickle with awareness, and she suddenly felt more tired than she ever had in her life.

Why was she still even here?

"Kitty?" he asked, and she still couldn't speak.

She closed whatever little distance was left between them. Despite the silence it took her a moment to locate his heartbeat; it thudded strong and sure against her palm.

"I should have told you earlier," he said, and his voice was sober.

"Why didn't you?"

"I didn't want you to back out of the deal."

The deal.

The only thing that had brought them together.

Those two words pulled Kitty back to herself, though she didn't move. It didn't matter how fleetingly kind he'd been to her once upon a time, or how good it felt to be in his arms. He was still Laurence Stone, and he would always put himself first.

That realization did not change the fact, however, that he was still close, and that she ached for him now even more than before, if that was possible. If anything, this had added layers to it.

He let out a sigh, and she decided in a flash to be honest. It wasn't as if things could get any worse.

"I still want you," she said, and gulped. "How is that even possible?"

"I don't know," he said.

And apparently he could read her mind, because he was nosing her face in the darkness, skimming that spot on her neck that made her shiver, whispering words that made no sense, and then finally—much to her relief—capturing her lips with his.

Kitty braced her hands on his chest, fisting the cashmere in her fingers, venting her frustration in little whimpers against his lips. She wanted it hard and fast and urgent, matching the way her pulse was racing, but Laurence was kissing her with the gentle intimacy of a lover who knew he had the entire night before him.

His hands were making a leisurely exploration of her hips, her waist, threading through her hair. She arched her chest up to meet them, greedy for them. His large palm cupped her right breast—finally—and even through the layers of her bra and the fine wool his thumb had no trouble locating her thrusting, aching nipple circling it almost lazily, a whisper of a touch.

Just as she was soothed in the gentle rhythm he tugged, with just the right amount of pressure, and she cried out—a soft exhalation of pleasure this time.

"We can't do this here," he said, with a modicum of his old briskness, and Kitty squeezed her eyes shut.

He was right, of course. This business between the two

of them was insanity in and of itself, but doing this here, with their past hovering round them in these halls like a malicious, disembodied spirit, was an entirely new level of *no*.

She shivered a little and he nodded, as if she'd confirmed something he had already been thinking.

"Come home with me," he said simply.

"Why?" she cried out.

He sighed. "Damned if I know."

She laughed—a short, shaky sound—and pushed her hair back over her shoulders. She couldn't have spoken even if she'd wanted to; she didn't trust her voice. Instead of walking, she reached out and took his hand, a little hesitantly. She felt such relief when his fingers closed over hers, warm and sure, that her heart seemed like it might burst in her chest.

Kissing Laurence Stone in a heated moment was one thing; giving him clearance to reject her was another. Knowing he wanted her, even if just physically, as much as she wanted him—

Two sides of her were warring now, but the need throbbing through her blood obliterated all reason. Once that fire had been doused, she thought a little hopelessly, perhaps she'd be able to think straight, to finally push Laurence Stone out of her life, precisely where he belonged.

"All right," she said quietly.

The moments after that were spent in the driveway, and then in the car, in a haze of heated kisses, frenzied groping, both alight with the frustration that came from not being able to get one's hands where one wanted them, *when* you wanted them. Laurence seemed intent on torturing her, on drawing out her want until she snapped.

When the car finally stopped he twisted away from her with great effort.

"Minx," he half growled, then took a deep breath before sliding out of the car, ahead of his driver, then going to open Kitty's door himself.

She ignored his hand and looked around instead in shock. "This is—"

"The harbor," he agreed, and began to walk toward the dock.

He'd only gone a few feet before he realized that Kitty was still peering out of the car, shivering in her thin evening dress.

"What are you doing?"

"I'm not following you. You said we were going to your place."

It took Laurence a moment to get it; then he began laughing uproariously.

"I live on a boat," he said, still chuckling. "I'm not planning to tie you to bricks and pitch you in the Hudson. Come on, Kitty."

"You live on...a *boat*?"

"Sometimes, yes."

Kitty was thunderstruck.

Laurence wrapped an arm around her as protection from the wind, and began to hustle her down the pier. When they reached a small motorboat with a man silently waiting inside, Laurence pointed into the gray mist on the horizon.

"There," he said, indicating a looming shape not far off the coast. "This is as far as they let me come in, usually. New York is fairly crowded; it'll take us about forty minutes to get there."

"What do you do during the winter?" Kitty demanded as he lifted her down, then swung himself over expertly and draped a soft waterproof blanket over her shoulders.

He huddled next to her. "I have a suite at the Plaza."

She could see him smile, even in the dim light.

"And all the room service you could want."

She reached out to hit his arm; he caught her and drew her close.

"You're lucky I don't get seasick," she murmured, then sighed a little as their lips met again, stoking her desire even more.

It felt unearthly now, as if they'd transported themselves to their own little dimension, where nothing mattered but being *alone*.

They could not be alone, though—not yet. She had to be welcomed aboard the massive yacht by a staff of thirty. She had to watch Laurence and the housekeeper, who greeted him with the deference due to the young master, had to watch him wave off the transport boat, muscles straining against the cotton confines of his sweater, had to hear about what food was in the fridge and what rooms had been prepared for them, then see the housekeeper off into the muggy damp of the night.

Kitty was so desperate for him by the time he'd finished that she was biting her lip raw.

"Let's go," he said, and then they were in an elevator, going below the main deck.

When the gilt doors closed her throat was dry as sandpaper and dampness was trickling down between her breasts, between her legs... She closed her eyes.

In one single movement Laurence wrapped her in his arms from behind and his hands were suddenly everywhere: cupping her backside, on her breasts. One rough, insistent hand was going further, parting her thighs...

Kitty came so fast she had no time to make a sound. There was little build-up—just the gentle stroke of blunt fingers between her folds before it overcame her, a fitting end to the tension of the past hour. She bent over, her skirt hitched to her waist, panting. She could feel the hard length of him against her backside, and barely had enough time to gain her bearings before he turned her around, kissed her hard.

"Now," she said, and her voice was a whimper.

"You must think I'm way more dexterous than I actually am," he said, and his voice was rough, his words disjointed.

"Laurence, *please*."

When he moved as if to exit the elevator she shook her head and backed up.

"Here," she said quietly, and leaned back against the wood-paneled wall.

His eyes darkened; she squeezed her own shut.

She had to do it this way to ensure that whatever happened between them remained meaningless, without the tenderness that would rope her heart into it. In a moment she heard foil tear, and arched her back as he hoisted her up. Then she was against the wall, the flimsy mesh of her underwear was wrenched to the side, and he was *finally* inside her.

"Kitty…" he groaned, and her answer was to dig her nails into his back as hard as she could.

She'd only had one partner before this—a sweet but bland boy in college who'd left her feeling decidedly indifferent. She'd never experienced the wild wanting that she did for this man who held her in his arms now. Not even close.

Laurence's breath was hot on her neck with an urgency she knew he rarely let show. There was a broken, "Please, sweetheart, *please*," and increasingly ragged breaths.

Kitty wrapped a leg round his waist, clutched him hard, and against all odds, against everything that made sense, she felt another orgasm coming—yes, there it was!

They sagged against the wall together, Kitty with her dress bunched round her waist, limp and useless, Laurence with his trousers unfastened but otherwise dressed.

There were a few moments before Laurence's hand crept

out, searching, tugging her to him. He wrapped his arms round her, held her close. "It shouldn't have been like this," he said, and his voice was ragged.

If she hadn't known him better she would have guessed that was actually emotion leaching through.

"Not the first time. Not *tonight*, Kitty—"

"I wanted it," she said softly, tracing a finger down his back.

She felt his muscles tighten and pulse in response, and then he released her, leaving her cold, bereft.

"Excuse me. I'm sorry. I'll be back in just a moment," he said roughly, and exited the elevator, doing up his trousers as he left and leaving her in a heap on the tiled floor.

He made it only a few feet before he stopped.

He just had to *breathe*.

It would serve him right, Laurence thought grimly, trying vainly to calm himself down, if he had a panic attack right at this moment.

Adrenaline was still coursing through him, making him shake, and his body had yet to come down from the high of taking Kitty Asare here, in the one place he used to escape from the world and all its ills.

His chest still ached with a longing that his climax had done nothing to assuage and, worse than that, guilt weighed heavy on him too—a guilt that made his stomach churn and his head ache.

He wished he'd never touched her.

He wished—

"Laurence?"

Kitty was behind him. He turned. He hadn't made it very far from the elevator, just halfway down the cream and gold tiled hallway that led to his stateroom. He didn't answer; if he did he might be sick. Instead he turned and glared.

She crept over in her bare feet, her shoes in her hand.

"Are you all right?" she asked, and for once he felt the stone facade he kept round himself begin to shift.

Each time Kitty spoke to him he felt like it cracked a little more—as if she were a light that shone beyond it, to the parts of him he kept hidden from everybody else. Maybe it was because she'd witnessed him at his lowest, before he'd amassed all this, but it was there.

"This is wrong," he muttered, and Kitty's face changed.

She placed her shoes on the floor and approached him. There was a moment of hesitation before she lifted her arms to encircle his neck. "You'll drive yourself mad," she said quietly, "trying to figure out why things happened. You're not your parents—you are Laurence Stone. And I came here because I wanted to be with *you*."

Hell, that was taking the knife and twisting it in.

"You said you weren't cynical, but I didn't think you were stupid," he said.

"I haven't—" She stopped, started again. "I've only been with one other person, Laurence. I don't *do* this. I wanted you."

What?

Shock tightened his chest, but then he remembered Kitty's trembling hands, and the wordless way she'd come undone in his arms, and knew it was true. Her response wasn't that of an experienced lover.

He should end this here, take her back to shore, communicate with her neutrally until they both got what they wanted and then he could leave, knowing that although he'd ruined her life in some ways, he'd set her up for life in others.

Kitty was his responsibility, whether she wanted to be or not, and knowing that—

He licked his lips to moisten them before he spoke. "We can talk in the morning."

"We have work in the morning," Kitty protested.

But she was melting into him, and he allowed himself a kiss…her mouth was simply too alluring. Kissing her was like getting drunk: each sip made you thirstier for more. Telling her his secret had unleashed something in him, a freedom to finally take what he wanted from her.

"*You* have work in the morning," he husked, "and your work for the moment is to let me help you. Part of the deal, remember? I can do that from anywhere. *Stay.*"

Back in control, he let his fingers find the zipper at the back of her dress. She did not resist when he tugged it down, nor when he pushed the fabric from her shoulders to reveal smooth, butter-soft skin.

"I have donors to court."

"We can fly them out here."

"You have problems…" Kitty gasped.

But Laurence's attention was on the gleaming flesh revealed by the relatively demure dress, and, *dear God*—

"Were you hiding these from me the whole time?" he murmured.

Her breasts were full and high, tightly restrained by lace and the softest silk he'd ever felt. The flimsy clasps opened easily, and he made a low sound deep in his throat as she spilled into his hands.

"They were right there the whole time," she said archly, although she was doing nothing to stop her dress's journey to the ground.

Laurence was completely lost in sensation, in taste, in the want that had consumed him since he'd laid eyes on her in the Park Hotel's dining room. His fingers slid up to her hair, catching in the soft waves. She made a little sound of protest, but he kissed the smooth, vulnerable column of her throat.

"Don't worry, I won't pull your extensions out," he said, allowing himself a laugh. *Yet.* "Will you stay?"

"Laurence—"

Inexplicably, he was near ready for her again, his body surging with desire. Kitty's naked form was so incredibly womanly, even in its slenderness, and the way she submitted to his touch inflamed him all the more. She was so very innocent, he thought, but in some ways she had the mind of a hardened cynic.

"Let me do this for you," he whispered. "I'd like to make love to you properly. *Please.*"

It was that word on his lips that did it. Kitty met his gaze with uncertain eyes, but she nodded.

"Room," he said, a little unsteady. "Behind you. And don't rush me this time."

Once inside his suite, Laurence brushed her cheek with the backs of his fingers; he couldn't help it. Her skin was soft and warm, and so very inviting. Tonight he was selfish enough to indulge the want that pooled low in his belly without thought, without reservation. Tomorrow he would think about the practicalities.

His hands were her on her thighs, on her firm round backside, and she was gasping soft and sweet against his mouth between kisses...

By the time they'd stumbled over the threshold Kitty had been shivering, even in the warmth of his entryway. Now, with the bedroom door closed, he slid his hands up the cool smoothness of her thighs to her waist.

"Help me with my shirt," he said.

The first two buttons were slow, undone with fumbling, hurried fingers. When his neck was bare she kissed it, a whisper-soft contact on warm skin. She let her lips linger for a moment as she steadied herself.

The intimacy of the touch was not lost on Laurence, but he allowed her soft, full mouth to skitter across his skin as she uncovered more. A small part of him was touched by the care she was taking. It was more than a technique to arouse him…she had a tenderness that was elemental, part of her being.

When she reached the hard, flat plane of his belly he reached down and caught her wrists in his hands. She looked up, confused and a little anxious, peering up at him through a curtain of glossy dark hair.

"You *never* want me to touch you," she said, a little accusingly.

"I'm not very good at that," he admitted. "Come to bed." His voice was hoarse.

In response she wrapped her arms round his waist and burrowed into the warm expanse of bare skin she had been kissing just moments before.

"Okay," she said, muffled against him.

He tucked her close to his side before he began the short walk to his bed, and lifted her fingers to his lips.

Laurence made her wait…made her work for it.

He held her in place with one rigid hand on her hip, teasing her with his fingers, showing her the best angle, watching her strain downwards with eyes that he knew had darkened with wanting. There wasn't any letting up on that swollen bud between her nether lips. When she bit her lip and spread her thighs wider, begging soundlessly, he gave her one finger, then two, then three.

He wanted her feverish, frantic. But when her walls locked on his fingers tight and drew him in, he nearly lost control himself. He loved the way she trembled. It was with desire, and a desire that belonged to him and no one else.

When she was at the precipice he slowly withdrew his fingers, ignored her whimper of protest, cupped her instead. He twisted silk and lace with his fingertips, tugging it up to rub against where she wanted it the most. He told her in a soft, husky murmur that he was going to wrench those panties right off her, but she had to *tell* him to.

"I—" She couldn't say it; she was biting her lip, instead.

He loved the way her face strained when she talked, as if passion forced the words from her despite her natural reticence. And the fact that he already loved something about her was disconcerting, but not surprising.

He rubbed one thumb slowly over the dusky nipples jutting out from smooth skin, followed it with a gentle scrape of his teeth. The other hand drifted down to where she was wet, swollen, ready for him. Again, she made attempts to touch him, to reciprocate, but he didn't let her. He waited until she was shuddering against his hand before his first thrust, and he was grateful for that, for he did not last long himself.

When Kitty finally slept, snuggled trustingly against his chest, Laurence looked at her face for a moment, more troubled than he'd been in years. He brushed her hair back and kissed her on the forehead before easing out of her embrace carefully. She was so lovely in sleep, and he couldn't look at her without feeling a palpable tug. His mind kept going back to their confrontation outside the Stone mansion, and in an instant he knew why he cared so much.

Laurence never wanted to see her cry again. *Never.* Whether she was angry with him, or pleased, or amused, he wanted her happy. *Fulfilled.*

Those cracks in the stone wall of his inner self had widened to proper gaps now, and Kitty had eased herself in. She was prickly and sweet and strong and kind, so unlike him, and he was transfixed.

Life had shown him to distrust love; he'd only ever seen it come with strings. Kitty's dedication to helping people was one thing; her coming here with him was another. She didn't despise him for what he'd done...she'd pushed her own pain aside to let him in, even if only for a night.

She deserves everything.

Laurence needed to open his computer, sit down, *plan.*

Take some action. He could not give Kitty back what she'd lost, and he couldn't rewrite the past. He could, however, ensure her future was secure—and he would, long before they disembarked!

Barefoot, Laurence crept out to the study adjacent to his suite. His mind was now remarkably clear, and his body hummed with purpose. He messaged Cordelia, warning her that he'd need her in ten minutes. There were people to call, properties to acquire, things to set in place.

Before the end of the week, One Step Ahead would be a trailblazer in its field and Kitty would finally be able to bury the demons that plagued them both.

He refused to think about what this might mean for them, or if there even *was* a "them." Considering that was like icy fingers around his neck. If he cared for Kitty...if he cared for her at all—

Laurence closed his eyes, took a deep breath, tried his damnedest not to think of the woman asleep next door, or how badly he wanted to go back to that bed, draw her into his arms again. This would be a fine distraction. It would be folly, with their history, to think they could ever be more than this, and he had to leave her with something to make up for their inevitable separation.

If he could think of Kitty as a problem that needed solving, rather than a woman he was growing to care about, he'd never be put in the position of hurting her again.

Kitty did not trust him, and he couldn't blame her.

He didn't trust himself.

CHAPTER THIRTEEN

KITTY FOUND HERSELF tangled in the Egyptian cotton sheets that covered Laurence's enormous bed when she woke up. She was stark naked and completely disheveled; he was nowhere to be found. She tumbled out of bed and hurried to the portholes that looked out to the sea. All she could see was watery gray, and she pressed her hands against her mouth, stifling a gasp.

He'd kidnapped her!

In disbelief Kitty reeled back, then scrambled over to the bed, looking for her clothes. She saw nothing but her lace underwear, tangled in the sheets, close to the foot of the bed.

"Good morning."

At the sound of Laurence's voice, lazy and languid, Kitty nearly fell. She recovered quickly and whirled around. Inexplicably, he looked as if he'd woken up from a full night's rest. His eyes were clear and bright, and he was dressed in a much more casual version of his usual office wear, a slim-cut cuffed linen shirt with matching trousers.

She drew the sheet tight over her breasts, embarrassed by her own dishabille. "Laurence, where are we?"

He squinted at the tablet in his hand. "The Atlantic."

Kitty felt very much as if she'd been turned unexpectedly on her head. "We're at *sea*?"

"Since a couple of hours after we got on board." His mouth twisted up into a mocking shape. "You didn't even notice when we started moving."

Kitty's face flamed. "I *did* notice!"

"Well, you didn't protest."

No, she hadn't—because he'd had her very distracted

at that particular time. But she forced herself not to go down that road. "Laurence…" she began, in her most no-nonsense voice.

"I did say we'd work from here for a few days, didn't I?" he added, then cast an eye over her. "I've been up since five-thirty and have had coffee already. But you can eat breakfast with me if you can shower and be dressed quickly. We can talk over our schedule. I've got an investment opportunity for you—"

At this point Kitty was gaping. She'd never seen him this way. His face was bright with an eagerness, an *energy* she'd never seen before.

"Anyway. I'll bring you up to speed as soon as you're ready."

Kitty looped up the hem of the bedsheet and began to walk rapidly, then broke into a run. She'd had no idea a man that size could move so quickly outside of a sports setting.

"Laurence—listen to me! You'll take me back to New York this minute—"

"We already talked about that."

"We didn't *talk* about anything!" Kitty panted. "I don't even have a current passport, for one thing."

"A yacht is a floating country, Kitty," he said in that patronizing voice she hated. "Send your details over and I'll have Cordelia sort it out. She'll have it waiting at the next port of call. Anything else?"

Port of call?

Kitty felt an urge to laugh, despite her anger. This was like a two-person cruise from hell.

Laurence stopped abruptly at the door, and Kitty plowed directly into his back. She swore and took a full step back, almost losing her hold on the sheet.

Laurence's eyebrows climbed as he turned around. "Why don't you get dressed?"

"My clothes are—"

And here, Kitty's face flamed. Her dress was on the back of an antique desk chair in his sitting room, where he'd unzipped her out of it so skillfully. The thin lace scrap of her bra was on the floor in the doorway, and she knew her lace underwear, damp from his skillful tongue and her own wetness, lay tangled in his sheets.

Laurence's brows lifted, as if he'd been reading her mind during this audit, and his chuckle made her spark with indignation.

"Do you need a moment?" he drawled.

"Oh—you—!" She stalked past him, throwing the sheet from her body rather dramatically, she knew.

She could feel him smiling, even though she could not see his face, and she was not afraid when she felt the hardness of his body press against her naked back. In fact, she sighed, felt her body relax.

His arms went around her and he kissed her neck. "You smell *delicious*," he said, and there it was: desire curling low in her belly.

There was a lightness in his voice that hadn't been there the night before. It was as if he'd exorcised something in the night, left it at the shore they'd sailed from.

"I smell like I've been out for twenty-four hours without changing my clothes," she said sulkily, trying not to shiver at the feel of his lips on her skin. "I want to bathe. And I want to get dressed."

"Just go with it, Katherine," he said, and there it was again, that hair-fine tension sparked by his voice caressing the vowels of her full name.

His big hands slid up her stomach, over her ribs, pausing to cup her breasts. They felt heavy and hot from their previous coupling, and so very sensitive. When his thumb circled the swollen bud of her left nipple her breath manifested itself in a stuttered gasp. When he pinched it none-too-gently she nearly lost her feet.

"Laurence…" she murmured.

"One more go?" he asked, as if he were asking if she wanted another helping of food.

His hand had left her breast and was descending to where her thighs pressed hard together. His fingers danced over her mound as if toying with the idea of her, and Kitty hesitated for a fraction of a second before rolling her hips, so that her backside was pressed directly into the cradle of his thighs.

"Is that a yes?"

He found her aching bud with gentle fingertips, using one digit to press before circling slowly—too slowly. His lips descended to her ear and Kitty couldn't have stopped squirming even if she'd wanted to, for he was telling her things, low and filthy in her ear…things he wanted to do to her that he hadn't before. But there was no time, because if he didn't have her that minute he was going to spend himself right here on her skin.

Kitty was so dazed by lust that she could do little but lick her lips, focusing on the sound of foil tearing, on how gentle he was when he finally lowered her to her hands and knees.

"Okay?" he asked, probing her quivering wet sheath from behind.

She heard a groan as her walls clamped hard against his exploring fingers. She wasn't sure if it was him or herself.

"You're so ready."

"Do it," she panted.

She was past dignity now—all she wanted was for him to fill her completely, to answer the need her body was screaming for.

"Or is that a you'll see?" he said, amusement coloring his voice.

She could feel the tip of him at her entrance. She strained backwards but he held her hips fast with one hand, while the other still circled the little bud between her thighs, almost idly.

Kitty almost cried in frustration. "You're insane!"

"Yes," he agreed. And then they both gasped, for he'd pushed completely inside her. Kitty felt her body soften, spasm, draw him in. "That doesn't affect this, though—"

Kitty began to laugh. She couldn't help it. Her laughter, though, was soon lost to husky breaths as he began to move, and then there was no sound in the room but that of skin rasping on skin.

Kitty had to bite back her moans. This was good, yes—the best she'd ever had, to be honest...not that she'd much experience to fall back on. It felt amazing to stop thinking, to finally drop her pretensions, her worries, and just—

Laurence breathed out something she couldn't hear, and then his fingers twisted, *just so*, and she let out a cry that she was sure he'd hold over her later. She pitched forward. He caught her just in time, cradling her to his chest for a fraction of a moment before lowering her to the rug. She took a moment just to breathe, trying to acquaint herself with the wanton stranger who was lying, panting, outside of Kitty Asare's body.

He quickly eased himself off her, rolling onto his back. Kitty lifted her head just enough to look at him. "Did you—?" she began, then bit her lip, suddenly shy. Her own climax had left her shattered, so absolutely *weak*.

His lips twisted up. "How considerate of you," he mocked, but it was good-natured. "Yes. I did. A little more quietly than you, but I did."

Kitty wanted to tell him to shut up, but she closed her eyes and let her head drop instead. The lush, soft wool of the carpet felt absolutely and welcomingly soft right now. Her lashes fluttered shut.

"Breakfast?" he said.

"Breakfast," she mumbled.

* * *

Laurence's yacht, the *Triumph*, was opulent in a way so gloriously over the top that new surprises seemed to appear each time she crossed the deck. Kitty found it fascinating, and had spent the first few minutes after she'd left Laurence's quarters walking after a blank-faced member of staff, her shoes in her hand, bundled up in an enormous dressing gown.

She was uncomfortable and, she supposed, none-too-fresh, but there was something curiously intimate about his scent on her skin. It hung around her in a gentle cloud after last night and this morning, tinted by the soft musk of sex. She felt marked, in a way, and was a little discomfited to discover that it did not bother her at all.

"Mr. Laurence said you're to have the Rose Room, miss," her escort informed her.

Whatever that meant.

"I'm very grateful," Kitty said, dryly.

"I'm to give you a quick tour as well," the woman said briskly.

The yacht was decorated in minimalist elegant shades of gold and cream, and its staterooms were all carefully planned and primed for dancing, dining, lounging, socializing. The top level featured a deck in hand-laid mosaic tiles, perfect for sunbathing, and there was a spa on the level below, complete with a full Moroccan bath tiled in white, coral, and the most brilliant blue Kitty had ever seen. An Olympic-sized saltwater pool took up a great deal of space on the main deck, hand-tiled with a scene that included a demon chasing a nymph.

Kitty clapped her hands when she saw it.

"It's a pain in the ass to clean," the woman said. "Come on—I'll show you the interior, and then we'll go to your stateroom."

"The interior" was decorated in an old English style,

with a library, an enormous dining room, and multiple staterooms—each decorated, the housekeeper explained, with a different theme. By the time they reached the Rose Room Kitty had dropped all pretense of indifference and her eyes were wide and delighted.

The massive stateroom had its own sitting area, full bathroom, a balcony and dining room, and was decorated in shades of blush, dusty rose, pearl-white, and the palest gray. Kitty's bare feet sank deep into a carpet so plush and soft it rivaled her best bedspread at home, and a massive arrangement of American beauties, the brightest colors in the room, filled the air with their sweet and heady scent.

She walked up to it, touched one of the petals with a finger. When would he have had the time to have flowers delivered, for goodness' sake?

"Have a nice stay here, miss," the woman said, interrupting her thoughts, then took the bag with Kitty's ruined dress in it. "Check the wardrobe. Mr. Laurence had a few things flown in for you this morning. Breakfast will be served on the Horizon Deck, one level up. Do ring if you need anything," she added with a rusty smile. "I'm Vera."

When she was gone Kitty crept into the bathroom, toying with the idea of showering instead of having a soak. Laurence was waiting for her, after all. Remembering how he'd all but kidnapped her, though, she rebelliously turned the taps to the hottest temperature she could stand and tipped half a jar of rose-and-vanilla-scented bath salts into the water.

She could use a soak. Their activities the night before and this morning had left her aching and sticky, in a guiltily pleasant way.

Half an hour later Kitty emerged from the Rose Room calm and fragrant, dressed in a cream sheath of the type of style and cut that she hadn't a prayer of affording, and flats that fit her perfectly. Her hair was pulled into a bun at the base of her neck; she'd touched gloss to her lips.

When Laurence saw her, his eyes became soft.

"I'm here to take you to breakfast," he said simply, then offered her an arm with an old-fashioned air that suited him very much.

When they were seated for breakfast, and Laurence had attacked a basket of bread, Kitty asked him about the yacht. "It's magnificent," she said.

"It's old," Laurence said.

It was just warm enough that they could eat together on the Horizon Deck, which featured a full bar where a server presided over mimosas and Bloody Marys and lifted silver lids off chafing dishes full of eggs, fresh fruit, and fresh bread so warm and fragrant that the smell lingered in the air long after it disappeared from their plates.

"World War II, I think. It's been refurbished several times—even been in a museum. I got it cheap, after graduation, mostly to piss the Senator off. It cost more to refurbish, even though it's not very big." He said that with a perfectly straight face. "Only a couple hundred feet."

Kitty chose to pass over that gem, and instead looked at him in curiosity. Over the few weeks they'd been involved he'd spoken very little about his past, or indeed about their shared history. Now, out in the balmy air of the open sea, he seemed more willing to talk.

As if he'd read her mind, Laurence looked up from his coffee and sighed. "What?"

Kitty felt her face grow hot. "I didn't—"

"You think it's strange that I live on the water?" he drawled.

"Well, it is a bit eccentric—"

"It's private," Laurence said, and his voice was curiously flat. "Privacy wasn't something I got a lot of when I was a kid. Anyone who follows us out here—" he gestured widely "—would be seen from miles out. Enough time to hunker down, issue a gag order…"

"It's dumb," Kitty said decisively. "A man your age should have an actual place to live."

"I'll keep that in mind."

Kitty leaned back into the softness of her chair. It was padded in some woven fabric that felt like linen but was twice as soft. "What do we do now?" she asked.

His mouth tipped up and his eyes slid down the length of her…deliberately. "You haven't had enough?" he teased.

Her body instantly ran hot. "Laurence—"

"There are many more things I'd like to do to you, and there will be plenty of time for that," he said. with a hunger in his eyes that made her press her thighs together. "Do you have any idea how long I've wanted to get you alone, Katherine Asare?"

She had to get him off this trail of conversation, and fast.

She groped for the nearest thing. "I wanted to ask you something," she said. "Last night."

"Oh?"

There was a lilt in his voice that she did not care to explore, so she barged forward. "After—"

"After what?"

"After what you did." She took a sip of tea, mostly to hide her face. "And I left. What happened when your father found out?"

Laurence's face went still. He was quiet for so long that she thought he wouldn't answer, but then he spoke.

"I'll tell you because you asked. But no more after this, okay? Let's look to the future, Kitty, not at the past."

She nodded, and he continued.

His voice had quieted, but his words were clear, if clipped and short. To her, he sounded like the young people she served, when they were recounting painful memories. It was always done like this…in brief, staccato sentences designed to get across the most information in the quickest, least damaging way.

Coping mechanism, she thought, and sank her teeth into her lower lip as he went on. She did not want to interrupt him…not for any reason.

"After I leaked that stuff to the reporter…" He lifted his shoulders. "My biggest mistake was bragging that I'd done it, that something big was coming. I posted about it, and my father was livid, but he couldn't do anything—not with everyone's eyes on him. The media took the story… ran with it. I picked up followers online…the opposition took me on—as some sort of a mascot, I guess."

He laughed, and his eyes were suddenly very far away, as if he were looking at something well beyond the yacht they were on, far beyond the swaying of the waves.

"He managed to hush it up, of course, and make me look like a liar. I was in way over my head."

He was silent for a long time—so long that Kitty reached out and placed a hand on his arm. Partly to bring him back, partly because she simply wanted to touch him. His muscles were so taut that she winced, and he flinched, then blinked down at her.

The emotion that had flitted across his face was gone, replaced by that oddly stoic expression, the iron mask he pulled over his face, bolted shut at the edges. He looked at her as if he were trying to gauge something.

"I don't know," he said, with marked gentleness, "what it is about you that makes me want to talk."

Kitty tried to smile, but didn't quite manage it.

Laurence heaved a sigh, then took her hand, tugged her into his lap. It was as close a position as they could be in, and Kitty was faced with the disconcerting sensation of not knowing where her body ended and his began.

Laurence picked up his tablet, touched the screen. One

swipe of his fingerprint and it was open, and he clicked on a series of files. His face was very still.

After a moment he handed it to her. "Take a look. Scroll down."

Kitty did so. The files held a series of scans of the pages of various newspapers: the *New York Times*, the *Journal*, the *Gazette*, the *Enquirer*. The headlines were in chronological order...

Troubled Teen Laurence Stone Caught in Drug Bust!

Stone Jr. leaked doctored tax documents while "under the influence," Stone family lawyer says...

Troubled teen son of New York politician enters rehab; family despondent...

Some headlines were more salacious than others, but they all told the same story. Laurence was at worst a manipulative liar, at best a troubled, drugged-up child worthy of pity rather than censure or admiration.

Kitty looked up, whispering the last one. "'*Stone Jr. enrolls at Sandhurst*'?"

Laurence nodded. "That was how it ended. It started when heroin was found in my bag," he said after a moment. "At an airport. Along with condoms and weed—that was a nice touch, and in a nice public place, with lots of witnesses. My father played the concerned parent to the max, of course. Shut down my social media accounts...suspended his...took some time off—enough to make sure I settled in well at what everyone assumed was rehab."

Kitty's stomach was twisting so violently it threatened to expel the breakfast she'd eaten. "The Senator did that to you?"

Laurence's mouth tipped up just a fraction. "I accused

him of it. He told me I couldn't prove it—which was entirely correct. He also told me I was no longer welcome in his home. He informed me that he'd continue to pay for my schooling—he couldn't have the scandal of estrangement after all the tax nastiness."

Kitty pressed her hand to her mouth and Laurence shook his head, shifting her so that their foreheads were almost touching. His voice had a forced lightness that twisted her stomach even harder.

"No, sweetheart. Remember? I'm an ass and you hate me?"

"But that's horrible!"

"It was a long time ago." He lifted his shoulders. "I thought that the leak would exonerate me—but, Kitty, the man has connections everywhere. That journalist printed a retraction of his story within the week, saying I'd falsified the information I'd provided. Who knows what the Senator did to the man…"

"Oh, my God," whispered Kitty.

"It's politics. I was too young to know better." His mouth twisted, just a little. "I promised to never say a word about him to the media again if he'd send me as far away as possible."

"Sandhurst?"

"Yes. He paid to get me in, I'm sure."

"And then…?"

Laurence's broad shoulders barely moved. "Nothing. I graduated, went to uni, went into business with Desmond. Last contact I had with the Senator, I handed him a check that covered every single penny I'd taken out of my trust fund to start the firm. Paid him back for school, too."

"And he took it?"

"He did."

Kitty sagged back, suddenly overwhelmed, feeling slow and stupid. "I'm sorry," she whispered.

"Don't be sorry for me," he said, with all the arrogance she would normally despise—except now her heart ached not only for herself, but for him and what he'd become. "I'm fine now. So are you. Take everything you've got... be everything you've ever wanted to be, Kitty Asare. Use me while you've got me because nothing else matters. Love doesn't matter, Kitty. It won't stop people from putting themselves first. And it shouldn't. Take what you can and be unapologetic about it. The sooner you know that, the freer you'll be."

Kitty suddenly felt very tired. Why was she here, then, if Laurence didn't believe in love? More than that, why did she care if he didn't? What had she been hoping to get from this?

The possible answers were absolutely terrifying, and she instinctively placed some distance between them, wrapping her arms around herself.

"Laurence?" she said after a moment.

"Mmm...?"

Kitty swallowed. This was going to take all her courage, every bit of it, but Laurence had opened up. He'd shared things with her that she sensed he never had with anyone, and... Well, in her work she knew how difficult that was for a victim to do. She could not let that go—not without giving him something of her own.

In one quick motion she twisted and pressed her body flush against his. "You are a *good* man, Laurence Stone," she whispered fiercely. "I don't care how you try to come off. I know that with all my heart."

His response was extraordinary: shock, followed by a softness of expression that swilled the contents of her stomach violently.

"I—"

"I mean it," Kitty said firmly, swallowing the lump

threatening to impede her speech. "I wouldn't have come here if I didn't think so. I *like* you. As yourself. I mean it."

"Oh." He blinked hard, once, and the fact that those simple words had affected him so much made Kitty a little misty-eyed herself.

"Don't look so shocked." She managed a smile. "Don't you believe me?"

Laurence coughed before he spoke, and Kitty braced her hand on his cheek. He looked so different. Naked. Open. *Vulnerable.*

"I consider it a victory."

Kitty laughed a little awkwardly, and the two of them sat in silence for a moment, looking out over the sea. Then he cleared his throat, eased her off his lap and stood up.

"We should finish breakfast," he said, regaining some of that cool nonchalance. "I'm sure the food is ice-cold."

Kitty tucked her hair behind her ears. "Okay," she said softly, and took her seat almost meekly.

Her heart was hammering strangely. Some strange energy had been released into the air in those moments of sharing, and she knew, deep down, that nothing would ever be the same again.

CHAPTER FOURTEEN

"If you could have anything, what would it be?" Laurence asked.

Kitty's eyes were closed, and she did not bother opening them. They were out on the deck, under a blazing afternoon sun. Laurence reclined on a deckchair to her left.

They were lazy, slow, languid from the lovemaking that had lasted most of the afternoon, fragrant with the jasmine and vanilla oil that Laurence was working into her skin with warm, capable hands.

"Kitty?" His voice was low, insistent.

Kitty didn't want to answer. She and Laurence had been at sea for three days—three delightfully hot, seamless, pleasure-soaked days that made the world they'd come from seem a faint and distant memory. They'd eaten and drunk, and bickered and laughed. They'd created their own little world, floating on the blue-gray water. A world where nothing mattered but pleasure, and the odd delight of discovering that they did get along where there were no expectations.

Kitty was also limp with exhaustion, wrung out from being brought to a climax over and over again. Now, as the rays of the sun penetrated her skin, and the faint stickiness of the cocktails they'd had earlier coated her tongue, tart and honey-sweet, she thought hazily that she'd never been so happy. The last time she'd been this happy was when she was a girl who'd thought she'd entered her own Cinderella story—until that life had shattered, and her heart with it.

"Kitty…" His voice rumbled low in his throat, a little impatient. "Roll over."

She didn't want to, and she squeezed her eyes a little

tighter. Laurence only used that tone of voice when he wanted to discuss something particularly unpleasant.

His voice took on a crafty lilt. "I need to do your front."

Even the mere suggestion in his voice made Kitty's breath catch in her throat, made her breasts feel heavy and hot. Could it be possible, she thought, to want someone all the time without even a moment to ruminate over how stupid she was being?

Dumbly, she acquiesced, venting breaths on a soundless whimper when his hands skimmed over her ribs, slid upwards to where her nipples already beaded, peaked and aching.

His fingers danced over the tips, then paused. Her eyes flew open.

"Thought that would get your attention," he said dryly.

Kitty glared and slapped his hands away, but with very little conviction, and when he returned them she tried very hard not to squirm.

"If you intend to start something, don't tease me," she gritted out, and his laughter rang out over the deck.

To her surprise, he slid over to her deckchair, hauled her up into his arms, then kissed her till she was breathless and warm. When they surfaced for breath he rested his forehead on hers.

"What would it be?" he asked softly, and shifted, positioning himself between her legs.

She immediately crossed her ankles, pressing them to his back so that the low-slung black trunks he wore abraded against her in a way that was shockingly, incredibly pleasurable.

"None of that," he warned.

She laughed softly, then reached up, touched his face with the flat of her hand. "There's no way I'm going to answer that question."

"Why not?"

"Because you're going to try and give it to me. And you can't," she said gently.

"I can do anything."

"Not this time."

"Try me."

She smiled, a little wanly. "I made wishes when I was a child, Laurence, but the problem with that is they were ephemeral."

He winced. "That's a little cynical, isn't it?"

She shook her head. "I'm not a cynic. I haven't got the stomach for it. But life has been good enough to me to make me see that dreaming serves no purpose."

Laurence's heavy brows came together; he looked thoughtful. "What was the last thing you wished for, then?"

"Clever man." She shook her head, then decided to keep the tone light. "That you would kiss me. And touch me."

He laughed. "Did you get what you wanted?"

"Yes." She shivered as one long finger traced her collarbone, moved down her chest, alighting on her nipple. "Yes. There," she said, and swallowed hard when his thumb began to circle the puckered swelling bud. Her eyes fluttered shut as waves of pleasure began going through her.

"So sweet," he whispered, and bent his head to capture the tip in his mouth.

There was one gentle scrape of his teeth, and she jumped, but he was holding her fast, and then his mouth was moving lower, growing gentler with each inch of quivering skin.

By the time he'd reached his destination she hardly knew which way was up.

Later, when they'd showered off the oil and had lunch, Laurence asked her to come to his study. It was the only cabin on the ship that stayed locked, and when he pushed open the large double doors with both hands Kitty blinked.

It was as if his Midtown office had been dropped in the center of this floating museum.

Despite herself, she was impressed. The entire east wall was a large, sleek digital screen that stretched from floor to ceiling. Laurence jogged over to it and flipped a switch, and Kitty gasped out loud, pressing her hands to her mouth.

It was a photograph of her from the television interview, larger than life. Laurence had been airbrushed out. The hair, the makeup, the dress—it all worked together to perfectly portray the image of a woman she'd been trying desperately to be for the past several years.

She crept forward, touched the screen with unsteady fingertips. The image dissolved, reverting to a clean, minimalist website.

Laurence came up behind her, pressed a slim remote into her hand. "Take a look," he whispered, and his arms wrapped around her, holding her close. "I thought we could refine it while we're at sea. Together."

Kitty swallowed and did so.

There was a location tab, with photographs of an enormous light-filled office. The address wasn't one she knew, but the location was one of the more fashionable streets in the Financial District. She clicked on another. There was a portal for applications, a donors' page, and another that featured her most recent contributors—including the Muellers.

"When did you have time to do this?" she whispered.

Laurence chuckled low in his throat. "Just keep looking."

The last page was dedicated to her clients, and this was the one that made Kitty's hand fly up, cover her mouth. Three of the young people she was currently helping flashed up in full color, styled impeccably, their smiling teenage faces flanked by concise biographies.

Proudly supported by Katherine Asare, they all said.

She felt a lump rise in her throat. "Laurence…"

He released her and stepped back, his eyes bright. "The

building is being renovated as we speak, and it will be ready when we disembark," he said briskly. "I know what you want most in life is to help people, so I want to give you that."

Oh, Laurence.

Overcome, Kitty stepped back, pressed her hands to her face.

Laurence tugged them away sternly. His own face was pleased, but he spoke briskly to cover it up.

"No time for that," he ordered. "There's a lot of work to do, and if we can do it here it'll be better. I've got a video conference set up with the team I've recruited for you; they'll bring you up to speed. And—"

"Laurence…"

"Desmond wants in as well. He's quite taken by you," Laurence added with some disgust.

"Laurence."

He blinked, looked at her and frowned. "What?"

She stood on tiptoe and pressed her lips to his.

"Oh," he said, when she pulled back to breathe.

His face was as she'd never seen it before…soft round the edges and almost tender.

"Kitty—" he began, reaching out to cup her face.

I can't do this.

No matter how much she wanted to, she couldn't.

The past three days with Laurence had proved something she'd always known in her heart of hearts: people were more complicated than they seemed, and Laurence was no exception. He was a link to her past, an antagonist, and recently, in the oddest way, a friend and a protector. He'd managed to penetrate the barriers she'd erected *because* of him, and this power left her more frightened than she'd ever been in her life. Not of Laurence, per se, but of herself, and how exposed he'd leave her if she let him in.

When he's done with you, he'll leave you.

And when he did, she'd be devastated.

She shook her head and stepped back before he could touch her, before he could say something else that would make this harder, that would crumble her resolve.

"Laurence, this is incredible. But I—" She took a deep breath, balled her hands into fists. *Courage.* "I can't accept it."

He actually reeled. "I'm sorry?"

"I can't accept any of it." She swallowed. "That office alone probably cost—"

"You are not to think about cost!"

Kitty shook her head gently. She could feel her mouth trembling the way it did when she wanted to cry; she hoped she'd be able to keep it together until she could get somewhere relatively private.

"Please," she whispered, and her voice cracked a little. She had never seen him look so absolutely fierce before.

"I don't understand," he said, and his voice was tight. Angry. "We had terms, yes, but that was before we—" Color rushed up to his face.

The air was heavy with unspoken words, and Kitty's heart gave a quick, traitorous beat. Before what? Before they'd had sex? Laurence certainly wasn't in love with her.

"It's my— I have values, Laurence. One of them is simplicity. This is—"

"It's modeled on one of the finest charities in the city," Laurence spat out. His face was stormy.

"I know." She took a deep shuddering breath. "But I don't want to run my foundation like that, Laurence. I've been in the same position as these kids, and I've seen what money can do to help them. But after my experience with your father I decided I'd only take money from people who had it and give it to people who didn't. I don't want to retain anything for myself, Laurence. I live simply. I use a shared office space—"

"Yes, you seem to enjoy mentioning that." Laurence was speaking through his teeth. "Very noble of you."

Kitty shook her head. "It's not about being noble." *Enough of the meandering. She had to be honest, now.* "I can't take money from you, Laurence."

"But you're all right hanging out on a yacht for three days and crashing parties?"

Kitty felt the blood drain from her face.

He's hurt, she told herself, swallowing hard. *Don't take it personally.*

"You brought me here," she said, taking a step back. "And you said this was about contacts, Laurence. I've never asked for anything else."

"What if I want to give you more?"

The words were soft, almost too soft to hear, and fear rushed up, paralyzed Kitty to the spot. She bit back what would have been a soft moan. *No.* Laurence couldn't mean this, not with his iron-clad control and his lack of trust, and she couldn't believe it even if he—

The fear grew inside her, obliterating the thought.

This wasn't real.

And if she gave in, let him in—

She'd recovered from losing his parents. She knew as much as she knew her own name that she'd never be able to recover from losing him.

"Laurence—"

There was frustration on his face. "I owe you this, at least. And besides that—"

Kitty swallowed once, twice, three times. Her heart was beating so fast she could hear it thrumming, liquid and hot in her ears. The look on Laurence's face…

Run. Get out. Now.

She could not allow Laurence to say something he wouldn't be able to take back, or something she wouldn't be able to forget he'd said.

Before he spoke she cut in, panic bleeding into her voice. "Laurence, I want to leave."

"Kitty—"

"No. Now."

Kitty concentrated on her breathing.

In. Out. In. Out.

"I'd like you to arrange me transport off the yacht, Laurence. Before nightfall. I can't stay here anymore. I'd like to go home."

What?

Laurence could not comprehend what she'd said—not at first. He simply stared at her, soft and lovely, in a filmy blue dress that blended perfectly into the sky behind them.

He'd picked it himself, after their lovemaking in the pool that morning when he'd caught her, wet and slippery as a mermaid, flush against the mosaic wall, palmed her breasts, her hips, lapped water off her skin and finally, after much wheedling, with her pink tongue darting softly across her lips, let her bend over her lap, take him in her mouth.

It had been as if they were driven by a sort of desperation to consume as much of each other as they could, and his skin still tingled at the thought.

Why the *hell* was he thinking about that *now*?

He worked his tongue round the inside of his mouth; it was dry as ash. He would have to speak, and he could not allow his voice to shake with anger, or with anything else.

There was pain on her beautiful face. "Laurence, please try to understand—"

Her *treacherous* face.

He turned his back, picked up his phone. In a few clipped words to Cordelia transport was arranged, and he turned back. He saw Kitty's face blanch, and she took a step back. *Good.* He wanted her to feel something as harsh as what was ripping out his insides now, even if it was fear.

"Laurence. Please don't be angry—"

Angry? That was an underestimation. He felt bruised inside, as if someone had been trying to claw their way out. He would lash out; he had to.

"You have refused," he said low, "an offer that took a *tremendous* amount of time and preparation—"

"I never asked for that!"

"After draping yourself in silk and letting me have you in every corner of this yacht?" His voice was growing low, malicious, and all too familiar. He'd heard his father use it many times—sometimes with staffers, sometimes with his mother, but mostly with Laurence himself.

Kitty's face had turned ashen, he noted, without much pleasure.

"I cannot believe you'd say something so hateful to me…" she whispered.

He lifted his shoulders. A dark ugliness was taking over his speech, dictating his movements. All he knew was that Kitty was leaving, that she'd bested him, and he must strike back. He stared her down, coldly, till she began to wring her hands and tears slowly made their way down her cheeks. He did not relent. He would not relent.

"Laurence," she said, and she swallowed hard. "Please. It was not my intention to hurt you—"

"Your choices are a matter of *supreme* indifference to me," he said icily. "Good thing we're close to the helipad. Let's get you up there, sweetheart. Now."

"Laurence, my things—"

"I'll have them shipped. Up. *Now.* Chopper will be ready to go in ten minutes, so you'll only have a short wait."

Kitty flinched, but he ignored it. He had to ignore it if he was to hold on to the rage that was the only thing that kept the sick feeling of dread at being left, being *abandoned*, from creeping up in his chest.

After he'd talked to her, opened up about things he'd told

no one else, even Desmond… Kitty was the first one he'd trusted to see the truth about him, because on some level he'd thought she'd *seen* him.

If she had, she must not have liked it, because she was doing *this*.

Laurence wrapped a hand round her forearm, tightened it slightly. "I'll carry you up if I have to."

"Laurence—"

"Now!"

A tiny sob broke from her throat but she obeyed—for once—drawing her skirt round those long, slim legs that had been wrapped tightly around him only hours ago. His skin heated at the memory, which made him even angrier.

"Move," he said shortly.

The walk to the helipad was short, and Kitty did not look at him. She might be crying, but he refused to verify it by looking directly at her. When she was gone—when she was out of his line of sight—he would lie down in his dark stateroom and face whatever demons she'd left him.

When they reached the little alcove that served as a waiting room for passengers, she turned a ravaged tear-stained face and tilted it up to his.

"Laurence…" she said.

He did not know what she wanted to say, and did not want to hear it. He shook his head and reached out to place his hands at her waist, lifting her in one smooth motion into the waiting chopper. The pilot was running checks, clearly flustered at the short notice.

Kitty did not settle into her seat; she leaned out through the door instead. "I'm sorry," she said.

There was pity on her face, along with regret, and he could not allow that. He could not let Kitty see how far inside his heart she'd managed to worm herself, or how much all this affected him.

This wasn't just about her turning down his offer. She'd

rejected *him*, and whatever had bloomed between them over the past couple of days. He hadn't even had a chance to put a name to it or realized that he wanted to before now.

The chopper's blades stilled while the pilot fiddled with the controls and they were thrown suddenly into an eerie silence. When he spoke, at first his voice seemed much too loud.

"Go," he said, roughly.

Then, he signaled to the pilot and stepped back to safety, both physical and emotional.

The thrumming of the blades drowned out all other sound, and the chopper lifted off into the sky.

CHAPTER FIFTEEN

WHEN KITTY WAS a child, placed in a particularly bad or lonely home, she'd sometimes cry till she was sick...until the tears left her with a headache so violent that she could do little but lie feebly in her bed and let sleep take her.

She hadn't cried a single tear in those years between her leaving the Stones and connecting with Laurence again. Now it was as if a floodgate had been unleashed and she cried. First in the chopper, then in the subway, and now in a taxicab , where the driver asked her, alarmed, if anyone had hurt her.

"No, I'm an idiot," she managed from the depths of her swollen face.

At last, in the safety of her room, she bolted her door, curled up in a ball on her bed, and wished quite frankly that she could disappear, fade away. Nothing had hurt this badly—not for years. It was the rawness of a heart that had been injured beyond repair, and the memory of the look on his face.

You did the right thing, she told herself. *You did the right thing.*

It was always less painful to give something up rather than have it taken away. She'd been proactive this time.

Then why did it hurt so badly?

Kitty could not trust that whatever had sparked between her and Laurence Stone would have blossomed into anything more than a few idyllic days on the open sea and a return to a full bank account. She did know, however, that she had been losing her heart, and losing it fast—and she'd needed to sever their connection on her terms.

Since that fateful night at the Park Hotel, Laurence had

steamrollered his way through her defenses, never giving her more than a cursory listen. But for once she'd escaped having the floor fall out from under her—by ripping it from under him.

Scorched earth. It was the only approach that would work with a man like Laurence. He'd never listen unless you made him…*insufferable* man.

The thought ended on a sob in the back of her throat. How she missed him already, though it had only been a few hours. Her bed seemed small and cold and inadequate—not because it was humble, but because it was empty, and she was alone.

Get used to it, she told herself savagely.

Laurence was never going to be an option, and doing what she had had achieved two goals in one swoop. One, she'd extracted herself from a situation that had grown more dangerous by the day, and two, she'd sent a message to Laurence Stone that he'd never be able to ignore.

You did the right thing.

Laurence lingered on the *Triumph* for a full day before he went ashore. He wanted to give Cordelia time to wipe all traces of Kitty Asare from his life.

He signed the Mueller contract the day he arrived, and the only mention of Kitty was from Cordelia.

"It's done," she said, in answer to his questioning look.

She added with a completely blank face that she would see to it that footage of the video that had started all this would be scrubbed from the Internet.

He laughed a bit sardonically and waved her out. He stared at a proposal from the art department for a full half-hour without reading anything, then went into his first official meeting with the Muellers feeling as if he was walking to his execution.

He'd gotten exactly what he wanted—and so had Kitty,

in a way. He'd denied her nothing. Yet he was left with a hollow feeling that only increased as the day went on—and for the first time in his life Laurence Stone left work early, waved his car off, and walked.

He couldn't go back to the *Triumph*, where he'd be reminded of that ugly scene…how he'd lashed out at her with his words. Her essence would be everywhere. In the air, in the staterooms where they'd eaten and laughed and made love.

How had she managed to worm her way into his inner sanctum and then, eventually, make a fool out of him? His skin prickled with humiliation as he remembered what he'd done for her and how she'd effectively thrown it back in his face. He who had never made a concentrated effort to go out of his way for anybody…

"Ungrateful," he gritted out through his teeth, and suddenly he wanted nothing more than to find Kitty Asare, make her lift that dimpled chin and look him in the eye and tell him why.

The thought cramped his lungs. He had to stop and take a breath, look around. He was surprised to see how far he was from the office. He reached for his phone, ready to call his car, then left it and continued to walk, thinking harder than he'd ever done in his life.

Before he knew it, he found himself descending into the subway. He hadn't taken it since he was a teen, but he remembered the anonymity of it, the gentle swaying of the cars on the tracks.

Laurence eased himself into one of the grimy orange seats on the Queens-bound F train. He couldn't go to Kitty's—he wasn't even sure how to get to her place from here, and he was one hundred percent certain he'd never pursue her again. But there was something soothing about being underground, where no one knew him.

If he'd been one of the hundreds of thousands who rode

this system every day, unencumbered by wealth, privilege, and a past that had snatched away all that was good, perhaps he'd have had a chance.

A chance to do what, Laurence?

The thought that perhaps he'd wanted a chance with Kitty Asare made him lift a hand to his throat, loosen his collar. He coughed hard, raked his fingers agitatedly through his hair.

Get a hold of yourself, he told himself sternly. *This isn't you.*

He hadn't been himself since the Park Hotel, what seemed a lifetime ago. And he wasn't sure he could find his way back to the man that person had been, or even if he wanted to.

When Laurence emerged in a part of Queens he didn't recognize, he eased himself onto a park bench, grimaced at what he was sure was years of grime, turned on his mobile, and dialed. His personal mobile, this time.

"Hello?"

"Aurelia," Laurence said dryly. He must be feeling better, he thought, feeling a hint of a smile take over his face, if the shock in his former companion's voice gave him so much pleasure. "Are you still in Dubai?"

"I'm not." Her voice was wary. "I'm back in New York. And I'm practically engaged," she added warningly.

"Don't worry, this is not a social call," Laurence said sarcastically. Then he remembered that he wanted to talk to her, and sarcasm probably wasn't the best way to start the conversation. Desmond would have been the most natural candidate for this, but Desmond wasn't a woman.

He hesitated, wondering how best to—

"How have you been, Laurence?"

Unwittingly, Aurelia gave him an opening.

"I see that you replaced me without much effort, with an absolutely tearing beauty. Who is she?"

That was all it took, and the story spilled out—an abbreviated version, anyway. The party, the proposal, Kitty's defection from the *Triumph*.

Aurelia was quiet at first. "Why are you telling me this?" she said finally.

Laurence exhaled noisily. "You're a *woman*. I need to know what you think."

He could practically feel Aurelia roll her eyes. "I think you need therapy."

"Aurelia," Laurence said, "this never happened with you. I just need an outsider's opinion."

Aurelia had known his parents, known him since childhood.

She was silent for a moment, and when she did speak her voice was grave. "I don't know," she said. "But don't go after her, Laurence. Not yet. Even if you are serious."

"Why?"

"I mean it. Let her reach out first." Aurelia paused. "She's proud, and you're overbearing." She stopped again, as if considering. "And self-centered. And arrogant. And pushy—"

"Okay, your point is made," Laurence said irritably.

"What I mean to say is you'll never know if she's in it because she wants to be or because you talked her into it, ad man."

Laurence compressed his lips.

"Sometimes I wonder if you can differentiate between what's real and what you've made up, and that can be pretty jarring for a woman. Let her know you're there, and then leave it alone." Aurelia paused. "She's had the rug yanked out from under her so many times it's ridiculous. If you want her, Laurence, you're going to have to make her believe that you're not going to abandon her. But to do that you also have to decide whether or not you want her to stay. *Do* you?"

For the first time in the conversation Laurence had no words, and after a long moment Aurelia laughed, soft and incredulous.

"My God, you really are in love, aren't you?"

"Aurelia—" He was *not*. He couldn't be. But he could not deny it out loud, and his face was hotter than it had ever been in his life.

"Listen… You don't have to take my advice," Aurelia said dryly. "Just know that if *I* were ever dumb enough to fall in love with you I'd want to be holding the controls."

CHAPTER SIXTEEN

KITTY HAD BEEN determined to escape her entanglement with Laurence with both her heart and her head intact—and she managed to do so for the most part. It had been a clean break. Everything, even down to the dress she'd been wearing the night she'd fled the *Triumph*, had been inventoried and given back to Cordelia. Every penny had been accounted for, and Kitty was left with the satisfaction of knowing that Laurence would never be able to take anything back because she hadn't allowed him to give her anything.

What Kitty couldn't shake, though, was the look on Laurence's face when she'd told him she was leaving. He'd looked…gutted. Betrayed. For the first time since she'd known him he'd looked as if he gave a damn about something.

Men like him don't need anybody, she told herself sternly.

Still, she couldn't get his face out of her mind.

The events of the past several weeks began playing in her head like a montage from a film, but they didn't concentrate on events as much as they did on the look on his face in certain moments. There had been that veiled interest the night he'd taken her to his suite, and she'd given in to impulse and kissed him. There had been amusement whenever she was angry, even more so when she flew into a rage. There had been a curious softness those one or two times when she was sad, an intensity that had burned through every part of her body when they made love…

The fact that she was even thinking of any of her sexual encounters with Laurence Stone as *making love* was terrifying in and of itself.

Still, there was something else that had sparked between them—something deeper, something both beautiful and heartbreaking. It had surfaced that last heated time they'd spoken…something she was terrified to seek a name for.

Why had Laurence done that for her?

More than that, why did she care so much?

Kitty's head ached.

She remembered who she had been, and who Laurence had been, and who they were now.

She dared not think about who they could have been…

Kitty launched her newly revitalized, expanded foundation on the last day of summer, when the hot, sticky days New Yorkers had been enduring for months had faded to something gentler, softer round the edges, balmier.

May, when she'd last seen Laurence, seemed years ago, but his imprint on her heart felt as fresh as ever. Perhaps, she thought, and swallowed hard. Perhaps *this* would finally be what eradicated him from her mind.

She'd chosen to have the party, after some consideration, at one of the many estates on Long Island out in the Hamptons that overlooked the water. Yes, it was a foundation for young people from the city—but it was a fundraiser, too. And after working with Laurence & Haddad, even for a short period of time, she'd picked up a thing or two about creating a fairy-tale facade to encourage people with too much money and too little imagination to buy into the fantasy. She'd even reached out to Cordelia, asking her for advice on a venue.

The woman had sounded surprised to hear from her, then cautiously pleased. "I'd suggest Long Island. The Hamptons," she'd said briskly, after sentiment had been done away with. "There's some lovely houses out there… very uncommon styles for New York, almost a West Coast look. I'll send you an agent."

She had, and the man had got back to her after a week with the perfect place—a large villa of white stone close to the beach, well within her price range. The owner, she'd been told, lived in the city and had only recently purchased it, so she'd be welcome to go the night before, give herself a little vacation.

Kitty had welcomed the opportunity. For the first time since she'd graduated she would allow herself time to rest, to enjoy herself. Work had been steady and had kept her incredibly busy. She'd had little time to think about Laurence Stone, though he occupied her thoughts during nearly every waking moment.

In an impulsive moment she knew she'd likely regret, Kitty had sent him an invitation—Cordelia and Desmond, too. The latter two had responded with enthusiasm and written generous checks, but she'd heard nothing from Laurence.

She'd grown so busy as the date approached that she forgot to be disappointed some days—except, she told herself sternly, what was she disappointed about? *She* had left *him*…deserted whatever had been budding between them. Perhaps there were some questions that simply would never be answered.

The day before the launch Kitty left for the Hamptons early, renting a car and driving out. She picked up her small, nervous, chain-smoking events manager at the train station, and they drove east together.

The two of them eventually reached a charming villa situated at the end of a shady street. It was completely ensconced in a flower garden and the vivid blooms, even this late in summer, nearly obscured the house, their heady scent filling the air. A mosaic garden path led to a door of smooth wood so silken the grain could not be felt. Beautiful figures were carved on it in relief.

Kitty focused on them before the events manager fumbled at the door, then pushed it open and handed Kitty a key. The villa was enormous, clearly ready for her vacation. Floor-to-ceiling windows were bolted tightly but would, she knew, let in sea breezes during the day, filling the villa with the scent of the ocean.

"Dining room is there," he said, pointing vaguely to the right. "Pool there. Stairs to roof there. I'll see you at eight." Yawning, he touched his cap and headed off.

Kitty was glad she'd come early; it would be heaven to spend some time at rest in this beautiful place. She'd soak in the tub, read a good book, take a long walk on the grounds before the caterers and decorators arrived in the morning. She took a moment to look around, straightening up in pride. *She'd* done this. By herself, with no help from anyone, and she was glad for it.

She stripped off her clothes methodically, had a long bath, then donned a filmy white nightdress that she'd bought on a whim because it was pretty. When the doorbell rang as she prepared a cup of tea she thought nothing of it. Perhaps it was the party planner, or maybe it was her host, bringing towels or milk or some other little luxury from his own estate miles away.

Anyway, this was the Hamptons, not Queens, she thought as she threw open the front door.

Her cry was muffled by Laurence Stone who, when he saw her, immediately reached out and pulled her into his arms.

"Don't scream," he said, but of course she did.

CHAPTER SEVENTEEN

"YOU," KITTY SAID, once they were inside the entryway and the door was bolted against the night, "are trespassing!"

"Kitty—"

"You're also unbelievable."

If Kitty kept talking, and at this speed, perhaps her heart would descend back into her chest cavity, where it belonged. She hadn't seen him in months, but her body, apparently, remembered precisely what her mind had tried to forget.

"I should have known when I sent you the invitation that you'd try something like this."

"I didn't—"

"The night before the launch, too," she said. "I knew you were outrageous, Laurence, but this—"

"Kitty."

"You didn't even have the courtesy to—"

"Kitty!"

She paused. There was absolutely nothing Laurence could say that would make her think he hadn't somehow planned to ruin this for her.

"Kitty."

She lifted her chin in her old gesture, forced herself to listen. "What?"

"Truly, I didn't know you were here until tonight." His mouth twitched, just a little. "And I'm not trespassing. I own the house."

I own the—

Kitty stared at him dumbly. "You don't own a house."

"I didn't. Not until a few weeks ago." Laurence rubbed a hand on his head a little sheepishly. "A girl I like told me it was stupid for me not to own one, so I went looking. I put it up to rent for events since…" He trailed off. "Since I'm not quite ready to move in yet."

Oh.

Kitty groped for the nearest chair and sank down into it. She couldn't imagine what her face must look like.

Laurence looked at her keenly for a moment, then eased into a chair of his own. "I presume you didn't know who the owner was," he said. "I also presume Cordelia suggested the place?"

"You bought a *house*?"

"I bought a house. I wasn't even going to open your invitation, but I did tonight. When I saw the address…" He trailed off. "Cordelia didn't even bother trying to hide what she did."

Kitty pressed her hands to her face. Laurence was looking at her intently, as if searching for something. He must not have found it, because he leaned back, his handsome face closing off.

"I'll leave you, then," he said. "You have my word…just think of me as the landlord. I won't show up tomorrow."

"Laurence…" said Kitty, softly.

"I didn't tell you all that rigmarole so you could give me Bambi eyes," Laurence said, sounding like his old self. "I am *fine*—"

"You bought a *house*…" Kitty said in wonder.

"Yes, we've covered that, and— What are you doing?"

Kitty was crossing the space between them, light-footed, with a look in her eyes that he'd never seen before without a veil of uncertainty over it.

She dropped clean into his lap with very little grace.

He grunted in surprise, but had no time to recover. Her long arms were looped round his neck and his senses were overwhelmed by everything he'd already grown to love about her body. Soft, yielding flesh. Warmth. The headiness of oil and the sweetness of powder. She pressed her warm cheek to his, and then her lips were at his ear. They were trembling, as was her body.

"I've missed you," she whispered. "You came."

She'd missed him.

"Well…" Laurence said. He was uncomfortably aware, once again, of her closeness, as well as of the warmth filling his chest so full he thought it might burst. "All right…"

An absolutely feral smile crept over Kitty's face. "You're blushing," she accused.

Damn his complexion. He chose to answer that by shooting her one of his famously hard looks, but she looked as amused as Desmond was prone to do, and reached out, cupped his face in her hands.

Her tenderness stole his breath. Slowly, deliberately, he palmed her thighs.

Kitty's breath hitched. "Laurence—"

It would be so easy to lift the barrier of her skirt, to relieve the need already surging through him, but Laurence didn't want to do that. This would be the scariest thing he'd ever done in his life—akin to throwing himself off a cliff—but he had to offer this to Kitty as a gift, not a bribe, when there was no expectation of a deal working out.

Laurence hated uncertainties, and the uncertainty of love was something he had not been able to risk—until now, when the alternative, losing Kitty, was simply…

"I love you," he said.

"I love you," he repeated, in a low husk that sounded nothing like she'd heard before.

And some wild, hungry thing inside of Kitty, where she'd kept it for so long, leapt at those three simple words, seized it so tightly she knew it would be impossible to release it.

She tried to speak but emotion tightened her throat. She could cling to him, however, and she did, gripping his mus-

cular forearms so tightly she worried she'd leave a mark.
She needn't have worried, though. Laurence was sweeping
her up, cradling her so tenderly she felt more secure than
she ever had in her life.

"I *love* you," he said a third time, so emphatically that
she had to smile. "Okay?"

"I know," she choked out. "Okay?"

Tears were running down her face, but somehow this
time she didn't mind.

Laurence whisked them away with his thumbs, an expression of tenderness on his face. "Are you all right?"

She nodded, unable to speak.

"First woman I've said that to—ever—and she starts
crying," he said to no one in particular.

Kitty laughed and hit his chest. "Put me down."

"Never," he said with remarkable gentleness, and he
sighed a little, and then he kissed her.

Kitty had never been kissed like that before—not by
him nor anyone else. He kissed her as if there were words
he wanted to say that had no language except for this. His
lips moved warm and slow over hers, not tentative, but savoring, and she knew her body's responding surge wasn't
lust, it was desire. A desire to be loved completely, and by
this man in particular.

When he finally set her on her feet Kitty was so wobbly
she leaned on him, closed her eyes. "I'm not very good at
this," she whispered.

There was so much she still wanted to say. She wanted
to say that she wanted them to be like this forever, in this
cocoon of warmth and love. She wanted to say that she'd
missed him so badly in the last few weeks it had become
a physical pain. She wanted to say—

"No, you're not," he agreed.

Indignant, Kitty looked up at him, and the smirk on his

face made her huff. She pushed back against his arms, but he held her fast.

"I meant what I said," he said, his eyes bright. "You don't have to say it back…not till you mean it. But I'd like us to— I mean, if you wanted—"

Laurence Stone at a loss for words was something she had never seen before—that was certain. She allowed herself to enjoy it for a fraction of a second before reaching up and lacing his fingers with hers.

"Thank you," he said, almost humbly, then lifted her hand to his lips.

Kitty took a breath. "What happens now?" she asked after a moment.

He leaned forward and rested his head on hers. Contact with him was heaven, and her body already ached, deliciously, in anticipation of the hours ahead of them.

Laurence smiled, just a little. "You could marry me, you know."

Kitty's head jerked up, her eyes flew open wide, and she attempted taking a step back before she could stop herself. "You're not serious—"

The smile widened into laughter. "I'm perfectly serious."

"I— Don't be ridiculous," Kitty faltered, but there was an odd fluttering in her chest that hadn't been there before. *Marriage?*

She'd be insane to consider it. But Laurence was turning over her left hand, a determined look in his dark eyes.

She tried to pull away, with little success. "I can't—"

"Not now," he agreed, and slid his arms down to span her waist. "But move in, at least. Test the car before you buy it."

Kitty sighed as her body softened into his; it wasn't even of her own volition anymore. She closed her eyes, rested her head on his broad shoulder. "You're the most absurd person I've ever met in my life," she said, and yelped when his hands slid down to squeeze her bottom.

When she opened her eyes, his were boring into hers. "Kitty," he said, and his voice was soft. "You know how deathly serious I am about my deals. Marriage is a contract, and once I manage to win you in matrimony—no matter how long it takes—you're *mine*. We'll make a home together..." he added.

His eyes looked distant, as if he were seeing something that did not exist yet but was still as real as the feel of his arms round her.

"Maybe here—maybe somewhere else. You'll run your charity and make me repurpose my clothes. And quite possibly, if you hate this place, we'll even live in *Queens*, and we can foster kids of our own...as many as you want—"

"I take offense to the 'even Queens' bit," Kitty said, but she was laughing. Happiness was filling her chest as sunlight would fill a room, warming, melting, and pushing outwards.

Home.

The word hit that tender, vulnerable place in the innermost recesses of a heart she hadn't realized was still so soft.

She managed to muster some acid into her voice when she answered, though. Although she suspected by the look in his eyes that he wasn't taking her seriously—not at all.

"I'm not a business deal, Laurence." Trust Laurence Stone to find the most unromantic way possible to propose and still have her considering it. "And I'm not going to marry you," she added. "Not now."

"Not *now*?" he repeated, a gleam appearing in his eyes at the caveat.

She felt herself blush, and ducked to press her face into the crook of his neck. This moment was for drinking him in and wondering how it was possible to want someone so absolutely. She would say she loved him, and soon—the words were already on the tip of her tongue—but in this moment she was overwhelmed.

The thought of being his bride, of belonging to him so completely—

"I can't right now…it's too much," she whispered, and slid her hands beneath his shirt to the hard wall of his chest.

Her body ached for him so badly she could barely speak. His muscles tensed, but he didn't pull away, didn't solidify his control. He let her hands wander, and when they skimmed where he already strained for her he did not redirect them. He took a deep breath instead, smiled a little as he looked down at her face.

"We both have a ways to go," he admitted.

Kitty nodded, tilted her lips up to meet his. They did. But, for the first time in her life, giving herself over to someone felt like a certainty rather than a risk. One day soon she'd be able to say aloud the words that her heart was whispering now.

I love you.

EPILOGUE

"IT GETS BETTER every year," Kitty murmured to her husband, looking out over the party.

The enormous courtyard of Kitty and Laurence's Southampton villa was filled with people—donors, potential donors, and some of the kids that Kitty had helped over the years. A pianist sat at a vintage Steinway, playing jazz tunes, servers circulated with ice-cold champagne, fruit, angel food cake piled high with fresh whipped cream.

One Step Ahead hosted this fete to celebrate its intake of young people each summer, and the event was becoming legendary, drawing donors from near and far who wanted to make a difference. They were expanding. There was talk of a similar program in Ghana, maybe an orphanage, a university…

She and Laurence were foster parents as well: for a year now they'd housed two chubby-cheeked pre-teen girls—sisters who were far more angelic, Laurence said, than he had ever been. Her union with Laurence had taken her vision beyond her wildest dreams, and two wandering spirits had merged to make the perfect home.

Home.

Kitty closed her eyes, indulging in a moment against the warmth of her husband's broad chest. She shifted so that she could look up at him and Laurence picked up her left hand, kissing the slim ring of Welsh gold that glowed against the deep tints of her skin.

I love you.

Those three elusive words had come out eventually, less than a month after she and Laurence had transitioned from a fake relationship to a real one. She'd whispered them against his mouth after they'd eaten yet another meal at the little Ghanaian restaurant in Hell's Kitchen. They had been huddled together on the sidewalk, kissing softly, and Kitty had been feeling safer in his arms than she ever had anywhere.

Laurence hadn't said much, but his grip had tightened on her, and that night when they'd reached home he had made love to her with so much intensity she'd covered her face, overwhelmed, as waves of pleasure pulled her body tight.

He'd cradled her to his chest, spoken softly against that tender spot on her neck of rings and weddings and honeymoons and future plans. For once Kitty had indulged him rather than arguing back. She'd known it didn't matter what became of the discussions. As long as they were together she would be content.

Home.

She had one now, and he did as well. They'd created it together, and it was perfect.

* * * * *

PROOF OF THEIR
ONE HOT NIGHT

EMMY GRAYSON

MILLS & BOON

To my editor, Charlotte.
I'm a better writer because of you.

To my husband and my mother.
Book Two is possible because of you.

To my Thursday night critique group.
For believing in me and loving me.

To my son. Baby Boy, you're our world.

CHAPTER ONE

CALANDRA SMYTHE'S EYES flew open as a warm, muscled arm curled around her stomach. She met her own gaze in the mirror above the bed and barely bit back a gasp.

Midnight-blue silk covered her chest and hips, but beneath the covers she was most definitely nude, the fabric a cool kiss against her bare skin. Her hair, which she normally kept contained in a bun, flared out in dark brown waves across her pillow. Lips swollen, cheeks tinged pink…

Oh, no. She looked like she belonged on the cover of a romance novel.

So did the naked man with his arm across her belly. His face was buried in his pillow, but his bare backside was on full display in the mirror. Dark hair curled across the nape of his neck; he had broad shoulders and a muscular back that begged for a woman's fingers to glide over every ridge before trailing lower…

Stop!

Slowly, Calandra got her racing heartbeat back under control. How the hell could she have let this happen? She never did anything this impulsive. Never let anyone get too close. But last night it was like someone else had taken over her body, made her respond with a smile and a flirtatious laugh instead of the cold stare she usually leveled at people who bothered her. If her boss found out what she'd done, or in this case *whom* she'd done, the career she'd fought tooth and nail for would be gone.

Sunlight streamed through the blinds and hit her square in the eyes. Squinting against the brightness, she managed to wiggle out from under the heat of her lover's arm and swing her legs over the edge of the bed. Her feet sank into the plush rug, belying the ache between her thighs. A marble fireplace dominated one side of the room, while a row of windows provided an incredible view of the sun rising over the Hudson River.

Once, a long time ago, she'd been surrounded by opulence like this. Endless toys, designer clothes, trips to France and Italy and Turkey.

She'd been miserable.

But easier to focus on the luxury than the stark-naked man sleeping peacefully behind her. Easier to evaluate details like the spa tub she glimpsed through the bathroom door than to recall the feel of lips trailing over her neck, her breasts, her stomach, leaving sparks of fire burning across her skin. To face the realization that she'd finally given up her virginity to a man whose company she'd despised for the past three years.

She grabbed her phone off the table and stifled a gasp. Six thirty in the morning? She hadn't slept past four in years.

A delicious shiver danced down her spine. Given how energetic their bed play had been, it shouldn't surprise her that she'd overslept.

Fortunately, there were no missed calls or texts from Adrian. No matter how incredible the night had been, no experience was worth risking her reputation.

Or her heart. She prided herself on her ability to keep everyone at arm's length. Indulging in a night of sex had never been worth testing that ability.

Until a night had suddenly seemed worth it. A night of incredible, mind-blowing, soul-stirring sex.

A quick glance over her shoulder verified that he was still sleeping. Sunshine fell upon his back, casting a golden glow over his chiseled muscles. Muscles that had sent a thrill through her veins as her fingers explored every inch of him.

Enough of that.

She turned away and stood. Where had her evening gown ended up? She needed to get dressed and get out of the suite before—

"*Buenos días*, Callie."

Alejandro Cabrera grinned as Calandra froze, her stunning body backlit by the morning sun. The light caressed her toned frame, from the delicateness of her swan-like neck to those long, long legs. Perhaps he could persuade her to join him back in bed and kiss his way up from the slender curve of her calves to those luscious lips, with some detours along the way.

Although judging by the tense set of her shoulders and the alarm in her gray eyes, a repeat of last night's performance wasn't happening anytime soon.

Too bad. The cold-blooded event manager with a heart of ice that he normally dealt with had thawed and revealed an enticing woman who had intoxicated him with heady kisses and passionate moans as he explored every inch of her supple body.

Her virgin body. That had been an unexpected shock. Yet it had filled him with a possessiveness he'd never experienced, one that had made him an even more attentive and gentle lover.

Although their second round had not been gentle. Calandra had responded with a passion that brought him to new heights of pleasure. Heights, he thought with a grin, he was more than happy to revisit.

He sat up and leaned against the headboard. Calandra's gaze flickered down to his groin. Just a glance made him stir. Two spots of red appeared in her cheeks, and she looked away.

His grin widened. "Nothing you haven't seen before."

A grimace passed over her face. "Please don't remind me."

Not the first thing women usually responded with after

sharing his bed. He frowned. Had he imagined the passionate temptress in his bed last night? Or worse, had he not been gentle enough? Her virginity had surprised him, but when he'd tried to pause, she'd grabbed his hips and pulled him deep with such demand he'd nearly embarrassed himself.

Before he could say anything else, she darted across the room and scooped her dress off the floor. She fumbled with the soft material before it slipped from her fingers and pooled in a black satin heap at her feet. She stared at it for a moment, as if willing the dress to levitate off the ground and cover her. Then, with a quick breath, she raised her chin and looked right at him.

There. The tiniest fire flickered in her eyes, smoky and defiant. Standing there in all her bare glory, hair unbound and falling in tousled waves over her alabaster shoulders, she looked like a dark-haired version of Aphrodite rising from the black folds of a stormy sea.

"Stop staring."

He tore his gaze away from the rose-colored tips of her breasts and refocused on her eyes.

Her flat, emotionless gray eyes. Something twisted in his chest. He missed the spark that had flickered to life just last night, then flamed into a blazing inferno as they'd left the empty ballroom behind.

Now that he'd glimpsed the real Calandra, he didn't want her to retreat back into the detached professional he'd come to know.

Not that it mattered, he reminded himself. He'd be on a plane to New Orleans this afternoon. Calandra would return to her career as event planner for his brother's company, Cabrera Wines. And their one night of passion, no matter how intensely pleasurable it had been, would gradually fade as time passed and new women graced his bed.

He covered his momentary lapse into maudlin territory with his customary playboy smile.

"Nothing I haven't seen already."

"Now, Alejandro."

With a disappointed sigh, he averted his gaze and stared out the windows at the towers of New York City sparkling in the early-morning light. He hadn't planned on dropping in for the release party of his brother's latest wine. But *maldición*, he was glad he had. It had been a solid month since he'd pleasured a woman. As much as he enjoyed teasing Calandra, he never would have guessed that she would be his next lover.

Or that she'd be untouched. Possession wound itself through his veins, hot and…desperate. Desperate to keep her all to himself, to not let anyone see the treasure that had been lurking beneath her dark clothing and stern expression.

A discreet glance over his shoulder made his chest tighten as he took in the sensual curve of her back, her tapered waist and those gorgeous legs disappearing into her dress.

Yes. Definitely glad.

"Well."

He suppressed another grin as he turned to fully face Calandra. The gown was in place, wrapped firmly around her body, her lips thin and tight as she stared at him, hands by her sides and curled into fists. The coldness in her gaze would send most men running.

But not him. Not anymore. Not after the delights she had placed within his grasp last night as she'd wrapped those stunning legs around his waist and—

"Sorry, what?" he asked, dragging his mind back from his lurid fantasies.

"Thank you for…" She waved her hand in the air, then shook her head. "I hope you have a safe trip to New Orleans."

Panic flared in his stomach, unexpected and unwelcome. He never panicked when a woman left his bed. Usually he was the one doing the leaving. So why did it bother him that Calandra was practically running into the living room of the suite? Easier to deal with a woman who left on her own than one who took a single night as a sign of something more.

But Calandra leaving bothered him. Before he could examine his emotions, he gave in to instinct and jumped out of bed, grabbed a pair of sweatpants he'd tossed over a chair and followed her.

She had her hand on the door handle when he walked into the living room. Her eyes widened and focused on his chest and then snapped back up, her face red.

Ah. The ice queen wasn't nearly as impervious as she portrayed herself to be.

"What are you doing?" Her tone, on the other hand, could have frozen hell. "I said goodbye."

"It would be rude of me not to walk you back to your room."

Her lips tightened even further. Ever since Adrian had hired her three years ago, Alejandro had delighted in teasing her, trying to get a rise out of the woman who seemed to prefer business over pleasure.

Until last night. Last night, she had definitely preferred pleasure when she'd gasped his name as her hands had clutched his shoulders. He could still feel the heat of her fingertips on his skin.

"I don't have a room here."

Alejandro frowned. "Why not?"

"I'm staying with a friend in the city."

Jealousy slithered through his chest. "A friend?"

She didn't bat an eye at the sudden tension in his tone. "Yes."

"Anyone I know?"

"No."

It shouldn't bother him. They'd had one night together. One night was usually all he made time for. If her fleeing his hotel suite was any indication, Calandra wasn't interested in anything more, either.

So why was he jealous?

She opened the door and walked out. Alejandro caught the door before she could close it and stepped out into the hall.

"Shouldn't you put on a shirt?" Calandra kept her gaze averted as she stalked down the hall to the elevator, the plush carpet masking the sound of her heels. An elderly couple walked past him, the woman's mouth dropping open as she took in his bare chest. The husband made a sound of disapproval and tugged his wife's hand, urging her along.

"I'm comfortable. Besides," he added with a grin as the elevator dinged and the doors whooshed open, "nothing you haven't seen before. Or kissed. Or nibbled—"

"I get it."

Before she could close the elevator doors in his face, he stepped in beside her and pressed the button for the first floor. The doors closed.

And suddenly they were alone once more in a very tight, very intimate space. He heard the sharp intake of her breath, felt the snap of electricity between them. He went hard in an instant, memories of their lovemaking rushing through his mind as his blood roared in his ears.

Mine, mine, mine.

He risked a glance down. Calandra stared straight ahead. She thrust her shoulders back, pressing her breasts against her neckline. That dark hair tumbled down her back, and he barely stopped himself from reaching out and tangling his fingers in the silky tresses.

The thought of her leaving the hotel room had filled him with a sense of urgency, almost a desperation to keep her in his sights. But now, as he took a step away from her and the temptation to press her up against the wall of the elevator and kiss those luscious lips, warning bells clanged.

Suddenly, he couldn't wait to be rid of her and the urges she inspired.

The elevator stopped and the doors opened, revealing the lobby. Grecian columns marched down the room, flanked by urns spilling over with deep pink blooms. A row of chandeliers hung from the ceiling. Soft instrumental music shut out most of the noise from Fifty-Third Street as taxis, buses and cars rushed by the floor-to-ceiling windows.

Calandra marched out of the elevator, heels clicking on the rosewood floor. Alejandro followed at a casual pace. As much as he wanted to return to his room, order breakfast in bed and catch a few more hours of sleep before his flight, he forced himself to do the right thing and at least see Calandra safely into a taxi.

The front desk attendant glanced up and did a double take as he passed, her eyes widening behind her enormous glasses.

"Um…sir—"

He winked at her. "I know, forgot my shirt. I'll make it right in a minute, I promise."

He quickened his pace as Calandra burst out the front doors and raised her arm. By the time he walked outside, she'd already hailed a cab and was reaching for the car door.

"Allow me."

Alejandro opened the door with a flourish and bowed. She tossed him a narrow-eyed glare as she climbed into the car.

"Thank you," she murmured stiffly.

"You're welcome."

She turned her head, probably to deliver a cutting remark, but whatever she was about to say was lost as their eyes met. The coldness disappeared once more, steel softening into misty gray that flared bright with desire, longing and…

He blinked. Something so sad it tugged at his heart.

"Calandra, I—"

She shook her head and reached for the door.

"Goodbye, Señor Cabrera."

The door slammed shut, and the taxi sped off. He watched it until it was swallowed up in the sea of New York traffic.

He glanced up at the legendary city's skyscrapers, despising the ache in his chest. The feeling that something wasn't quite right had been building for the past few months, a dissatisfaction with the endless parties and, if he dared to be honest with himself, a longing for something more. Something permanent. The two upcoming new ships that would be added to Cabrera Shipping's fleet had assuaged some of the emptiness. So had the tentative approval of the board to move forward on the *La Reina* project, despite his father's increasingly pointed comments about all the things that could go wrong. Not unexpected. He'd gotten used to Javier Cabrera's disapproval a long time ago.

The future was bright. So why did this longing for something more persist? And why had his night with Calandra tilted his world even farther off its axis?

He didn't know how long he stood there, staring at the spot where she'd disappeared, an uncomfortable ache tugging at his heart. But a sudden whoop, followed by a "Hey, sexy" from a bleary-eyed woman with smudged eyeliner hanging out the window of a passing cab, yanked him out of whatever nostalgic land he'd ventured to and back into reality.

One night. One night of mind-blowing sex. That's all it was, and that's all he wanted it to be.

With that final thought, he turned and walked back into the hotel. The clerk stood behind the desk, arms folded and eyes narrowed. Her black-and-gold name tag proclaimed her name to be Leia.

"Sir, we ask that all our guests wear a shirt, pants and shoes in the lobby."

He grinned and leaned against the counter. Instead of swooning or eyeballing his chest, her eyes tapered into slits.

Two women who'd resisted him in one morning. Maybe he was losing his touch.

He held up a hand in surrender. "I'm sorry. I wasn't paying attention. It won't happen again."

She stared at him for another long moment, then nodded toward the door.

"I hope your friend enjoyed her stay with us."

The smile disappeared from his face. "Yeah." Why did it bother him that Calandra had fled? He'd left plenty of beds without even a goodbye. He didn't care for being on the receiving end.

A flicker of compassion crossed Leia's face. "It could work out."

He returned Leia's gaze before smiling slightly. "Thanks. And I am sorry."

She pushed her glasses up the bridge of her nose and nodded briskly. "Yes, well…just don't do it again, Mr. Cabrera."

He backed away with his hands held up in surrender, shot her another thousand-watt smile that did nothing more than make her roll her eyes and headed for the elevator. The door swished open and a beautiful blonde woman rushed out, head down, hand clutched tightly around her suitcase. She glanced up. Recognition flared. He'd seen her dance with Adrian last night, seen the way his normally uptight brother had looked at her.

He started to say hello, to at least glean her name, but she dashed by so quickly he didn't even have a chance.

Oh, well. He had problems of his own. Like keeping his

company moving forward and forgetting the woman who had run from his bed like the hounds of hell were nipping at her heels.

All while looking insanely sexy and deliciously rumpled.

Step one: cold shower. Step two: get dressed, grab breakfast. Step three: head to the airport. Step four: put Calandra Smythe and their incredible night together out of his mind.

CHAPTER TWO

Four months later

CALANDRA SURVEYED THE crowd gathered on the lawn of Adrian Cabrera's Paris home, her fingers curled around her champagne flute like it was a lifeline. People moved in a sea of summer colors, mint-green gowns and pale blue dress shirts, as they sipped on champagne and snacked on mushroom tartlets.

To think, the crème de la crème of European society considered this an intimate gathering. She'd been a part of this crowd when she worked for Adrian, not to mention the first thirteen years of her life.

But that was the past. A problem demanded her immediate attention. She would prefer to be home in North Carolina curled up in bed with a book and a cup of tea, but her conscience demanded that she address it.

A quick conversation. Just a couple minutes, and then you can leave.

Slowly, she eased the death grip on her glass before she broke it. He had no reason to be upset. She had a plan and would take care of everything, just like she always did. Besides, how many times, during their verbal sparring at various Cabrera Wine events, had he said he was a no-strings kind of guy? He eschewed commitment of any kind.

When he'd walked her down to that cab, she'd seen him in the rearview mirror standing on the sidewalk, gazing after her. And in that moment, a terrifying emotion had taken root—*want*. Not the burning, physical attraction she'd experienced that night, but a desire for the safety she'd experienced curled up in his arms.

She'd given herself a stern talking-to about all the reasons why such an emotion was dangerous. It implied commitment, something Alejandro clearly wanted no part of. Commitment she didn't want, either. Marriage had been crossed off her list long ago.

Even after she'd explained why she had no interest in getting him involved, her sister, Johanna, had encouraged her to reach out. After her younger sibling's relentless guilt tripping, she'd finally tried getting in touch. First by email, then by phone. Her emails went unanswered, her calls stonewalled by a terribly efficient secretary.

So she'd resorted to crashing an engagement party for the boss she'd walked out on over three months ago. She wouldn't have bothered if she hadn't been in London, she told herself, and the ticket from London to Paris had been manageable on her limited budget. Her final round of interviews for an event planner position with an elite European fashion house had included a round-trip plane ticket. An indicator, Johanna had excitedly said, that interview or not, the job was hers.

The interview that had gone south when they'd asked if they could contact Adrian Cabrera for a reference if they offered her the job. Her fourth interview in six weeks. Another reason why coming to this party was a good idea. Perhaps, along with sharing her important news with Alejandro, she could also somehow finagle a recommendation from Adrian. She might not have left on the best of terms, but she'd done damned good work for him in the time she'd given to Cabrera Wines.

She longed to sip the champagne in her hands, to feel the bubbles dance down her throat and soothe her galloping heartbeat. It had quickened into a fast-paced tempo when her plane had landed yesterday morning. It had kicked into a frantic pace this afternoon as she'd pulled on one of her last remaining evening gowns, the rest sold to give a feeble boost to her rapidly dwindling savings. And ever since she had boldly walked into the party like she belonged, her heart had pounded so ferociously she was amazed no one else could hear it.

"Beautiful, isn't it?"

Calandra reined in her runaway thoughts and schooled her features into a politely blank mask before turning to see who had interrupted her musings.

A tall brunette stood next to her, eyes fixed on the Eiffel Tower, standing tall and proud against the backdrop of a darkening sky.

"First time in Paris?"

As much as she loathed small talk, something about the young woman's waiflike innocence tugged at her. When she turned to look at Calandra, she bit back a gasp. The innocent wonder in the young woman's gaze was enhanced by her two differently colored eyes, one the palest shade of blue, the other a bright amber.

The young woman nodded eagerly. "Yes. I've lived in Spain since I was ten. I always dreamed of seeing Paris."

Protectiveness unexpectedly reared its head. Calandra kept her hands wrapped around her glass and resisted the urge to drag her away. Away from the glitter and shine that concealed far too many wolves in sheep's clothing.

"My name's Annistyn, but my friends call me Anna."

"Calandra."

"How do you know Adrian and Everleigh?"

"I used to work for Cabrera Wines."

Anna's eyes lit up. "I live at Casa de Cabrera in Granada. My uncle Diego is the butler."

Calandra smiled slightly. She had fond memories of the silver-haired steward of the Cabrera mansion.

"Oh."

Calandra followed Anna's gaze to where Adrian and his fiancée, Everleigh, stood on the terrace overlooking the lawn. Blood roared in her ears. Had they seen her? Would they call security and have her thrown out before she could accomplish her mission?

Breathe. Stay in control.

They weren't even looking in her direction. No, they only had eyes for each other. A handsome young man approached them, his smile flashing white against his dark brown beard. Adrian laughed and hugged him.

Calandra blinked. She could count on one hand the number of times she'd seen Adrian laugh.

"Um, excuse me."

Before Calandra could say another word, Anna turned and disappeared down a garden path. Calandra turned back in time to see Everleigh kiss the younger man on the cheek. Judging by the similarities in appearance, she was finally seeing Antonio Cabrera for the first time. The youngest brother had never attended Adrian's events, at least while she'd been working for Cabrera Wines.

Unlike Alejandro, who had attended almost every one and sought her out. He'd thrived on vexing her, tugging at the loose threads of her patience that only he seemed to be able to find. With everyone else she stayed calm, cool, unaffected.

With him, she turned into someone she didn't recognize. Someone who, for one wicked night, had thrilled at the touch of a hand on her face, a whisper in her ear, who now craved the closeness of sleeping next to someone and feeling their heartbeat beneath her fingertips.

A fool. He turned her into an irrational, dreamy-eyed fool.

She glanced around the party once more. No sign of him. She exhaled, long and slow, the tension melting from her shoulders. A soft breath in, followed by another long exhale.

She could do this.

One more glance over the crowds. No glimpse of the

long, dark curling hair or deep blue eyes glinting with a lethal combination of seduction and humor.

Her eyes sought out Adrian and Everleigh once more. Conviction charged through her veins as she lifted her chin.

Before her resolve wavered, she set her untouched glass of champagne on a tray, pulled up the hem of her dress and marched across the lawn, keeping Adrian and Everleigh in her sights. As she advanced up the stairs, Adrian's head turned and he saw Calandra. Recognition widened his eyes, followed by a narrowing as his gaze turned stone-cold.

Should she have expected anything less? She'd abandoned her boss during his time of need, and had done so in a very unprofessional way. If Adrian knew the real reason she'd left, she had no doubt he would turn her life into a living hell.

One foot in front of the other. With each step her courage grew, propelling her forward as she reached the top of the stairs.

"*Buenos días*, Señor Cabrera."

Her voice came out firm, steady, a touch of friendliness in her tone. She held out her hand and kept it there, waiting.

Adrian stared at her for a long moment before finally shaking her hand. "It's been a while, Calandra. How are you?"

Everleigh elbowed her fiancé in the side even as she sneaked a curious glance at Calandra. "Be nice, Adrian."

"I am."

Everleigh rolled her eyes and, before Calandra could say anything, enveloped her in a hug.

Calandra froze for a moment before her brain kicked in. She tentatively patted Everleigh on the back. Everleigh released her, her face wreathed in a huge smile.

"I'm guessing you're Calandra Smythe? I've heard a lot about you."

"Nothing good, I'm sure."

Everleigh waved a hand. "I've only heard Adrian's side of the story. I'm sorry he's being discourteous. And at our engagement party, too."

Adrian's lips thinned. "Speaking of, I don't recall seeing you on the guest list."

"Adrian!" Everleigh exclaimed. "That's just rude."

"There's no need to apologize," Calandra said quickly. "I'm the one who should apologize. I came without an invitation. And I behaved very unprofessionally and left you in a bind." She looked directly at Adrian. "I'm sorry. I let a personal situation affect my work, and you bore the consequences."

Adrian returned her gaze with his trademark stare, the one that made men with years of experience quake in their boots. She didn't like talking, she didn't like apologizing and she definitely did not want to be around the Cabrera family any longer than she had to.

But she didn't back down.

At last, Adrian bowed his head briefly toward her. "Apology accepted."

Relief flooded through her. "Thank you."

Everleigh went up on her tiptoes and kissed his cheek. "I knew you had it in you."

Seeing the adoration in Adrian's eyes as he kissed his fiancée made Calandra's chest tighten. Her father's philandering and her mother's pining for the man who would never love her the way she loved him had ruined any girlhood dreams of Prince Charming. Love wasn't wedding bells and rosy baby cheeks. Love was crying until there were no tears left. A fairy tale with a monster lurking on the last page.

"Congratulations to you both. I'm very happy for you, Adrian."

She didn't believe in love or marriage, but that didn't mean she wished ill for anyone pursuing the elusive dream of true love. She meant her well wishes to the couple, every word. There were traces of the Adrian she had worked for, but he seemed happier, more relaxed.

Hopefully, unlike the early years of her parents' marriage that had turned from bliss to nightmare, his happiness would last.

"Thank you, Calandra." He snaked a possessive arm around his fiancée's waist and pulled her close. "But I can't help thinking that you didn't come to Paris just to wish us a happy engagement."

The perfect opening. She took a deep breath. First, recommendation. Second, where his brother was. She could do this.

"Hello, Calandra."

The world screeched to a halt as her hair stood on end, that sensual, deep voice sliding over her skin and touching the deepest parts of her illicit desires. Blood pounded in her veins so loudly the rest of the party noises faded around her. She turned, slowly, desperately trying to stay calm as her gaze locked onto a familiar pair of deep blue eyes.

Alejandro Cabrera. The father of her child.

CHAPTER THREE

THE CALANDRA SMYTHE standing before him was not the one he'd seen disappearing into the sea of New York traffic. That Calandra had been vulnerable, desire lingering in the uncertain gaze she'd shot him before running away. This Calandra was the one he remembered from her years at Cabrera Wines: dark, impervious, ice-cold as she stared at him with silver eyes so sharp they could cut a man to ribbons with a mere glance.

But he knew better now. He knew that beneath the ice ran a current of hot passion that had kept him awake for weeks after their tryst. Just the memory of making love to her, of her nails raking down his back as he'd slid in and out of her wet heat, sent raw hunger pulsing through him for the first time in four months.

Obsessiveness spread through his veins and rooted him to the spot. Even as he nodded to Adrian and kissed Everleigh on the cheek, he soaked in every detail of Calandra's appearance. The dark hair wrapped into a bun at the nape of her neck. The dash of deep burgundy on her lips. The swish of black satin that clung to her torso and flared out just below her breasts into a soft, loose skirt that fell in ripples to her ankles. A surprisingly whimsical style on her. He never would have thought her the romantic type.

Just a month ago, he'd typed her name into Google, his finger hovering over the Enter key. He didn't know how long he'd sat there, contemplating what he would do if he actually found her, called her. Really, what was there to say? They'd had a one-night stand and, less than three weeks later, she'd quit his brother's company without notice and disappeared.

A sting to his pride. Nothing more. He'd never had a

woman flee as if the devil were on her heels. Calandra's sudden departure and ensuing silence had been a novelty. That was the only reason he'd thought about her since.

At least that's what he'd told himself.

In the last few weeks, he'd barely thought of her at all. Javier's interferences had monopolized his thoughts day and night.

With the slightest shake of his head, he slipped into his playboy persona and flashed a smile in her direction.

"I'm surprised to see you here. And dressed in almost not black. What's the occasion?"

Everleigh sucked in a breath.

"Don't worry," Adrian said wryly. "They bicker like brother and sister."

Oh, no. Bickering like two people who couldn't stand that they were so attracted to each other, yes.

Most definitely not like brother and sister.

Unlike their previous encounters, though, Calandra did not take the bait. Her eyes darted to the side as she bit down on her lower lip. Her hand drifted to her stomach before she clenched her fingers into a fist.

Initially she'd seemed calm and collected. But now she seemed…nervous.

His eyes narrowed. He'd seen Calandra nervous exactly one time, and one time only—right after she'd kissed him senseless in an elevator in New York City.

Something was wrong.

She shot a stiff smile at Everleigh. "It's okay. I've gotten used to his teasing. It brings back memories of high school, actually. Same levels of maturity, too."

A grin tugged at his lips. Yes, the sex had been amazing, but even before they'd seen each other naked, he'd thoroughly enjoyed their verbal sparring. Calandra was the one woman who hadn't been afraid to stand up to him, to call him out or flat-out roll her eyes.

She was the only woman he'd ever felt truly comfortable around.

She turned those gray eyes on him, and his chest tightened. Yes, something was definitely wrong. Calandra kept herself aloof, always in control of any situation. He'd watched her navigate everything from drunk guests to a caterer who'd shown up thirty minutes before dinner was supposed to be served. She never batted an eye at the myriad things that had gone wrong in the years that she'd worked for Cabrera Wines. She'd simply adapted and overcome.

So what problem had caused this unrest in her, this nervous energy that practically sizzled across her alabaster skin? Adrian and Everleigh appeared unfazed. Could no one see the unease in her eyes, in the slight drumming of her fingers on the balcony railing?

"Alejandro, I need to speak with you."

Adrian's head whipped around, his eyes narrowing. Before Alejandro could open his mouth and come up with some witty retort, Everleigh, God bless her sweet soul, wound her arm through her fiancé's and tugged him toward the stairs.

"I think the fireworks are about to start, my love."

"But—"

"Off we go."

And just like that, they were alone. The seconds stretched out, each one longer than the last, as Calandra's gaze darted from the crowd gathered on the lawn to the marble staircase to the darkening Parisian sky.

Everywhere but him. Frustration tightened his jaw. She was the one who had sought him out, who had blazed her way into his brother's anniversary party to talk with him and now couldn't even look at him.

"What did you want to talk to me about?"

His direct question seemed to startle her out of her uncharacteristic state. Her lips parted as she sucked in a breath and started to speak…

Only for the boom of fireworks to cut off whatever she'd been about to say. Alejandro turned just as sparks burst above them, a shower of green and silver streaks that lit up the sky.

Below him, Adrian drew Everleigh into the circle of his arms, resting his chin on her golden head as she snuggled into his embrace.

A vise tightened around Alejandro's heart. The possibility of a long-term relationship, let alone marriage, was off the table. He'd sworn off long-term anything the day he'd walked into the library and discovered that his father wasn't an emotionally distant taskmaster with a fondness for rule following. No, he was much worse—a sanctimonious bastard who deserved to rot in hell for his selfishness.

It had nearly killed him to keep that secret all these years. But Madre was happy. He couldn't bear to shatter the illusion that Javier had somehow managed to maintain all these years. So he'd taken to punishing his father the one way he could—by engaging in the activities Javier loathed. The vices he indulged in had the added benefit of suspending the pain of rejection. Temporarily. Which was why he sought them out again and again.

He glanced at Calandra out of the corner of his eye. Her flight had added insult to injury, ripping off the bandages he'd been slapping over his wounds with reserved tables at the most exclusive clubs across Europe, casual sex and luxury cars.

But he'd also invested, scheduled the construction of two new ships to bring Cabrera's cargo freighters into the twenty-first century. Now, the first project that was truly his and his alone, *La Reina*, bordered on the brink of disaster, brought there by Javier's machinations. He wouldn't back down, though.

"Alejandro?" Calandra appeared next to him, a small V between her brows. He'd never pictured her as the emotional type. "Are you all right?"

"Yes. Got lost in my own thoughts. It's been an interesting couple of months."

A breathy laugh escaped her lips. "You have no idea."

He turned to see her face lit up by the constant stream of fireworks bursting overhead. Shades of blue, red and gold caressed her skin. His depressing thoughts faded away as he remembered just how good they'd been together, how tightly her body had wrapped around him as he'd moved inside her, the flare of emotion in her eyes when she'd looked up at him as if seeing him for the first time.

He'd always shied away from bringing emotions into sex. Hard to remain a bachelor when feelings got involved. But with her, the unexpected tenderness he'd experienced had added a heightened pleasure that had burned inside him long after she'd fled.

His groin tightened.

"Let's go inside where it's quieter. This sounds like a serious conversation."

She hesitated, then nodded. Triumph emboldened him as he reached out, grabbed her elbow and steered her toward the balcony doors that led into the library. He gestured for her to enter and closed the doors behind him. A quick tug and green velvet drapes fell over the glass, throwing the room into darkness, save for the dim light filtering in from the windows up above.

Something clicked. A lamp blinked on as Calandra looked around the room. Alejandro quelled his irritation. Light wasn't suitable for seduction. Although, he amended as the light shone through the fabric of her skirt and illuminated the curves of her legs, maybe it wasn't a bad thing.

Calandra circled the room, arms wrapped around her waist. Her eyes took in the books crowding the floor-to-ceiling shelves.

"Reminds me of the library from *Beauty and the Beast*."

"Singing teapots and a magical rose? Doesn't seem like your kind of movie."

A bitter smile twisted her lips. "Ice and snow and a beast with a cold heart. Seems just like me."

Normally he would have responded with a witty joke or some pithy comment about her remarkable resemblance to the ice sculptures that had often stood guard over the food at his brother's events. But the pain in her voice stopped him, as did the hurt that tightened her jaw as she pulled a book off the shelf.

"I beg to differ," he replied as he walked toward her. "You remind me of the candelabra that's always ordering everyone about."

She glanced at him over her shoulder, her prim expression somehow sexy. "I can't recall ever being on fire."

Oh, but I can. If she realized what she'd said, she gave no indication as she looked back down at the book in her hands. He walked toward her, each step upping his desire. His fingertips burned at the memory of how hot her bare skin had been beneath his touch. Excitement and lust heightened his senses as he stopped just a foot away.

"What did you want to talk about?" he whispered into her ear.

Her head snapped up and she turned, her mouth so close to his all he had to do was lean forward and claim her.

Her lips parted. He leaned in, ready to kiss her.

"Your child."

The words hung in the air. He drew back and stared down at her. He'd heard the words, knew they'd been spoken, but couldn't fully comprehend.

"My what?"

Her fingers came up and clenched the pendant around her neck so tight her knuckles turned white. "Your child, Alejandro. I'm pregnant."

CHAPTER FOUR

THE SECONDS DRAGGED on, each one growing longer as Alejandro stared at her.

Nothing. Not a flicker of emotion in those dark blue eyes. A blank visage, lips turned up slightly at the corners. The perfect poker face. A moment ago he'd been about to kiss her, and weakling that she was, she'd considered letting him, just to have one more taste before she dropped her bombshell.

Her brain had come to her rescue, and she'd forced out the words that would drive a wedge between them. Yet she hadn't expected this. Anger, shock, even a snide remark or a ribald joke. But of the myriad scenarios she'd planned for, complete and total silence was not one of them. Silence that stretched and filled the library with its oppressing presence, pushing against her until she was thrust back into the past and those terrible, awful mornings of endless quiet, save for the whisper of her mother's labored breathing.

Say something!

One last boom of fireworks reverberated outside. Another moment of even more oppressive silence. Then music struck up once more, sultrier, more seductive.

Just like that night. Try as she might, she couldn't shake the memory of a darkened ballroom and a handsome man with his sleeves rolled up to his elbows, tan skin contrasting sharply with the white of his shirt.

The shirt she'd ripped off him less than an hour later in a passionate frenzy she'd never thought herself capable of.

Her lips thinned. Alejandro was dangerous. He brought her to the edge of control. Like now. Anyone else could have given her the silent treatment and she would have shrugged, turned and left.

But for him, she lingered. Waited. She hated it, yet she couldn't seem to walk away.

At last, he moved. He slid his hands into his pockets, broke eye contact and looked down at the balcony.

"Huh."

Blood pounded in her ears. She'd flown across an ocean, nearly two thousand dollars on plane tickets, a hotel room and a cab to sweet-talk her way into a party to tell the spoiled second son of a billionaire family she was pregnant with his child, and all she got was a damn *huh*!

She shouldn't have expected anything more. But she had.

In that moment, she hated Alejandro Cabrera. Hated him and his cavalier attitude, his lack of thought for anyone but himself. Common sense kept her from slapping him across the face. It would only be another display of emotions, a sign of weakness.

No matter how satisfying it would be.

Alejandro walked over to the balcony door, opened it and signaled to someone outside. Moments later, a waiter dressed in a silky black vest and bow tie appeared in the doorway, a silver tray with bubbling flutes of champagne perfectly balanced on his gloved hand. Alejandro plucked a glass from the tray and dismissed the waiter before he moved to a bank of windows. With a quick tug on a cord, the curtains fell back to reveal the sparkling lights of Paris on the horizon. The way he leaned against the windowsill, one trousered leg crossed casually over the other, glass in hand, looked like an ad selling thousand-dollar bottles of champagne.

"I'm not here for money. I'm taking care of everything." *Barely.* "But she—"

"Have you picked out names?"

Calandra blinked. A simple question, and yet how strange coming from his lips.

"We've picked out a few."

His head whipped around. She barely stopped herself from taking a step back at his darkening eyes.

"We?"

He uttered the word in a silky voice, but uncharacteristic anger lurked in his tone.

"My sister, Johanna." His shoulders relaxed. "She lives with me."

He looked back down at his drink. "So, if it's not about money, then what do you want?"

"To do the right thing. To let you know you have a child on the way."

His smile flashed once more, but this time it held an edge to it. She blinked, and it was gone.

"How quaint."

He took another long drink of his champagne and turned, eyes fixing on her face. She resisted the urge to squirm under his scrutiny.

"You flew all the way to Paris just to tell me?"

"I tried emailing. And calling."

He frowned. "I never received anything from you."

"If the secretary who refused to put my calls through also answers your emails, that explains it."

His lips twitched. "Yes, Laura is frighteningly efficient." His fingers tapped out a rhythm on his glass. "How much is all this going to cost you, anyway?"

"I have it handled."

No smile, no glint of teasing. Just a hard stare that made her want to squirm.

"Where do you work?"

"None of your concern." Her words whipped out, sharp and cold. She barely stopped herself from wincing. Why could she not keep her cool around this man?

He didn't even flinch.

"So," she continued, her voice calmer, "now that you know about the…the baby, I can keep you updated." Just saying *baby* made her feel possessive, protective. Strange, because she'd never imagined having children before. But ever since she'd seen the heartbeat pulsing across the monitor, she'd known she would do anything for the tiny human growing inside her, including keeping it safe.

Even from its own father.

"Updated?" Alejandro repeated.

"Photos, things like that. We can discuss events like birthdays and such later if you want to attend. But I know this is the exact opposite of your preferred lifestyle. And I have everything handled," she repeated.

There. She'd done it. She'd told him, set her boundaries. She suddenly felt lighter than she had in months. Now she could go home, close the door on this chapter of her life and move on with Johanna and her baby. Despite the gravity of the situation, a tiny seed of happiness sprouted inside her. She been so focused on this confrontation, on telling Alejandro and getting it over with, that she'd barely thought about life with her child. But now that she had done the right thing, she was free. Free to buy books and booties and finally let Johanna drag her to the nearest store and start planning the nursery. A thought she would have turned up her nose at just a few months ago, but now…now she was going to be a mother. A mother who would never, ever let her child experience the pain she had.

She reached into her clutch and pulled out a card. Not having Alejandro involved in her and the baby's life was the best gift she could possibly give it.

"Here's my number and email if you have questions. Now that you know and know how to get ahold of me, I'll—"

He moved suddenly, crossing the floor and stopping within inches of her. She took a step back without thinking and bumped into a bookcase.

"You're not leaving, are you?"

"Yes. What else is there to say?"

His eyes narrowed. "You have a very clear idea of how this is going to work."

"Well, yes."

That smile reappeared, the one with the bite to it that revealed a glimpse of a darker, more serious Alejandro. She didn't like it.

"But you haven't asked me what I want."

"Given your history, it's obvious what you want."

He leaned in, balancing his hands on the bookcase and caging her between his arms. Her breath caught. He was so close she could see flecks of gold in the blue of his eyes, inhale the erotic aroma of pine that always clung to him.

"What do I want, Calandra?"

His voice came out husky and made heat pool between her thighs.

"To be free."

"I'll give you that. I used to want nothing more than freedom. To do what I want, with whom I wanted, when I wanted. But I've also had a tumultuous four months. And I've found that I want something else besides freedom. Something you've just handed me."

Warning pricked the back of her neck. "What?"

He stepped back, tucking his hands in his pockets and shooting her his thousand-watt grin. "I want to be a part of our child's life."

What? Her mouth dropped open, but no words came out. For once, she was speechless.

"Is that acceptable to you?"

"Um… I…"

He laughed, the rich sound breaking through the shock and drifting over her skin with disturbing sensuality.

"I need to mark this on my calendar. The first time you didn't have a snappy comeback."

"No, because I…" At last she found her voice. "You hate commitment."

The smile disappeared. The sight of him, lips tight, shoulders tense, jaw clenched, made her uneasy. What had happened to him? It wasn't just this moment, but something had been off all night, a darkness lurking behind the smile.

"Used to. People change, Calandra."

People did change. And other times, you thought they'd changed, only to have them take your trust and rip it into tiny shreds.

"I don't think I'm comfortable with that."

"Because of my past?"

"I've seen enough pictures of what you've been up to the past four months. It's not your past that concerns me, but your present." Somehow her voice came out collected and cool. "My own father was like that. My childhood was a living hell. I won't have that for my child."

"Our child."

"*My* child," she repeated heatedly. "I'm going to be the one raising it, loving it, paying for it—"

"One million dollars."

She blinked. "What?"

"Or two million. Whatever you and the child need to live comfortably."

"You can't buy our child," she snapped.

"I'm not." Annoyance laced his voice. "I'm doing the right thing for *our* child, Calandra. The one I have a right to see."

Threads of fear tightened her chest into a fearful knot. She knew just how easily a man of Alejandro's resources and power could crush her, could use his wealth and lawyers to get shared or even sole custody. The reminder of who he was behind the charm only exacerbated the worry she'd been carrying since she'd decided to tell him about the baby.

Finally, she closed her eyes and let her head drop. Defeat sucked the energy from her limbs. Like it or not, it would be far easier to meet Alejandro halfway than fight him. Fighting could lead to a legal battle she couldn't even begin to afford.

"What do you want?"

The wooden floor creaked beneath his feet. A warm hand cupped her face. Startled, her eyes flew open and she looked up.

"I would like to be a part of our child's life." He held up a hand as she started to speak. "You have misgivings. Our relationship up until now has been...tempestuous."

Despite the gravity of the situation, amusement lightened her mood. "Fancy word for 'barely didn't kill each other.'"

His grin made her chest flutter. It had to be the excessive hormones pumping through her veins.

"You're the one who wanted to kill me. I just enjoyed teasing you. But we barely know each other. Not really."

She looked away. She didn't want to get to know him. Knowing someone meant time, emotions, investment. Things she wanted nothing to do with.

"What are you suggesting?"

"Stay tonight. Here. We'll talk in the morning."

"And if I refuse?"

Determination hardened his eyes and chased the pleasantness from his face. "If you refuse, then it becomes a legal problem."

His threat shocked her into silence. If this went to court, she would lose in a heartbeat. She couldn't even begin to compete with Alejandro's wealth or the lawyers he could buy. His menacing words solidified what she had suspected—beneath the smiles and gallant charm, he was just like her father. He toyed with people's emotions, manipulated them until he had what he wanted and then revealed his true self.

Her hand settled over her stomach as she lifted her chin. She'd play his game for now, maybe use the time to figure out why exactly he was so interested in becoming a father. Was there a business angle, like securing an heir—archaic as that notion seemed—or was it just male pride?

"Fine. We can talk tomorrow," she replied stiffly.

"Excellent."

"But I have a hotel room."

"Where are you staying?"

"Nearby."

He stepped closer. She stood firm. She despised him, hated him for having the power of wealth, for fooling her, for giving her a taste of what she thought had been true passion only to find out it was just a mirage.

Most of all, she hated that despite everything she'd discovered in the last five minutes, her body still responded to his dark, sensual masculinity.

"Stay here tonight."

Her spine straightened. Just because she was playing his game didn't mean she would take orders.

"No. Thank you."

His expression softened, but she kept her heart hard. She wouldn't be trapped in the vicious cycle her father had kept her mother in for years. Expensive trips, lavish gifts, a compliment designed to make the heart sing...until the next time he'd cheated. The next time he disappeared for a week and they'd had no idea if he was running wild in Europe or if he was lying in a ditch somewhere.

"It would be easier—"

"I said no." She spit out the words with such ferocity that she almost blinked in surprise.

Sadness darkened his eyes as he turned away. Her hand came up to...what? Stop him from leaving? Comfort him? *Don't fall for it.*

He pulled back the curtain from the balcony doors and

stepped outside, then looked back at her expectantly. He'd managed to turn this into a dismissal even though she was the one who was leaving.

Her defenses hardened. The last three years of conversations and bantering had revealed a keen mind and a sharp wit. Traits many people, including herself, had brushed aside because he seemed so utterly ridiculous. But then last year they'd talked more, delving into business, politics and travel. She'd learned that he was intelligent.

An intelligence she needed to be wary of as they moved into battle.

She walked across the library slowly, not giving him the satisfaction of hurrying to his side. As she started to move past him into the summer night, he caught her hand in his. Slowly, so achingly slowly, he brought her fingers up. She should pull away, should call him every insult she could think of. But no. No, she watched her fingers travel up to his mouth, bit down on her bottom lip as he pressed a kiss to her knuckles.

"Until tomorrow."

And with that he walked down the stairs to join the partygoers below. She watched his tall figure cut through the crowd with ease, pausing here and there to greet someone.

More than one female someone, she noticed.

It shouldn't bother her. It *didn't* bother her, she sternly told herself. The man had just threatened to take her to court over their child. He was a selfish, spoiled rich boy who, hopefully after she outlined all the responsibilities being a parent entailed, would run as far away from her as he could.

She would remain on guard. Rational. Logical.

Those thoughts did nothing to erase the burning sensation on the back of her hand where his lips had rested.

CHAPTER FIVE

THE NEXT MORNING, when Calandra rang the doorbell, a
sweet-faced maid answered and ushered her into the grand
hall of Adrian's Paris mansion, presided over by a crystal
chandelier that probably cost as much as the mortgage on
Aunt Norine's house. The maid murmured that Monsieur
Cabrera would be out in a moment and disappeared. Moments later, the sound of raised male voices cut through the
silence from one of the doorways off the hall.

"...don't know the first thing about being a father!"

Adrian's voice lashed out. Another voice responded, the
faintest murmur, but it still sent a dangerous shiver down
her spine.

Alejandro.

"How do you know she's telling the truth?"

Adrian's words cut deep. Shame rose in her throat, thick
and bitter. The baby deserved so much better than her, a
cold woman who'd succumbed to a moment of weakness
with the last person she thought she would have slept with,
much less taken as her first lover.

I'll do better, baby. I'll be better. For you.

Alejandro responded once more, his voice still so low
she couldn't make out his words. Silence ensued for several seconds. Then a door slammed.

"He's gone now."

She froze. Was he talking to her?

"I'm not going to bite, Calandra."

Another memory appeared with no warning, of his
lips on her breasts, his teeth nibbling on her flesh as she'd
arched up into his embrace.

She gritted her teeth. If she'd known sex would have

caused this many moments of vulnerability, she never would have given up her virginity so easily. Or ever.

"Callie?"

"My name," she snapped as she advanced into the dining room, "is Calandra…"

Her voice trailed off as she stopped in the doorway.

The dining room, like the rest of the home, was elegant in the extreme. Black-and-white photographs of Paris, from the glass pyramid of the Louvre to the sweeping gardens of Versailles, decorated the cream-colored walls. Two-story windows marched along the far wall, sun streaming in to dance over the crystal chandelier that hung over a long, white table trimmed in gold.

On the left sat Alejandro, bare-chested, hair tousled and wearing a smirk that deepened the sexy dimple in his cheek. Clad only in burgundy lounge pants with a newspaper draped across his lap and his feet resting on the table, he raised his coffee mug to her in salute.

She tried to focus on those details, like the steam rising off the cup, and not on his chest.

His naked, tanned, muscular chest.

"Do you ever wear clothes?"

"They get in the way."

She rolled her eyes. Hopefully her outward irritation masked the unwelcome heat winding its way through her veins, leaving behind the desire to run her fingers over the carved muscles of his biceps.

"Your brother thinks I'm lying."

His smile grew, but this time his eyes crinkled at the corners. Funny, she'd never noticed that before. Almost like the smile he'd given her before was practiced, false, whereas this one was genuine.

"I missed that," he said before he took a sip of his coffee.

"What?"

"Your bluntness."

Not the most swoonworthy of compliments. So why did his words fill her with warmth?

Because you're just like your mother. You thought you were so strong all these years, but you're not. You're weak.

Her spine straightened as the heat in her veins turned to ice. The child growing inside her needed her to be strong. Needed her to stop her fantasizing and take charge of the situation.

"If you're hungry, the chef laid out quite the spread." He nodded toward a table on the far side of the room.

She nodded and walked over. She needed time to think, to regroup. Seeing him barely clothed had knocked her off balance. But as she put toast, sliced banana and a hard-boiled egg on her plate, her resolve strengthened. When she turned back toward the table, her walls were firmly back in place.

"How did you know I was here?"

He pointed to a mirror hanging on the far wall as she sat. "Not very sneaky."

"I wasn't trying to sneak." She took a bite of bread and let out a sigh. Lightly buttered, toasted to perfection.

A strangled sound came from across the table. But when she looked up, Alejandro was reading the paper in his lap.

"It sounded like Adrian thinks I'm trying to trap you."

Alejandro shrugged. "Doesn't really matter what he thinks. He's in big brother mode. Wants to make sure I don't make a mistake."

"Like marrying me?"

He let out a bark of laughter as he looked up. "I think we both know that would never happen."

Even though she had absolutely no desire to be shackled to him, or anyone for that matter, his emphatic statement still hurt.

"You do. I do. But your brother doesn't."

Years of suppressing her emotions helped her stay calm

as she continued to eat her breakfast under his watchful gaze. But finally, after she'd taken another bite of toast and eaten half the banana, she looked up at him in irritation.

"It's rude to watch someone eat."

"Shouldn't you be eating more?"

Her fingers tightened around her fork. "On the list of things you can't tell me what to do, how much I eat is number two."

One eyebrow arched as his lips quirked. "And what's the first?"

"How to raise my child."

His feet dropped down as he spun in his chair, sitting up straight and leaning forward over the table. It should have looked comical, a shirtless man sitting amid the backdrop of so much luxury.

But the look on his face was anything but funny. Eyes narrowed and crackling with intensity, lips thinned, jaw tight. In that moment, he looked more like his brother than she'd ever seen him.

Except this was...*more*. She and Adrian had shared a similar disposition. When they took charge, they grew cold. Their command partially came from their ability to show as little emotion as possible.

Alejandro, on the other hand, channeled his usual charm and energy into a threatening force that threw her off balance.

"*Our* child."

His voice vibrated with suppressed anger.

"I acknowledge your anatomical contribution. And while I had not expected your interest in being a parent—"

"How could I not be interested?" he bit out.

"I don't have enough fingers and toes to count the times you told me and anyone within earshot that jumping into a shark-infested pool would be more preferable than marriage."

"Marriage, yes. Fatherhood, no."

Her confusion only heightened her own anger.

"How could you possibly expect me to separate those two? Oh, the man who sleeps with at least one new supermodel every week also wants to burp a baby and change diapers. A logical conclusion. How could I have missed it?"

Some of his anger faded as he leaned back in his chair and rubbed the bridge of his nose. "Why do you always have to be so cold?"

He was excelling at hurtful comments this morning. She wanted to respond truthfully, to snap out that she didn't like being cold. The world had made her this way.

Cold wasn't by choice. Cold was by necessity.

"If you'd leave me alone, you wouldn't be subjected to my company."

He sighed. "This is not how I wanted this conversation to go." He nodded toward her plate. "I'm not trying to control you, Calandra. I've never been around a pregnant woman before, much less one who's carrying *my* child."

Ignoring his emphasis on *my*, she focused on her water glass. "Impressive given your history."

"You're the first I've been irresponsible with." He grimaced. "I had condoms in my damn pocket. But I wanted you so much I just…forgot."

Damn her traitorous heart and the little jump it gave upon hearing those words.

"I see."

"I just want to make sure you're getting everything you need, including nutrients. I've heard the phrase *eating for two*." He nodded at her plate. "And that's barely enough to feed a bird."

She inhaled deeply. Condescending as his voice was, her mind pointed out that, surprisingly, he was just trying to help.

"I appreciate your concern. I wish I could eat more.

I'm experiencing horrible nausea. Small meals are best right now."

He nodded, then glanced around the room. "What do you say we reconvene in the main hallway in ten minutes? I find walking and talking helps me relax."

"Walk to where?"

He smiled, his jovial nature restored. "It's a surprise."

She groaned. "Alejandro, I'm really not—"

"Please."

And just like that, he cut through her resolve, wielding sincerity like a sword. His use of a simple word laid waste to her armor like no sensual assault could.

"Fine."

He stood. She kept her eyes on his face.

"Ten minutes."

And with those parting words he scooped up his coffee and his newspaper and walked out of the dining room without a backward glance. Once his footsteps faded, she sank back into her chair and hung her head.

Years. For years she'd been impervious to men, to their looks, their attempts at seduction, their harshness when they didn't get their way. Anytime she'd entertained even the slightest thought of allowing one into her life, all she'd had to do was summon an image of her mother as she'd last seen her, paled by death and lying in a casket, and it had kept her armor in place.

She sighed. The doctor had told her it would be another few weeks at least before the baby would move. Aside from the nausea, most days it didn't seem real, that a child was growing inside her. But when she stopped and thought about it, really thought about it, she was overcome with a love so fierce it stole her breath away.

The first time she'd experienced that rush of emotion, she almost cried. Deep down, she realized, she'd sometimes wondered if she was truly good at suppressing her emotions or if she just couldn't feel them. She loved Aunt Norine and Johanna, but she'd never experienced emotions the way others had described them. The highs, the lows and everything in between.

Until Alejandro. And then their child. With Alejandro, it was dangerous. But with her child...yes, she could love her child with all her heart.

No one, not even Alejandro, with his fortune and power, would take her away from her baby. She'd make sure of it.

CHAPTER SIX

ALEJANDRO GLANCED AT Calandra out of the corner of his eye as they walked up the stairs of the Eiffel Tower. She moved with purpose, her gaze evaluating her surroundings with cool indifference, as if she wasn't walking up one of the most iconic monuments in the world. He'd offered the elevator; weren't pregnant women supposed to rest as much as possible? But she'd dismissed that idea with a shake of her head and started for the stairs before he had even finished paying for the tickets.

A gaggle of giggling young women hurried past them, their excited voices labeling them as American. One, a pert brunette with painted red lips and a deep V-cut shirt, flashed him a sexy smile and brazenly raked him from head to toe with her green eyes.

An invitation he normally would have leaped on in a heartbeat. He smiled slightly and shook his head. The girl shrugged and continued on with her friends.

It wasn't just that the mother of his child was by his side. In the past four months, he'd had almost zero interest in other women. He'd only been on one date—dinner in London with a popular actress. When he accompanied her back to her hotel, walked her to her door and she'd kissed him, he'd experienced…nothing. He'd made an excuse. She'd flown into a rage, thrown a barrage of creative insults at his manhood and slammed the door in his face.

Production delays in the construction of Cabrera Shipping's latest freighter had consumed much of his time the first four weeks after New York. Concerned clients, worried stakeholders and an increasingly hostile board had led to late-night conference calls, plane trips around the world and endless pots of coffee. Toss in his mother's car accident, his older brother nearly drowning himself in alcohol and then Alejandro assisting Adrian in locking his future fiancée out on a balcony to propose to her, and he'd been downright swamped.

And the last three months…preparing how best to respond to his father's interference and threats had occupied the majority of his waking hours. It never mattered how many times Alejandro met the bar Javier had set, there was always room for him to raise it further still.

This little jaunt into Paris was a welcome break from the crisis mode he'd been operating in since Javier had set out to ruin his middle son. Serious discussion looming in the near future aside, he took the time to enjoy the warm sunshine on his skin, the sight of Paris laid out in all her historic splendor and the classic beauty of the woman at his side. Dressed in her customary black, a pencil skirt and loose-fitting silk shirt, hair coiled into a bun at the nape of her neck, she looked every inch the modern French woman. Elegant, sophisticated, untouchable.

He'd expected more of a reaction when she'd entered the dining room this morning. A flustered mumbling, an openmouthed stare. Her ice-cold response had simultaneously flummoxed him and flamed the banked coals of desire that had been smoldering inside his chest ever since he'd seen her on the balcony last night.

Never had he had to fight so hard to retain a woman's interest. It had always been that way with Calandra—perhaps it was why he'd sought her out over and over again at Adrian's events. She'd been an anomaly, the woman who resisted his charms. Not only had it been fun to see how far he could push the boundaries, but it had been refreshing. Most women fawned over his wealth, his flashy cars, his familial connection to the internationally recognized Cabrera name.

Not Calandra. When she'd simply rolled her eyes at him and gotten breakfast in response to his half-dressed state, it had taken every ounce of self-control not to close the doors to the dining room, drape her across the table and kiss her senseless until she moaned his name.

His eyes dropped from her pert nose and nude lipstick to her belly. Possession reared its head. No matter what sins he'd committed, he would never abandon his own flesh and blood. His child would know their father, would know they were wanted.

"Stunning, isn't it?" he asked, nodding in the direction of the grassy lawns of the Champ-de-Mars and, in the distance, the Corinthian architecture of the École Militaire school complex.

"Mmm-hmm."

She'd barely said "boo" when he'd escorted her out the front door to his Jaguar convertible. She hadn't batted an eye when they'd pulled up in front of the Tower and received exclusive valet service. All the tricks that normally worked on every other woman he'd met didn't faze her.

Uncertainty tugged at him. If he couldn't wow her with his wealth, with all the resources, gifts and support he could bestow upon their child, then what would work?

They reached the second floor. Calandra wandered to the edge of the observation deck and leaned against the railing. He pointed out the Louvre, the Champs-Élysées, lined with some of the most luxurious shops in the world, and the Arc de Triomphe.

She blinked in response.

"I've never met anyone more unimpressed by life," he said with a shake of his head as he leaned against the railing.

Out of the corner of his eye, he caught the barest flinch in her shoulders. Had he imagined it? A quick glance revealed nothing in the stoniness of her expression.

Yet he'd noticed the same thing this morning when he'd

told her point-blank he would not be offering marriage. A nagging feeling that he'd hurt her.

Unfathomable, given her stalwart personality.

But she's not impervious.

He'd seen another side of her. A much more emotional and passionate side.

"Just because I don't share the story of my life with you doesn't mean I'm not impressed."

He turned and faced her. "Then tell me."

She frowned. "Tell you what?"

"What you're thinking."

"I don't see how that's relevant to the discussion we need to have."

The more she resisted, the more he wanted to know. It hit him that, despite having been acquainted with her for the past three years, he really didn't know anything about her. Other than that she had worked for Cabrera Wines, had a sister named Johanna and, until four months ago, she'd been a virgin.

"Humor me. Answer one question and then I'll devote myself to an entire five minutes of serious discussion. Ten," he conceded as she opened her mouth to object. "Ten whole minutes."

"Probably ten minutes longer than you've ever gone," she grumbled.

He started to correct her, to tell her about the hours he'd spent poring over numbers and reports with his chief financial officer or the seven board members he'd taken out to individual lunches, spending anywhere from an hour to three explaining why Cabrera Shipping should remain in his hands.

But he stopped. That part of his life, the reality that took place behind the media's coverage of his supposedly glamorous existence, was private. Calandra had already shown herself to be difficult to impress on multiple occasions. The thought of sharing that little bit of himself, the one piece of his life he took pride in, only to be faced with her judgmental silence, was not something his pride cared to experience. God knew he'd faced enough indifference from Javier to last a lifetime. Setting himself up for the same disappointment with the woman who was carrying his child was not an option.

Coward, the little devil on his shoulder whispered.

Yep, he mentally replied.

"Well?" he asked, his voice light and not showing an ounce of his inner turmoil. "Ten minutes for your thoughts?"

She looked out again, her gray eyes roving over the rooftops of Paris.

"I was thinking…" She paused. Her chest rose and fell. He noticed the swell of her breasts—how could he not—but also the look of resolve on her pale face.

Again, that little flicker that he was missing something. There was so much he didn't know about her.

"I was thinking how good it will be to bring my…our," she amended with a glare in his direction, "our child to the top of the Tower one day."

Her words surprised him. She didn't strike him as the type to daydream or think about the future, unless it involved the seating charts she'd laid out oh so meticulously for Adrian's events.

"That sounds nice."

"I've met my part of the bargain." She glanced at the silver watch clasped around her wrist. "Ten minutes starts now."

Right back to business.

"I want to be involved in our…" His voice trailed off. "Are we having a boy or a girl?"

"I don't know."

He frowned. "Aren't they supposed to be able to tell by now?"

"I want to be surprised."

Another unexpected revelation. "But you plan everything. You counted how many roses were in each vase at that party in Switzerland. All fifty vases."

"And now I want to be surprised," she retorted.

He held up his hands in surrender. "I'm not opposed."

Silence and that frigid stare. He sighed. This was not going well at all.

"Calandra, as I stated before, I have no interest in taking the baby away from you. I don't know the first thing about kids. And I have no desire to part a child from a parent who obviously loves it so much already."

Her eyes softened. The effect was almost jaw-dropping. Her face relaxed, her mouth going from its customary strict line to tilting up at the corners. Instead of rigid and powerful, she appeared…approachable. Feminine.

Desirable.

"Thank you, Alejandro."

The words punched him in the gut. Her voice came out husky as her shoulders relaxed and she tucked a stray wisp of hair behind her ear.

"You're welcome," he responded dryly in an attempt to mask the effect she had on him. He glanced down at his watch. "I believe we ate through nearly three minutes with that little drama, so let's cut to the chase—I have two proposals for you."

Her guard immediately came back up. "Oh?"

Two proposals he'd stayed up until well past midnight contemplating. "Yes. My first—I will be involved in our child's life."

"Define involved."

"I want to visit. Regularly. As in," he continued as she opened her mouth, no doubt to ask for a definition, "a minimum of one week a month. Most likely two."

A frown crossed her face. Irritation tightened his muscles as his lust ebbed. Did she truly think so little of him that she could barely stand the thought of him being around their child?

"I can't just fly to France or Spain or wherever it is you jet off to for your parties."

"First, I have my own jet. I'll fly to you. I won't be exposing a child to parties, either."

He'd hoped she would refute his last statement, that she didn't think him that stupid. Her silence gave him his answer. He should be used to rejection and low expectations by now. Why did hers feel like someone had just carved his heart from his chest?

"Second," he continued, "an investigator friend of mine informed me you don't have a job."

Two bright red spots appeared in her cheeks. "You had no right to pry into my private life."

"I had every right." He kept his tone friendly but his voice firm. "You know so much about me. Fair is fair. Which brings me to my second proposal."

The V between her eyebrows deepened. "You're not giving me money."

"I am giving you money, but for the child."

"No."

"There's no room for disagreement on the money. I have more than I know what to do with. I'm not going to let our child grow up without the things they deserve—a good education, a nice home, security."

"I can provide all that."

"Without a job?" He knew the remark was harsh, but she had to understand, had to see the reality of her situation.

Her shoulders dropped. Just a fraction, but enough that guilt fizzled on the edge of his conscience. She turned to look out over Paris, her face averted.

"Your second proposal?"

Her voice was so quiet he instantly regretted his severe

remark. Calandra was a fighter. She stood up to anyone and everyone, including him. To see her withdraw into herself was disheartening.

Before he could reply, a swarm of tourists disembarked from an elevator. A cacophony of languages swirled around them. Mothers grabbed onto errant children as excited couples, faces bright with awe and romance, grasped hands and rushed to the railing. One overly eager young man knocked into Calandra, and she stumbled. Alejandro moved fast, catching her in his arms and pulling her tight against his chest.

"Sorry, mate, I..." The young man's voice trailed off as he took in the cold fury in Alejandro's eyes. "S-sorry." He swallowed hard, grabbed his wide-eyed girlfriend and steered her away.

Slowly, the thundering of his heart abated. There were protections all over the Tower to keep the millions of tourists who visited it every year safe. But for one horrific moment Alejandro had seen Calandra pitch to the side, had envisioned her toppling over the railing to the pavement below.

His arms tightened around her.

"I can't breathe, Alejandro."

He almost missed it, the faint breathiness beneath the frigid tone. But when he looked down and saw her eyes burning like molten silver, assessed the color blooming in her normally pale cheeks, he knew that she felt it, too. Not just the desire but the magnetic pull that had drawn them together night after night for the past three years.

A satisfied smile spread across his face. Perhaps it wouldn't be so hard to convince her.

"Breathing is overrated."

She pushed him back. "I know a few billion people who would disagree with you." She smoothed the folds of her skirt as she turned back to the railing. Once again in control.

But not always. He had an effect on her. He wouldn't hesitate to use their chemistry to get what he wanted.

"I believe you had a second proposal for me."

He leaned on the railing and looked out over Paris. "Yes. I'd like to hire you as an event planner."

CHAPTER SEVEN

CALANDRA KEPT HER gaze focused on the scorched yet still proud towers of Notre Dame, standing resolute against the blue morning sky, as she processed Alejandro's words.

The first emotion to reveal itself in the tangled mess inside her chest: anger. Anger that he was only proposing this as a way of giving her money because he knew she wouldn't just accept a check.

Embarrassment was next, that hot, uncomfortable emotion that burned her cheeks. Before her epic fall from grace, she'd courted offers every year from industries around the world wanting to steal her away from Cabrera Wines. But she'd liked her job.

A job she'd thrown away. A blood test her doctor had ordered after she reported trouble sleeping had revealed her pregnancy. Hours later, Alejandro's name had jumped out at her on the proposed guest list for the party celebrating the joining of Cabrera Wines with Fox Vineyards. Images had cascaded through her mind, ranging from her blurting out her secret in the middle of the party to rushing to the nearest trash can with morning sickness as he paraded around the room with an actress or model or heiress, whatever flavor of the week he was indulging in.

Uncertainty and panic had driven her to do something impulsive—she'd quit. Better that than make a fool of herself. Her job hadn't been worth her pride, her self-respect. A week later, those pictures of Alejandro walking into a hotel in London with a famous actress had confirmed that she'd made the right decision.

Until a few weeks after that when she started receiving rejections and had faced the reality that, rather than make a smart decision, she'd once again done something uncharacteristic—she'd made a huge decision based on emotion, not practicality. She'd given up a job she enjoyed and a sizable paycheck that allowed her to pay for Johanna's nursing school as well as the rest of Aunt Norine's mortgage on her beachside cottage, on the possibility that she might see her one and only former lover.

A paycheck that had fueled a lovely savings account that was dwindling under the constant onslaught of bills and expenses.

Which brought her to her third and final emotion: hope. Hope that maybe this job, whatever it was, would not only provide her with a financial foundation before the baby was born, but might lead to her hearing *You're hired* instead of the copy-and-paste *Thanks for your time, but we've decided to go with another candidate* email she'd received too many of lately.

Her pride didn't like it. Actually, her pride hated it. Accepting any type of help made her skin prickle.

But it wasn't just about her anymore. Johanna, bless her, had taken on a part-time job at a nearby hospital and secured two scholarships that would see her through to graduation.

"Something I should have been doing all along," she'd chirped cheerfully when she'd shared the scholarship letter with Calandra. "Don't worry about me, sis." She'd rubbed Calandra's belly excitedly. "It's my turn to take care of you."

And that's what Calandra needed to focus on. Much as she preferred to do this alone, and as much as she didn't want to be around the man who put her into such a state of confusion, the baby was now the most important thing in her life. If that meant making some sacrifices, like accepting a little help from the devil himself, then so be it.

"Doing what?" she finally asked.

"Overseeing final preparations for a party."

She turned to look at him, then wished she hadn't. When

she looked out over the buildings of Paris, she could admire the history, the architecture, map out the arrondissements and neighborhoods in her head if she needed something to focus on.

But when she looked at Alejandro, dressed to the nines in chestnut-brown shoes, tan slacks that clung to his muscular legs and a sky-blue shirt molded to his tall, burly frame, all rational thought fled. She envied the relaxation she'd spied on his face as they walked to the Tower. She'd been both tempted and terrified of the passion in his eyes when he'd held her close. It made her remember what it was like to have a man look at her with desire. With passion. To hold her like she was the most treasured thing he'd ever encountered.

Dangerous. Men like him were so dangerous. Her father had been like that, flashing his winning smile and showering her mother with compliments that would make any woman swoon…or he had until he'd turned his attentions elsewhere.

His eyes pinned her in place. A smile lurked about his lips, but now she knew better. After seeing how quickly he'd flipped this morning, taking charge of a situation and letting his facade slip to reveal the strength that ran beneath the surface, she kept her guard up. She'd always treated him like a puppy—silly, at times humorous and more often annoying.

Now she wondered how much of that was Alejandro and how much of it was a mask.

"I don't see cargo ships hosting the kind of parties I usually plan."

"I'm diversifying."

"To what?"

He joined her at the railing. A summer breeze teased his dark curls.

"We're in the process of completing construction on two

new ships. Two more will join them over the next three years. Instead of scrapping one of the ships being replaced, I'm having it retrofitted into a floating hotel off the coast of Marseille."

Admiration rose in her chest. "An interesting concept."

He smiled. When he smiled like that, a real smile where his eyes crinkled at the corners and warmth brightened those dark blue depths, he was even more frustratingly handsome.

"I wish I could take credit for it. The Cunard Line did something similar with the *Queen Mary*. The ship we're retiring, *La Reina*, is in good condition. She's just old. Once a ship hits the thirty-year mark, clients and stakeholders get nervous."

The change in tone caught her attention, the serious, businesslike tone he'd occasionally let slip into their past conversations.

"Still, it must cost a lot to remake a cargo ship into a hotel."

"Yes and no. We're not doing the whole ship. Just the upper portions where guests will be staying and eating. The lower portion will be left as is."

Pride ran deep in his voice. His eyes usually glimmered with amusement or teasing, but it was excitement that lit them now. It lit a similar fire in her, all the possibility that *La Reina* offered. Crafting events from scratch and seeing her ideas come to life had been her favorite part of working for Cabrera Wines. "You could offer tours. Make use of the space."

His smile deepened. She fought the pleasant sensation that spread through her veins upon realizing that his smile was directed entirely at her.

"This is why I'd like to hire you. The board must approve my proposal. At the end of every fiscal year, we have a final meeting, vote on any major issues and then celebrate with a small party at my villa in Marseille. This year, a week from now, I'm hosting it on *La Reina*."

"So where do I fit into this?"

His face darkened as his eyes hardened. "My father is the majority stakeholder of Cabrera Shipping. He thinks I'm throwing money away on this idea. If the board votes against my proposal, let's just say my life will look very different."

She wanted to ask how, but his expression offered zero room for inquiries.

"I'm still not sure why you need me."

"One of the things that will make *La Reina* a success is if I give a glimpse into the luxury experience we'll offer. You specialize in such events. Help me sway them."

Her thoughts turned to the young man she'd seen on the balcony with Adrian and Everleigh the night before. "What about Antonio? He already runs successful resorts."

"He's helped me with the renovations, suite designs, that sort of thing. But he's busy with his own upcoming launch in Italy. And you," he said with a seductive smile, "have all the experience I need."

"Planning a party of that magnitude will take more than a week."

"Most of it has already been planned. But I need someone to bring all the pieces together, to supervise. Still a lot, which is why I'm prepared to pay you half a million dollars."

Her hands tightened on the railing.

"That's too much."

"No, it's not." He held up a hand as she started to object. "Whatever plans you put together have the potential to make my company, and therefore me, a lot of money."

"What if the board votes no?"

"They'll vote yes."

She envied his assurance, the complete and total confidence she'd had before she'd had sex. Was sex always so complicated?

"Two bonuses from this arrangement," he continued, oblivious to her questioning herself. "One—once completed, you'll have my personal reference that will secure you any job you want. And two, we get to know each other better so you're comfortable with me being involved as a father and we avoid the nasty legal battles."

Oh, it was a neat solution, all tied up with a pretty bow. Never mind it scared the hell out of her—a week alone with a man she could barely control herself around.

"I'll also help beyond the job. Financially."

She pinched the bridge of her nose. "Alejandro, you're already offering an outrageous salary—"

He grasped her hand and gave it a gentle but firm squeeze. "That part is nonnegotiable, Calandra."

She stalled for a moment, trying to think of something, anything else that might change his mind.

Nothing. Finally, grudgingly, she murmured, "All right."

The lock slammed on the door to the private hell she'd just created for herself. She'd spent her whole life avoiding becoming trapped by her circumstances the way her mother had. Wooed by a Swiss millionaire on a spring break trip in college and whisked from her modest home in the Carolinas to a mansion tucked between the Alps and Lake Geneva, her mother had been helpless when the dream had turned into a nightmare.

And now here she was, accepting a job offer, money, allowing herself to become a kept woman.

You're not your mother. Much as she'd loved her mom, what Lila Smythe lacked in strength and determination, Calandra had more than made up for over the years. Yes, she had to hand over a little bit of power now. But she would prevail.

"Scared, Calandra?"

His voice, so deep and yet so silky, so dangerous, wrapped around her, tantalizing, tempting, seducing.

She didn't immediately answer, because yes, she was scared, terrified even, that after only one night together he still stirred such longing in her. Time and experience had taught her that men like Alejandro were fun, until they weren't. Her child would grow up without the pain that had been her constant companions through childhood.

Which meant keeping men like Alejandro at arm's length.

Or an ocean's length, she thought as Alejandro took another step, the heat from his body kissing her skin.

What had she just done?

He leaned in. She stayed still, hand clutched around the railing of the Eiffel Tower like it was the only thing keeping her tethered to reason. She would not back down, would not succumb.

"Don't be scared." His smile deepened. "What's the worst that could happen?"

CHAPTER EIGHT

CALANDRA STRODE TOWARD the double doors of her boutique bed-and-breakfast. Beyond the glass and down the boulevard, the stone walls and elegant pillars of the entrance to the Louvre stood tall and proud.

Museums and tourist spots, from the Statue of Liberty in New York to the Eiffel Tower, had failed to pique her interest in the past. They were notable only in that others liked them, dreamed of them, crafted entire trips around seeing a monument. She'd worked plenty of icons into her events because the guests appreciated them—it had been good business, even if she'd failed to see the allure.

Yet when she stood on the deck of the Eiffel Tower yesterday, she'd meant what she had said to Alejandro. Some might say the magic of Paris had worked its way into her blood. Or perhaps she was just embracing the prospect of motherhood more as her waistline slowly but steadily expanded.

Whatever the reason, the thought of seeing her child squeal in delight as they saw Paris laid out before them filled her with a maternal warmth.

That she'd briefly entertained an image of Alejandro standing next to her, one hand intimately entwined with hers and the other on their child's shoulder, had irritated her.

Weak. Foolish.

She steeled her spine as her heels clicked on the wood floors. One week. One week to do a job that might reopen all the doors that had been slammed shut because of her brief but disastrous foray into the world of emotions.

One week to let Alejandro live out whatever fantasy he'd concocted of being involved. At the first sign of morning sickness or a reminder of how little sleep new parents achieved, he'd be gone.

The possibility that he would stick around frightened her in more ways than one.

She pushed open the door and stepped into the warm French sunshine, a bag hanging from her shoulder and a suitcase in hand. A couple stops on the Metro and she'd be at the station in plenty of time to catch her train to Marseille. Unexpected anticipation lent a barely discernible bounce to her step. Even without a job keeping her tied to a rigorous schedule, she'd spent her weeks editing her résumé, following up on job leads and staying busy. As always.

An uninterrupted train ride through the French countryside sounded like heaven.

"Mademoiselle Smythe?"

Calandra's head snapped up. A young man stood in front of her, dressed in a dark gray suit with a navy tie. Almost as young as Johanna, but with a much more serious air. A sleek black limo stood behind him, windows tinted so dark she couldn't see the interior.

"Who are you?"

The man bowed his head. "Your chauffeur."

"I didn't order a car."

"Monsieur Cabrera did, mademoiselle, with his compliments."

Her fingers tightened on the phone. Suspicion slithered up her spine as she barely bit back the retort that rose in her throat.

"Did he now?"

If the man sensed the danger lurking in her tone, he didn't reveal it.

"*Oui*, mademoiselle. I'm to take you to your destination before you continue to Marseille."

Hard to be angry at a thoughtful gesture even though

her instincts were screaming at her to be cautious. Warily, she allowed the chauffeur to put her suitcase in the trunk and open the door. Black leather and cool air welcomed her into the luxurious interior.

The chauffeur hurried around and pulled away from the curb before she could change her mind. They passed the glass pyramid outside the Louvre, the sparkling waters of the Seine and the vivid green storefront of the legendary Shakespeare & Company, the sidewalk outside the shop crowded with shelves of books and tourists.

Just as she started to relax and enjoy the sights, her phone pinged. She pulled it out of her pocket and frowned as she read the message.

"'Your train ticket has been refunded'?" she read aloud. She looked up just in time to see the limo pass by the bridge that would have led to the train station.

Realization hit first, followed by a swift rush of anger so intense she barely stopped herself from cursing out loud. So much for Alejandro letting her make her own decisions. Did he think he could arrange everything to his liking?

By the time the limo pulled into a private airfield thirty minutes later, she had reined in her temper to a manageable level. The limo drove straight onto the tarmac and stopped next to a jet with the letter *C* emblazoned on the side in scarlet. Alejandro stood at the bottom of the stairs, eyes hidden behind his sunglasses, dark hair falling about his chiseled face. He looked like he'd just come from a magazine cover shoot—V-neck navy shirt stretched across his muscular chest, blue jeans hanging casually from his tapered waist. The grin he aimed at the window of the limo was playful. But beneath the casual smirk she now saw the edge, the determination in the firmness of his lips.

She'd underestimated Alejandro. Again. But, she reminded herself, each event like this gave her more insight into what she was fighting. It was a learning experience, not a failure.

"Buenos días, sol."

She arched a brow as she drew nearer, hardening her heart with every click of her heels. "Sunshine?"

"You brighten up my day by accepting my invitation."

"Invitation?" She returned his smile with a frigid one of her own. One that clearly let him know she would not be bought off nor controlled. "You and I have different definitions of invitation. *Threat* would be more accurate."

He stepped closer and whipped off his sunglasses. The intensity in his dark blue gaze almost made her step back. Almost. She stood straighter, one arm instinctively crossing over her waist.

Alejandro's gaze dropped down to her belly, and he frowned.

"Do you truly think I would harm you? Harm our child?"

"*My* child. And no, not physically," she admitted at the flash of what almost looked like hurt in his eyes. "But I don't appreciate you rearranging my schedule or canceling my train tickets. That's a violation of my privacy."

The hint of emotion disappeared as swiftly as it had appeared, replaced by something hard and unsettling. Not the affable, immature playboy, but the man who had brought Cabrera Shipping back from the brink of ruin. An intelligent, driven man who, she was finding out the hard way, went after what he wanted.

What did it say about her, that instead of being angry or afraid, a thrill shot through her veins at the sight of that strength?

"You agreed to spend time with me, Calandra. To get to know me better. A three-hour train ride by yourself is not the way to accomplish that."

"You canceled my ticket," she repeated.

"Of course. How rude of me. Next time I'll just let you pay for a ticket you're not going to use."

She didn't know which was worse—that he had interfered in her travel plans and was showing absolutely no remorse, or that he was at least partially right. When he'd brought up traveling to Marseille as he escorted her back to her bed-and-breakfast after their trip to the Eiffel Tower, she'd interrupted him with a plea of a headache and rushed inside, away from what she'd known would be his suggestion that they travel together.

Before she stuck her foot in her mouth or, worse, apologized, she started to climb the stairs into the plane. A hand settled on her waist, and she bit back a gasp as electricity skipped across her skin and sent frissons of crackling warmth straight to her thighs. She turned and nearly came nose to nose with Alejandro. He stood on the step behind her, but with his impressive height, they were face-to-face. He kept his hand at her waist, his touch burning through the thin cloth of her dress.

Could he hear her heartbeat as it galloped through her chest? Did he see the rise and fall of her breasts as she tried to keep her breathing steady?

Slowly, ever so slowly, his fingers trailed from her hip, delicious, traitorous shivers radiating from his fingertips throughout her body.

And then he laid his hand flat across her belly. Possession tightened his face as his lips parted and his eyes grew dark. She was caught in a whirlwind of conflicting desires—the need to run away, far away, and the desire to lean in, to let go of her control and let him in.

"This child is ours, Calandra." He leaned in, and for one brief, horrific, glorious moment, she thought he was going to kiss her. "Ours."

Before she could gather her wildly spinning thoughts and utter a retort, a voice called out from behind her.

"Ready to leave in five, Monsieur Cabrera."

She turned away and walked up the stairs with measured steps. She wasn't going to give him the satisfaction of letting him see how much his touch, his words, had unsettled her.

She entered the plane, trying to ignore the mahogany wood floors, beige leather seats and computer screens installed in the back of each chair. A dim memory of flying in a similar plane when she was eight surfaced, her mother sitting limply toward the front and her father in back behind a curtain. When she'd sneaked out of her seat and peeked behind the curtain, it had been to see her father with his hands buried in the gold curls of the flight attendant as he'd kissed her.

Nausea rolled in her stomach. She quickened her pace, determined to get to her seat before she made a fool of herself.

And then stopped at the sight of the robin's egg–blue package tied up with silver string sitting in one of the seats.

She glanced over her shoulder. "For me?"

Alejandro dropped into a chair and propped his feet up on the seat of another across the aisle. A casual move, but one that made her feel trapped. No last mad dash to the exit before they closed the doors.

"Perhaps."

She rolled her eyes and leaned down to read the gift tag attached to the outrageous bow.

A mi bebe.

Her throat tightened. Her heart followed suit. *For my baby.* The passion Alejandro had displayed yesterday, his desire to be involved in their child's life, this… He'd shown more interest in the little one growing inside her in the last twenty-four hours than her father ever had in his own children.

Swallowing her emotions, she picked up the box and turned. "Should I save it for the baby to open?"

Alejandro grinned. "I dare you to wait that long."

With a shake of her head, she undid the bow and lifted the lid. Nestled inside among white and blue wrapping paper lay a chestnut-colored teddy bear with blue paws that matched the gift box and a silver heart around its neck.

The simple gift touched her. She hadn't bought the baby any toys. Her fingers glided over the soft fur as she lifted it out of the box, then rested on the silver script on one of the bear's feet.

Recognizing the luxury brand, she looked back at Alejandro. "These cost almost a thousand dollars."

He shrugged. "I'm rich. I want our child to have the best."

Her heart sank. He wasn't her father, no. But he still rated things by how much they cost, placed value on the price tag instead of the intrinsic value. If her child were anything like Johanna, the teddy bear would be covered in sand and dampened by the ocean air in no time. The baby wouldn't care if the teddy bear had cost five dollars or five thousand.

"What's wrong?" Alejandro asked as she sat.

"Nothing."

She didn't like that he could read her so easily. Sometimes Aunt Norine and even Johanna had trouble discerning her moods. She'd liked it that way. Smooth, unreadable, unflappable. Less room for mistakes, for heartache, when you kept yourself locked up so tight no one could penetrate.

"Something's stirring behind those daggers in your eyes." He nodded at the bear. "Not expensive enough?"

She sat, the bear cradled carefully on her lap, as another possibility crept in, ugly and insidious. The limo, the fancy jet, the expensive gift…he'd said he wasn't going to buy access to their child. But his actions said otherwise.

A flight attendant came by and set a drink on her table, green and frothy with a sprig of mint perched across the rim of the glass.

"Oh, I can't—"

"It's a virgin mojito, Mademoiselle Smythe," she said with a smile. "Monsieur Cabrera provided us with your dietary restrictions and preferences this morning. But please let us know if there's anything else you require."

Calandra glanced at her watch as the flight attendant waltzed down the length of the plane, keeping her gaze on Alejandro out of the corner of her eye. To his credit, he didn't even glance at the woman's hips swaying beneath her tight skirt.

"Cocktails before noon?" she asked as the flight attendant returned and set before him a highball glass with thin ribbon of amber liquid at the bottom.

"Ten thirty here is three thirty in the morning in New York." He shot her a heated smile. "I recall both of us having a refreshing beverage around that time."

Oh, yes. He'd ordered champagne after their first bout of lovemaking. They'd sipped it in bed as he demanded she share something she'd never told anyone else. Her quip that she'd already given him her virginity had made him smile, but he hadn't relented, pressing until she'd revealed her early-morning walks on the beach and the collection of shells beneath her bed. Silly, but a ritual she'd developed her first summer living with Aunt Norine.

She should have known then, the way he hadn't let her pull away, that he was so much *more*. But she'd been in a first-time-sex-induced haze of euphoria, not paying attention to the warning signs like the tug on her heart.

Shrugging off the memories, she grabbed her mojito glass, took a sip and moaned. Her eyes drifted shut as the tart taste of lime mingled with the soothing scent of mint. She'd never thought to make herself virgin cocktails, but she'd have to make this a part of her evening routine. Utterly relaxing.

Her eyes opened, and she nearly choked. Alejandro's eyes were fixed on her, blazing with intense desire.

And then it was gone, so quick she wondered if her own traitorous body had conjured up the image.

Apparently, pregnancy did not inhibit her libido.

"Tasty?"

"Yes, thank you." She'd had her one night with Alejandro, just like dozens of women before her. If she ever entertained the possibility of succumbing to temptation again, all she had to do was conjure up the paparazzi photos of Alejandro getting out of a limo with that slim, dark-haired actress in a clingy red dress in the same week she'd found out she was pregnant.

The reminder dashed a much-needed splash of cold water on her passion.

"Tell me more about this project." Business was a safe topic. "I understand wanting *La Reina* to be a success, but you mentioned something else."

"Ah, yes." Alejandro laughed, the sound unexpectedly harsh. "If the board doesn't accept my proposal, I will be replaced as head of Cabrera Shipping."

"What? By whom?"

Alejandro's smile was so sharp it could have cut glass. "My father."

CHAPTER NINE

CALANDRA'S EYES WIDENED, just a fraction, but enough to show her surprise.

God, he'd missed this. Four months of no witty banter, no gray eyes snapping at him, no cool retorts that heated his blood. Compared to the uncertainty regarding Cabrera Shipping's future and his father's threats, Calandra's familiar presence, not to mention her incredible revelation, were rays of light warming him during one of the most challenging times of his life.

His eyes drifted down once more to her stomach. In five months, he would meet his child.

His child. He hadn't really contemplated having children before. His casual romances and liaisons had excluded that type of commitment, one even more binding than a marriage license. Most probably assumed his first thought would have been horror.

Surprisingly, the more he'd thought about it after their conversation yesterday, reflected on Calandra's dream of taking their child to the top of the Eiffel Tower, the chief emotion had been wonder. Wonder and excitement.

However, he reminded himself, only if the woman across from him would let him be a part of their child's life. Yes, he could absolutely throw his weight around, hire lawyers and drag her to court. And if he had to, he would.

But that was something his father would do. Wowing, charming or even seducing what he wanted from Calandra was preferable to following in his father's footsteps in any fashion.

The thought of Javier taking away the one thing he'd dedicated himself to, the company he'd literally poured blood and sweat into, made his chest burn with the same fury he'd felt the day he'd discovered Javier in the library with his cheating bitch.

Now, though, it wasn't Javier's threats and attempts to control his life that pushed him. The determination to be the father Javier never had been added a light to the darkness. Even if Cabrera Shipping fell apart, he'd have a son or daughter. He'd fought for Cabrera Shipping, poured his soul into something for the first time in years. But it was something that had been gifted to him, a scrap thrown to the mongrel of the family. *La Reina* was the first thing in his life that would be his. Yet Javier had even managed to taint that with his interference.

The baby was the first thing he'd cared about that his father couldn't take away from him. And he'd be damned if he was going to let Calandra keep him from his child.

Alejandro grinned at Calandra, his casual smile hiding his turmoil. By the end of this week, she'd agree to his terms.

"Your father wants to head Cabrera Shipping?"

Her cold question snapped him out of his erotic musings. Anyone would have thought her completely in control, ivory skin so smooth and pale she could have been carved from marble.

Only he saw the drum of her fingers on her thigh, the pulse beating just below the elegant curve of her jaw.

"Yes."

A tiny V appeared between her brows. "Why? Doesn't he already oversee multiple other businesses?"

He glanced down at his drink, his muscles tightening as the memory of that phone call echoed in his head.

"Cabrera Shipping is losing money, Alejandro. Fix it." A heavy sigh. *"Or I'll have to fix it for you."*

"I mentioned we're behind on construction, yes?"

"Yes. Two ships?"

"Yes. By about a month on one and three on another.

It may not seem like much, but four weeks behind means two to three trips down the drain. Millions upon millions of dollars in cargo going to other shippers."

"I'm sorry."

"Thank you. Unfortunate," he added with a flippancy he didn't feel. "But the loss has, understandably, made stakeholders and the board nervous. Convincing them to spend more money on renovating an aging ship when we just lost so much and saw clients move, at least temporarily, to other companies is not an easy feat." He leaned into the plush cushions of his seat and closed his eyes as the enormity of the task before him weighed on his shoulders. "My father, the majority stakeholder, does not support the alternative use of *La Reina*. He holds considerable influence over the board. If they vote no on this proposal, Cabrera Shipping will no longer be mine."

"That seems harsh."

He shrugged, the casual gesture masking decades of pain. "He's not a kind man. I see the loss in revenue as a temporary setback. He sees it as a catastrophic blow to our bottom line. Not that he was a fan of my idea about *La Reina* to begin with. In his mind it's further evidence that I have no head for business. I'm squandering company finances to create a playground for the rich."

Sentiments his father had expressed multiple times over the last few weeks. Thankfully, the comments had been delivered over the phone so Javier couldn't see the effect his lack of faith had on his middle son.

Ridiculous, really. Alejandro loathed his father. Had for over twenty years now. His opinion shouldn't matter.

Silence. At last, he opened his eyes. Calandra stared out the window at the ground passing by, one hand resting lightly on her belly.

Despite the warmth of the afternoon, she wore her customary black. Slashes of black eyeliner reminded him of war paint instead of makeup.

Still, she'd softened since he'd last seen her. He'd first glimpsed it on the Eiffel Tower yesterday, but now he saw it in more vivid detail. Perhaps it was the gentle curve of her lips as her fingers traced back and forth over her stomach. Or maybe it was the occasional flashes of emotion he caught on her face, glimpses into the woman who'd seduced him with her intelligence and no-nonsense attitude.

"Why do you want to repurpose *La Reina*?"

An innocent question he wanted to answer glibly. But she sounded like she truly wanted to know, a notion that made his chest swell with pride.

"*La Reina* was the first ship I sailed on when I took over." He could still taste the salt of the sea the first time the bow had carved through the waves of the Atlantic. His first bit of freedom from the confines of the persona he'd trapped himself in. "Helped out on the crew to understand how everything worked. She's thirty years old, which is ancient in cargo ship years. But it's hard to picture the old girl being sailed off to a graveyard and stripped down to nothing."

"That's an expensive endeavor for the sake of nostalgia."

"Nostalgia's part of it," he conceded. "But I want Cabrera Shipping to go in a new direction. Our latest ships are being constructed to meet new environmental standards. I want *La Reina* to be a part of that trend, not contributing to waste but being reused."

An unexpected wistfulness crossed Calandra's face. "I wasn't expecting that sort of viewpoint from someone so..."

"So what?"

Naked pain flashed in her eyes before she shut down, misty silver shifting to steel gray in a heartbeat. Her fingers clenched around the armrest for the briefest of moments before he saw her intentionally relax her body and recline back.

"Someone who views people as inconsequential, playthings to be discarded when they cease being interesting."

The harsh remark hit him hard. He started to retort, to snap out a comment that both covered his pain and delivered a blow of his own, but stopped. Unlike his father, her words weren't designed to hurt. They were coming from a different place, something rooted in Calandra's past.

"Do you truly think that of me?"

She continued to stare, so intensely that he had to stop himself from shifting in his seat beneath her perusal.

"I don't know what to think," she finally said. The coldness slipped, and he got a glimpse of vulnerability in the crinkling of her eyes, the little V between her brows. "One minute I think I have you figured out and the next…"

She blinked and the vulnerability disappeared. "Tell me more about the event. What you want to accomplish, what you envision, what still needs to be done."

So, he did. He talked for what felt like forever, though a glance at his watch revealed it had only been thirty minutes or so. No one, not even the board members who supported *La Reina*, had shown as much interest as Calandra did.

It was unsettling, the way she watched him so attentively. Like she could see everything about him. The women he'd dated the past year had been the exact opposite. They'd never looked past his money, the fancy cars or the glamorous vacations he whisked them off to on his private jet.

However, no matter how much he was embracing this new phase of life, he had no desire to invite a woman into it permanently. As far as the world knew, he was having too much too fun to settle down.

Let them think whatever they like.

Being a father to their child would enable him to step up and be a parent the way Javier had never been. But marriage…no one, not even his parents, had managed to maintain a true and loving relationship. His mother didn't know it, but she was married to a lie.

He didn't want to even tempt that kind of fate. Nor, that nasty little voice in his head whispered, did he want to risk the other possibility.

That he was more like his father than he wanted to admit. That one woman would never be enough.

"Before you dive in, you need to see the ship." He glanced out the window and spied the deep blue waters of the Mediterranean on the horizon. "We're close. Once we land, I've arranged for you to tour *La Reina*."

"Good idea. Who's giving me the tour?" she asked.

He grinned. "Me."

An hour later, he watched Calandra as she circled around the ballroom for what had to be the ninth time. Eyes flickering over every last detail, her face revealing nothing.

He glanced over the ballroom. Most of the floor had been done in white marble flecked with gray, with a light gray wood for the dance floor in the middle. White columns soared up to the ceiling. A custom, hand-blown glass chandelier dominated the room, casting a warm glow over the tables below.

The all white had not been his first choice. Adrian's dining room in Paris was all white. Boring. Flat. Interesting to see how long that color scheme lasted once his and Everleigh's child started running around.

But here…here it screamed elegance. Wealth. Power.

Even if the board voted against this endeavor and Javier yanked Cabrera Shipping away from him, he would make *La Reina* a success. Everyone, including his father, thought he squandered his money. Few knew that ever since he'd taken over a year after college, he'd stashed away most of his profits in a Swiss bank account. He'd spend every last dime he had until the very end if he had to.

Well, almost every last dime, he amended as he glanced again at Calandra. Hiring her had solved two problems— knowing his event was in good hands and finding a way to get her to accept money. He'd had a private investigator look into her circumstances. He knew she and her sister were living in a tiny house in a little town on the coast. He knew the exact amount of her bank account. Her savings, while admirable, would barely cover her medical bills and living expenses through the end of the year.

Stubborn woman.

"It's beautiful," she said as she joined him.

Having her approval shouldn't affect him. But it did.

"Gracias."

"I have an appointment tomorrow with the caterer to confirm details. Then Thursday for final planning and evaluation—"

"And hopefully some time in there for us to spend together."

Her brows drew together. "What?"

"We're supposed to be getting to know each other. Not in the biblical sense, of course, since we already checked that box."

"Twice," she replied dryly with that so-sexy arched brow. But sadly, the flirtatious glint disappeared as quickly as it had unexpectedly appeared. "I have a lot of work to do, Alejandro."

"I'll accompany you."

She held up a hand. "No. I work best alone."

He frowned. Being told no was not something he was used to. Nor, he acknowledged as his jaw tightened, did he like it.

"Dinner, then. This week."

The narrowing of her eyes indicated a protest was incoming.

"I insist."

She chewed on her lower lip, a gesture of consternation but one that nonetheless conjured images of her naked, stretched across his bed and watching him not with an icy gaze but a hot stare that demanded he come over, strip off his clothes and join her.

It had been way too long since he'd had sex.

"Fine."

She turned and started toward the exit. For some reason, the sight of her walking away nicked his pride. He caught up to her in several swift strides.

"Where are you going?"

"Into Marseille. I have a lot of work to do."

"You do know most of the vendors have phone numbers. There's no need to traipse around and tire yourself. I can take you back, or," he added testily, "if you've tired of my company, I can send for the limo."

She stopped so quickly and turned around that he nearly careened into her.

And then they were close. Too close.

"I don't need your limo." Her voice was eerily calm, devoid of emotion, as was the rest of her countenance.

Save her eyes. Those glittered with some emotion he couldn't discern. Normally he could read women with astonishing accuracy. It's why they enjoyed him so much. He knew, and gave, exactly what they wanted.

What did Calandra Smythe want?

He watched her for a moment, eyes sliding down the curve of her neck, the slenderness of her waist, although now as he looked closer he saw the tiniest swell beneath her black dress.

That's my child.

The thought simultaneously thrilled and terrified him. He wanted to be a part of that child's life more than anything. But could he do it? Could he be a better father than his own?

"I was very successful when I worked for Cabrera Wines," Calandra replied testily. "That is why you hired me, right?"

"Of course."

"Not because you're trying to pad my bank account?"

"I would never be so underhanded."

She stared at him for a long, long moment. Then leaned in closer.

He went hard. Almost instantly. His eyes caressed her smooth, pale face, the column of her neck, the enticing place where her pulse pounded at the base of her throat...

His gaze snapped up. Calandra Smythe was just as affected as he was. Her pupils dilated as a slow smile curved across his face. Her lips parted. Her quick intake of breath sent heat careening through his veins.

"Let me do my job, Alejandro." Her words came out breathy this time, all sense of calm laid waste by the attraction crackling between them. "And for the rest of the day, please leave me alone."

She turned away again and started for the door. This time, he didn't pursue. The uncharted territories of parenthood and interest in a woman beyond her body were unfamiliar and uncomfortable.

But the game of seduction was one he knew very well.

He had one week. One week to impress, to woo, to get her to agree not only to let him be involved in their child's life, but to perhaps have her in his bed once more. The thought of feeling her body beneath him, of the novelty of making love to the woman who carried his child within her, made him positively giddy.

"Your wish is my command."

She didn't respond, didn't even acknowledge she'd heard him, as she disappeared into the main corridor.

Unexpected parenthood. His company on the brink of being torn from his grasp. His arrogant bastard of a father still interfering in his life. With all the uncertainty, and all the things that could possibly go wrong, he should have felt concerned, on edge, nervous.

All that paled in comparison to the memory of that sharp intake of breath.

His smile grew wider still. In one week, he would achieve his desires. Cabrera Shipping. *La Reina*. His child.

And Calandra Smythe in his bed.

CHAPTER TEN

CALANDRA WATCHED THE boats drifting across the waters of the Vieux-Port de Marseille from her spot at a little café with red-and-white-striped umbrellas. The scent of fresh-baked bread had guided her feet to this little haven as she killed time before her appointment.

The city was a welcome distraction from the luxury of Alejandro's seaside villa. The teal-blue furniture, floor-to-ceiling windows and her own private guest quarters at the end of a long hallway had screamed wealth. Only one thing had stood out as truly Alejandro among the carefully chosen name-brand items—artsy photographs of ships, from the historic floating palaces of the early twentieth century to romantic sailboats, tucked here and there among more recognizable pieces.

A far cry from the tiny house Aunt Norine had raised her and Johanna in. A reminder of everything Alejandro was, no matter how charming or seductive he could be.

Pride had made her take a cab to the villa yesterday afternoon once she realized that there really wasn't a lot to be done in town. She'd managed to work successfully at a table on the patio, surrounded by lush blooms and the greenest grass she'd ever seen as she confirmed vendors and created schedules.

It had been heaven working again. Feeling useful. And this morning, when her first emergency had arisen, she'd thrilled at making last-minute arrangements to put out what had the potential to be a very large fire.

One more step, two more steps at most, and *La Reina*'s party would be back on track.

Would Alejandro be proud of her quick response and her unique solution?

She shoved away the unwelcome thought. She didn't need his approval. She had done her job just fine without begging for compliments and praise before. No need to start now.

The *garçon* came out and set a plate with a fluffy croissant, wild berry jam and a tiny bowl of fruit on the table with a flourish.

"Pour vous, mademoiselle."

"Merci."

She reached for the knife when nausea hit so hard she could barely move.

"Oh, baby, what are you doing to me?" she whispered. Already she loved the little one growing inside her so much. But moments like these, she could do without.

The nausea slowly subsided, and she sat back in her chair, her breathing heavy, her forehead damp. A long drink of water further settled her stomach.

Maybe a combination of pregnancy and concern. Concern that she was headed down the same path as Mother. She'd tossed and turned a good portion of the night as she replayed the scene on *La Reina* over and over again, trying to figure out how she'd let go of her control and let him see that he still affected her.

The exhaustion that invaded her bones could be chalked up to the energy her body required to grow her child. But there was no excuse for the fragility she'd developed. Her child needed her to be the strong woman she'd been for the last seventeen years.

She grabbed the knife once more and slathered jam on the croissant. She bit into it, savoring the sweet burst of berries on her tongue, and sighed. At least one thing had gone right today. Nothing beat the simple pleasures of eating a freshly baked French croissant.

"Does the baby have a sweet tooth?"

She choked on the croissant and coughed. Someone

pressed a glass of water into her hand. She brought it to her lips and gulped it down.

Alejandro dropped into the chair across from her. A frown marred his handsome features. The sleeves of his brick-red polo shirt clung to his biceps, the blue jeans conforming to his thighs. Irritation buzzed inside her head. Did the man always have to look so put together?

"Are you all right?"

Gulls cawed overhead. Languages from around the world flowing around them in a bewitching hymn of sounds and accents as shoppers and tourists bustled by. A breeze blew in from the harbor, light and cool to combat the growing heat of the morning. Details Calandra would have soaked up in her new quest to enjoy life a little more had her mutinous body not gone rigid the instant it registered Alejandro's presence.

"Are you having me followed?" she replied. She kept her voice neutral, even though his banal question put her guard up. A normal person might think his interest sweet. But to her, it was the top of a very slippery slope. One where she let herself be lured in by his supposed kindness, gifts and, damn it, desire, only to have the rug yanked out from under her when he got bored.

It's what men like him did.

A light breeze stirred his hair. The knot in her chest twisted painfully. Was this what it was like for her mother? Fingers aching to touch the man who stirred such powerful emotions in her? Knowing all along that the more she gave him, the harder she'd fall when he left?

Because men like her father—like Alejandro—didn't stay. They never stayed.

Alejandro pointed toward the bay, where a yacht gently bobbed next to one of the docks. Even from this distance, she could see the name painted in bright red letters.

"La Pimpinela Escarlata?"

"Your Spanish is very good."

"Not good enough. *Escarlata* is 'scarlet,' but *pimpinela*?"

"The scarlet pimpernel. A plant with scarlet flowers." His lips quirked up at the corners. "Also the name of a movie I watched with Madre as a child."

The name teased her memory. "Isn't it a book, too?"

"One of the few times I have enjoyed the movie more than the book. Featuring a devastatingly handsome hero with a flair for fashion and seduction."

"I didn't know you liked to read."

"There are a lot of things you don't know about me." He tapped his hand on the table. "Which is why, when my yacht docked and I spied a woman in black seated at a bayside café, I decided to take advantage so we could spend a little time together."

An emphatic *No!* sounded from her more rational mind. Her heart, that useless muscle that had gone from iron-clad and frosty to weak and feeling, disagreed.

"Alejandro—"

"Calandra," he broke in, "you set the terms of this arrangement." He leaned across the table and, before she could stop him, grabbed her hand in his. "And you're avoiding me." His finger traced a circle on the back of her hand, his delicate touch as light as butterfly wings, yet no less potent than the sensual attack he'd unleashed on her body four months ago. "I just want to get to know you better."

The pattern he'd traced on her skin burned as if he'd etched it into her. She snapped her gaze off his hand and refocused on her half-eaten croissant.

"Which leaves me with only one course of action. To show the mother of my child that I'm not the evil man she thinks I am."

She sighed. "You're not evil. I never accused you of that."

He glanced toward the bay, his hand staying on top of hers as if he was afraid she might flee.

Which she had. Multiple times. But in this moment, running was the furthest thing from her mind. What was first and forefront was the hint of discomfort she'd heard in his voice.

"I don't think you're evil," she repeated. She tugged her hand out, but before he could move settled her fingers on top of his. Warmth blossomed in her fingertips as she registered the slight dusting of black hair on the back of his hand, the heat of his skin, the erotic contrast of dark tan skin beneath her own pale white.

"Then why?"

When he turned to look at her, there was no arousal in his eyes. No artifice, no seduction. Just a simple question and, if she looked a little deeper, pain lurking in those dark blue depths.

She had no desire to air her family's deepest secrets. But the longer she looked at Alejandro, *really* looked at him, the guiltier she felt. Yes, he was a playboy. Unlike her father, however, she'd never seen evidence of him being cruel, of using money to try and slap a Band-Aid over a heart he'd crushed to smithereens with his selfishness.

"My father…he liked to have fun. Too much fun." Her mind raced as she tried to condense years of pain, rage and loss into as few words as possible. "His actions, especially his infidelity, hurt my mother. To the point that she became very depressed and eventually passed away."

A simplified and very watered-down version of the truth. But it was the best she could manage for now.

"I'm sorry."

She swallowed hard and nodded. "Thank you." She sat back, pulling her hand away. The moment of reassurance had been nice, but the longer she allowed it, the more likely she was to share more. Sharing led to vulnerability. Vulnerability led to feelings. In her experience, feelings led to heartbreaking situations like a young girl being forced to grow up into a mother and caregiver before her tenth birthday.

Or two daughters watching their mother's coffin being lowered into the ground, one still just a child, the other forced into adulthood far too fast.

But, she reminded herself as she put the brakes on her maudlin reminiscing, the genuine empathy in Alejandro's eyes let her know she'd done the right thing. If he was truly interested in being a father to their child, he deserved to know why she was struggling so hard with letting him be a part of her life.

Johanna would be proud, she thought wryly. Her sister was always encouraging her to open up and share her feelings more.

"I better understand your reticence to let me into our child's life." He leaned back in his chair. "One thing I'd like to reassure you on, Calandra. I won't be parading women in and out of their life. I want him, or her, to have some stability."

She swallowed the insult that rose in her throat, harsh words powered by bias and an unwelcome bit of jealousy.

"Thank you."

"What can I do to make you feel more comfortable with the idea of me being involved?"

A small smile tugged at her lips. "Just you asking makes me feel a little better. My father didn't have an interest in my mother's opinion."

"Your opinion matters a great deal, Calandra."

There was magic in those words. Powerful, seductive magic coupled with a devastatingly handsome man who wanted to be a father to her child.

"Then we'll find opportunities to get to know each other better over the next few days." She nodded toward the myriad of streets and shops that lay just beyond the port's edge. "I have a one o'clock with a prospective caterer."

Alejandro frowned. "I already had a caterer lined up."

"A caterer whose owner was tossed in jail last night for driving drunk and is now facing a PR nightmare." She set enough euros on the table to cover her bill and stood. "You're welcome to walk with me if you'd like."

Five minutes later, they strolled down one of the many charming alleys Marseille had to offer. A casual walk with at least three feet of distance between them. It didn't stop every nerve ending in her body from sizzling.

"Who do you have in mind to replace my caterer?" Alejandro asked.

She started to respond, excitement humming at the prospect of finding the perfect vendor who fit seamlessly into the plan.

Until a flash of sunshine caught her eye.

She couldn't help it; her head jerked around. There in the window of a small boutique was the most exquisite gown she'd ever seen. Buttery yellow and sleeveless, with a sweetheart bodice that followed the curves of the mannequin like a lover's hand, layer upon layer of gauzy skirt that fell to the floor...

A dream. A dress that would make any girl feel like a princess.

She looked away. Not her. She'd never been a princess. Efficient, professional, all work and no play. That was Calandra Smythe.

"Calandra?"

She blinked and looked away, continuing forward.

"Sorry. For the catering..."

Her voice trailed off as Alejandro's hand settled on her shoulder.

"What?"

His eyes searched, probed, delving so deep she barely resisted squirming under the intensity of his gaze.

"What?"

"The dress."

"It's just a dress."

"It may be just a dress, but you do have a special event coming up. Something other than black, perhaps."

"Black is a versatile color."

His eyes narrowed thoughtfully. "You know, I don't think I've ever seen you in anything other than black. Well," he added, his voice lowering and making her stomach flip-flop, "once."

She refused to blush. "I like black."

"Yes, but why?"

She barely resisted squirming under his scrutiny. No one had ever asked why before. Everyone else had just labeled her as falling into the goth phase or joked that she must attend a lot of funerals. One young man she'd rejected in college had said she dressed in the same color as her soul. Dramatic and petulant, but the comment still crept under her skin. Johanna and Aunt Norine were the only ones who knew that to her black meant armor. Strength. Security. It had since the day of Mother's funeral, when she'd walked into her father's study in her black mourning dress and wielded power over him for the first time in her life.

"I just do."

"You hide so much of yourself."

With a deep breath, she turned and met his gaze head-on. "Spoken like someone who also hides behind a mask."

He jerked back. Surprise flashed in his eyes. Then it disappeared as he gave her one of those insincere smiles.

"Touché. So are you going to try it on?"

"It's not me."

Pride, and a little bit of shame, refused to let her admit that she wanted to try on the dress very badly.

Her phone beeped. She glanced down and sucked in a relieved breath. "Five minutes until my appointment."

She took off down the boulevard, her pace quick, not giving him enough time to reply. He caught up to her, his long legs eating up the distance she'd put between them. They walked in uneasy silence, passing more shops and cafés, until a violet-colored sign with white lettering caught her eye. She slowed her pace.

"Here we are."

He glanced up at the sign and frowned.

"Le Giordano École Culinaire. A culinary school? I thought you were going to meet with a caterer."

She held up her phone. "I am. Suzanne Giordano's culinary school offers catering."

His frown deepened. "Maybe I didn't make my wishes clear. This event has to impress some of the richest men in the world to not only continue to invest in *La Reina*, but let me keep Cabrera Shipping. Burned bread and attempts at an appetizer some kid saw online won't cut it."

Her heart thumped hard again, but this time in anger.

"Spoken like a spoiled billionaire."

He leaned in, eyes narrowing, that dangerous intensity she'd glimpsed back in Paris on full display.

"You don't know a thing about me."

"Judging by your elitist comment, I know all I need to know," she snapped back. "Your brother trusted me implicitly, and every event I executed for Cabrera Wines was a success. You said you trusted me. Clearly you don't."

"I don't trust a bunch of aspiring chefs who might give my guests food poisoning."

She punched in a website on her phone and held the screen up to his face. "Suzie Giordano has trained multiple two-and three-star Michelin chefs. She's won awards all around the world. The chef who cooked your fancy meal in London a few months ago is a graduate of her school."

His handsome features hardened until it looked like his face had been chiseled out of granite.

"London?" Silky menace laced the word. "How did you know about London?"

"Don't flatter yourself." She swallowed her bitterness. "I didn't stalk you. I didn't have to. There were photos everywhere." Somehow, she managed to keep her voice from cracking underneath the weight of her pain. Which was worse? The sharp sting of remembering how quickly her one and only lover had replaced her? Or the icy fingers of memory clutching her heart and squeezing as the echoes of her mother's sobs at discovering yet another mistress played over and over in her head?

"London wasn't what you think."

"Of course it wasn't." She waved a hand. "But it's not important anyway. What is important is that you're questioning my ability to do a job you hired me for."

He blew out a breath and ran a frustrated hand through his curls. "Calandra, this is not—"

"Perhaps," she interrupted, "if you don't trust me, I should go home."

Nothing. Absolute silence as he stared at her, eyes blank, face smooth, without the slightest hint of expression.

Like looking in a mirror.

Was this what people saw when they talked to her? The thought made her sick to her stomach. It would have been better to see something, anything.

Anything but complete and utter disinterest. Because this was what she feared seeing. A month, six months, a year. Whenever the allure of this novelty wore off, this would be the look she'd see.

Although perhaps it was better to see it now. Remind herself that he might be able to shove his way into their child's life legally. But that didn't mean she had to let him into hers. And she would move heaven and earth to keep her son or daughter from having to see that same look on his face, from ever falling into the trap their grandmother had of wondering if they just weren't enough.

She turned and continued down the road. She didn't look back. If he didn't trust her, better to cut the cord now before she got any deeper.

CHAPTER ELEVEN

CALANDRA CUPPED HER hands around her mug of tea as she watched the waves crash along the beach. The rising sun warmed her skin as she relaxed at what she'd come to think of as her table on the patio. Sea salt danced on the air. The perfect setting for rest and relaxation.

Or it would have been if her damn heart would stop kicking into overdrive every time she thought she heard someone approach. Even though her time at the culinary school had served as a welcome distraction, Alejandro had been ever-present in her mind, intruding and refusing to let her eject him from her thoughts. Already she'd made a mistake; she'd lowered her defenses at the harbor, on their walk. She'd taken the olive branch he'd offered too easily. Had it been his simple, sweet plea that he wanted to get to know her better? Or the feeling of his hand rubbing circles on the back of her hand and stirring memories of that same hand closing over her breast with a possessive heat?

Whatever it was, she'd caved. Not five minutes later, he'd shown that he didn't trust her, that money was more important than anything else and, worst of all, that once something or someone challenged him, he shut them out.

She'd entertained the idea of calling his bluff and booking a flight back to North Carolina. But she'd be running away, tail between her legs, and merely putting off a battle that would turn into a full-scale legal war.

So she'd forced herself to carry on yesterday. She'd spent nearly three hours at the school, a three-story building with creamy blue walls covered with photos of beaming graduates and colorful culinary concoctions. Her mood had been significantly bolstered, partially because of the delectable food and partially because of the energetic company of Suzie Giordano, a short woman with a long silver braid draped over one shoulder and a booming voice. The crinkles etched into her skin that told a story of years of smiling and laughter had reminded Calandra of Aunt Norine. She'd relaxed almost instantly and even smiled back.

Suzie had given her a tour of the school, weaving in and out of the classes in session, providing tips to eager students and the occasional joke in rapid-fire French. By the time she'd sat Calandra down at a small table on the balcony on the third floor, she was almost certain that she'd found the right place. One bite of canapés Lorenzo had settled it, savoring the taste of the crispy parmesan cheese and hearty crabmeat.

Part of what had made her so successful as an event planner, especially in New York, had been her ability to identify talent and solidify new relationships. She had known as soon as she'd seen the arrangement at a floral show that the girl who'd dropped out of college would be the next sought-after florist. She'd locked in an exclusive deal with a string quartet made up of a schoolteacher, a retired army colonel and twins who ran a bookstore in SoHo.

Most would have laughed at the notion that Calandra Smythe, the ice queen herself, was capable of building relationships. When it came to the billionaires and lofty business professionals she'd worked with, that was absolutely true.

But when it came to the people those billionaires and professionals looked down on, she thrived. Her blunt words, her loyalty to those who showed up and did their job, had made her successful.

Calandra glanced up. Nine o'clock in the morning as the sun climbed higher into the Mediterranean sky. In Kitty Hawk the moon would still be up, turning the surface of the ocean into an ethereal silver that lit up her attic bedroom.

Ever since finding out about the baby, she'd looked at

Aunt Norine's house with new eyes. While it had been a refuge after her mother's funeral, she'd resisted calling it "home." Now, thousands of miles away, she longed for the creaky porch and the worn but stark white lace curtains that hung in the windows.

Lace curtains that, despite their overly bleached, frayed appearance, reminded her of the gauzy curtains hanging in the suite in New York, filtering the streetlights and casting shifting shadows over Alejandro's incredible body as they'd made love.

Another memory blazed forth before she could stop it. The night of the party in New York, when four members of the cleaning crew had failed to show, she'd kicked off her heels, grabbed a trash bag and started cleaning up. It had been just after midnight, she'd been exhausted and had wanted nothing more than to crawl in bed.

She'd turned after clearing one of the tables and nearly run into Alejandro, sleeves of his dress shirt rolled up, tie undone and hanging around his neck.

"What can I do?"

Those four words had rocked the foundation of who she thought him to be. He stayed for two hours, helping her pack away centerpieces, toss tablecloths into laundry baskets and, just as they'd been about to call it a night, had taken the mop he'd been wielding and performed a tango across the ballroom floor.

She'd laughed. He'd grinned, not a playboy's smirk but a friendly, heart-melting smile that had heated her blood. They'd gotten into the elevator. Who moved first, she'd never know. They'd crashed into each other, drawn in by the power of a desire they'd been suppressing for years that had suddenly burst free and claimed them in one soul-altering kiss.

The man he'd been that night was the man her heart remembered. The man she could accept, even embrace, as the father of her child.

Although the more he talked about *La Reina*, the more he revealed of himself, the more she remembered their interactions over the years, how she'd started to become aware when he walked into a room or even looked forward to the conversations they'd have.

Was the man she'd started to see real? Or an illusion?

Doesn't matter. He doesn't trust you, her brain reminded her with cruel honesty.

Adrian had trusted her. Yes, he'd required evidence, plans, documentation. When she'd suggested an appetizer for the last release party that included BBQ sauce, she'd had to show him sales of the condiment in the United States and the recipe she'd obtained from a famous chef.

But he'd trusted her. Alejandro, on the other hand, only cared about impressing his board.

For one brief moment, when he'd tried to persuade her to try on the dress, she thought he'd seen something most people missed. That she had dreams, hopes, desires, beyond her career. That she exuded coldness because, ever since her mother's passing, she'd had to, to stay sane, to stay strong for Johanna.

Stupid. If she just clung to the memories of him with his parade of women, the overly cheery insults he'd lobbed at her over the years, she could keep him at arm's length.

"How was the food?" His husky voice interrupted her thoughts. Her heart jumped, but her hands stayed steady on her tea mug. She could do this.

"Delicious," she replied. "Too bad you missed it."

He circled the table and walked into her line of sight.

She'd only ever thought of food as delicious before. But the sight of Alejandro clad only in navy swim shorts that clung to his perfectly muscled backside had her rethinking the term.

Sun gleamed off his tan skin. Her eyes ran over his chest, the dark hair that trailed down his stomach and disappeared into the waistband of his trunks. Despite the dark-colored fabric, the bulge between his thighs wasn't hard to miss.

Her head snapped up in time to see his satisfied smirk. "Hungry?"

The word penetrated her, stabbed her deep as it conjured up images of naked bodies, glistening with sweat and arching against each other, moving in sensual harmony. What would it be like to say yes, to take his hand and lead him back to the guest suite? She'd been a quick study their first time together. Taking control, embracing the emotions coursing through her, delighting in the approval that had glittered in his eyes as his hands had tightened on her hips and guided her up and down…

She closed her eyes for a moment. Savored the memory. Then released it.

"I've already had breakfast." She nodded toward her plate, empty except for a few bread crumbs and some strawberry leaves. "Also delicious."

It took every ounce of self-control she had not to laugh at his look of consternation as he sat across from her.

"Glad the cooking is at least to your liking," he muttered. He leaned over, snatched a bagel out of the basket a maid had brought out and sat back. She kept her gaze trained on his face and off his chiseled abs.

"Suzie is hosting a final tasting this evening. Appetizers, main course samplers, desserts."

"Hmm."

Irritation nipped any lingering attraction in the bud. "Hmm?"

He took a bite of his bagel. "Mmm-hmm."

She barely stopped herself from slamming her mug on the table as she stood. "Well, I will tell Suzie you agreed to everything with an 'mmm-hmm.'"

"Suzie already knows I agree."

"What?"

He didn't even look at her as he slathered cream cheese on his bagel. "I called her this morning. Nice woman."

She sucked in a slow, deep breath—a better alternative to reaching across the table, grabbing the bagel basket and dumping the contents on his lap. When he did look up, those damned blue eyes were wide and innocent. The devious twinkle and quirked corner of his full lips said he was full of it and up to no good.

As usual.

"You all right, Callie?"

Her obstetrician would probably have had a fit if she could see Calandra's blood pressure right now. She tamped down her rising irritation, at least outwardly, and summoned her iciest smile.

"What did you chat about?"

He bit into the bagel, chewing slowly and leaning farther back in his chair. She silently willed the universe to break one of the chair legs and send him tumbling back onto his arrogant ass.

"We made a few changes to tonight's tasting."

A throbbing started at her temples, low but persistent. "Oh?"

If he heard the warning in her tone, he blazed right past it as he bestowed his most dazzling smile on her. "You'll like them."

"And if I don't?"

"You will."

She laughed. It was that or commit murder with a bagel basket. "Of course. I should have anticipated—what did *Variety* call you? 'Every commitment-minded woman's worst nightmare'—to hire a professional to manage an event that his entire dream rests on and then interfere whenever he feels like it."

He set the bagel down, stood and in three seconds was standing less than a foot away.

"Everyone thinks they know me from those articles." No hint of a smile. His voice was low and dangerous. "Keep in mind, the public sees what I want them to see."

"Ah. So you put on a show?"

"Yes." His eyes narrowed before his gaze dipped down to her lips, then back up. "I'm not the only one in this villa who hides."

The past ripped through her defenses and rendered her speechless. She stared at him, fighting back the retort that she wanted to deliver, that explained why she hid. Hiding had saved her in the past, saved Johanna.

Slowly, she eased herself back into her chair. The irritation slipped from Alejandro's face as he watched her.

"What's wrong?"

She held up a hand, gathering strength before she spoke. Alejandro sat across from her, face serious and eyes searching for answers. She resisted turning away. To do so would only invite more scrutiny. But as she lifted her mug to her lips, she glanced at him from beneath her lashes.

It wasn't just that the depth of her feelings for Alejandro and her lack of control over them terrified the hell out of her, that made her hide and push him away. It wasn't just the possibility of him breaking her heart. It was what would happen to her child when Alejandro left that drove her to keep him at arm's length. She'd had years of being her mother's caregiver to build up her walls, to cocoon herself in apathy and coldness, reserving her emotions only for Mother and Johanna.

It was the one thing that had saved her from suffering the same anguish her mother had when her father had lost interest in her, had abandoned her to living in a lakeside mansion bursting at the seams with everything a little girl could want.

Everything except love.

Love. When Alejandro had helped her in New York,

when he'd treated not just her body but *her* with such tenderness, she'd wondered if she'd fallen a little in love. Definitely lust. But his interest in the baby, his dedication to his company…she'd gotten glimpses over the years of the real man he hid away, but she'd never anticipated a leader, a caregiver, a provider.

A lover.

She refocused on her tea. She was not in a position to evaluate him accurately.

"Morning sickness," she finally said as he continued to stare at her.

"Bullshit."

She arched a brow. "You might want to work on that mouth of yours before the baby arrives."

"Don't distract me. It's not just the pregnancy that's bothering you."

A quick shrug of her shoulders. "It's not important."

"It is to me."

Her hands tightened on the mug as her heart swooned. It was scary how much she wanted to believe him, to curl up in his arms and confide every dark event, every secret, surrender to being cared for.

"I appreciate that, Alejandro. I do," she insisted when his eyes narrowed. "However, as kind as that sentiment is, I believe you're using it to distract me from the fact that you messed up my evening."

Her phone buzzed on the table. She picked it up and frowned as she read the text.

Confirming the change of venue for tonight's tasting. Excited to see the yacht!

She had to read it twice before it sank in.

"Your yacht?"

Alejandro frowned. "I wanted to tell you."

"Why?"

"So I could see a glimmer of excitement in those normally staid eyes. That or daggers." He squinted. "Guess I got my wish. If looks could kill—"

"You would have been dead a long time ago." She set her phone and mug on the table and gave in to the desire—no, the need—to massage her temples as the headache grew. "What game are you playing, Alejandro?"

"No game."

"I sincerely doubt that."

The teasing smile disappeared as his lips straightened once more. "Perhaps, instead of assuming I'm playing a game or devising a devious plot, you might instead question how your actions forced me to do this."

Her mouth dropped. "What?"

"This week wasn't supposed to be about work. It was to get to know each other. How is that possible when you're running around Marseille and staying as far away as possible from me?"

The headache unleashed its fury, little pickaxes hacking away inside her head as she tried to find her footing in the conversation that had seriously spiraled out of control.

"You still had no right to interfere with my work without talking to me first."

"So you could make an excuse?" Brittle laughter tumbled from his lips. "I have no doubt that, had I approached you, you would have tried to find a way around me just like you did when you tried to flee Paris."

"Fleeing is an over exaggeration," she replied coolly. *Calm.* She had to stay calm to maintain the upper hand.

He started to retort, then stopped and pinched the bridge of his nose. "Regardless, the venue has been moved to my yacht. Be ready outside the villa at six."

"Somewhere in that order I heard an invitation."

"Hear what you want." Alejandro stood, his body tense,

frustration rolling off him in palpable waves. "So long as you're outside by six."

Perhaps she could accidentally knock him overboard.

"Who will be there?" she asked as he started to turn away.

"You, me, Suzie and whoever she brings. Plus my crew."

The headache faded as warning whispered across the back of her neck. "But...just us? For dinner?"

It was like watching a predator realize it had its prey within its grasp. He leaned forward, hands tightening on the back of the chair as a sensual smile spread across his too-handsome face. "Is that a problem?"

Judging by the electricity that had slowly begun to sizzle in her veins, yes, it was a major problem.

"No. Just curious."

The deepening smile told her he knew better. Knew that right now that heat was pooling between her thighs no matter how sternly she lectured herself to keep it together.

There would be other people on the yacht. But for all intents and purposes, they would be alone.

"Don't think you can seduce me to get what you want."

Alejandro circled the table, muscles rippling as he moved like a panther, swift and confident. Sun gleamed on his bare skin, and she had a frantic recollection of the golden lights from a nearby building creating the same glow on his chest as he'd slid inside her for the first time, big and hard and yet so gentle as the initial discomfort had faded, replaced with a wondrous pleasure that rippled through her with each tender thrust.

"I will get what I want, Calandra," he said as he placed one hand on the table and one on the back of her chair, caging her between his powerful arms. "But not by seduction. When we make love again, it will be because you want me as badly as I want you."

Even she was impressed by her own willpower and ability to keep her face blank. Because if he saw the effect he was having on her, the swirl of heat and need combined with that emotional pull that was so tempting and yet so frightening, she had no doubt he would use it in a heartbeat to make her surrender herself to him. Body and soul.

"Hold on to that fantasy, Alejandro. Because that's the only place you're going to see me naked ever again."

A wolfish smile crossed his face. "We'll see."

Before she could pull back, he leaned down…and placed a kiss on her forehead. She should have pushed him away, far away, instead of closing her eyes and, for one brief, reckless moment, allowing herself to just *feel*.

And then he straightened.

"Six tonight. Don't be late."

And then he was gone, leaving her with the sinking feeling that she had just made a colossal mistake.

CHAPTER TWELVE

THE BLACK SHIRT and skirt Calandra wore as she walked down the front steps of the villa only made her look paler. Beautiful, Alejandro acknowledged, but aloof, distant. She walked toward the vintage Rolls-Royce, a purse slung across her body, hair pulled back in a tight braid. If she thought he wouldn't be attracted to her when she dressed like she was going to a funeral, she was dead wrong. The braid bared her face to his gaze, a sight he consumed greedily. Dark brows bringing out her gray eyes, sharp cheekbones offset by that intoxicating, rosebud-shaped mouth.

Beautiful. He knew how to work with beautiful. But as she drew closer, her hand straying to the tiny bump beneath her shirt, he knew a moment of uncertainty. The women he'd known before had been easy to deal with and, most of the time, fun. For some, he'd been a shoulder to lean on. For others, he'd been a body to enjoy as they pushed memories of past lovers out of their mind. For a select few who had not heeded his caution that he was only interested in a good time, he'd been the target of angry tears and smeared mascara as they'd thrown shoes, hairbrushes or, in the case of a beautiful symphony percussionist with a passionate temper, a glockenspiel.

But this…this was new territory. Not just because she carried his child inside her. She fought him at every turn, resisted his usually successful charms and scorned the wealth that previous women of his acquaintance fawned over.

She fascinated him.

He glanced down at his watch, not ready to have her see how much she affected him beyond the physical attraction. "Five fifty-nine. I'm impressed."

Her eyes flickered over him, her gaze opaque.

"I'm impressed you're wearing clothes."

He cracked a grin. "Figured I'd try something new since my state of undress doesn't seem to affect you."

"Fishing for compliments, are we?"

"I'm not above begging."

She stopped in front of him. The faintest scent of sandalwood mixed with something surprisingly soft and fruity—cherries?—teased him. He resisted the urge to lean in, inhale her scent and place the faintest of kisses on her lovely neck.

He dragged his gaze from where her pulse beat at the base of her throat up to meet her eyes. Not dark and flinty, but soft and gray.

"You look handsome tonight, Alejandro."

The simple compliment floored him. No over-the-top words, no excessive batting of the eyelashes. Just five words that shot straight into his chest.

He opened the door and gave her an exaggerated bow. "It's a start. After you, mademoiselle."

How big of a bastard was he that he was encouraging her to open up to him while throwing up his own defenses? His conscience bugged him the entire ride into Marseille as he regaled her with the history of the town and pointed out various landmarks.

They arrived at the harbor, and he escorted her onto the teakwood deck of the yacht.

"*Bonjour*, Mademoiselle Smythe!" Suzie said happily as Calandra walked onboard. "I am so excited for this opportunity."

"Thank you for changing your plans so quickly."

He ignored Calandra's barb and, with a quick murmur of thanks to Suzie, guided Calandra in the direction of the stairs.

"Al fresco dining on the sundeck as we cruise around

the Gulf. Suzie and her team will cater, and we'll have some privacy."

She tossed him her signature raised brow. "I'm not having sex with you on the deck of your yacht."

"Ah. Well, since you figured out my sneaky plan, should we just cancel the tasting and go back to the villa?"

A roll of the eyes, but she didn't turn quickly enough to hide the smile that quirked her lips.

They reached the deck, and he had the pleasure of seeing her eyes widen as she took in the splendor of *La Pimpinela Escarlata*. Plush couches were arranged around a small fire pit filled with glittering glass. Beyond the couches, a crystal-clear pool glimmered beneath the lights of the port and the emerging moon. And on the far side of the sundeck, two red velvet chairs and a white table decked with votive candles and set for two.

He turned to Calandra, waiting for her compliments on the custom wood decking, the hand-stitched silk pillows or any of the other details former lovers had gushed over when he'd brought them here.

Nothing. Nothing but that analytical stare sweeping over everything.

"It's nice," she finally said.

He bit down on his own tongue as he clasped her elbow and walked across the sundeck toward the table.

"Glad it's satisfactory."

If she sensed the irritation in his voice, she didn't acknowledge it. She sat down, crossed her legs and watched the buildings of Marseille grow smaller as the yacht pulled away from the port.

Suzie bustled over to the table and set two plates in front of them with a flourish.

"Monsieur Cabrera, Mademoiselle Smythe told me of your appreciation for old-world glamour."

He glanced at Calandra, who was examining the food on her plate with a critical eye.

"Yes. *La Reina*'s renovation was inspired by cruises from an earlier generation. My mother and I used to watch old movies." A smile tugged at his lips. "One of my favorite memories."

Suzie grinned as Calandra looked up, her gaze searching. He'd never shared that tidbit before. A small fact, so why did he feel bare, like he'd just revealed something deep?

"That makes me happy to hear. Like *Gentlemen Prefer Blondes*, yes? Or *An Affair to Remember*?"

Hearing the familiar names brought on a rush of nostalgia. "Two of my mother's favorites, actually."

"Good." Suzie gestured to the plate in front of him. "I also share an affinity for such films. For your tasting tonight, you have oysters Rockefeller, baked in a butter sauce, *socca* flatbread with a salmon tartare and baked camembert with honey and red pepper. And for you," she said, turning to Calandra, "I have prepared a traditional French dish, coquilles St. Jacques, seared scallops on cucumber slices. And then brie fondant au pesto, topped with pine nuts and served with grapes and toasted baguette slices." She put her hands on her hips and beamed. "A mix of your old-world glamour and French favorites."

As much as he'd balked at the idea of a culinary school catering the party that could make or break his company, he found himself eyeing the food with appreciation. Not only did it smell incredible, but the delicate touches, from the sprinkling of chives over the scallops to the lemon wedges arranged artfully around the oysters, lent an artistic flair.

"This looks wonderful," Calandra said. The smile she bestowed on Suzie had him blinking in shock. Sweet, feminine, kind. He realized with a jolt that he was now privy to one of the reasons why Calandra had been so successful in her job with Cabrera Wines. She hid her warm and fuzzy side well. But when she pulled it out of wherever she'd been hiding it, she dazzled.

"My students were very excited at the prospect of cooking for a famous billionaire, not to mention on his personal yacht." Suzie beamed. "But we shall see what you think of the food. Eat!"

And with that pronouncement, she left. The yacht cut across the water, the brilliant sapphire of the sky stretching down to meet the darker blue of the ocean. The bell tower and stone walls of the Notre-Dame de la Garde stood proudly on a hill overlooking Marseille as the port grew smaller on the horizon.

"It is beautiful."

Alejandro glanced at Calandra. With her face turned toward Marseille, her pale profile stood out in stark, stunning contrast against the sky.

"How much did it cost you to admit that?"

Instead of her customary silence or a sharp retort, she surprised him with a small smile that twisted his stomach into a tight knot.

"It's too beautiful not to acknowledge."

Before he could say anything else, he picked up a scallop and cucumber slice and popped it into her mouth. Her eyes widened.

"Oh, my."

Her moan of pleasure made his blood boil. Pushing past his lust, he scooped up a piece of baked camembert with the flatbread, then sat back in surprise as the sweetness of honey and spice of red pepper hit his tongue.

"Well?"

"Decent."

"Decent?" she repeated. "This is wonderful and you know it."

He shrugged and took a sip of water, enjoying stretching out the moment. "Better than some places I've eaten."

She started to retort, but then her eyes narrowed. "You're teasing me."

"I would never."

She scooped a generous helping of brie and pine nuts onto a baguette slice and held it out. "Try this."

He leaned forward and, before she could snatch her hand away, bit into the bread. Her eyes widened as she sucked in a breath. Her hand trembled. He reached out and caught her wrist before she dropped the baguette. Beneath his fingertips, her pulse pounded so furiously it echoed in his head.

"Delicious."

Her cheeks flamed pink. No, not immune to him at all.

Food first. Then, perhaps later, he could offer her a private tour of the master suite. Optimism and lust had directed his instructions to the staff to make the king-size bed up with black silk sheets and a red rose on the pillow just in case the tide really turned in his favor.

Suzie distracted him from his lascivious thoughts with the next course. Over the next hour she kept up a steady delivery of culinary treasures. In between bites, Alejandro peppered Calandra with questions about her life back in Kitty Hawk, her time in college, the internship that had led her to Cabrera Wines. She, in turn, surprised him by asking not about business, but his movie marathons with his mother, his years at university and his time as a deckhand. His story of nearly getting swept overboard during a nasty storm on the Atlantic elicited more reaction than the luxury surrounding her.

"I don't think most heads of corporations would do that."

"It was fun. I actually enjoyed it. I earned the respect of my crew. When I presented everything I wanted to change to the board, they liked what I had to say."

"And your father?"

The relaxation that had settled in vanished at the mention of his sire.

"My father pointed out Adrian's sales of Cabrera Wines and told me once I hit that level of profit, then he would congratulate me."

She stabbed her fork into the salmon sitting atop a pile of creamy risotto. "I may not approve of all aspects of your lifestyle, but that's just cruel to do to your son, let alone someone who accomplished so much in such a short time."

Her defense of him was surprisingly touching. When had anyone paid attention to him? Just him?

He couldn't really recall.

After the last course was served, Suzie's students replaced the table and chairs with the lounge chaises that normally occupied that spot. Calandra sat down and stretched out, her face content as the sun sank behind the waves of the Mediterranean, leaving behind fingers of pink and orange clinging to the sky as stars started to twinkle, little pinwheels of light against the darkening sky.

"You were right."

She glanced up at him. "Oh?"

"Some of the best food I've ever had."

Another smile that kicked him hard. "I'm glad you liked it. If the board wasn't already planning to vote yes, they'll have to after a meal like that."

Her belief in his plan touched him in a way he didn't care to examine too closely. At least not now. He shrugged. "Hopefully."

Her eyes latched onto him, gray and pensive and searching. "I've noticed when you shrug, it means you care about something."

"Come again?"

"When you shrug, others see a casual, fly-by-the-seat-of-his-pants, spoiled billionaire. Nothing fazes you." She tilted her head. "I think it's how you hide."

"Hide?" he echoed as he sat down on the lounge next to her.

"You're more than just a playboy, Alejandro." Her unexpected words made him pause. Was her view of him changing? "If your board knows anything about business, they'll know that voting yes on *La Reina* is the best thing to do. You have a solid business plan, and more importantly, you believe in it." Her eyes stayed trained on his, and, God help him, he couldn't look away. "You're more than most people think you are. I have no idea why you act otherwise."

Because I don't know any other way.

Suddenly, the possibility of altering her perceptions, of showing her the man he was just coming to know himself, made him extremely uncomfortable. The few times he'd opened that door with Javier, the rejections had cut deeper and deeper until he'd locked the door and thrown away the key.

"Perhaps it's not an act."

He sensed her disappointment with his answer but steeled himself against saying anything else. His campaign to woo Calandra had been based on wowing her with his wealth and showing her that he didn't spend every waking hour drinking and smoking cigars. He hadn't anticipated this deep dive into emotions that were better left untouched.

"How long until we're back in port?" she asked.

His lips parted. What would she say if he told her everything?

Fear snatched his confession away, leaving him hollow and cold. He glanced at the passing rocky cliffs of Calanques National Park.

"Less than an hour."

She pulled a notebook out of her purse. "In that case, I did have some details I wanted to verify for the party—"

"Don't you ever take a break?"

She looked up at him in surprise.

"When there's time, yes."

"It's after eight o'clock. Nighttime," he added.

"I'm not surprised that you view this as a time to…relax or enjoy." She kept her eyes trained on her damned list. "But not all of us have the luxury of drinking and seducing our way through the evening."

The frosty tone rankled him. Even if he hadn't confessed all, he'd let her see more of *him*, whoever he was, than he'd ever shared with another woman. Because he hadn't responded the way she wanted, she'd resorted to jabs that once would have made him laugh, but now just made his teeth grind.

"All right." He leaned back against the chaise and closed his eyes.

"All right?"

"Mmm-hmm."

"Was there something else you wanted to discuss?"

"Just persuading you to let me be involved in my child's life."

For a moment there was only the distant sound of the ocean waves.

"When you say it like that, it sounds awful," she said.

Irritation flared into anger. He opened his eyes, swung his legs over so his feet rested on the deck and faced her, letting her see the depth of his displeasure.

"It is awful, Calandra. You're threatening to not let me be involved in my own child's life."

"That's not what I said. I just—"

"'Birthday parties and such,'" he quoted back at her. "Isn't that what you said in Paris?"

"I didn't mean you couldn't ever see the baby, I just…"

"Just what?" When she continued to stare at him, her face blank, he barely stopped himself from grabbing her shoulders. "Just be involved when you say it's allowed? Maybe that's once a year, maybe once every three years?"

She came to life, exploding with passion and energy as she leaned forward, eyes blazing.

"Fine, then! Take me to court, sue me for custody or whatever it is you want. God knows you have enough money to get whatever you want."

"What I want," he ground out, trying to figure out how this conversation had spiraled so quickly out of control, "is not to force the mother of my child into doing something she doesn't want to do. Yes, I slept with dozens of women. I swung from the chandelier at the Venetian Hotel. I've spent money on God knows what. But I've always tried to do right by the people in my life, and that includes you. Why are you so afraid of me?"

"I'm not afraid of you!"

He leaned in then, his lips just a breath away from hers. Her breathing stopped, then resumed with a deep, shuddering inhale.

"Perhaps you should be, Calandra." Just a touch closer. "Perhaps I make you feel things that frighten you. Things you want but for whatever reason won't let yourself have."

She swallowed hard. "I'm not going to make the same mistake my mother did."

As she started to stand, the deck tilted. A small movement from the lapping of the waves, but enough of a surprise that it threw Calandra off balance. He stood and caught her.

And then she was in his arms and he didn't know whether it was the roaring of the ocean or the blood thundering in his ears. All he knew was that her hands still lay on his chest, his arms were still wrapped around her waist. They stared at each other, waiting.

Just when he thought he wouldn't be able to contain himself any longer, her arms wrapped around his neck and she pressed her lips flush against his.

CHAPTER THIRTEEN

HE BURST INTO FLAMES. His body hardened everywhere as he crushed her against him, running his tongue along the seam of her lips, demanding entry. She gasped, opened beneath him, moaning as he tasted her.

Their lips fused together as he sat down on the chaise, stretched out with her body clutched against his. His hand slid under her shirt. Her mouth opened on a gasp as he cupped her swollen breast. He teased her by tracing his tongue over her lips as his fingers plucked at her nipple.

Until she nearly undid him by grabbing the back of his head and crushing his lips to hers, slipping her own tongue inside in a brazen, seductive move that made him so hard it almost hurt.

Dios, she was incredible. Fiery, strong, fearless. He couldn't get enough of her, needed more. He pulled her shirt up, the cup of her bra down and sucked her nipple into his mouth.

"Alejandro!"

A tiny thread of sanity pushed through, whispering that they could be discovered at any moment. But he didn't care. This was his yacht and she was *his*. His, and he couldn't have stopped touching her even if he wanted to.

He reached down as he continued to kiss and suck her breasts, bunched up the material of her skirt until his fingertips met the bare skin of her thigh. She arched against him and—*querido Dios*—he could feel the heat of her core against his erection straining against his jeans.

"Alejandro…"

Hearing her name tumble from his lips drove him mad. He tore his mouth from her breast, trailed kisses over her cheek and down her neck. With a quick yank, her skirt ended up around her waist and he peeled away her panties.

Her red, lacy panties that made him so hot with desire it was all he could do to keep himself from stripping them both naked and making love to her right then and there on the sundeck.

"I just…they're not…" She stumbled over her words, withdrawing into herself. "I don't—"

He tucked the panties into his pocket, rolled and laid her beneath him. Then he pulled her skirt up and placed his mouth on her. She arched, thrusting her hips against him as he tasted her sweetness.

"Alejandro!"

She was liquid fire in his arms. Stripped bare of not just the unexpected lingerie but all her defenses. He looked up, caught her gaze in his and watched as her eyes flamed molten silver as his tongue danced over her most sensitive skin. Knowing that he had been her first, that he was her only, made his fingers tighten on her thighs as he upped his sensual assault. A maddening urge drove him onward as he used the cues of her body—the hitch in her breathing, the clench of her thighs, the arch of her back—to guide his lovemaking and ensure she never even entertained the thought of sharing her body with another man.

Just the idea of another man touching her, let alone engaging in this kind of intimacy, made him see red. Jealousy like he'd never known before shot through his veins and he buried his face between her legs, savored the sound of her crying out his name.

Mine, mine, mine, an inner beast roared.

Her fingers tangled in his hair. He paused. He hadn't planned on ravishing her like this, of being brought to the edge of his control. It would be a very long night, but if she wanted him to stop, he would.

And then her fingers tightened and she spread her thighs

even more with a whispered "Please" that made his blood boil. He licked her, kissed, nibbled, experimented with what made her whimper, what made her gasp, what made her demand more.

Her thighs clenched. Her breathing grew more frantic, her hips thrusting harder. He buried his tongue inside her as he envisioned what it would be like to finally sheath himself inside her tight wetness again.

She exploded, writhing against the chaise as he kissed her most vulnerable spot, made love to her with his tongue until she collapsed, body shuddering, fingers still tangled in his hair but limp.

He stretched out next to her, tugging her skirt back into place as he cradled her body against his. She leaned into his embrace, her head resting on his shoulder.

Something sparked inside him. Not just the lust that was roaring through his veins, not the desire that was tightening his chest until he thought he would explode if he couldn't feel her luscious body wrapped around him.

No, this was something else. A protectiveness, a need to not only claim her body with his own but to keep her safe. To wipe away whatever pain had fueled the defenses she normally kept in place with icy precision.

Slowly, she raised her head. Her eyes glowed silver under the light of the stars. Luminous, bright with satisfaction and…

Fear. He saw the fear flickering deep in the gray depths, felt her uncertainty as her hands rested on his shoulders.

"Calandra, what just happened—"

"Can't happen again."

Her words stopped him cold. "What?"

It almost hurt to watch the change that came over her. The coldness that eclipsed the lingering passion in her eyes. The straightening of her shoulders as she pulled away from him. The firming of her lips as she stood, smoothed her skirt and sat down on the other chaise.

That a woman could box him up and push away so neatly after such a heated, passionate encounter—in the middle of the damned ocean—and then react with all the cool efficiency of a military general rubbed him raw.

That that woman was also carrying his child made the wound especially grievous.

"I'm sorry, Alejandro. I kissed you first and started our...that is—"

"Our lovemaking?"

He hadn't thought it possible, but her face grew harder. "Don't call it that."

If he hadn't just held her in his arms, felt her come apart beneath his lips, he would never have thought the ice queen sitting before him capable of the passion she'd just displayed.

But she had. Others might confuse this withdrawal for her being rude, or even a "stone-cold bitch," as he'd heard one waiter snap at an event when Calandra had taken him to task for showing up late in wrinkled clothing. Was he the only one who had glimpsed her pain? The only one who had seen her staunch loyalty to those she believed in, like Suzie and her culinary students?

"What would you like me to call it?"

"A mistake."

It wasn't just his pride that she hurt. No, those two words crawled beneath his skin and lodged somewhere near his heart, seeping into his body with a black, poisonous pain that made him question himself.

Not enough. He'd wondered over the years what it would be like to surrender his playboy image, to settle into a relationship. Most marriages in his world were power plays. But that hadn't stopped the curiosity, nor the loneliness that sometimes invaded after he left yet another bed at the crack of dawn. A hell of his own making, but one that had grown tiresome.

Yet he'd never wanted to risk trying. Who was he without his money, his power, his reputation? The women who had expected more from him hadn't wanted *him*. They'd wanted his lifestyle, possessions, notoriety.

Until Calandra. The woman who had given herself to him, then turned around and presented him with yet another gift. Who made him want more, to be more.

And then crushed him before he could even try.

He smiled, the distant smile he'd perfected over the years. She blinked, some of the glacial condemnation slipping from her face.

"Alejandro, I—"

"You're absolutely right." He nodded at the lights of Marseille on the horizon. "I might enjoy seducing women all over the world, but on the deck of a ship when we could have been caught was crass to say the least."

She started to reach out, to settle her fingers on his arm, but he stood and stepped out of reach.

"I hope this incident hasn't ruined my chances of being involved with our child."

She shook her head. Her eyes gleamed, and for a moment his commitment wavered. Were those tears?

Doesn't matter.

"No. And I'm sorry, Alejandro."

He bowed his head before she could say anything else. "Me, too. I took advantage of you."

"No!"

"Yes. It won't happen again." He turned and walked away. She'd done it to him twice now. Once in New York, and once on the deck of his own yacht.

It probably made him cruel, no better than his father. But he couldn't stop the grim satisfaction that settled in his bones as his footsteps carried him farther away from the one woman who he had realized, too late, held too much power over him.

A positive of his facade. When he hurt, when he felt too much, he could pull the mantle of his pretense around him like a shield and distract himself with the vices he'd indulged in over the years.

For tonight, at least, the vices would keep the heart-wrenching pain at bay.

CHAPTER FOURTEEN

THE WAVES OF the Mediterranean were sharper this morning, capped white as a brisk wind barreled over the water. Clouds darkened the horizon, puffy gray transitioning to a dark slate that advanced ever closer toward land.

Memories assailed her, of another stormy day long ago when rain had fallen into Lake Geneva as she sat on the window seat of her mother's room. Johanna and she had escaped into the luxury of their mother's suite as thunder had roared. Mom had been in bed, her skin so papery thin Calandra had imagined she could see her bones just below the surface.

Johanna had climbed into bed and snuggled against Mom's listless body. Calandra, unable to stomach the knowledge that their mother was wasting away from a broken heart, had gone to the window seat, leaned her head against the cold glass and watched the drops fall onto the lake.

"Calandra," her mother had whispered at last. Calandra had turned to look back at her, dark hair spread across the pillow, lips pale so that when she smiled, she looked like a ghost.

And then she'd uttered the words that had governed Calandra's life ever since.

You're so strong.

Was it the weather taking her to such dark memories? Or her own cringeworthy actions from the night before? She'd relived seeing that smile on his face, that horrid smile that she had put there with her cold words and her casual dismissal of the passion they'd shared, at least a dozen times since she'd gotten up.

It hadn't been his fault. Far from it. *She* had been the one to kiss *him*. Once she started, she hadn't been able to stop, her desire an addiction she'd needed to sate.

And then she'd been so angry with herself, so horrified at her behavior, that she'd taken it out on him.

Alejandro had called a driver to pick her up at the port and take her back to the villa. After spending an hour crafting half a dozen statements as she'd paced the guest quarters, she'd tossed them all out the window and decided that maybe, just for once, she'd wing it, let her emotions and remorse speak for themselves when Alejandro returned.

But he hadn't come back. She'd sat up until nearly one in the morning waiting for his headlights to appear on the drive. Doubt had crept in with every passing of the hand on the clock in her room. She'd found her release under his skillful lovemaking. He'd had none. What if he had decided to seek out someone in Marseille? It wouldn't be any of her business; they weren't a couple, and her treatment of him—her employer, the father of her child, her only lover to date—had been abhorrent.

She had absolutely no business being jealous. No reason for experiencing the same kind of hurt she'd felt when she'd spotted that tabloid magazine at the supermarket and seen him walking into the hotel in London with that actress on his arm, gazing up at him in adoration.

At least that's what she kept telling herself as she sipped her tea.

Thunder rumbled across the water, soft yet so deep she felt it in her bones. The sensation relaxed her muscles as she leaned back into her chair.

An angry voice yanked away her precious moment of peace. She sat straight up, her head whipping around as furious Spanish filled the air.

Calandra's breath caught when she caught full sight of him. His hair was combed back from his face, damp like he'd just come out of the shower. With a loose gray shirt hanging off his broad shoulders, blue jeans clinging to those muscular legs and bare feet padding against the patio stones, the sexily casual look fanned the lust that seemed to always be within arm's reach these days.

It wasn't just how perfectly his clothes molded to his physique, though. No, it was the firmness in his granite jaw, the blazing anger in his stormy eyes, the tautness of his biceps beneath the shirtsleeves as he cursed into the phone.

"Terminamos con esta conversación. Adiós."

He dropped into the chair opposite her. He blinked, then suddenly focused on her as if seeing her for the first time. The anger disappeared as he flashed her a cocky grin. One that didn't quite reach his eyes.

"Parents. Hopefully I do better in that role than my father."

He said it in jest, but his words caught her attention. "He wasn't a good father?"

It was like watching a door being slammed shut as his face hardened. Just as it had last night. He grabbed an orange from the fruit bowl and focused his attention on peeling it.

"Room for improvement. How are you feeling this morning?"

A deft change of subject. But she followed his lead.

"Good." She sucked in a breath. Time to apologize. Except the words froze in her throat as he bit into an orange slice. Juice dribbled down his chin. He swiped a hand across his chin and sucked the juice off a finger. Her heartbeat kicked into overdrive, remembering the way he'd sucked her nipple into his mouth last night as his hands had drifted…

"Calandra?"

"Sorry." She mentally shook her head as she met his amused gaze. The bastard knew exactly what she'd been thinking. "What did you say?"

"I told the crew about the change in caterers. They're excited to have Suzie and her crew."

When the words registered, a thrill shot through her. "Really?"

"Yes. The food was spectacular, the service impeccable." He shrugged. "Wasn't expecting it, but they did well. And supporting a local school will bring in good publicity and earn us some points with the community."

She didn't even bother hiding her satisfied smile. "Thank you."

He cocked his head, his eyes narrowed as he assessed her for a moment. "It's I who should be thanking you." His bark of laughter was harsh. "Well, that and that I'm the one making the decisions regarding this event. Javier told me I was ruining my chances at swaying the board before I even started."

"Is that what you were arguing about?"

"That and you. Not about…" He gestured toward her stomach with the half-eaten orange. "That."

"That?"

"What am I supposed to call it? We don't know if it's a boy or a girl."

"The baby?"

Alejandro rolled his eyes. "That's so…plain."

The conversation was so…normal, she realized with a start. As if they were an ordinary couple bickering good-naturedly over finding out the sex of their child. It stirred a longing for other normal things, like having a partner to share that first smile with.

"Anyway," Alejandro continued, unaware of her inner turmoil, "I told him I hired you to oversee the last details. He already thinks I'm wasting time and money on this venture as it is."

"I imagine your half-a-million-dollar payout for one week didn't sit well."

"None of his business. Yes, I'm paying you more because I impregnated you." He held up a hand as she opened her mouth to retort. "But I'm also paying you what you're worth. You earned an MBA from MIT and you worked for Cabrera Wines for three years. That's after your four-year stint at another firm as an associate event planner."

The retort died as she sat back, stunned. "You know all that about me?"

"Yes." He held her gaze for a long moment. "I didn't just stare at your cleavage at those events."

She arched a brow. "You looked at my ass, too?"

"It's a great ass." A grin flashed, then was unexpectedly replaced by a serious countenance. "But I listened, too. I know you increased Cabrera Wines' event attendance by two hundred percent over two years. I know you got Adrian that feature in *Time* because they heard about his parties. I'm paying you what you're worth, Calandra."

Other than Aunt Norine, no one had ever stood up for her. She'd learned early and she'd learned hard. She had no one to depend on but herself.

Until now. Even when she'd found out about the baby, every time she'd envisioned the future, it had been with Johanna those first couple of years, then alone as Johanna moved on with her life. Just her and her child. But every time Alejandro did something like this, the image of a family became more vivid, more enticing.

That he'd still defend her after last night meant even more. It also laid bare a truth she could no longer deny—he had hired her for *her*. Unlike Father, who'd used money to manipulate situations and people to his advantage, Alejandro believed in her.

Seconds ticked by. Calandra kept her eyes trained on the ocean, the rise and fall of the turquoise waves, and off Alejandro.

She could feel him, though. Watching her. That gaze, the

color of the sea, laying waste to the wall she'd built over the years and stripping her bare until she felt naked. Exposed.

"Your father is a fool," she finally said. A fool for doubting his son, for trying to micromanage a brilliant mind. For whatever he'd done to hurt his son.

Alejandro ran a hand through his hair, dark curls pulled back to reveal the sharpness of his cheekbones, the strong cut of his jaw, before falling back down to graze the tanned column of his neck.

"He is. But I spent years acting like a fool just to try to piss him off." His teeth flashed white in the morning sunlight. "Although I've been quite successful."

She shook her head, trying and failing to suppress a smile. "You do excel at pissing people off."

Alejandro's grin disappeared as he glanced down to where her hand still lay protectively over the slight swell of her stomach.

Calandra's nose wrinkled. "When will you tell him?"

"I don't know. I doubt he'll be excited by his greatest disappointment siring offspring. But don't worry," he added with a reassuring smile. "The rest of the family will be more supportive. And kind. Especially my mother. She'll be thrilled."

His words sliced through the camaraderie and brought her crashing back to reality. Since the age of twelve, it had been her, Johanna and Aunt Norine. And Aunt Norine had been gone for almost two years now.

Just the thought of Alejandro being involved had been hard to digest. Toss in his mother, two billionaire brothers, a fiancée and a bastard of a father, and she could barely keep her tea down.

But that was for another time. She paused. He'd been the one to initiate their encounters so far. As he'd pointed out, if they were truly going to get to know each other better, they needed to spend time together.

"I have a few details to confirm for the party, but if the storm passes, I thought about going to Calanques National Park this afternoon." She inhaled deeply. "Would you like to join me?"

He blinked. Time passed, each second stretching longer than the last. Another rumble of thunder rolled across the landscape, louder and more aggressive as the amber liquid in her teacup trembled.

"Unfortunately," Alejandro finally said, "I have a virtual meeting with my father most of the day and tomorrow to discuss the construction delays and review finances."

His rejection sliced through her. No animosity in his words, no cruelty on his face. But she had no doubt that, had she not let her fear get the better of her last night, he would have been interested, perhaps even excited, to spend time with her.

"I hope it goes well," she managed to force out.

He stood and bowed his head to her and started to walk off, head held high, his stride steady. Something, though, was amiss. It should frighten her, how easily she was able to pick up on his moods now, discern that something was wrong.

"Alejandro."

He turned and glanced back at her.

"I'm sorry. About last night." She looked down at her hands. "I took out my own insecurities on you."

A shrug. "Happens. I could have handled it better."

She swallowed hard. He was accepting her apology. Time to let it go.

"Thank you. And…" She floundered for a moment, trying to find the right words. "I know how much the renovation of *La Reina* means to you. I thought hiring me was just a way to give me money. Even though I think you're still overpaying me—" his lips quirked "—I know it wasn't just that."

He nodded. "You're welcome."

And then he left. Still the confident walk, back straight, head tall. Yet something dark seemed to cling to his shoulders, slow his stride as he walked away and didn't look back.

Leaving her alone with the encroaching thunder, the dark swirl of the sea and her own storm of emotions waging war inside her chest.

CHAPTER FIFTEEN

ALEJANDRO KNOCKED ON Calandra's door. He'd closed the laptop on his meeting in the library and come straight to the guest suite. Over the last eleven hours, eight of them had been spent poring over records and reports or engaging in heated arguments with his sire.

If he wasn't exhausted, he would question why his first thought had been to come see Calandra. However, since he could barely keep his eyes open, he didn't care to examine his reasoning. He just wanted to see her. Her offer of time together had been an olive branch, one that had surprised him after last night's acrimonious parting. Pride had inspired his refusal. Pain had flared in her eyes, spurring his flight from the patio.

Coward.

This time, he didn't shove the thought aside. He'd labeled his previous departures from uncomfortable situations as spur-of-the-moment, a distaste for conflict or, in the case of his father, survival.

But the more he thought about it, the more he realized those had just been excuses. Excuses for running away.

Just like your father.

The thought angered him. He was nothing like his father.

But aren't you? that nasty little voice whispered. Javier had rarely been a part of family functions, from dinners to vacations. But after Alejandro's discovery, he'd been even more absent.

He hadn't been lying about his meetings with Javier. Yet he'd grabbed onto that excuse with both hands. Had seen the hurt flare in her eyes, felt the vulnerable price she'd paid and the pain of rejection in his soul.

The same rejection he'd experienced when she called last

night a mistake. The same rejection that, no matter how many successes he'd accumulated, his father still heaped on his shoulders with every criticism of Cabrera Shipping, every snide remark about the women he spent time with—as if the bastard had any room to talk.

The truth of what had happened that morning—that instead of savoring the victory of having Calandra finally offer him what he wanted, he'd run away like a damned *pollo*—had clung to him like a shroud. The stronger the rain had pounded against the window of his office, the blacker his mood had grown. To the point that when Javier had asked in that brisk, holier-than-thou tone if Alejandro would prefer to continue their review at a later date, he hadn't hesitated to say yes.

Javier had blinked, eyes so round with surprise he'd reminded Alejandro of an owl.

"What?"

"I said *sí.*"

"But—"

"We both know you'll make the decisions in the end, Javier, especially if you get your way Saturday night. So," he continued, ignoring his father's gaping mouth, "if you don't mind, I have something more important to deal with."

Slamming the computer screen shut on Javier's face had been gratifying and fortified him for the long trek through the villa to the guest quarters.

And now he stood there, waiting to see which Calandra would open the door. The cold, efficient planner? The passionate lover? Or the vulnerable woman who hid so well behind her wall of ice?

He rubbed the bridge of his nose. A couple days ago, everything had seemed so simple. But he'd been so focused on getting her to see him that he hadn't thought about what getting to know her would do to him. To be reminded not just of their mind-numbing, body-tingling sexual heat, but of the rapport they'd unknowingly developed over the years.

Knowing her better, seeing the woman who cared about supporting a small culinary school and who would fight tooth and nail for her baby, and feeling the urge to share more and more of himself, placed him at a crossroads. He was free-falling into an intoxicating, terrifying emotional tangle he'd never experienced before.

The temptation to go to one of Marseille's lavish clubs, imbibe too many cocktails and leave with some beautiful dancer who would make him forget the last twenty-four hours had been strong last night. But when he thought about actually kissing another woman, touching someone else after what he'd shared with Calandra, he couldn't do it.

He didn't want to seduce just for the sake of physical pleasure. Not anymore. He wanted something more. If someone were to ask him what, he wouldn't be able to answer. Not yet.

Calandra was at the crux of all this confusion. Maybe more time would not only get him what he wanted in regard to their child, but some answers for this web of feelings he'd become ensnared in.

A shuffling came from behind the door. A moment later a click sounded, and the door swung open.

"Alejandro?"

He didn't even bother trying to hide his stare. In loose linen pants and a seashell-pink tank top, hair unbound and flowing over her shoulders, she looked stunning. The shirt brought out the faintest rosiness in her cheeks. She wore no makeup, no battle paint slashed across her eyelids or bloodred stain on her lips that made women eye her with envy and men with desire and intimidation.

This was Calandra at her rawest. And he couldn't stop looking.

"Is everything all right?" she asked hesitantly.

"You're wearing color."

She glanced down with a frown. "Yes. My usual pants are a little tight. My sister insisted on helping me pack before I flew out and must have snuck them into my suitcase." She tugged at the shirt hem. "The last time I let her do that."

"You look beautiful." Her eyes narrowed, and she opened her mouth. He held up his hand. "Just take the compliment."

She stared at him for a moment, then inclined her head toward him. "Thank you."

He bit back a grin.

"Would you like to take a walk with me?"

She eyed his outstretched hand with uncertainty. "A walk?"

"Yes. You move one foot in front of the other and—"

"Thank you." She shook her head. "You'll fit right in with a child since you have the humor of one."

His heart beat a little faster. After last night, he'd been certain that their heated encounter on the yacht had done anything but convince her he was father material. He'd never been good at waiting, had wanted to press her for an answer, but he didn't. This was by far the most important thing he had ever wanted. It was worth a little patience.

The most important thing?

He pondered that for a moment, held the thought in his hand and weighed being a father against maintaining control over Cabrera Shipping.

Yes.

"Where are we walking to?"

"Just along the beach. The storm has passed and the sun's setting."

Calandra arched a brow. "I thought you were busy with your father?"

"I was. But an entire day with him is more than enough."

Finally, she reached out and took his hand. His fingers closed around hers for the second time in less than twenty-four hours as possession reared its head.

"Shall we?"

He managed to escort her out onto the back patio without dropping a kiss on her bare shoulder. Impressive, given that last night he'd locked himself in his suite with an erection so hard even stroking himself hadn't helped. It had taken a very, very cold shower to cool his ardor.

And even that hadn't stopped him from waking up with his hardness throbbing, muscles taut with desire.

If all he could do right now was hold her hand, then he would do it.

They walked along the beach, the sand still warm from the sun.

"If you're free tomorrow, I've canceled my meeting with him."

Her hand tightened in his. A quick glance at her face revealed nothing.

Then, finally, "I can make some time. Where are we going?"

"Somewhere."

"Somewhere like…?"

"Somewhere like it's a secret."

Her customary roll of the eyes, but this time it was coupled with a small twitch of her lips.

Companionable silence descended, backlit by the ocean waves crashing onto the beach and the damp sand clinging to their bare feet. They circled a bleached hunk of driftwood and headed back toward the house.

"I met your father a couple years ago. I don't recall him coming across as controlling or patronizing."

Alejandro's laughter sounded just like his *padre*'s—sharp and harsh.

"No, he doesn't. He presents one face to the 'genteel

world' and another to those he thinks are beneath him. I fall into the latter category."

"What makes you say that?"

Did she see the sudden rise in his chest as he breathed in deeply, trying to control the anger that was never far out of reach when he thought about Javier?

"He's been breathing down my neck since I took over Cabrera Shipping. Every time I've brought up *La Reina*, he points out every possible scenario where the whole plan falls apart. Never anything that could go right."

Calandra frowned. "Perhaps he's worried about you."

This time his laughter rang out down the beach, startling a couple of seagulls who squawked in indignation and took flight.

"My father doesn't get worried about me. He gets worried about three things—my mother, business and if I'm going to do something to embarrass him."

Her frown deepened. "Have you embarrassed him often?"

"Oh, all the time," he responded cheerfully. "It became a bit of a game in my Eton days. How far could I push him until he snapped."

"Oh."

The way she said it made it sound as if she'd just had a revelation.

"Oh?"

"Sometimes I see a different side of you. This morning when you stood up to your father. Yesterday with Suzie. That night in New York…"

"That night in New York?" His casual tone belied his erection hardening once more, so heavy the cloth of his jeans rubbed against his hot skin. "Hmm…not coming to mind. Perhaps you can describe it for me. In lurid detail, please. My mind's a bit fuzzy."

"If I did describe it, I imagine you wouldn't be able to finish our walk," she said dryly.

"Touché. By the way…" He leaned in, savored the flare of heat in her gaze. "If we ever make love again, it'll be because you initiated."

Her eyes narrowed. "I did last night."

The pert response, delivered with such class, made him grin.

"I want you." He leaned in closer still. There would be no doubt in her mind that he wanted her. "But I'm not going to jeopardize my future with our child by overstepping."

As soon as she made that first move, he would take up the reins and show her everything one night of sex and a hot session of foreplay hadn't afforded them.

"Now that that's established, back to your fascinating psychological profile of my father."

She glanced at him from beneath her lashes. Would she choose now to challenge him?

"I just wonder if, deep down, your father responds like that because he's worried about you. Worried you'll get caught by some gold digger."

Nothing like talking about his father to cool his libido. "Not his style." The cavalier response covered a bone-deep hurt, that of a young boy whose father had no time for him as he traveled the world.

They reached the stone path leading back up to the villa. Electric lanterns lit the walk, casting a romantic glow over the landscape.

"I pulled out the file I've been keeping on *La Reina*, some of the old ships that inspired her renovation." He nodded toward the floor-to-ceiling windows of his office, glinting in the light from the setting sun. "I can show them to you."

"I'd like that. I got a good impression when I toured, but more information is always better."

Pride straightened his shoulders. He'd shown the plans to plenty of people, some who had appreciated, some who had seen dollar signs and some who had seen nothing but an old ship. Sharing the plans with someone who would not only see the business possibilities but the motivation, the inspiration, made him feel as excited as a child showing off their first school drawing.

They walked across the lawn and up the stairs to the glass doors that led into his office. Calandra stopped in the doorway as he flicked on the lights.

"What?"

She surveyed the room for a moment, narrowed eyes darting back and forth. "Just looking."

He turned and looked over the cathedral-size room, trying to see it through her eyes. Sleek gold-and-white office furniture sat atop a shiny, black marble floor. A modern white desk was positioned in one corner, the black executive chair facing the bank of windows that looked out over the backyard.

The first time his father had set foot in this office, it had done exactly what it was supposed to do—made him grimace and shift uncomfortably in the chair placed in the middle of the room, directly across from Alejandro's desk. A trick he'd learned from Adrian's office in Granada.

But now, as Calandra walked through, her eagle eyes missing nothing, something shifted. Something uncomfortable. She saw the office for what it was. Something he'd picked because it was what people expected, not because it was what he wanted.

Her eyes landed on the one untidy space in the room—the mound of paperwork spread across the desk.

"What's all this?"

"Research. If the worst should happen, at least I'll go down fighting. Use the money I have saved up to make a go of *La Reina* on my own."

Her gray eyes fixed on him.

"I stand by what I said."

He arched a brow. "Which part?"

She gestured to the stack of papers. "I knew you were in charge of Cabrera Shipping. But I didn't realize you took such an active interest in the company."

"Thought I just drank and smoked cigars and laid about with models while much lesser paid men took care of the real work?"

Her blush reappeared, but she didn't blink. "Yes."

"I do. Did," he amended. "Not as much the past year."

"Why?"

"Cabrera Shipping took up more of my time." He glanced down at the two-dimensional rendering of *La Reina*'s top deck, his fingers tracing the lines with pride. "The company has always been the one thing I felt tied to. But it was still given to me by my father. I didn't earn it." Bitterness warred with the discomfort of knowing his increasingly outrageous antics in college had not given Javier any incentive to bestow one of his more lucrative holdings upon his middle son. "At the time I inherited it, I hadn't done much with my life. The company was not in good shape. My father probably thought it was a safe bet to give me because they were already planning for it to die."

"And then you did the impossible."

It was ridiculous how much warmth her words triggered.

"I did. Ruined my father's expectations again," he added with a cheerful note that belied the pain of rejection that still stung so many years later, "just in a different way. But *La Reina* is the first thing that's truly mine. Well, that and…" He nodded toward her stomach. "Two things now. So long as I didn't make too big of a mistake last night."

She flinched, and he inwardly cursed.

"I wasn't trying to make you feel bad, Calandra, just—"

She held up a hand. "Don't. I said it this morning, but

I'll say it again. I'm so very sorry, Alejandro, for the way I treated you last night. I was embarrassed by my own behavior and I took it out on you."

He risked a step in her direction. "Why?"

"Because I've never acted like that. And I..." Her voice trailed off, grew quiet. "I don't want to make the same mistakes."

"The same mistakes as your mother?"

She moved over to a window and looked out over the ocean, the waves capped with the oranges and reds of the setting sun, her back to him. Her hair tumbled uncharacteristically down her back, but her neck was straight as a board, shoulders thrust back proudly.

But now he knew to look for the other signs. The tension tightening her muscles, arms wrapped around her waist. Funny how he'd always thought of those gestures as cold, a lack of interest in people or relationships. He knew better now, the depth of emotion she was capable of, the relationships she could build with people like Suzie in a matter of hours.

"My father..." She paused and inhaled deeply. "My father was very wealthy. Not quite Cabrera level of wealth, but wealthy enough that we had a house on Lake Geneva."

Alejandro's eyebrows shot up. "Oh?"

Her gaze stayed trained on the landscape outside, but he noted the slight tightening of her arms, as if she were hugging herself tighter. An ache built in his chest and he almost stepped forward, to pull her back against his chest and cradle her, to make her feel safe as she finally opened up.

That last thought stopped him. Would she lean into his embrace? Or would his touch snap her out of her confession and drive her away? It wasn't worth the risk to find out. So he fisted his hands at his sides and listened.

"The wealth didn't last. After he died and Aunt Norine came to collect Johanna and me, we found out that he'd maxed out his credit, held two mortgages on the house and hadn't paid on loans for his car in months. He used money to control, to manipulate."

A piece of the puzzle slid into place. Her aversion to money, her insistence on paying for everything. No wonder she had reacted to the teddy bear with such disdain. He'd taken her lack of enjoyment personally, a rejection of him and his attempt to start being a part of their child's life. And she hadn't wanted to be manipulated by lavish gifts.

"He sounds like an ass."

His bald comment startled a small laugh from her. She glanced over her shoulder, the sunlight playing with her dark hair and creating beautiful streaks of orangish gold that brought out the rosiness in her cheeks. She looked as she had last night when she'd smiled up at Suzie—soft. Warm. Alive.

How had he ever thought her cold?

"My early years with him were pleasant." She started to circle around the room, eyes roving over everything but him. "Picnics on the lakeshore. Train rides around Europe. Summers at beach resorts. He and my mother were happy." She stopped by a globe in the corner, the map covered with little red *C*s that marked the location of a Cabrera business, and ran a finger over the blue of an ocean. "Until they weren't. Until my mother realized she, and I, were nothing more than passing fancies. The more she held on, the more my father tried to escape through spending sprees and other women." She spun the globe, eyes focused on the earth as it revolved. "He loved new things, the more expensive the better. So he tried to appease her with things he thought would make her happy. Jewelry. Clothes. A new car. And all she wanted was his love."

Beneath her detached recitation of her parents' failed marriage, he caught something else.

"What did you want, Calandra?"

Silence descended, save for the soft whish of the globe as it spun.

And then, so softly he almost didn't hear it: "The same thing."

He moved to her then, reached out and took her limp hand in his. When she didn't look, didn't respond to his touch, he gave in to a desire he'd never experienced before and laid his fingers gently on her cheek, guiding her face up until her eyes met his.

Eyes that had turned steely once more. Except this time he wasn't going to back away. Not when he knew so much more about her, about why one minute she was passion incarnate and the next disappeared behind her icy exterior. He'd seen in it in her eyes last night, felt it in her lips beneath his, heard it the tiny sigh that had set his body aflame with desire.

She wanted him. She wanted him just as badly as he wanted her.

"How is wanting lovemaking the same mistake as your mother?"

"She died," Calandra said flatly. "I loved her. But by the end she was weak. She left two daughters alone with a father who treated us more like dolls to be dressed up in couture as a sign of his prominence instead of his children." Her free hand drifted to her stomach, fingers splaying across her belly. "I will never let my child experience the pain of being abandoned."

"And you think I would abandon it?"

Her face twisted into a frown of confusion. "I did… I don't know…" A heavy sigh escaped her lips. "I don't know what to think anymore, Alejandro. You tie me up in knots and I can't think straight."

Focus. Focus on the fact that she wasn't running away, that she wasn't pushing him out, and not on how she had, at least at one point, thought he would abandon their child once he got bored. That someone else thought so little of him.

Although, his mind argued, he had brought it on himself. Until recently, Calandra had seen mainly what he'd allowed the world to see. A carousing billionaire without a care in the world. Few saw the serious side, the dedicated CEO, the hard worker. Easier, and more fun, to live up to the expectation of not doing much except partying his life away.

Safer, too, if he was being completely honest with himself. Safer than trying and risking failure. Hurt. Rejection.

"Let's take a break from the serious talk." For her sake, he assured himself. Not because he was trying to avoid confronting unpleasant truths of his own. "But know this, Calandra—I will never abandon our child."

No scoffing. No roll of the eyes. Just the slightest nod that filled him with relief and a touch of panic. What if he couldn't fulfill that promise? What if he did fail and hurt not just his child, but Calandra, too?

Calandra yawned, and he jumped onto the reprieve she offered. "I'll escort you back to your room so you can get some sleep. We have a busy day tomorrow."

"Where are we going, anyway?" she asked as he tugged her toward the door.

"It's a surprise." One that, despite his inner turmoil, he was very grateful he'd planned out given her revelations tonight. "Trust me."

CHAPTER SIXTEEN

CALANDRA KEPT HER eyes focused on the passing scenery and tried to keep her thoughts, and her gaze, off Alejandro as he guided the car through the French countryside. She'd awoken that morning feeling surprisingly refreshed after her confession and, after seeing she had a text from him asking how she was feeling, giddy. *Giddy.* A giddiness she couldn't shake no matter how sternly she talked to her reflection in the mirror as she'd gotten ready.

He'd been waiting outside the villa, looking like he'd walked straight out of a fashion ad in black jeans and a dark blue polo shirt fitted perfectly to his broad chest and muscular arms. The car ride had been surprisingly relaxing as they talked about everything from their past travels to his favorite movies and her favorite books.

Alejandro gestured to the north. A village perched on a hilltop, the collection of white stone buildings arranged in a charming cluster on the mountainside.

"The village of Gordes."

"It's lovely."

"Glad you like it."

"Did you think I wouldn't?"

"Most women I've known wouldn't enjoy this. They would want something fancy."

"Sounds like most women you know are stuck-up."

"Pretty much." That thousand-watt plastic smile flashed, not the genuine grin or teasing twist of his lips. "They date me because they want the fantasy, not the reality."

Sadness crept over her.

"Is that what you think, Alejandro? That if they knew the real you they wouldn't want you?"

The smile faltered, a slip in his carefree mask that spoke volumes.

He didn't answer. Awkwardness filled the space between them until all she wanted to do was escape the car and disappear down one of the little cobblestone streets she spied. They continued on past Gordes as the sun rose in the sky. Surely they were close to wherever Alejandro was taking them. She needed to get out, stretch her legs and have some time to think.

Why was Alejandro hiding behind this pretense of being spoiled? In the years she'd known him, she would have described him as one of the most confident, self-assured men she knew. Yet she'd seen the cracks in his persona this week, as well as views of a man who intrigued her, who made her long for more than just a hot tryst in a hotel room.

Or on a yacht, her mind taunted.

She thrust that thought away and reflected on what she'd seen of Alejandro this week. The man she'd seen onboard *La Reina* with a deep passion for his work. The man who stood up to his father on her behalf even after she'd hurt him. The man who watched classic movies with his mother and wanted to go into business with his brothers because he respected their work. In the moments he'd tried to impress her with his wealth, the similarities with her father and her genuine disinterest in having anything in common with his previous paramours had helped her stay aloof.

It was the moments when he hadn't tried that had broken through her resolve to keep him at arm's length. When she'd seen the man he was beneath the money and glamour.

The hill on the right sloped down, and the sight before her drew her out of her reverie. She gasped.

"Oh!"

She'd heard of the legendary lavender fields of Provence. But she wasn't prepared for the stunning beauty of it in person. A stone church sat at the base of tree-covered hills, surrounded by thick bushes nearly bursting with violet-colored flowers lined up, one after another.

"Sénanque Abbey," Alejandro said. "Built in 1148."

They drove by the front two lavender fields, the first a large open area with at least a dozen rows of thick, bushy lavender plants. Across a small bridge and behind a line of trees lay another field, smaller but still boasting the same vibrant purple flowers.

"This is incredible," she breathed.

"One of my mother's favorite sites."

"Thank you, Alejandro. For sharing this with me." She tucked a wisp of hair behind her ear. "I never would have gone to a place like this on my own."

He pulled his sunglasses off and gave her one of those genuine smiles that made her heart flip in her chest.

"Calandra Smythe, are you thanking your arch nemesis?"

His joking tone teased a reluctant smile from her. "I wouldn't describe you as a nemesis. Just a thorn in my side."

"A thorn? How flattering. I would have hoped I might compare to something a bit larger."

"No comment."

He chuckled. "You're certainly good for bringing a man down a peg or two."

"So I've been told." She grabbed her purse off the floor, surprisingly eager to see the abbey and the lavender fields up close.

They walked up the drive, the walls of the abbey growing larger as they neared. She found herself entranced by the ancient stone, the elegantly carved windows and the tower that stood proudly against the backdrop of the tree-covered hills. The soothing scent of the lavender surrounded them, floral and sweet.

"It doesn't seem real," Calandra finally said. "Like a

fairy tale." She glanced back at the almost empty parking lot. "I guess not many people know of it."

"They do. Peak tourist season for Provence occurs in July." He shot her a smug smile. "Hence why lavender field excursions for *La Reina*'s guests will occur in late June. Two weeks of exclusive access to some of the most beautiful fields in France, minus the elbowing and clamoring for space among the crowds of tourists."

"Smart." Her eyes softened as she gazed at the abbey. "It's the kind of place you're so grateful to discover, but you don't want too many others to know."

When he slipped his arms around her waist and pulled her back against his muscular chest, she gave in to temptation and leaned against him.

"I'd like to share something with you."

The seriousness in his tone made her freeze. For a moment she said nothing, her breath caught in her chest. If she said no, she'd be doing what she'd been doing from the beginning—staying safe inside her little fortress of solitude while taking away his chances of proving himself.

If she said yes, the door she'd slowly been opening all week as she'd spent time with him, confided in him, would be flung wide-open. The potential for so much joy. So much heartbreak.

She breathed in deeply and leaned deeper into his embrace.

A heartbeat passed. Then his arms tightened around her and he started to speak.

"I had a good childhood. My mother was incredible, always there for Antonio and me."

"Not Adrian?"

"They didn't have the best relationship for a long time. But it's getting better." He huffed out a breath. "I can't say the same for my father and me. It's always been terrible. My first memory of him is showing him a drawing I'd done when I was about four. He'd just gotten back from one of his trips. He didn't even look, just ruffled my hair as he walked into his study and shut the door."

Her heart ached for the little boy who'd just wanted his father's love. Such a simple thing, and yet one that, at least in her experience, was too much to ask.

"I imagine it wasn't the first time he ignored me, or the second or the third, because I remember grabbing a lamp off the table. It broke all over the floor. My father came out, berated me, put me in time-out. I was in trouble, but I had something I hadn't had before—his attention."

A small group wandered past, chattering in English and snapping photos of everything in sight. Alejandro released her and drew her away, his body angled protectively between her and the tourists as he kept one arm wrapped firmly around her waist. As they walked toward a smaller lavender field, he continued.

"I only misbehaved when he was around. It became a game. What could I do when he was home to get his attention, to make him react. The more I did, the angrier he got. I never did it around my mother, and I don't think he ever told her. We kept at it, me acting out and him losing his temper. Adrian didn't attend Eton until he was fifteen, but Padre sent me there when I was thirteen. He told me point-blank the less he saw of me, the better."

They stopped next to a tree with long, crooked branches and thick leaves that provided welcome shade from the growing heat of the afternoon sun. Alejandro's arm dropped from her waist and he stepped forward, hands tucked in his pockets as he stared at the green hills beyond the abbey.

"One day I came back early for a holiday. My father was with a woman in the library." Anger edged into his voice. "I knew the moment I saw them. I knew that my father had betrayed my mother. When he saw me in the doorway, he became enraged. I accused him of cheating on her. He said if I ever told my mother, he would deny everything, insist that I was lying and acting out the way I always had. I had no intention of telling her—she loves him." The smile that crossed his face was almost cruel in its harshness. "So I decided to punish him instead. Breaking lamps was nothing compared to what I would do the rest of his life."

The parallel between his parents and hers, between how he'd threatened his father and her last conversation with hers, made the ache in her chest intensify. She knew exactly what that moment felt like, when one discovered that a parent had committed such a grievous sin against the other.

"I mentioned my father presents a priggish front. He grew up from nothing, so he's obsessed with the image he maintains. Every article that's published, every photo that's snapped, is just another knife in his chest."

It was almost surreal, this glimpse into what could have been her life had Father not died a week after Mom's funeral. Would she have pursued his punishment so zealously? Crafted her entire life around reminding him of his transgressions every chance she got? While she'd never wished him dead, she found herself grateful for the silver lining his death had granted her.

"What does your mother think?"

"Not a fan of the parties." A fond smile temporarily chased away the gloom that had settled over his handsome features. "We were so close, though, that when I started to make the papers, she asked if I was happy. Probably knew I wasn't, but knew me well enough not to push. I wasn't doing anything illegal. I overheard her tell my father once she thought I needed to find myself." His bark of laughter startled a bird out of the tree. It tweeted its dismay, spread its wings and soared up into the summer sky.

"She sounds like a good mom."

"She was. Summers when I was off from school, we watched *The Black Pirate* with Douglas Fairbanks and

The Court Jester with Danny Kaye. My father discouraged rough play. My mother and Diego, our butler, strung up a rope in the backyard so Antonio and I could pretend we were pirates and swing off one of the trees into the pool."

"That sounds wonderful," Calandra said with a touch of longing.

"It was." He scrubbed a hand over his face. "It should have been enough. But for whatever reason, I wasn't able to let go of this fixation with my father. By the time I graduated from Eton, we barely spoke. When I graduated from Oxford, Padre put me in charge of the weakest of all his holdings—Cabrera Shipping. Five ships, three of them rusty and behind on maintenance. Crews full of dissatisfied men working long hours for horrid pay. He'd given Adrian Cabrera Wines. Antonio was a year behind me at Oxford and had already interned for some luxury resort, so he was in line to head the hospitality management side of Cabrera holdings. Javier had to give me something to save face with the outside world."

"But you turned Cabrera Shipping into a success."

"I pointed out the same thing to Javier about a year ago. He said he'd given me everything to make Cabrera a success and that anyone could have made it profitable." He laughed, the sound hollow. "It shouldn't have made an impression, but it did." He let out a long, slow breath. "I spent the majority of my life acting out, breaking the rules, for my father. First to get his attention. Then to punish him. Every time I ended up in the papers, every time my picture was splashed across some magazine, I got a phone call or a text from him. It embarrassed him. Not being embarrassed mattered more to him than being a part of our family. So I did it more."

Sunlight kissed his cheekbones, highlighting his chiseled features, the strength in his jaw. A man so handsome and yet hurting so deeply it twisted her heart. How many times had she dismissed him as her boss's spoiled little brother? She'd been clinging to her own pain and prejudice so tightly she hadn't been able to look past the surface.

"And here we are." Alejandro spread his hands. "The spoiled, billionaire playboy who wanted to get his father's attention through sex, parties and alcohol. Except the last year I've realized that my hard-earned reputation that was designed to punish my father instead kept me from pursuing what I really wanted. I enjoyed my work for Cabrera. I worked hard to make it a success. But again, to prove my father wrong. So I went after what I wanted."

His eyes fell to her, then drifted down to her stomach.

"Once I set my mind to something, I'm invested." He took a step closer, then another. Her heart jumped into her throat at the raw emotion in his eyes. Sadness, anger and need. "I want to be the father mine never was. That includes being there for our child."

His words settled deep into her bones. In that moment, she knew he meant every word. If she could let herself trust him, be just as vulnerable with him as he'd been with her, their child could grow up with two parents who adored it.

Was it too selfish to hope that, perhaps, there was a possibility for them, too?

CHAPTER SEVENTEEN

A RUMBLING CUT through her thoughts. She stepped out from under the tree branches and looked up as stone-colored clouds raced over the hilltop to the west. A brisk wind barreled down the hillside and whipped the lavender bushes into a frenzy.

Alejandro grabbed her hand.

"Time to go."

They hurried to the car, the first cool drops of rain hitting her skin as he opened the door for her. He ran around the front of the car and got in just as the clouds released a torrent of rain so thick they could barely see ten feet in front of them. She pulled out her phone and checked the weather forecast.

"Rain for hours. And possible hail."

"There's a bed-and-breakfast nearby we can take shelter at."

Alejandro's words cut through the thundering of the rain as he pulled out of the parking lot. Her hands tightened on the seat of the car, grasping at anything that would anchor her even as her breathing quickened.

"A bed-and-breakfast?" she repeated in as casual a voice as she could muster. "Sure."

They stayed silent as Alejandro drove at a crawl through the summer squall. It gave her time to think. Too much time. Alejandro had just opened up and shared himself with her. Not the hints and bites of information he'd been giving her throughout the week, but a baring of his soul.

She no longer wondered if she was in love with him. She knew. Now she just needed to know what to do next.

Five minutes and one winding road up a hillside later and they pulled under the awning of L'Auberge de la Lavande.

They walked through the double glass doors into the lobby. Calandra kept her mouth from dropping open. When she heard the words *bed-and-breakfast* or *inn*, as the sign on the outside had proclaimed, she thought of quilt-covered beds, pancakes and a long porch with rocking chairs.

The Lavender Inn catered to an entirely different clientele. The lobby boasted dark wooden floors polished to a shine beneath the lamps dripping with crystals that had been artfully scattered among white and lavender-colored furniture. Elegant armchairs, chaise lounges and a few sofas offered rest and places to visit. The walls were covered in professional photographs of the lavender fields, the abbey and the village of Gordes. One side of the lobby was glass that she guessed, on a sunny day, provided incredible views of the valley beneath the inn.

Even the air carried the faint, floral scent.

A sweet-faced girl in a violet suit jacket and starched white shirt smiled at them.

"Bonjour."

"Bonjour," Alejandro replied. "Do you have any rooms available?"

The girl smiled, her cheeks dimpling. "You're in luck! We were all booked, but we just had a cancellation for our honeymoon suite."

"Honeymoon suite?" Calandra repeated.

The girl nodded enthusiastically. "Top floor. Once the rain passes, you'll have the best view of the lavender field from a private balcony."

"I don't think—"

"Perfect," Alejandro interrupted as he passed the clerk a credit card. "Monsieur and Madame Cabrera, please."

His casual use of such a title made her want to laugh and cry at the same time. Laugh, because a week ago she would have shuddered at the thought of Alejandro being involved in her child's life, much less being tied to him herself.

Cry, because in the last couple of days, she'd thought more and more of what it would be like to have Alejandro not just in their child's life but in *her* life.

After checking in, Alejandro guided her to the elevator. The doors swooshed open, and she paused. The last time they'd gotten into an elevator, they hadn't been able to keep their hands off each other.

"I promise not to kiss you this time."

"But what if I want you to?"

The words slipped out before she could stop them. She sneaked a glance at Alejandro. He stood next to her, his body tight, eyes straight forward. Her throat constricted. Had she waited too long?

"Are you sure?"

Those three words, the barely constrained passion in his dark, sensual voice, broke down the last remaining threads of her defenses. Confidence emboldened her to walk into the elevator, turn and meet his eyes, allowing him to see the naked desire in her own gaze.

"You coming?"

Her breath hitched as he stalked toward her, eyes on fire as his presence filled the elevator. The door slid shut.

He started to reach for her. But she didn't want to leave any doubt in his mind that she was initiating, that she wanted him. She moved forward, pushed him against the wall of the elevator, slid her arms around his neck and kissed him.

Just like that, she was tumbling, falling deeper into the complicated mess of emotions she felt toward this man. Yet instead of being afraid, she threw caution to the wind as her fingers tangled in his hair and she wantonly pressed her body against his.

What have I done?

One last rational thought pounded through her head before Alejandro groaned and leaned in. His tongue swept the seam of her lips. She opened her mouth, moaned when he tasted her.

Without stopping their frantic kissing, Alejandro grabbed her hips, turned and pressed her against the wall. The firmness of his erection pressed against her thighs. She wriggled against him, sliding her core up and down his length with wanton abandon.

"Stop!"

The whispered word penetrated the haze of desire. She reared back, humiliation creeping in. She was very inexperienced, but she'd thought, based on their last time, that she'd at least pleased him.

Alejandro grabbed her face between his hands and rested his forehead against hers, his breathing labored.

"If you keep doing that, I'm not going to last."

The thrill of knowing she had that kind of effect on him emboldened her. She twisted, wrapped her legs around his waist and brought her body flush against his. She brazenly rubbed herself against his length, moaning as he hardened even more beneath her.

"Then I guess you better find a way to distract me."

Before he could respond, the elevator dinged and the doors whooshed open. She got a brief impression of a four-poster bed with gauzy curtains and a vine-covered balcony before he whisked her inside.

Where this fire, this passion came from, she couldn't say. But she loved it, this side of her that she'd only let out once to play. Loved seeing his eyes darken, feeling his shoulders tighten beneath her fingers.

He took up her challenge. And devoured her.

Before she could do anything else, he hooked his fingers in the straps of her dress and pulled them down, baring her breasts to his hungry gaze. Then he wrapped his strong arms around her body and pulled her against him.

She cried out, the sensation of her bare nipples rubbing against his chest making her throb with need.

"Alejandro, please..."

He kissed her once more, keeping her arms pinned to her sides. His lips trailed over her jaw, up to her ear, where he placed the most delicate of kisses before sucking the lobe into his hot mouth and nibbling. She nearly came apart then and there.

But he was just getting started. As she moaned and begged and writhed, he pulled her onto his lap and continued his sensual onslaught, dragging his mouth down her neck with excruciating slowness, over the pulse beating wildly in her throat. Fire burned at every spot his lips touched, sparks skipping over her skin, making her feel feverish with need.

And then he sucked a nipple into his mouth. She arched against him, cried out his name. He released one of her arms to cup her other breast in his hand, his fingers cupping her flesh and stroking it with long, skillful caresses. He continued to suck and nip and nibble and kiss until she was almost sobbing.

Then he moved to the other, repeating the same sensuous seduction as she rubbed herself against him, that fire building and building until she couldn't stand it anymore and came apart. She fell against him, shuddering, her free hand tangled in his hair.

He softened his caresses, gently kissing the globes of her breasts as she drifted back down from the incredible heights he'd sent her to.

"Alejandro... I..."

He kissed her on the lips, silencing whatever she'd been about to say. Then he moved her off his lap onto the bed and stood. She huffed in protest.

Until he grabbed the dress gathered about her waist,

tugged it down along with her underwear and tossed it to the side.

Leaving her completely naked.

She started to cover herself, to cross her legs and cover her breasts with her arms. He caught one of her hands in his, brought it to his lips and kissed her fingers.

"Do you trust me?"

Trust. It always came back to trust between the two of them. Could he trust her to give him a fair chance at being a parent? Could she trust him to not repeat the sins of her father and hurt her, hurt their child?

Yes. Yes, she could. This man trusted her. Not just with her job, but with his secrets, his past, his hopes and dreams. He wanted to be a good father, a partner, and she loved him for it.

Slowly, she nodded.

He knelt between her legs. He stroked the folds of her most intimate skin with one finger, sliding up and down with a light touch that drove her crazy.

"Alejandro...please..."

Her hips bucked as his finger touched her *there*. Then he pulled back, and she whimpered. A whimper followed by a cry as he leaned down and replaced his finger with his mouth. His tongue moved over, dancing over her skin as heat pulsed through her, carrying her higher as she tangled her fingers in his hair and begged for release.

He slid a finger inside her, her heat clenching down around him. He sucked her into his mouth, and she came apart again. Her entire body shattered, sensation rippling over her skin as she closed her eyes against the pinwheels of light dancing in her vision.

Her body went limp, the coolness of the sheets a pleasing contrast against her heated body. Her heart pounded against her ribs. Slowly, with deep, cleansing breaths, her lust receded.

"Calandra…"

She opened her eyes to see him braced above her, that devilish smirk lurking on his lips.

"See what happens when you trust me?"

If he hadn't just given her such pleasure, she'd be tempted to do something utterly childish, like pinch him. Instead, she sat up, reached forward and laid her hand on the growing bulge in his pants, savoring the darkening of his eyes as he let out a hiss. "What are you doing?"

"Do you trust me?"

He groaned as she tightened her grasp on him.

"Guess I'll have to."

She unzipped his pants, her fingers curling around his thick length. He sucked in a breath. His eyes blazed as he watched her hand slide up and down, trailing over every inch of him.

And then she leaned down to suck him into her mouth. He groaned, his fingers tangling in her hair. She loved the taste of him, the musky, masculine scent. It made her feel wild, passionate, *free*.

"Calandra…"

He stood and removed his clothes. Then he sat next to her on the bed, picked her up and tugged her onto his lap. He paused, the tip of his sex resting against her core.

"Calandra…" She started to ease down, but he stopped her. "You need to know—"

"No conversation," she whispered as she tried to sink down. She needed him inside her, needed to feel him.

"London."

The word stopped her cold. She stared down at him, hurt and jealousy splashing cold water on her lust.

"What about London?"

His fingers tightened on her thighs. "Nothing happened. It's only been you. Ever since New York. No one but you."

Her heart burst. She slid down his length, then leaned

forward, pressed her naked skin against his and kissed him with all the love and desire she could pour into a single act. He kissed her back, fingers tangling in her hair as he marked her as his.

Then she sat up and moved, slowly at first, relearning his body, how he felt inside her. His hands stayed on her hips, his eyes fixed on hers as she rode him.

She burst once more, a kaleidoscope of colors obscuring her vision as she arched back and cried out his name. He jerked against her, returned her call with one of his own as he groaned her name, then shuddered. She collapsed against him, keeping at bay all the wild, rational thoughts trying to maneuver their way in.

For now, just for a little while, she wanted to savor this moment when she'd thrown off the shackles of her past and embraced the present.

And the man who, no matter how hard she had tried, was now firmly lodged deep inside her heart.

CHAPTER EIGHTEEN

A LIGHT AWAKENED ALEJANDRO. He opened his eyes to see the trumpet flowers on the balcony glowing as the setting sun lit them from behind. A quick glance confirmed the bed was empty. Concerned, he threw back the covers, tugged on his discarded pants and padded over to the glass doors, his heartbeat slowing as he spied Calandra on the cream-colored divan on the balcony.

Long legs, bare and sleek. That incredible body wrapped in a lavender bathrobe, the top parted just enough to hint at her stunning breasts. Her face, smooth and serene, eyelashes dark against her skin, eyes closed.

Sexy, yes. Sensual. Beautiful. But it wasn't just her beauty that drew him in. It was her strength, the gentle nature she hid from all but the privileged few who got to see her commitment and loyalty.

When they'd gazed at the abbey, standing almost in the exact spot he remembered first viewing those ancient walls with his mother, a sense of rightness had settled over him. Just as Calandra had envisioned taking their child to the top of the Eiffel Tower, he saw himself standing with his son or daughter in the midst of the lavender, their tiny hand engulfed in his grasp.

That vision had included Calandra by his side. Where she was meant to be.

So he'd done what he'd been pushing her to do all week—he'd opened up. Told her everything. Either she could accept him, all of him, or she couldn't.

Yes, she'd initiated sex. She'd responded with even more wild abandon, more passion than he had ever dreamed of.

But for the first time, sex wasn't enough. He needed her to trust him, to believe him capable of managing whatever life they were going to forge together as much as she believed in his ability to make *La Reina* a success.

He distracted himself from his tumultuous thoughts by tugging his phone out of his pocket and checking his email. An update that one of the new ships was on track to be completed next month, pending a final inspection. Another about how the news of the impending new ship had spread and seventy-two percent of their cargo space had been booked in the past twenty-four hours alone, with more calls coming in.

All excellent news. More positives he could bring to the meeting and the vote on Saturday. Already he'd received emails congratulating him from three of the seven board members. Just one more on his side and he'd be clear.

So why could he not focus? Why, when everything he wanted was within reach, was he so distracted?

Distracted by the woman out on the balcony who had worked her way into his heart long ago and he was only just now realizing it? He'd been falling for her for years. It had taken a night of incredible, mind-blowing, soul-searing sex and an unexpected child to make him realize that how he felt about her went far deeper than casual attraction.

Yet still she held back.

Calandra opened her eyes, not seeing him in the shadows beyond the door. She stood and slowly moved to the edge of the balcony, her back to him. Drawn like a moth to a flame, he stood and walked out onto the balcony, his eyes fixed on her. Her shoulders tensed with every step he took.

She didn't look back at him, just kept her eyes trained on the lavender fields laid out below them. The setting sun bathed the fields in a golden light that made the flowers glow like violet fire.

One of the most romantic places he'd ever been. His hand started to come up, to slide around Calandra's waist and pull her against him, savor the warmth of her body. A natural reaction to being in such a relaxed setting with an attractive woman by his side.

The urge to press a kiss to her hair, to slide his hand around and let it rest over the gentle swell of her stomach, was unnatural.

Without Alejandro Cabrera, international playboy extraordinaire, he didn't know who to be. But every time he thought about Calandra, not as an employee or business partner, but as a woman, as the mother of his child, he saw whom he wanted to become.

Calandra closed her eyes and leaned back into Alejandro's embrace. She forced herself to breathe as she felt the warmth of his body kiss her skin.

"I remember as a child I was afraid of heights." She let her hands settle over his and opened her eyes, savoring the incredible landscape before her. "I'm so glad I overcame that."

"I won't let you fall."

Too late. I've already fallen.

His words made her want to melt. For years, she'd been the one to keep Johanna safe. Aunt Norine had been a wonderful guardian, but her age, coupled with her health, had made Calandra the one who ensured Johanna got off to school in the morning, who helped with cleaning and other chores around the house. She'd been in charge ever since she was seven and Mother had stopped getting out of bed. It had gotten lonely, leading all the time. But she'd gotten used to it.

Until now. Until now when this man cradled her in his arms like she was the most delicate of treasures. When the slightest touch seared her skin.

When he'd opened his heart to her.

"I told you that my father was larger than life. He also

had a proclivity for living to the fullest. At least that's how he'd termed it."

Words she'd never thought she'd express bubbled up inside her, threatened to suffocate her as they piled up in her throat. She'd kept everything inside for so long. People had labeled her stuck-up and bitchy when she kept her distance. Gradually, she came to think of herself as such. Cold, calculating, unsympathetic. Once in a while she experienced a flash of emotion. But she kept to herself because she didn't know how to handle them, how to be anything but detached. Detached was safe. Detached was bulletproof.

Detached was lonely. And the more time she spent around Alejandro, the more she suspected she had done herself a great disservice living so distantly from other human beings.

As if he sensed the dark place she'd slipped into, he pressed a kiss to her cheek.

Strength. He gave her strength.

"I don't know when my mother found out he was cheating. I do know that around the time I turned seven, she started to fade. Didn't come down as often to meals, didn't go out on family drives. My father also started spending more and more time away. I would get up in the morning, bring tea to my mother and beg her to drink something. She eventually would, but I usually had to cry to get her to." She blinked hard. "I remember the first magazine one of the girls brought in. A photo of Dad getting out of a car in Bora Bora, a young lady in the front seat with him, his secretary. He had his hand up, like he was trying to cover up the camera lens."

She could still see the woman in her mind's eyes, the tiny red dress, the sky-high heels.

"I was upset. I wanted to be comforted, to have my mother tell me that our family was still okay. So I took the magazine to her. She said she'd asked my father about it, too, that he'd insisted it was a business trip. But over time there were more photos. I stopped bringing the magazines to her, because every time I did, she got weaker."

She gripped his hands, soaked up the warmth of his skin, as her voice grew thick. "When I was nine, Johanna was born. I don't know what happened between Mom and Dad, but just before and for about six months after, they were happy again." Amazing how clearly she could remember sitting on Dad's lap, smell his spicy aftershave as he helped her hold baby Johanna wrapped in a soft pink blanket. Mom had looked on from her bed, a rosy glow in her cheeks and a sparkle in her eyes.

"It didn't last. Nothing did with Dad. Around the time Johanna turned one, he started going out again. Filled his absences with toys for Johanna and me, gifts for Mom. Every time one of those gift boxes arrived, she faded a little more. One night I heard Johanna screaming." Her throat constricted so tightly she nearly choked. "I found her in her bassinet, wet and cold. No blanket. Mom had started taking sleeping pills. She slept right through it."

Alejandro's arms tightened around her waist.

"So I started taking care of Johanna. And Mom."

"What about servants?"

It was almost a shock, hearing Alejandro's voice after she'd been speaking so long.

"We had maids and a housekeeper. A cook during the week. But I was ashamed. Ashamed of my father for abandoning us. Ashamed of my mother for abandoning us, too, in her own way. So I did what I could by myself."

She closed her eyes. Exhaustion and memories tugged at her, made her weary.

"I remember the last night I had with her. I was twelve. Johanna was three. I took her to Mom's room for a visit and Mom was…happy." Her eyes grew hot and she scrunched her eyes tight against the tears. "I was so…hopeful. She was dressed in this beautiful gown she hadn't worn in years. She'd had the cook bring up treats. There were chocolates and strawberries and ice cream, and she even let me have a sip of champagne." A tear escaped and traced a burning trail down her cheek. "She…she told me she was so proud of me. Her big girl."

Somewhere in the distance, a bird tweeted. She opened her eyes. The sight of the French countryside lit by the warm glow of the sun calmed her racing pulse, tethered her to this moment enough for her to force out her next words.

"We put Johanna to bed together. She tucked me in and kissed my forehead. I thought we would finally go back to the way things were. That I would get to be a kid again. I went to bed happy."

Her voice cracked. Alejandro started to say something, but she plowed forward. "I found her the next morning. She'd overdosed on sleeping pills."

"Calandra…"

He turned her in the circle of his arms and cupped her face. She met his eyes, sucking in one shuddering breath after another.

"She said in her note…that she couldn't go on…any longer." All the emotions she'd suppressed, all the grief she'd stuffed down deep inside, rose up at once, a tidal wave of sorrow that threatened to drown her. "I confronted Dad… after the funeral. He cared more about his reputation and whether anyone knew that she'd killed herself than the fact that his wife had committed suicide because of him. And then a week later…he died. In a car accident with his mistress."

She broke. Years of restrained sobs escaped. Had Alejandro not been holding her, cradling her, she would have sunk to the floor of the balcony.

He scooped her up in his arms, carried her inside and laid her on the bed. She started to reach for him, to ask him to stay, but before she could, he laid down next to her and drew her back into his embrace. How long she cried, she couldn't say. Alejandro stayed by her side the entire time, stroking her hair, kissing her forehead, whispering words in Spanish she didn't understand but still took comfort in.

At last, her tears dried. When she looked into Alejandro's eyes, saw the emotion brimming his dark blue gaze, she couldn't stop herself from kissing him. He paused, as if waiting to see if this was just a reaction to unburdening herself or if she truly wanted him.

She smiled against his mouth. Then sat up, rolled and straddled his hips.

His eyes flared. "Calandra…"

She leaned down and pressed her lips to his again. She nipped his bottom lip, thrilled at the groan that escaped him as his hands gripped her thighs. With one tug, she loosened the belt of the robe and shrugged out of the sleeves. Seeing his gaze darken with passion as he gazed at her naked body made her feel beautiful, sexy…

Strong.

She reached down, grabbed his hands in hers and guided them to her breasts. His fingers settled on her flesh, sliding down to stroke her nipples into hard points. She gasped, arched, moaned.

"Alejandro…make love to me."

Before she could take a breath, he sat up, one arm circling around her waist, and laid her back onto the bed with a strength that stole her breath. He stripped himself of his clothes in record time and laid his naked body on top of hers. He kissed her as he slid inside her, claiming her body with his.

They moved together, their pace almost frantic as they arched against each other, hands grasping, lips tasting, fire building until they came apart in each other's arms.

As they drifted down from the peak of pleasure, three words rose to her lips. She almost whispered them.

Wait.

Just a little longer. A little more time to think, to process.

Her eyes fluttered shut as he pulled the sheet up over them and she snuggled into his embrace.

"Calandra…"

"Hmm?"

Silence. Then another soft kiss on her temple. "Nothing. Go to sleep."

Something in his tone filtered through, a hesitancy that sent off a distant warning bell. But the satisfaction from their lovemaking, coupled with the events of the day, silenced it, and she drifted off to sleep.

CHAPTER NINETEEN

THE ELEGANT STRAINS of a violin carried across the ballroom of *La Reina*. Sequins sparkled under the light of the chandelier, silk flashed as dancers spun across the floor and champagne bubbled in over a hundred glasses.

"I'm still irritated that you chose champagne over my wine," Adrian said as he took a sip.

Everleigh patted her belly. "And I'm still irritated that I can't drink any of it."

They stood off to the side of the ballroom with Alejandro, watching as guests arrived. Even though the event was designed primarily to show off *La Reina* to the board, Alejandro had followed Adrian's lead from the merger party he and Everleigh had hosted a couple months ago and invited his employees.

"Not too bad." Antonio appeared next to Alejandro and clapped him on the shoulder. "Perhaps we should go into business together more often."

Alejandro smiled as his eyes roamed over the crowds. "Perhaps."

"Looking for someone?"

Adrian's voice was light, but Alejandro didn't miss the edge in his older brother's tone.

"Perhaps."

Everleigh leaned in. "Did you decide what you're going to do?"

Alejandro's eyes snapped to Adrian's face. "You told her?"

"Told her what?" Antonio asked, his gaze swinging back and forth like he was watching a tennis match.

Everleigh blushed. "I'm sorry. He was so irritable in Paris that I pried it out of him."

"I wasn't irritable!" Adrian retorted.

Before his family could drive him nuts, Alejandro walked away. He would deal with his brothers and soon-to-be sister-in-law later. Now, he wanted to find Calandra.

She had truly outdone herself. The food, brochures full of pictures of *La Reina*'s completed rooms and a story about where the ship would be in a year, sprigs of lavender she'd added to the rose centerpieces in a nod to some of the excursions they'd be offering—all of it was better than he could have ever envisioned.

"Alejandro!"

He turned, unable to contain his grin as his mother approached him, arms open wide.

"I'm so proud of you!" she gushed as she hugged him. "You've turned this ship into a marvel."

"*Gracias*, Madre."

He started to say more when a flash of yellow caught his eye. He turned. His heart stopped in his chest.

He hadn't been sure she'd wear it. But after he dropped her off in Marseille to do a final walkthrough of *La Reina* yesterday morning with a heated kiss and a whispered goodbye, his feet had guided him down the lane to the boutique. He'd wanted to give it to her in person, see her face when she opened it. By the time he was done with his own preparations for the party, and he'd cracked open the door to the guest suite, Calandra had been fast asleep. He'd had to settle for leaving the petal-pink box with a white ribbon on the table.

The longing to crawl into bed with her, to wake her with kisses and hear her say his name as he slid inside her again, had been almost unbearable. But something held him back. They hadn't talked the rest of the night in Provence, aside from whispering each other's names as they'd woken sometime around midnight and made love again. Then once more in the morning when they climbed into the shower together and she'd sunk to her knees and taken him in her mouth. He'd nearly come undone before he'd grabbed her by her elbows, lifted her up, wrapped her legs around his waist and thrust inside her as hot water had poured over their naked skin.

The car ride had been spent in pleasant, companionable silence, their fingers woven together. Talk had been unnecessary.

Until they did talk, clarified what this new development meant and how she felt about him, he wouldn't push his luck and risk pushing her away.

Although he'd worried if he'd crossed a boundary by buying her the dress. Now he had his answer.

She'd mentioned the little girl who hid in the shadow of her father, who had continued to hide all her life. But not tonight. Tonight she shone, the yellow of the dress making her skin glow. She'd left her hair unbound, loose curls falling over her shoulders as she made her rounds, whispering a word to a server here and propping up a rose in an arrangement there.

Still the same confidence. Still the same power. Unlike four months ago, though, tonight her shoulders were relaxed. Her movements less rigid, more assured and less tense.

And she smiled. His heart clenched as their eyes met. She glanced down at her dress, then back at him and mouthed *Thank you*.

"You care for her."

His mother startled him out of his musings. He swung his head around, summoning a jovial grin.

"She's a good friend."

"Ah. I didn't realize you were capable of being so discreet."

He arched an eyebrow in her direction. "When have I ever not been discreet?"

She snorted. "The Venetian Hotel…"

"Everyone brings that up."

"The Louvre," she continued.

"A minor misunderstanding."

She shook her head. "I worried about you, you know."

He paused. Her comments had always been sparse on his activities. He loathed the idea that he'd caused her stress. "I'm sorry."

She waved her hand. "I worried. All mothers do. I wondered if you were truly happy. And," she added with a twist of her lips, "I didn't like the insinuations of the tabloids. There's so much more to you than what the world sees."

The same words Calandra had spoken to him. Words that warmed his chest.

Had it been just four months ago? Four months since he'd seen Calandra standing in the midst of the chaos left by Adrian's guests, resolution firming her face even as her shoulders had sagged the tiniest fraction? That night, all he'd wanted to do was help. Be someone's savior, for once, instead of their curse. And the more time he'd spent with her, the more he'd seen something all too familiar.

Someone hiding behind a mask no one bothered to look past.

Perhaps that's why they had such explosive chemistry. In those moments, they didn't just lust after each other and sate their desire with sex. They ripped their masks off for the only other person in the world they could be themselves with.

His eyes drifted to Calandra. He'd felt possessive over *La Reina*, but it was a mere flicker compared to the inferno that blazed anytime he pictured Calandra round with his child.

Doubt slithered into his mind. Was it possible, to go from wanting nothing to do with matrimony a week ago to contemplating a marriage proposal? What if his feelings for Calandra, his desire to be a dad, were misplaced? If *La Reina* succeeded, would he be this focused on being a father?

"Alejandro?"

His father's voice cut through his dark musings and made his spine straighten. Slowly, he turned.

"*Padre.*"

If his mother sensed the sudden tension between father and son, she didn't let on. She crossed to her husband, who took her hands in his and smiled at her like she was the most precious thing in the world.

The look on his mother's face, one of happiness and love, was the only thing that had made him hold his tongue over the years. Made him hold it now despite the red haze of anger that colored his view of the room.

"Good evening, my dear."

"Good evening." Madre kissed him on the cheek, then gestured to the ballroom. "Our son has achieved something wonderful here tonight."

"He has."

Alejandro resisted rolling his eyes. Always an act, always the supportive father in public and his number one critic in private.

"Alejandro, may I have a word?"

He wanted to say no, to tell his father that until the board held their vote at nine o'clock, he had no interest in being within a dozen feet of him.

But with his mother looking on with such pride and exuding pure happiness, he had no choice but to incline his head and follow his father out of the ballroom.

As they walked out, he looked up. Calandra watched him, eyes flitting between them, a frown on her face. He gave her a small smile. Knowing she would be waiting for him gave him a boost, one he desperately needed if he was going to face Javier.

He strode past his father and led the way into an alcove

off the grand foyer. He stood off to the side, waited for Javier to follow him inside and then moved in front of the doorway. One wrong word and he was gone. He would not have his night of triumph ruined.

"The board has already informed me of their decision."

His stomach sank, followed by a swift rush of anger. Based on the emails, the conversations he'd had as he circulated the ballroom, he thought they'd vote in favor. The impulsive part of him wanted to turn around, walk back to the ballroom and demand an explanation for their duplicity. Few of them had seen him at his angriest. Perhaps it was time.

"Seems like you won this round, then."

Javier blinked. "What do you mean?"

"Getting the board to vote against *La Reina*." He leaned in, flashing a devil's smile. "No matter. *La Reina* will succeed. All that money you accuse me of wasting has been accumulating a nice bit of interest in a Swiss bank account. More than enough to see her through her first year of operations."

His father frowned. "There's been a misunderstanding. The board is voting unanimously to complete the renovation of *La Reina* and support its opening later this year."

Triumph zinged through his veins. He raised his chin. "I'm glad they saw sense."

Javier clasped his hands behind his back and started to pace. "Is that what you truly think? That I was trying to beat my own son, to make him fail?"

Alejandro bit back the first words he wanted to utter. He tucked his hands in his pockets and leaned against one of the pillars.

"When have you ever given me cause to believe otherwise?"

Javier sagged. Suddenly, his father looked very old, his wrinkles deepening as he sank down onto a settee and hung his head. Alejandro never would have guessed himself capable of pity for his sire. But the sight of the patriarch of the Cabrera empire, shoulders drooped, skin gray, inspired just that.

"I've been too hard on you."

He must have misheard.

"What?"

Javier scrubbed a hand over his face. "I was a terrible father to you. To your brothers." He let out a hoarse laugh. "I don't even know why your mother stayed with me."

"I don't, either. How long did you cheat on her?" Javier's head snapped up. "Or are you cheating on her still?"

"No!"

His father's denial echoed down the foyer. Alejandro arched a brow.

"Careful, Padre. Unless you want to draw attention to who you really are."

"Who I…"

Javier's voice trailed off as his eyes widened slightly. "Minerva."

"Minerva?"

"The woman you saw me with in the library." Javier swallowed. "You're right. I cheated on your mother."

Cold anger chilled his veins and tightened his fists. He'd known for years. But hearing the confirmation elevated his hatred to a new level.

"Although not the time you saw me."

Alejandro barked a laugh. "Does it matter?"

"It does." Javier hung his head. "You know your mother lost a child, a daughter, between you and Adrian, yes?" At Alejandro's nod, he continued. "I loved…love," he corrected, "your brother. You. Antonio."

The closest his father had ever come to saying "I love you."

"But I'd really looked forward to having a girl." Another emotion he'd never expected to see on his father's face: sorrow. "When we lost the baby...your mother retreated into herself. And I buried myself in work." He stared down at the floor, lost in memory. "Losing a baby wasn't as talked about back then. It's not an excuse for how I behaved. It just...counseling, mental health, they weren't as accepted.

"When your mother got pregnant with you, she barely got out of bed. The doctor encouraged her to rest. But she was so scared that she hardly ever left her room. And then I met Minerva. It's because of her that I worried about the women you associated with." He scrubbed a hand over his face. "I met Minerva at a hotel bar. I'd been drinking. A lot. Before I knew it, we went back to my room and..." He waved a hand in the air. "One time. The biggest mistake of my life."

"I don't believe you."

"Because you saw us together at our house in Granada? Yes, I can see why." He ran a hand through his hair. Hair that, Alejandro now noticed, was thinning at the top.

"Minerva, it turns out, wanted more. Much more. I told her in the morning that I had made a mistake. I told her about losing the baby, your mother being pregnant with you, everything. She didn't care. She wanted a ring on her finger. And if she couldn't get that, she wanted money."

Alejandro arched a brow. "She blackmailed you?"

Javier nodded once. "For almost twenty years, until I found evidence that she had embezzled funds from a charity she managed. A stalemate, but I haven't heard from her in thirteen years. The day you found us in the library, she had just upped her demands and provided a picture she'd taken of us in bed together while I'd been asleep."

Alejandro's stomach rolled. Such a photo would ruin his mother.

"Every time I saw you...knowing that my weakness had

led to such a mistake, I could barely look at you. When you started to act out more, I saw myself in you." His lips quirked up into a sad smile. "I became determined to make sure you didn't duplicate my mistakes. So instead of focusing on the good, I came down hard. The more you misbehaved, the harder I tried to correct you."

"You didn't just come down hard." He hadn't even known himself capable of the wrath that infused his voice. "You abandoned me, then brought me to my lowest point."

"I'm sorry, son."

"Sorry?"

Javier stood, slowly, as if a great weight rested on his shoulders.

"What else can I say? I'm sorry I placed the burden of my mistakes on your shoulders so young. That I pushed you into the life you lead now." Javier huffed. "Ironically enough, turned you into me."

A hum started in his head, low but steadily building to a roar.

"What do you mean?"

"I was just like you when I met your mother. Different women, clubs, spending money left and right."

Just like your father.

The world tilted. His father might be making amends now, but that didn't erase decades of pain. Madre had often spoken of how quickly they'd fallen in love, how absolutely certain they both had been about their future together.

Just like him and Calandra.

"I hope if you ever have children, son, you can avoid the many, many mistakes I've made." Javier took a tentative step forward. "Chief among them ever making you doubt that I didn't want you to succeed. I was harsh. Unnecessarily so. I wanted you to succeed, wanted you to be the man I knew you could be."

If the situation wasn't so sad, he would laugh. Finally,

he had an explanation, an apology, even words of support from his father.

Words that had come at a price. He'd based his entire existence, the man he was today, on what had transpired in that library. And for what? Nothing. And now he had to confront the possibility that, if he continued to pursue a life with Calandra, he would fall into the same trap his father had. Trying to turn himself into someone capable of love, fidelity, fatherhood, only to fail and leave Calandra broken, just as her father had done to her mother, and their child alone, just as he'd been. Just as Calandra had been because of the sins of her father.

"What if I can't break the cycle?"

He hadn't meant to utter the words aloud. They echoed in the stillness.

Javier gazed at him with sad eyes. "You're a strong man. You're capable."

"But if I can't?" Alejandro demanded, his voice hoarse.

His father breathed in deeply. "If you can't, then don't get married. Don't have children. Don't risk hurting a woman who deserves none of the pain men like us are capable of causing. If you don't know for sure that you want that in your life, then it's not worth it."

CHAPTER TWENTY

THE YELLOW MUSLIN whispered over Calandra's skin as she moved about the ballroom, the fabric as soft as a lover's touch, as delicate as butterfly wings. When she'd seen herself in the mirror for the first time, she couldn't stop the smile from breaking across her face.

When she worked for Cabrera Wines, she'd been based in New York, and she'd shopped at the same designer's store on Madison Avenue. A wonderfully competent saleswoman named Brittany had known her preferences: dark colors, clean lines and simple silhouettes. The clothing had made her feel powerful, in control and, when needed, it gave her the ability to fade in the background and let her work take center stage.

Now, for the second time in her life, she felt beautiful. Not authoritative, not proficient, but feminine, lovely.

If she'd known herself capable of this level of happiness, she would have let down her walls much sooner. *La Reina*'s event was a success. Judging by the whispers she overhead as she'd walked around the ballroom, the board would vote in Alejandro's favor.

And tonight, after the meeting, she would tell Alejandro she loved him. The attraction that had taken root in New York had only strengthened. Except last night it been more than just physical attraction. That blind trust had reached out and ensnared her, heart and soul.

Because she wasn't just counting down the days until she could fly home, check in hand and Alejandro out of her life. No, she was dreaming of her and Alejandro, standing together, a baby cradled between them as he kissed her on the forehead.

Because I'm in love.

As soon as she'd seen the box, she'd known what was inside. She'd reverently undone the bow and unwrapped the tissue paper. Her first glimpse of the sunshine-yellow fabric had brought tears to her eyes.

When she donned the gown, along with the accompanying silver sandals, she'd never felt so beautiful in her entire life. She'd even twirled in front of the mirror. Johanna wouldn't have believed it even if she'd seen it.

She glanced around the ballroom. Adrian and Everleigh were off to the side. Judging by Everleigh's failed attempts at covertly glancing at her stomach, Adrian had told her about the baby.

The older woman she'd seen in Paris was with them, too. She caught Calandra's eye and raised her champagne glass with a smile. Calandra cautiously smiled back. Had Alejandro told her about them? About the baby?

Although there wasn't really a "them" to speak of yet. Yes, they'd had another incredible night of sex. They'd shared their deepest secrets. They'd held hands on the drive back to Marseille and he'd gifted her this beautiful dress.

Uncertainty flickered through her. He wanted to be involved with the baby. She thought she'd seen the same emotion, the same passion in his eyes.

But he hadn't said it. His voice, too, just before they'd fallen asleep at the inn, lurked on the edges of her memory. He'd been on the verge of saying something.

Stop.

She was borrowing trouble. The meeting would happen in an hour. Then she'd tell him how she felt.

Five minutes later, Alejandro still hadn't reappeared with his father. A quick glance confirmed everything was continuing smoothly. After a quick word to the assistant she'd hired for the evening from a local agency—one she'd strongly recommend Alejandro hire full-time—she walked out of the ballroom.

He doesn't need rescuing.

No, Alejandro most certainly could handle himself. But he didn't have to face his father and whatever eleventh-hour obstacle he was trying to throw in his path.

The low murmur of voices reached her ears. As she continued down the grand foyer, they grew louder. She started to call out when Alejandro's voice, harsh with anguish, echoed down the hall.

"What if I can't break the cycle?"

Cycle? Had something else happened to the ships in construction?

"You're a strong man. You're capable."

Unexpected words from Javier.

"But if I can't?"

She continued forward, ready to break in, to tell Javier once and for all to end his attacks on his middle son.

And then the older Cabrera's words froze her in place.

"If you can't, then don't get married. Don't have children. Don't risk hurting a woman who deserves none of the pain men like us are capable of causing. If you don't know for sure that you want that in your life, then it's not worth it."

She waited for Alejandro's rebuttal, for him to tell Javier that he was indeed having a child, that he and Calandra had discovered something special in the midst of their mutually painful histories.

Each beat of silence drove the stake deeper into her heart. Her vision blurred, and for a moment she was standing next to her mother's bedside, hand on her cool cheek and frantically whispered words begging her mother not to leave her. Not when they'd been so close to having everything back to the way it should be.

The memory faded, replaced by the sparkling chandeliers brightening *La Reina*'s halls. Just as she had that morning so many years ago, she drew up, drawing strength from some inner source as she locked her emotions away where they couldn't betray her. She backed away and walked back to the ballroom, her footsteps thankfully muffled by the thick carpet.

This was why she'd kept the walls around her heart, why love and marriage had never been an option after Mom's death. Because the brief, exquisite happiness she'd found this past week made the fall so much worse.

Her initial fear had been accurate. She'd fallen into the same trap as her mother, drawn in by a handsome face and charming words, dreaming of forever when she'd only been a fleeting interest, a novelty in his glitzy world. She'd thought he'd truly wanted her. The baby. After yesterday… a life. Together.

But he'd stayed silent. Alejandro, the man who always had a snappy comeback or a witty comment at the ready, had stayed silent. She'd heard his answer in that silence, loud and clear.

At least, she consoled herself as she moved around the room, she'd found out before she did something stupid like confess her feelings to him. She would be strong. Stronger than her mother. Stronger than the weak woman she'd allowed herself to be this past week. A temporary lapse. But one that tonight, after the party, she would rectify.

After another round of the ballroom, a few words of direction to a slightly harried-looking server and a check-in with her assistant later, Alejandro reentered.

His gaze landed on her. The cracks in her heart ripped open.

He came up to her, eyes blank, face devoid of a smile.

"I'd like to speak with you after the party." The smallest glimmer came into his eyes. "The board voted unanimously to support *La Reina*."

Somehow she smiled and forced herself to reach out, pat him on the arm. "Congratulations."

He leaned down, kissed her cheek and moved away toward a group of older gentlemen. She barely stopped herself from reaching up to the touch the spot where his lips had brushed. The light caress had been casual, like a kiss you might give a friend you hadn't seen in a while. Not a woman you loved.

The final confirmation, like a dagger to the heart.

The next three hours passed agonizingly slowly. But finally the last guest left, the band started to pack up and Suzie's students began to clear the tables.

Alejandro appeared by her side.

"Ready to go home?"

"Yes." More than ready. She never wanted to set foot in France again. It would be too painful.

He held out an arm. She took it, her fingers settling on his sleeve, and allowed him to escort her down the elegant hallway of the ship. A ship she'd come to care about, to see as a grand old lady getting a second chance at life.

Another loss. Another reason why forming emotional attachments was such a bad idea.

The drive back to the villa was silent. Unlike the comfort of yesterday's drive back from Provence, this one was fraught with tension. Alejandro either ignored her cool detachment or was too consumed by his own thoughts to notice.

No matter, she reassured herself. She didn't need him. Not anymore.

He pulled up in front of the villa, the white stairs glowing in the moonlight. He got out, came round before she had her seat belt unbuckled and opened the door for her.

"Home."

She breathed in. "No. It's not."

Her words hung in the stillness of the night as Alejandro's attention suddenly riveted on her.

"What?"

"I heard what you and your father were talking about."

* * *

How had everything gone so wrong so quickly? Alejandro rubbed the bridge of his nose. Four hours ago he'd been in love, his certainty in the success of the first project that was truly his allowing him to entertain thoughts of shopping for a ring for the mother of his child.

And then his father, with surprisingly good intentions, had once again taken his life and turned it on its head.

"You don't think you're capable, do you? Of being a father, of..." Her voice trailed off, choked with emotion. He moved forward, to hold her close like he had at the inn, but she held up a hand. "Of committing," she finished.

It was all happening at once. Too much. Too much swirling around inside like a hurricane, destroying everything in its path. He'd built his life around what his father had done, had pursued women and notoriety to punish him.

Except it had been a mistake. One mistake committed out of pain instead of a calculated affair. He'd lived nearly twenty years of his life on a myth that he'd been too angry, too hurt, to examine more closely. To act like an adult and talk with his father.

His entire reality had been called into question in one conversation. Much as he wanted to blame his father—how much easier that would have been—he had no one to blame but himself. And Javier's words of warning had made him wonder...did he really want to be a father? A husband? Or was this just another twisted trick of his psyche?

He didn't have an answer. Which was probably an answer in itself.

"Calandra...if you heard everything..." He spread his hands helplessly. "I don't know what to think."

He watched whatever they'd had end as her shoulders straightened, her chin came up and her mask slid back into place, all within a few seconds. His heart, his chest, his whole damn body ached to hold her, to erase the last few hours and recapture the magic they'd found in Provence.

But he kept his hands by his sides. He'd borne witness to the painful price her parents' abandonment had demanded of Calandra. How could he risk doing the same thing to the baby? Risk putting Calandra through yet another rejection? Like his father had said, if he didn't know one hundred percent that he wanted this, it was better to let her go. Let their child go.

"It seems, then, that I have my answer." A heartbeat where she hesitated, where the ice in her eyes cracked and revealed the insurmountable pain he'd caused her. Even if he did find an answer, he'd never be able to come back from this. From hurting her so deeply.

"Goodbye, Señor Cabrera."

Somehow, he thought as he watched her walk up the stairs and disappear into the villa, he'd always known Calandra Smythe would walk out of his life.

He'd just had no idea he'd be the one to drive her away.

CHAPTER TWENTY-ONE

Three weeks later

SILVER MOONLIGHT CREATED a mystical glow on the ocean, the waves rising and falling beneath a dark sky speckled with stars. Calandra sat on the beach, one hand draped across her belly.

The ocean had looked incredible from the porch, the muffled roar calling to her. The view from her attic bedroom was nothing compared to the beauty laid out before her. Waves crashed on a smooth beach, the white-capped peaks glowing in the moonlight, the water tumbling over itself in frothy splendor to almost kiss her bare feet before receding. Stars spiraled above her head.

She kept her eyes on the barest glint of a horizon, where the midnight blue of the sky met the even darker blue of the ocean. Beneath her fingertips, something fluttered.

A sad smile tugged at her lips. She'd felt it this morning, the briefest twinge. She'd chalked it up to muscle spasms. But the fluttering had grown stronger, until it had been impossible to deny that she was feeling her baby move inside her for the first time.

Johanna had insisted on baking a cake to celebrate the occasion. A yellow cake frosted with caramel and topped off with sprinkles in the shape of baby rattles she'd served after dinner.

For all the years that Calandra had spent taking care of Johanna, her sister had repaid the favor twice over in the three weeks Calandra had been home. She'd picked her up at the airport, held her while she forced out the whole story on the couch with thankfully minimal tears. She'd arranged a meeting for Calandra with a finance student from her college to help her decide how best to manage the five-hundred-thousand-dollar deposit that had appeared in her account twenty-four hours after she'd left Marseille.

An email had also been sent with an attachment, a formal letter of recommendation from Alejandro Cabrera himself, head of Cabrera Shipping.

Last week she'd been mindlessly flipping through late-night movies, unable to sleep, when *The Scarlet Pimpernel* had come on. She'd changed the channel with a savage push of a button, then changed it back again. Landing on the scene where the beautiful, tortured Marguerite had looked at Percy with sad eyes and whispered, "This is some absurd role you're playing. I don't know why. But I'm sure it is. Perhaps to keep the world at a distance. Only now you're shutting me out as well," it had plunged a knife into her heart so deep it had made her eyes burn.

She'd done the right thing. He hadn't been playing a role when he'd flat-out told her he didn't know if he wanted her in his life, wanted their child in his life. A definitive answer. One that had nearly killed her.

Better to know now, before the baby came and could get attached to a father who would disappear from its life, than to suffer that heartache later.

It didn't stop the wondering. Or the memories. The dreadful, horrid, wonderful memories of a week when she'd climbed the Eiffel Tower, seen the Mediterranean from the deck of a yacht and knelt down to smell a sprig of lavender in front of a historic abbey.

At least Alejandro had given her that, she consoled herself. She'd lived more in the past week than she had in years. That little taste of life had come just in time. When their—her, she corrected herself—her child arrived, she would make sure it got that same taste of life, that same joy in both the big and small.

And through that, her child would at least know their father a little.

A breeze blew in, bringing with it the scent of sea salt. Out of the corner of her eye, something appeared. She turned her head and gasped. A yacht glided across the water, elegant and glowing white under the kiss of moonlight. If she squinted, she could just make out letters written in graceful red cursive.

Her heart thudded. It wasn't possible. She was imagining things. Or hallucinating.

The yacht stilled, bobbing gently up and down on the waves. She pushed to her feet, eyes trained on the boat as her heart pounded in her throat. Was it him? Did she want it to be him? After nearly a month of silence—no texts, no phone calls, no letters—what was left to be said?

A shape appeared out of the ocean, a ghost emerging from the water. She took a few steps back, fear mixing in with her adrenaline.

"Kitty Hawk's nice this time of year."

The husky voice echoed up over the beach. Her mouth dropped open as Alejandro walked out of the water, white shirt clinging like a second skin to his muscular chest, black pants pasted to his legs. With dark curls plastered to his forehead and that wicked grin flashing in the dark, he looked like a hero from one of her old paperback romances.

"You're wet."

His laughter, deep and rich, chased away the chill that had settled on her skin when she'd first seen the yacht.

"Nothing gets by you, does it?"

"Rarely." She crossed her arms over her middle, partly out of instinct to protect the baby now fluttering wildly in her stomach, and partly to keep herself from running down the beach and throwing herself into his arms. "Once in a while, though, I've been known to make a mistake."

The barb hit home. His grin faded as he smoothed the wet hair out of his face.

"So have I. In fact, I made a big one pretty recently."

"Aside from swimming in the Atlantic at night?"

"Yeah." He took a step toward her. She didn't move. She wouldn't back down. "I let the woman I love walk away."

Love. That word echoed in her head, over and over again. She wanted to reach out, grab it, hug it to her chest. He loved her?

Don't. Don't let him in.

"Hmm."

"Hmm," he repeated. "As in, 'hmm, I like what I'm hearing' or 'hmm, go jump in the ocean, you bastard'?"

"I haven't heard enough to make a decision." Her eyes slid back to the yacht. "Seriously, why did you jump in the ocean?"

"I wasn't planning on it." He gestured at his soaking-wet clothes. "Believe me, I wouldn't have worn this to go swimming. I planned on mooring the boat, coming ashore via the dinghy and kidnapping you. Unfortunately, I haven't taken it out by myself in quite some time." He gestured at the dark waves. "It's now a permanent addition to the bottom of the Atlantic. But I'm a good swimmer, and that's not important. What is important is I need…" Even at this distance, she could see, *feel*, the intensity of his gaze sharpen as he stared at her like they'd been parted for years instead of just a few weeks.

"I need you, Calandra."

Hadn't she just been ruminating on how she hadn't really been living her life? Had let fear mask itself as discipline and kept herself emotionally distant from everyone and everything? Alejandro was offering her the chance to break free from the past.

"You were going to kidnap me?" she finally asked.

"Romantically kidnap you. With your permission, of course."

Damn her lips for twitching. She'd missed him. His humor. His charm. The way he looked at her like she was the only one in the world. But she'd allowed herself to be suckered in once. To open her heart and believe he could be different. Would it be fear to reject him, or practicality?

"Do you still feel about me the way you did when we left Provence?"

Her mouth dried up as heat blossomed inside her. "What do you mean?"

"You know exactly what I mean, Calandra. I saw it in your eyes. I know what you were going to tell me the night of the party."

"You said we both had our answer. Nothing more needs to be said."

Long strides ate up the distance between them. She stood, frozen in place by desire and want and the dread that if she moved a muscle she'd break down, throw her arms around his neck and ask him to never leave again.

"Much more needs to be said." He laid a hand on her cheek, the gesture so gentle and tender it brought a lump to her throat. "For starters, I am not like my father."

He sucked in a deep breath as he savored the feel of her skin. He'd been an idiot to wait as long as he had to come for her. But it had taken the past three weeks and several long, difficult conversations with his father, his mother, Adrian and even Everleigh to make him see sense.

"Do something incredibly romantic," Everleigh had encouraged.

So he'd ordered *The Scarlet Pimpernel* to make the crossing from Marseille to Kitty Hawk, North Carolina, and moor right in front of her aunt Norine's ramshackle beachfront cottage. A storm had slowed their journey by a few hours so that instead of arriving just before sunset as he'd planned, they'd sailed in under the light of the moon. His captain had tried to discourage him from taking the dinghy out with the waves as high as they were, had offered to take the yacht to the nearest marina and call Alejandro a car. But the marina was an hour away by boat, and he hadn't wanted to wait.

His pride smarted a little from getting tossed into the ocean. He'd envisioned striding up the beach with the confidence and swagger of Douglas Fairbanks, not a drowned rat. But it had been worth it to reach Calandra as soon as he could.

God, she was beautiful. Dark hair flowing past her shoulders, arms crossed over her belly, now slightly rounded and peeking out from beneath the hem of her shirt. The need to hold her, cradle her stomach and the life growing inside her, feel her curl into his body the way she had all those nights ago, almost overpowered him.

First things first. Apology. Explanation. More apology.

"I'm so sorry, Calandra." He placed his forehead against hers, exhaled sharply when she didn't pull away. Even if she pushed him into the ocean and told him she never wanted to see him again, he would savor every touch she allowed him. "That night on *La Reina*, what you overheard was the first time my father and I have had a conversation about anything other than my behavior or business. He told me things about his affair that put it in a very different light. That rendered most of my life obsolete."

Calandra leaned back and his stomach dropped.

"I don't understand."

"I lived most of my life, my flings, my ability to remain unattached, my exploits, to punish my father." He closed his eyes for a moment. "Only to find out that my entire existence was built on a misunderstanding. An assumption I made that turned out not to be true. Suddenly…" He raked a hand through his hair. "I had no idea who I was. I was faced with nearly twenty years of distance and foolish decisions and a persona I'd concocted that wasn't really me. It made me question everything. Including whether I was pursuing you and being a father for the right reasons."

He waited for the shutter to drop down, for her beautiful, misty eyes to turn steely gray and her voice to whip out an order to leave and never come back.

Hope bloomed, tiny but fierce, as she stayed put, continued to look at him thoughtfully instead of with the disgust and fury he'd anticipated.

"So what did you decide?"

He barely resisted kissing her for uttering her question in that prim, controlled voice that drove him crazy. Crazy because he admired her, how she managed to lead and coordinate and do all the amazing things she did for her career. Crazy, too, because he wanted to kiss her senseless until the primness was replaced by that breathy moan that set his blood on fire.

"Cabrera Shipping became the first thing I really wanted in life for me. Making it a success because I wanted to build something. *La Reina* was the second, and the first thing that was truly my own. I never thought anything could be more important than *La Reina*."

He reached out, slowly, giving her plenty of time to back up, before he placed his hand on her belly. She didn't lean into him, but she didn't pull away. He knelt down in the sand, gave in to temptation and placed the softest of kisses on her stomach.

"You, and our child, are more important to me than anything in the world, Calandra." He looked up at her, letting every emotion he'd repressed show. If he lost, at least he'd know he gave it his all. "It started out with me wanting more purpose in my life. The chance to be the father mine had never been. And then I realized that it wasn't just our child, but you that I wanted, too. The woman I've been falling in love with for the past three years."

A tear traced its way down her face, leaving behind a trail on her cheek that glistened in the silver light. He stood and hurriedly wiped it away.

"Calandra, I—"

"I'm sorry!" she cried out and flung her arms around his neck. He hesitated for half a second before wrapping his arms around her waist and hauling her against him, burying his face in her hair and breathing her in.

"You have nothing to be sorry for," he whispered in her ear as he cradled her in his arms.

"But I do." She pulled back to look him in the eye, her hands settling on his cheeks. "I heard enough of your conversation with your father to know how serious it was. You told me about your relationship with him, how tumultuous it was, but I focused on the little bit I heard and made it all about me and my past." She wiped away more tears with the back of her hand. "I should have given you grace. I should have trusted you and told you how much I respect your drive, your dedication…how much I loved you. And instead I assumed the worst and I ran."

He cradled her face in his hands and kissed the tears from her cheeks as joy filled him, true joy like he'd never known before.

"I'm not perfect, Calandra."

A smile broke through her tears. "Trust me, I know."

"Minx." He kissed the tip of her nose. "I mean that I'm just starting to get to know myself. It's going to take a while. There will be days I struggle. It's a lot to ask anyone to take on. Selfish, really."

"And I'm just starting to confront my past," Calandra said as she laid her hands on top of his. "I have trust issues. Big ones. I buried myself in routines and checklists and a job that required order. I struggle to share my emotions. I have a lot to deal with regarding my parents."

"Well…" So much. So much pain on both sides. "Aren't we a pair?"

Her eyes dimmed a fraction. "Do you think…"

"I think," he replied as her voice trailed off, "that we both love each other. That we know each other better than anyone else does. And," he added as he placed a hand on her stomach once more, "that that's enough for a new start. I want to marry you, Calandra. I want to wake up to your face the rest of my life, to our baby in the nursery. I want you to drag me to little culinary schools and remind me that I'm being an ass and not let me get away with anything."

A wobbly smile crossed her face as more tears spilled down her cheeks.

"Was that a proposal?"

He dropped back down on one knee and grabbed both her hands in his. "A horrible one, but yes. Let me try that again. Calandra Smythe, love of my life, will you marry me?"

With her breathy "yes" echoing in his ears, he surged to his feet, swept her into his arms and kissed her beneath a sea of stars.

* * * * *

COMING SOON!

We really hope you enjoyed reading this book.
If you're looking for more romance, be sure to
head to the shops when new books are
available on

Thursday 28th October

To see which titles are coming soon, please visit
millsandboon.co.uk/nextmonth

MILLS & BOON

THE HEART OF ROMANCE

A ROMANCE FOR EVERY READER

MODERN — Prepare to be swept off your feet by sophisticated, sexy and seductive heroes, in some of the world's most glamourous and romantic locations, where power and passion collide.

HISTORICAL — Escape with historical heroes from time gone by. Whether your passion is for wicked Regency Rakes, muscled Vikings or rugged Highlanders, await the romance of the past.

MEDICAL — Set your pulse racing with dedicated, delectable doctors in the high-pressure world of medicine, where emotions run high and passion, comfort and love are the best medicine.

True Love — Celebrate true love with tender stories of heartfelt romance, from the rush of falling in love to the joy a new baby can bring, and a focus on the emotional heart of a relationship.

Desire — Indulge in secrets and scandal, intense drama and plenty of sizzling hot action with powerful and passionate heroes who have it all: wealth, status, good looks…everything but the right woman.

HEROES — Experience all the excitement of a gripping thriller, with an intense romance at its heart. Resourceful, true-to-life women and strong, fearless men face danger and desire - a killer combination!

To see which titles are coming soon, please visit

millsandboon.co.uk/nextmonth

MILLS & BOON

Coming next month

UNWRAPPED BY HER ITALIAN BOSS
Michelle Smart

'I know how important this maiden voyage is, so I'll give it my best shot.'

What choice did Meredith have? Accept the last-minute secondment or lose her job. Those were the only choices. If she lost her job, what would happen to her? She'd be forced to return to England while she sought another job. Forced to live in the bleak, unhappy home of her childhood. All the joy and light she'd experienced these past three years would be gone and she'd return to grey.

'What role do you play in it all?' she asked into the silence.

He raised a thick black eyebrow.

'Are you part of Cannavaro Travel?' she queried. 'Sorry, my mind went blank when we were introduced.'

The other eyebrow rose.

A tiny dart of amusement at his expression—it was definitely the expression of someone outragedly thinking, *How can you not know who I am?*—cut through Merry's guilt and anguish. The guilt came from having spent two months praying for the forthcoming trip home to be cancelled. The anguish came from her having to be the one to do it, and with just two days' notice. The early Christmas dinner her sister-in-law had spent weeks and weeks planning had all been for nothing.

The only good thing she had to hold on to was that she hadn't clobbered an actual guest with the Christmas tree, although, judging by the cut of his suit, Cheekbones was on a huge salary, so must be high up in Cannavaro Travel, and all the signs were that he had an ego to match that salary.

She relaxed her chest with an exhale. 'Your role?' she asked again.

Dark blue eyes glittered. Tingles laced her spine and spread through her skin.

Cheekbones folded his hands together on the table. 'My role…? Think of me as the boss.'

His deep, musical accent set more tingles off in her. Crossing her legs, thankful that she'd come to her senses before mouthing off about being forced into a temporary job she'd rather eat fetid fruit than do, Merry made a mark in her notebook. 'I report to you?'

'*Si*.'

'Are you going on the train ride?'

Strong nostrils flared with distaste. 'It is no "train ride", lady.'

'You know what I mean.' She laughed. She couldn't help it. Something about his presence unnerved her. Greek god looks clashing with a glacial demeanour, warmed up again by the sexiest Italian accent she'd ever heard.

'I know what you mean and, *si*, I will be on the voyage.'

Unnerved further by the swoop of her belly at this, she made another nonsense mark in her book before looking back up at him and smiling ruefully. 'In that case, I should confess that I didn't catch your name. I'm Merry,' she added, so he wouldn't have any excuse to keep addressing her as 'lady'.

His fingers drummed on the table. 'I know your name, lady. *I* pay attention.'

For some unfathomable reason, this tickled her. 'Well done. Go to the top of the class. And your name?'

'Giovanni Cannavaro.'

All the blood in Merry's head pooled down to her feet in one strong gush.

Continue reading
UNWRAPPED BY HER ITALIAN BOSS
Michelle Smart

Available next month
www.millsandboon.co.uk